Praise for Nancy Thayer and *Belonging*

"This is Nancy Thayer's best book yet. She has created in Joanna Jones a woman very much of the nineties: smart, savvy , self-sufficient, and filled with love and concern for others. *Belonging* is about all the things women care about: having a nice home, building a strong self-image, creating intimate relationships, and belonging to a family, no matter how it is defined."
—Leslie Linsley, author of *Nantucket Style*

"Anyone who wants to get inside the skin of a contemporary woman simply has to open Nancy Thayer and start reading."
—Elizabeth Forsythe Hailey

"Satisfying . . . A modern fairy tale."
—*Publishers Weekly*

"Engrossing . . . Thayer's story of a woman's quest for self-identity and self-affirmation does inspire."
—*Booklist*

"A book you will not want to end . . . In novel after novel, Nancy Thayer has kept her readers obsessively turning pages, living the lives of her characters and consumed by their adventure; she has done it again with *Belonging*."
—William Martin, author of *Back Bay* and *Cape Cod*

Belonging

NANCY THAYER

St. Martin's Paperbacks

This book is dedicated to
Jill Hunter Wickes
with much love and gratitude
for her literate, generous, reliable friendship

I would like to thank many people who helped with this book: Lisa Hale and Tony DiGioviny of the Massachusetts General Hospital Sumner Redstone Burn Center; Bruce Watts, chief of the superlative Nantucket Fire Department; Jane Bonvini of Nantucket Cottage Hospital; attorney Kevin Dale; Nantucket historian Nat Philbrick; Charlotte Maison and Janice O'Mara of the Nantucket Atheneum; Patrick and Riley Wynn, who reminded me how delicious babies and children are; the lights of my life, Josh Thayer and Sam Thayer; and Charley Walters, my husband, my home.

There is an old Indian tradition that some time previous to the settlement of the island by the whites, a French ship, having on board a quantity of specie, came ashore at the east end of the island in a severe storm, and was driven up into what is called the "Gulch," a trifle to the westward of Siasconset, and wrecked. The island at the time was so thickly wooded in that vicinity that they were compelled to cut their way through the forest to reach the Indian settlements. Such is substantially the tradition, as remembered by many of our older inhabitants, and it is submitted for what it is worth. That the story was not wholly regarded as a myth by our ancestors is shown from the fact that the beach in that vicinity has been thoroughly dug over within a hundred years, in the vain hope of unearthing the ship's treasure, which was said to have been buried there.

Wrecks Around Nantucket, compiled by Arthur H. Gardner (New Bedford, Mass.: Reynolds Printing, Inc., 1913, 1943)

John Coffin built a house at Quaise, on one of the harbor's eastern coves, and it became known as Kezia's country estate. Watching Kezia Coffin profit at what they considered their expense, many Nantucketers spread rumors about her dealings with the enemy. The Patriots on the island were the most vociferous because they felt the most aggrieved. Kezia Coffin was trading regularly with the British, they claimed. Coffin ships were running the British blockade with impunity. And Kezia's country house at Quaise was the collection point for smuggled goods and a rendezvous for secret deals with the enemy. So went the rumors, including a claim that Kezia had had a tunnel dug from her house to the beach, and that the tunnel was jammed with illicit merchandise.

A. B. C. Whipple
Vintage Nantucket, revised edition

Part One

One

~

*T*he television screen showed a family and their guest at ease in a luxuriant garden. The man wore white flannels and held on his lap, recumbent in the curve of his arm, his curly-haired daughter, fresh as peppermint in a pink sundress. Leaning toward them in indolent possession, a pregnant woman clad in a floral smock reclined on a white wicker chaise, her hand with its glinting diamonds draped complacently against her abdomen.

The other woman wore a crisp silk suit of a green so pale it was nearly white. She was not pregnant, and she wore no rings.

She spoke: "Until next time, this is Joanna Jones with *Fabulous Homes.*"

Joanna Jones smiled, tilting her head slowly so that her blond hair slid rippling against her shoulder, catching the sun. The camera moved steadily back, opening up the scene to focus on the house. Massive and stony as a castle, it was softened by trellises of roses and window boxes spilling with flowers. In the open door a black Lab and a white cat sat side by side in a shower of sun.

Theme music sparkled in. The credits began to roll.

Joanna flicked the remote control and the scene vanished. She was glad. She'd taped this Tennessee segment just last month, and now, watching the final version from her office in the CVN building on Third Avenue, she was surprised to find that this particular home stirred her emotions just as it had during her interview and tour. Joanna did not usually lust for possessions or envy others their lives, but the pretty little curly-haired girl and her smug pregnant mother made her feel oddly lonely and filled her with an unsettling, powerful longing.

Secretly she chided herself: she should feel exhilarated. *She* should feel smug. She'd completed another show for next year's series. This one was slotted for next March. It would be a welcome spot of fresh air and flowery bloom right when her audience would be most desperate, most receptive, most eager for spring to come. It would cheer everyone.

"That's it!" she announced to the two men watching with her.

"It's good," Jake told her.

Jake Corcoran was vice-president in charge of network programming for CVN; a benevolent dictator, his opinions were famous in the cable television business for being precocious, brilliant, and trend-setting. Jake had been the first to endorse Joanna's show, and she had not let him down.

Jake was right; this show was really good. Her shows kept getting better and better. The fan mail proved it, as did the caliber of guests who opened their homes to her. And before all that, before the airing of the produced shows and the response of the audience, before the praise of her employers and the compliments from her colleagues, before she even saw the first videotapes on the monitor, she knew as she was planning and writing and hosting the shows that they were so good, so substantial, so *meaty,* that they were no longer merely entertaining. They were significant. They were worthwhile.

The essential focus of *Joanna Jones' Fabulous Homes* was not on the celebrity of the owners or the costliness of the statues in the garden or the prestige of the architect or interior decorator. The homes Joanna profiled were not museums of fabulously expensive, fragile, and unusable antiques. In FH houses there were cookie crumbs on the counters, silk shirts flung on the chaise longues, dog hair under the sofas, and opened novels lying on the sunroom floors. The air was electric, ringing with calls down the stairwell and doors slamming shut and bathwater bubbling and little boys wrestling and maids muttering over their caviar ceviche. Joanna Jones' Fabulous Homes were lived in by families, and although they were families of notable people—writers, painters, movie directors, actors, corporate leaders, statesmen, professors—the emphasis was not on the fame or wealth, but on the family life.

Joanna had a talent for discovering homes full of movement, contentment, beauty, and warmth, and a gift for graciously displaying those homes and their families in the richest, most generous light.

If, during the past two years as she produced and presented her show, she came to realize that this knack was like that of a starving person sniffing out a bakery, or a cold person locating heat, she ignored that old news, shrugging it off as irrelevant. She was a practical woman. She could not change the past, only the future.

Carter Amberson, who coproduced the show, remarked, "We thought it was quite a coup to get the senator's permission."

"It was," Jake agreed, adding, "Joanna's reputation is pure gold."

A whisper of tension rang in the room then like the reverberation of a struck gong. From the beginning, Carter had been scrupulously careful to see that Joanna got full credit for her achievements; now that *Fabulous Homes* was two years old and successful, he no longer had to be vigilant on her behalf, but rather on his.

Carter was one of the network's producers, working behind the scenes, handling a complicated spectrum of tasks. He was responsible for the dry work of contracts and logistics, but provided necessary conceptual advice on both the taping and the postproduction editing. The crucial procurement of in-house production financing and advertising hookups was also in his charge. He had to be creative and analytical; he had to deal with small print and with giant egos. He could do it all; and he did do it all beautifully.

But Jake was not willing to give Carter any praise these days, and Joanna was always putting herself into the position of peacemaker between these two men, both of whom she loved in complicated ways.

"I'm off, then," Jake declared, rising.

Joanna's heart stirred with pity. The Jake Corcoran she'd grown to admire and even to worship during her tenure at

CVN had always been a vigorous, dynamic man, an industry giant, capable of flashing lightning bolts when angry or engendering joy with his great, heart-lifting smile.

But now the blaze in his dark eyes was nearly extinguished, and premature silver swirled among his black curls, and his hand-tailored suits hung loosely over what had once been a robust, even burly, torso. Emily, his wife of twenty-five years, had recently died, a wretched death, of liver cancer. Joanna, like some of the others in the network family, was not certain Jake would survive the loss, but Joanna believed firmly that if anything would save him, work would, and for that reason alone she'd asked him to sit in on this viewing before the three went their separate ways during August. She wanted him to remember how much she valued his opinion and needed his counsel. She wished there were more she could do to ease his burden of grief.

"Where are you spending your vacation, Jake?" Joanna asked.

"Adirondacks. My son's fiancée's family has a house up there. Mark and I will do some trout fishing, some sailing, some hiking." He smiled at Joanna with affection. "I'll be fine."

In response, Joanna stepped forward and embraced Jake, wrapping him in a tight hug in an instinctive, irresistible act of affection and consolation.

She'd never been this bold before, although Jake was a natural toucher. He crunched his staff in his great bear hugs during celebrations and ruffled hair and patted backs. Joanna considered Jake patriarchal, or avuncular, but suddenly as she stood holding her great, heart-bruised boss, she realized that he had never fit into any tidy category—nor did her emotions, which stunned her now with their inappropriateness.

She and Jake were almost of equal height; he was five feet nine inches of muscular male; she was five eight, and large-boned though slender. As her body pressed Jake's, Joanna experienced a rush of pleasure at the feel and smell and warmth of this powerful, emotional man. She didn't want to let him go, and she was at once so startled and so ashamed that she nearly shoved him away.

She stepped back. "Take care of yourself, boss."

Jake's eyes were kind. He didn't notice her confusion. "You, too, kid."

She never minded Jake calling her "kid." He was ten years older than she, but eons more experienced at the cable television game, and he had always given her excellent advice; he had always been on her side. Her ally. Her mentor. Her trusted and esteemed *friend,* a rare thing in this competitive business.

Looking past her, Jake said, "Carter, I hope you and your family have a great time in Europe." He held out his hand.

For a split second Carter hesitated, and his icy blue eyes sparked. Then he stepped forward and shook Jake's hand. Jake was after all his superior at the network, and Carter was, above all else, self-protective. What a force field those two created, Joanna thought, looking at them. Jake was massive and dark and emotionally open; Carter was nearly beautiful in a cold, blond, aristocratic way, and tense and guarded. It was possible that Jake guessed that Carter and Joanna were lovers; if he did, he was bound to disapprove.

"Thanks. We will," Carter replied. "We're flying to France tonight. Blair and I honeymooned in Paris. We're sending Chip to his grandmother's after the tour and spending a week in Paris, just the two of us, a sort of second honeymoon. Walking by the Seine at midnight, sipping champagne on the balcony of our hotel suite, strolling down the Champs-Elysée. All that mushy stuff. I'll come home a new man."

"That should be interesting," Jake remarked dryly. Nodding to them both, he said, "Good night," and went out the door.

Joanna looked at Carter. "Ouch."

He seemed genuinely surprised. "What do you mean?"

"I mean it wasn't very kind—either to Jake or to me—to make it quite so crystal-clear that you have a loving wife with whom to share your vacation."

Carter looked crestfallen. "God, Joanna, I see what you mean." With the heel of his hand, he struck his forehead. "I'm sorry. I was just trying . . . Look, Joanna, I'm sure he suspects us. And neither one of us needs the network hassle for that. I thought that if I romanticized my wife in front of the woman who might very well be my lover, I'd deflect suspicion."

For a long moment Joanna stared at Carter, relishing as always the sight of his exceedingly handsome face and the sheer blissful lean height of the man. The tantalizing glitter of his arctic-blue eyes. The iceberg planes of his cheekbones and shoulder blades and chin. The cutting white sail of his smile.

"Oh, it's all right, Carter. I guess I'm just overreacting." But she couldn't keep the emotion from her voice.

Coming close to her, but not yet touching her, Carter said, "Joanna, you know I have to do this. It has nothing to do with honeymooning with Blair. I was determined not to be an absent father, and I don't think I've lived up to my goal. The least I can do is give Chip a family vacation."

"I know." She crossed her arms over her breasts, steadying herself.

"But God. I'm going to miss you." Approaching her, Carter put his hands on her shoulders, and with great deliberation moved them down along the curve of her arms, so that his thumbs lightly brushed the swelling arch of her breasts. His warm breath stirred her hair. His body loomed against hers like a dark shadow. "Joanna. You know I need you."

Torn by pride and desire, Joanna did not reply. Carter gently kissed her hair. Her temple. Her throat.

"It's so late," Joanna protested. "You'll miss your plane."

"It's not until nine. We've got plenty of time." Already his hand had found its way beneath the lapels of her jacket and was slipping under the lace of her bra.

"Yes, but, Carter—" she protested, attempting to pull away from him.

"I love you, Joanna. You know I love you."

"I love you, too, Carter," she murmured, and that was true. Lifting her arms around his neck, she swayed against him.

"I need you. I need you now."

"Yes," she agreed, surrendering, for she needed him, too, and together they sank down onto her office sofa.

Because it was the last time they'd be together until Carter returned from Europe, he took his time making love to Joanna, holding himself back so that her pleasure could mount and expansively unfold, and when finally they had col lapsed together, Joanna was pleasurably mussed and crushed and breathless. Twisting languidly onto her side and out from under the mass of his body, she maneuvered herself so that she faced his chest. She listened to his powerful heart pounding beneath the white arc of ribs, the tough warp of muscles, the taut stretch of white skin, and she imagined that his heart was like a hot, determined engine booming steadily in the depths of an ultramodern vessel—an icebreaker, cold, clean, gleaming, Olympian.

As she listened, his heart slowed and steadied. Childlike, she wrapped her arms around him, clinging. Eyes shut tightly, she tried to absorb into her being just one more moment to take with her into the coming month. Since they'd become lovers, they had not been separated for such a length of time and now, against all reason, she ached at the thought of his coming absence.

"What's our next shoot?" he asked, and Joanna heard his voice rumbling in his chest.

Smiling against him—like Joanna, Carter was obsessed with his work, and perhaps that was assurance enough—she answered, "Santa Fe. That assistant of mine, the Flawless Gloria, has everything in control. Next, the Chicago penthouse."

"I've been thinking about that." The sofa rose and sank beneath them as he changed positions, nudging more closely against her. "Why not do it all at night?"

Joanna visualized the starkly stylized, phantasmagorically lit, Art Deco grottoes and chambers of the smart young married couple whose avant-garde apartment she and Carter had examined last month. The owners of a successful new restaurant and nightclub in Chicago's Wrigleyville district, Joel and Jolen Braski spent their days sleeping and worked at night. A striking, even startling couple, of exactly the same height and ballerina slightness, the Braskis both had buzz cuts dyed Dracula-black, and identical obscure signs tattooed high on their left cheeks, and nipple rings which showed through their matte-black clothing. Originally from Peoria, they had decorated and streamlined their bodies and their dwelling to reflect their carefully invented radical images. At night their rooms would glow eerily from their neon tube and fluorescent lamps, cutting the sharp, slightly off-kilter furniture out from the blank walls and floors with a hallucinatory clarity.

"You're right." This was why she loved him. He could be brilliant. "Of course. That's just divine, Carter. I'll have Bill Shorter fly out there with me to check it out at night."

"Let's do a shot of their club, too. It's in the same genre of 'nouveau psychotic' the young wealthy seem to go for these days."

Joanna mused a moment. "Their club . . . I don't know . . . all those decapitated, amputated torsos . . . what about the censors?"

"Hey, those statues are art. Besides, they'll be in the background, and CVN has an adult audience. No problem." Carter stretched and edged up into a sitting position. "That cold green light at the bistro is the same at their apartment. Very dramatic."

Joanna sat up, too. "The Braskis will be delighted to have the publicity."

Throwing his shirt over his shoulder, Carter rose and went into the private bathroom.

"Another thought," he called through the half-opened door. "Check out the possibilities of beginning this program with a telephoto shot from outside—from another apartment window, or even a helicopter if we have to—zooming in toward the building . . . a sort of voyeuristic approach."

"Mmm," Joanna responded. "I'll have to think about that. Maybe a little too sinister . . . but it might work . . ." She was surprised to find she could only halfheartedly consider the show just now.

Quickly she pulled on her clothes—she would bathe later, at her apartment—and smoothed her hair. Hurriedly checking in her compact mirror for mascara smudges beneath her eyes, she noticed how her face had the bee-stung, blurry, compliant look of sensual contentment. She clicked the compact shut, as if to enclose that look and that moment of emotional peace as a keepsake to take with her into the next few days. Now, she thought, here come the brief words, the preoccupied kiss, the goodbye.

Carter emerged from the bathroom, his shirt buttoned and tucked into his trousers, his tie hanging loosely around his neck. Joanna saw him clearly: a handsome, tense, ambitious man. At forty-two, he was balding, but he wore it well. It made his already long face look longer, his forehead higher; he looked even more intellectual than he was. Tennis, riding, skiing, sailing, all the sports he loved and did so well, kept him trim and lean. He wore elegant, expensive clothing; today a pinstripe suit of a blue as inky-dark and soap-smooth as carbon paper. His eyes were an electric, frosty, computer-screen blue, a judicious consequence of his laserlike intelligence and his carefully chosen contact lenses.

Carter stared at Joanna, drinking her in with his eyes, then reached out and brought her close to him. Hiding his face against her hair, he confessed, "I don't know how I'm going to get through this next month. Christ, Joanna, I'm going to miss you."

This was almost worse than anything, Joanna thought, this sensation of love which made her heart swell with joy and hope and confusion. She held her breath, trying to stem the welling tide of tears which threatened to embarrass her.

Only when she'd regained her composure did she allow herself to say calmly, "I'll miss you, too."

Carter pulled away, and suddenly he was smiling, his relaxed, almost piercingly beautiful smile that made him seem years younger. "I've got a present for you. Wait."

In a few strides he crossed the room, exited Joanna's office, and returned, bearing in his arms a large, heavy box of brown cardboard. A red bow had been fastened to the top.

"Good Lord!" Joanna laughed with pleasure and surprise. "What is it?"

As he bent down to set it on the floor before her, his face flushed with exertion and his own delight, Carter answered, "Open it and find out." He handed her a paper knife from the desk.

She ripped off the bow and tossed it aside, slit through the cellophane tape, and, pulling back the sections of the lid, discovered the gleaming sumptuous cover of *Houses along the Hudson* staring up at her.

"Carter!"

When she picked up the top book, she found a book on castles on the Loire, and beneath that a book on manor houses and country estates in England. Then a book on southern plantation homes. She lifted the books out and stacked them on the coffee table. A book devoted to conservatories and sunrooms in houses throughout the United States. Two books filled with elaborate architectural drawings and watercolors of the rooms and furnishings from famous novels, from the House of Seven Gables to Tara. All were filled with fascinating text.

"Oh, Carter," Joanna cried. "These are just delicious! I could just . . . *eat* them!"

"Better not," Carter replied gruffly, pleased by her pleasure.

Joanna ran her hands over the pile of books, which glowed like jewels with their rich, vibrant colors. She was deeply moved by Carter's gesture and, wanting to do something equally generous for him, she cocked her head and said lightly, "I can't wait to curl up with these. Now I won't even know you're gone."

Looking up, she met his eyes. She managed to keep the smile on her face. Carter's gaze was dense with love and pain.

"I've got to go." Taking up his briefcase, he gave the office a quick last look.

They kissed quickly, solemnly.

"I'll see you in a month," Carter told her. Then he left.

Joanna stood in her darkening office without moving for a while, then crossed behind her desk to sink into the familiar confines of her desk chair. It was growing late. Time for an evening meal, she supposed, but she had no food at her apartment, she never did, and really she wasn't very hungry, although a void was opening up within her that felt very much like hunger.

She fancied she could actually feel the silence of the offices in the building tonight. If she wanted, she could summon up the presence of any number of colleagues, even Carter, by slipping on an unedited working video- or audiocassette. But she needn't indulge herself now; she'd have all the time in the world to be maudlin as the month progressed.

Behind her, outside her window, the city blossomed into night like a time-lapse photograph of a marvelous glittering electronic rose. She was encapsulated from the street sounds by the hushed humming of the building's air-conditioning system. If she began to feel too lonely, she could call a friend, or she could simply remain here, where she felt most at home. She could sleep on the sofa, where she and Carter had made love, where she and Jake and Carter had earlier watched the Tennessee senator's show.

She would be all right. She was fine. This imposed solitude could actually be good for her, she decided. It had been a long time since she had had the time to sit peacefully, alone. Kicking off her pumps, she put her feet up on a fat pile of folders on her desk, leaned back into the padded leather chair, and considered her life.

Two

~

$\mathcal{A}$ll in all, she was glad to be where she was, a successful career woman, a "media personality" at the age of thirty-eight, with her own New York apartment and a substantial bank account. A few good friends. A rich, rewarding life. She'd never married, but then she'd never expected to. Because her parents had divorced, had never found "true love," she'd calmly, if ruefully, assumed she wouldn't, either. It had been the most wonderful surprise of her life, the miracle of adulthood, a completely unexpected bolt from out of the blue, that she loved her work, that she and her work fit so well together it had become a sort of marriage for her. Her deepest personal satisfaction, her sense of identity, even the most enduring visceral pleasures and deep abiding joys, came from planning and producing her television show.

It was an odd talent, she supposed, that she could immediately, instinctively, detect the core and strengths of other people's homes when she had grown up without a home of her own. When she was younger, she had envied others their memories of home: a split-level ranch house or a backyard with a swing set or a bedroom filigreed by sunlight through a maple tree's leaves or a kitchen table or the worn corner of a favorite chair. She hadn't had any of that, not her own room with stuffed animals and curtains matching the bedspread, or a cat or a dog or a hamster, or even an apartment steeped with familiar, welcoming smells.

She was the only child of Erica and Vincent Jones, a handsome, charming, ill-matched, and finally irresponsible couple. When adorable Erica was a young woman at Vanderbilt, everyone told her she was gorgeous enough to work as a model; after she'd heard that enough and found herself bored with her studies, she moved to New York, visited the agencies, and actually worked on the runways in fashion shows for three months. During that time, at a nightclub, she met Vincent, who was just finishing his residency in plastic surgery. They fell in love, married, had Joanna, moved to Palm Beach, had affairs, got divorced.

Joanna's father quickly became a popular, socially visible plastic surgeon, with offices in Palm Beach and New York. Her mother smoothly evolved into a professional optimist, always trusting that her ex-husband would come back to her or that one of the many debonair men she loved would marry her. She was very pleased to live her life in transit, meandering around the country, staying with lovers, or in bed-and-breakfasts, or in the homes of friends, and, occasionally, briefly, in rented furnished apartments.

Erica—for her mother had insisted that Joanna call her by her "real" name—had been lighthearted, good-natured, frivolous, great fun. She always had so many friends that finding a place to stay for a week or a month or the holidays or the summer was never a problem, even with her little girl around. Erica had been loved by many people, people who worked hard and worried late into the night, who enjoyed coming home to Erica with her perfume and laughter, gin and tonics and nail polish, and her well-mannered beautiful daughter.

Joanna's father became a shape passing by, a check in the mail, a distracted voice on the telephone. Joanna was never able to separate who he truly was from the complicated Romeo dissected for her by his girlfriends. Whenever Joanna visited her father, he was living with a new woman who grudgingly designated some small space in her home for Joanna and her suitcase. As she grew older, many of the women confided in Joanna, hoping that she'd have the key to her father. But she had no key. And no female was permanent in her father's life. He was always changing apartments and women, and along the way Joanna learned things about men in general that made her realize she should never depend on one financially or emotionally.

Both her parents had died within the past decade; her father from a heart attack, her mother from cirrhosis of the liver. They hadn't lived to see Joanna's success, and certainly they would have been puzzled, if they'd had any reaction at all, by her chosen profession.

Joanna had begun her career with accidental good luck when she was a senior at the University of Missouri at Kansas City. Needing money, she took a job on the *Kansas City Star,* assisting the social editor, who hired her as a favor to her mother. She was assigned to cover retirement parties, wedding showers, costume balls, but time after time her accounts contained brief mention of the guests and lavish descriptions of the homes where the parties were held. The social editor yelled, cut, rewrote, and complained to the features editor, and suddenly Joanna found herself writing a weekly column for the Home section. That eventually led to her move to New York to write for small magazines, then for a big magazine, and finally the leap to television, to the newly formed CVN cable network.

Two years ago while Joanna was an assistant writer/researcher for CVN's morning news and entertainment show, she secretly worked up her idea for *Fabulous Homes,* and when she was ready, she made an appointment with Jake Corcoran, the all-powerful network programming vice-president. With a reputation for brilliance and always furiously busy, Jake Corcoran still found space for her in his schedule one day. Jake was so enthusiastic about her idea that he took the time to advise her in the preparation of her pitch, counseling her to work up a concise, vivid outline of the show, backed up by a fifty-page document detailing what the weekly half-hour show would encompass over a span of nine months, the proposed skeleton production staff, and a production budget estimate. Jake advised her to research and be prepared to discuss just what segment of the American audience would watch her show and what kinds of advertisers would support it. She did all that, as well as using her vacation time to search out, examine, and compile photographs and specs of the first eight houses she planned to show. She had letters of acceptance from the owners.

The more she actually dug into the details and shaped the show, the more excited Joanna grew. She could envision every shot, every room, every millisecond. She worked furiously, speeding through her duties for the morning news and entertainment magazine so that she'd have time to devote to her project, not bothering with regular meals or shopping for clothes or for dates with men or friends. Just slaving with a feverish, delicious, nearly maniacal determination. She'd never been happier in her life.

She'd also never been as frightened—or as proud—as she was the Monday afternoon when she was given fifteen minutes to present her idea to five of the network's most terrifying executives. Jake Corcoran had called the meeting, and the sheer fact of his presence made it clear to the others that he approved of the show, and gave Joanna courage. Still she knew that her show—and it seemed now, the meaning and texture and zest of her life—hung in the balance.

At that point she didn't have an agent to go to bat for her; at that time she didn't need one and couldn't have afforded one. But she was thirty-six, slender, a tall, broad-shouldered, honeyed blonde with her heavy hair sweeping down over one side of her face, giving her a sultry look that balanced out her businesslike demeanor. She wore a simple suit of creamy gray wool with a white silk blouse. She looked good in person; she'd look good on camera. She was comfortable with that, and she was confident of the worth of her idea.

Calmly Joanna made her pitch. She needed to get one of the five executives so excited about the show he'd take on the difficult job of arranging in-house production financing as well as exploring outside marketing and all the other various production tasks.

Ronnie Dantz, the network's baby genius, yawned openly and picked at his dirty fingernails; he loved animation, science fiction, computers, and the future.

Sandra Mattlebury, the old cow who produced the afternoon tabloidesque talk show, watched Joanna suspiciously; obviously she'd come to this meeting only to watch out for competition.

Meticulous, nervous Phil Curtis with his hyena's laugh and jerky mannerisms had been in Joanna's mind the most likely possibility. He produced the network's cooking and gardening shows and had made it known he was looking for a new challenge. Whatever he'd touched had turned to gold, so Joanna found herself aiming her pitch his way, and was relieved to see him take copious notes as she talked.

White-haired, red-faced Shamus Reilly, the network's veteran, gnawed on an unlit cigar and popped Tums like candy into his mouth, nodding and grunting in what Joanna interpreted as positive reinforcements.

Carter Amberson was there, too. Joanna had heard about Carter and seen him across the room at network parties. At forty, he'd made a name for himself from the shows he'd produced. An almost chillingly handsome man, he was known for his abrupt, no-nonsense demeanor and his ability to work hard. As a coproducer he was, rumors went, fair but tough. But she could get no reading from him as she talked. His face was impassive.

Joanna talked for exactly fifteen minutes, then smiled and concluded, "That's it. Thank you for your time."

From the other end of the table, Jake nodded his curly black head in approval.

"What time slots are you thinking of?" Phil Curtis asked suspiciously. "Saturday afternoon is nicely packed already."

"I'm thinking of Friday evening, around seven," Joanna quickly responded, leaning forward eagerly. "The audience this would draw would be professional; they work hard, they make a lot of money, they want to know how to spend their money. They go out on Saturday nights, help the kids with homework on school nights. Friday nights they relax, watch TV, check out how the competition lives, see what they've been working for."

"Your show will make the audience envious. They love that. Can't get enough of it." It was Carter Amberson speaking. "I want the show. I'll do it."

Joanna's eyes met his across the table and she felt an electric jolt zap between them so that her heart thumped loudly. Her knees went weak. It took all her determination not to collapse at the table. That was it? It was done? She was going to have her show? She could have rushed across the room and smothered Carter Amberson with kisses of gratitude if he hadn't been so forbiddingly aloof.

So at once, in a tumbling, exhilarating, breathtaking rush of activity, an entire new phase of her life began. Joanna was busier than she'd ever been, and happier. The pilot went off beautifully and *Fabulous Homes* premiered its first three shows that spring. The network committed to a contract that summer, and the series began in late September. Within months *Fabulous Homes* was high in the ratings, written up in trade rags and popular magazines.

Joanna was so good at what she did she seemed to have been born exactly for *Fabulous Homes.* She could quickly spot the warm true center of any house; she could draw out the most laconic family member; she had a gift for knowing how long to linger on any subject or furnishing or architectural detail. On camera she discovered she was a natural, relaxed and efficient and quick and slightly humorous. The more shows she produced, the better she got. The fan mail began piling in. Celebrities approached her, wanting their homes to be spotlighted. The network asked her to sign a five-year contract. She found an agent to represent her both to the network and to the magazines who wanted to profile her, the charities who wanted her to donate her name or time, the talk shows on other networks who asked her for an interview. She was given her own office at the CVN building and her own secretary.

At first Joanna was concerned about collaborating with Carter, but immediately they discovered that their minds worked with the same speed: in brilliant, dense, rapid flashes that often left others behind. It was not merely that they thought the same way, agreeing on what was important; their minds ran in similar channels, arriving at point D from point A while everyone else was stumbling over point B. They had similar energies: on the way to one location they could spend an entire plane ride arranging the details for the next show; when problems arose, they didn't panic or waste time tearing their hair but simply grabbed hold and twisted the situation to their advantage. They loved their profession with a passion and recognized that in the other.

Her status and Carter's were clearly spelled out in the myriad and complicated contracts they had signed with the network and with each other, but each show required hundreds of decisions. Joanna had heard that Carter was used to getting his own way. She knew the time would come when she would have to confront Carter, to fight him, and as she worked with him, she studied him in preparation. Carter

Amberson was cool and contained, hard to read.

Early in their first year, the occasion she'd been expecting arose. Vern Cook, a young, capable, reliable assistant lighting technician, presented himself humbly in Joanna's office one day. In spite of the constant praise and encouragement, Mitch, the head lighting tech, showered on Vern, the young man was still painfully timid. Joanna knew it was something crucial that had forced him to come to her office by himself.

"Hi, Vern, what's up?" Joanna asked, continuing to sort through her correspondence in order not to seem to be staring at the guy.

His voice trembled. "Mr. Amberson fired me."

"What?" Joanna dropped her stack of mail. "Why?"

Vern's pitifully pockmarked face burned red with embarrassment. "I, uh, Mr. Amberson got a letter, uh, I, uh, you know . . . with Mr. Bently's daughter."

Joanna gaped, dumbfounded. FH had just taped a show at the estate of a Texas oil magnate who entertained himself with a ranch of exotic wildlife. He was a big, pie-faced man with a brood of big, pie-faced, loud-voiced, ambling, gun-toting sons, and a big, pie-faced, loud-voiced, ambling, gun-toting daughter who had just been kicked out of her eastern boarding school two months before graduation for drunkenness and improper conduct. Clearly bored with the entire majestic sprawl of land and animals and with her fabulously furnished home, as vast and ornate and beautiful as an air-conditioned Taj Mahal, Sapphire had trailed around sulkily with the FH crew during every second of the shoot; the only time Joanna had caught the young woman smiling was when she was being interviewed.

"Wait." Joanna stood up. Leaning on her desk, she stared at Vern. "You did exactly what with Mr. Bently's daughter?"

Vern's teeth were nearly chattering with fear. "You know. I . . . did it with her."

"You went to bed with Sapphire Bently?"

Vern nodded so hard he nearly went into spasms.

It was all Joanna could do to keep from laughing. A more unlikely love match was inconceivable.

"All right," she sighed. "Let's go see Carter and straighten this out."

As they made their way along the hall and in the elevator

to Carter's corner office on the twentieth floor, they didn't speak, and Vern seemed to regain some equanimity, but after Joanna announced to Carter's secretary that she wanted to see him immediately and the two of them were shown into Carter's posh inner sanctum, Vern's anxiety level shot up again. She could nearly smell the fear steaming off him.

"Carter," Joanna explained pleasantly, "it seems we've got a little problem here." She gestured to some chairs. "May we sit down?" Without waiting for him to assent, she sat, and Vern gratefully followed suit. "Vern says you've fired him."

In reply, Carter winged a sheet of paper across the desk toward Joanna. "I think this explains everything."

Quickly Joanna scanned the page, a letter from Beau Bently castigating the entire CVN network because for the week that they were on the Bently ranch, their employee Vern Cook had taken advantage of his daughter, Sapphire Bently.

"He's threatening to sue us," Carter pointed out.

"Actually he's not," Joanna retorted. "He's only blowing hot air around. If a man like Beau Bently were going to sue, he'd have done it by now. Instead of this overwrought letter, we'd have a kick-ass legal document."

"I hope you're right. At any rate, Vern has been informed of our policies before. Messing around with any of our guests or their relatives is verboten, and—"

Ignoring Carter, Joanna looked at the assistant lighting technician, who had gone gray. "Vern," she prompted kindly, "what can you tell us about all this? Is it true?"

Vern nodded, looking as if he were about to be ill. "But . . . she came after me," he confided. "I swear. She followed me around. She invited me to her room." He turned red again. "She begged me."

"Oh, well, that makes all the difference," Carter cut in, his voice as sharp and chilly as ice. "Vern's not responsible, since she went after him. I'll simply draft a letter to Beau Bently and explain it. Still, since Vern's such a hunk, he's a danger to the show. The only thing to do is to fire him."

Joanna could feel the heat of anger burning in her own cheeks now.

Staring at Carter, her voice as cold as his, she overruled

him. *"I'll* write the letter to Beau. I have no doubt that I'll be able to smooth this all over. As for Vern, I'm certain he won't do anything like this ever again, no matter how tempting the circumstances." Looking at the pathetic young man, she softened her voice. "You're not fired, Vern. Don't worry. We'll work it out. You can go now."

Vern rose on shaky legs and made his escape.

Joanna glared at Carter. "Why were you so unkind?"

"Unkind? Hell, Joanna, if Beau Bently had sued—"

"You know he's not going to sue. That daughter of his must be twice Vern's size and eighty times as experienced. Carter, I really object to your language and your style. My crew—"

"—will take advantage of you at every turn if limits aren't set."

"What is your problem! That poor young man—"

Carter interrupted her again. "That 'poor young man' can't keep his fly zipped. He pulled a stunt just like this on one of the shows I was producing last year. This year he got Linda Rosenbloom over in Legal pregnant."

Joanna's jaw dropped. "Vern Cook?"

"Vern Cook." Carter paused to let this sink in, then continued, "It's a mystery to me, but some women go wild for him. After Linda had the abortion, I called him in and told him in no uncertain terms that if anything like this ever happened again, he was out of CVN for good."

Quickly the implications of what had just happened raced through Joanna's mind. "Carter, I apologize for countermanding you in front of an employee. I acted hastily."

"That's right," Carter said.

"On the other hand, all this wouldn't have happened if you hadn't made a unilateral decision to fire Vern without consulting with me," Joanna pointed out. "If you'd told me about Vern's background, and asked my opinion, I probably would have agreed with you."

"Look, I'm trying to save you some time and trouble. You shouldn't have to attend to every detail."

"I consider our crew more than a detail," Joanna retorted. "Look, let's agree not to make major decisions without consulting the other first. Okay?"

"Okay."

* * *

After the first confrontation, the others were easier to navigate and Joanna found that to Carter's credit, once a decision was made, even one Carter didn't like, he did not try to subvert her, and he did not carry any kind of grudge. Carter wanted the show to be a success; that was his first priority, and he didn't let petty disagreements distract him.

Even better and completely unexpected was the elegant balance their personal styles provided. Joanna's vision was soft, warm, diffuse, forgiving; Carter's electric, cold, swift, critical. At first this difference was an irritant. Eventually they were able to discuss their managerial styles, to analyze and anticipate and even to use them in a kind of good cop/bad cop way with their staff. Joanna was so reasonable and personable that she was often inefficient, and people took liberties with her they'd never think of in dealing with Carter, who managed with clear-cut and unflinching authority.

Their alliance was especially helpful in dealing with Dhon Rodriguez, the lovable, theatrical, adorably witty and easily wounded young man who took care of Joanna's makeup and hair for the show, working the miracles that kept her looking gorgeous on camera in spite of heat, humidity, or cold. He entertained the FH crew while they traveled, cheering them through the most cataclysmic shoots with wickedly realistic imitations of celebrities and network dignitaries, singing Ethel Merman songs when the rest of the crew was exhausted and depressed. Dhon was priceless. Everyone loved him, and Joanna didn't want to face a camera without him. But Dhon had never learned to appreciate solitude or even to accept that few seconds of silence that helped people regain their equanimity. He didn't know when to stop and there seemed to be no subtle way to get through to him. Once when a rainstorm persisting over an entire week ruined their plans for a shoot in a house on the Vineyard, Joanna snapped at Dhon, "For God's sake, will you close your mouth a moment so the rest of us can think?" Dhon had instantly gone into a major sulk which didn't end until Joanna sent him red roses. She and Carter had a private discussion about Dhon after that, and from then on if Dhon needed subduing, it was Carter who did it, in his cool, indifferent way. Dhon accepted it from Carter; Carter was known for his heartlessness and

Dhon didn't take it personally, as he did with Joanna.

As Carter and Joanna smoothed out the rough spots in their affiliation, they brought each show to its ultimate pace and look. *Fabulous Homes* entered its second season, and Joanna and Carter began to reap rewards: great leaps in salary, network bonuses, industry awards, a fine fat share of fame and fortune. But that wasn't why they worked so relentlessly. The truth for both of them was that they loved their work, loved *working* more than anything else in the world. No matter how they muttered and cursed about the endless hours they put in, producing FH together was a pleasure so intensely rich it was almost sexual.

But not overtly sexual. That was never Carter's style. Joanna observed time and again how his startling good looks drew stares and smiles from women he passed on the street and in offices and restaurants and airport terminals, while Carter never responded or even seemed to notice. He didn't flirt with or even react to the most seductive invitations from various women who worked at the network.

Still, because they spent so much time alone with each other traveling across the country in planes and limos and in vans with camera crews, they gradually developed a comfortable alliance that was nearly a friendship. When Joanna told Carter a little about her lonely, nomadic childhood, Carter confided in return what few others knew about him: he had been dirt-poor and had struggled to get his education at a state college in the Midwest. He did not work as hard as he did only for the money, but money was terribly important to him; it meant security.

During the first year of her show, Joanna didn't really have a private life. She spent every minute working, or sleeping until she went back to work. She was completely happy, and then one morning she boarded a 727 to Jackson Hole and discovered Carter's assistant, Hank Cunningham, on the plane instead of Carter. A network emergency had kept Carter in New York. Hank was personable, pleasant, and efficient, and the production went along smoothly enough, but something was lacking. As they flew home after their week's work, Joanna closed her eyes and leaned against the seat back and realized that without Carter around, much of the excitement and zest—the electric deliciousness—was missing.

She realized she was in love with Carter.

But wait, she told herself. Was it really love, or something more complicated, mixed of admiration and gratitude?

Earlier that month CVN had held its annual banquet in a ballroom at the Waldorf-Astoria. There had been a feast and speeches, and there had been awards presented at the head table. Silver-haired, whiskey-voiced, sequin-drenched Bea Blake, the doyenne of cable TV and one of CVN's CEOs, read out the name of the producer of that year's best new show: Carter Amberson for *Fabulous Homes.* The room filled with applause as Carter was pecked on his cheek by his serene wife and as he made his way to Bea Blake's side. He wore a tux with diamond studs which glittered when he reached the podium, where the light glinted off his blond hair like the sun off a suit of armor, and there was something medieval about him in his lean aristocratic fineness and in his bearing.

And in his courtliness, too, for instead of reaching for the silver award shaped like a globe with a garland around it, Carter leaned to the microphone and said, "I cannot accept this award. It belongs to Joanna Jones. She conceived the show, did the first research on it, wrote it, structured it, hosted it, and she is the one who has been its artistic guide. I have been only her coproducer, her assistant."

Bea Blake stood with the trophy in her hand and her mouth open in shock. No one had ever refused an award before or challenged the judgment of the executives who decided who would receive them.

"I would like to see this award given to Joanna Jones," Carter declared, turning his powerful gaze on Bea Blake, who was pretty powerful herself.

"Here, here!" Jake called from the audience, and then a multitude of other resounding cries rang out.

Bea Blake quickly regained her composure. "In that case," she announced, "I will be delighted to present this award for best new CVN show to Joanna Jones for—"

Carter leaned into the microphone. "—for *Joanna Jones' Fabulous Homes.*"

Joanna was amazed. She was accustomed to the steady eye of the television camera on her and the hot beat of lights, but the quick cold flick of flashbulbs against her vision was unsettling as she rose from the table where she sat with Gloria, her assistant, and Dhon, her makeup man, and Bill Shorter, the director, and their escorts. Jake and Emily were at the head table, and Carter and Blair were seated at a table at the front of the room, and as she dazedly approached the dais, she passed Blair, who was not smiling. Well, why should she; a network award was a major achievement, not to be easily passed up.

"I just want to say," Bea Blake was speaking, "that this is the first time a woman has won this award." She kissed Joanna's cheek.

Later, Joanna was told how dignified she'd been as she accepted the award, how almost regal she had looked, and how elegant had been her very few words of acceptance. In fact, she had been nearly stupefied with surprise and nervousness.

Later, too, she had tried to thank Carter for his generosity, but he had been impatient with her gratitude, each time changing the subject, turning their talk toward the next show.

Few men had given Joanna her just due as Carter had, and no one else had done it quite so spectacularly. But during her career there had been other men, and women, too, who had given her a significant boost up the ladder of success. She had felt gratitude and affection for them, but what she felt now for Carter Amberson was galaxies more complex than that. What she felt for Carter Amberson overwhelmed her body as well as her mind and emotions.

That would never do. Over the years she'd had a series of love affairs of varying intensity with more or less appropriate men—some too old, some far too young—but never had she slept with another woman's husband, and she'd vowed she never would. She'd grown up hearing women crying over men: her mother over unfaithful lovers, and all the pretty women her father, a compulsive Don Juan, had romanced, and moved in with, and left . . . No, she would not be the cause of another woman's tears.

Cold rain, as bleak and pitiless as her memories, slashed at the plane's windows. The plane landed. Joanna walked down the long ramp into the terminal, automatically calling out goodbyes and thanks to Hank and the other members of the crew, already mentally making a list of single men she should start seeing immediately, must start sleeping with, so she could exorcise herself of her desire for Carter Amberson.

As she moved briskly along, she was unusually aware of the health of her body easily bearing the weight of her shoulder bag and briefcase, her skirt sliding sleekly over her long strong legs. This body that did her bidding so well—how long had it been since she'd pleasured it? Since she'd had a lover? She couldn't remember. Automatically she received and ignored the stares of the people in the crowd who recognized her. She kept her face, partially hidden by sunglasses even on this rainy day, blank. How would it feel to lie next to Carter? She could not give in to such thoughts, not even in fantasies. She had to get control of herself.

She was in such a state of miserably determined renunciation that when she turned out of the gate into the broad terminal, she nearly plowed past a man before realizing it was Carter. He reached out for her. Grabbing her shoulders, he stopped her in her tracks.

She stared at him. "What are you doing here?"

Carter looked terrible and wonderful, simultaneously pale and shadowed, his usually immaculate clothes as rumpled as if he'd slept in them.

"I need to talk to you," he said.

"What's wrong?"

Because his mind seemed to run on so many levels at once, Carter had a habit of not looking at the person he was talking to, but now his vivid blue eyes were focused right on Joanna's face. All his energy, all his powerful intellect, was directed toward Joanna. She was mesmerized.

But he seemed to be nearly paralyzed. "Wait," he said. "Not here."

She let him pull her along through the crowded halls, out the automatic doors past porters and travelers and security guards, and into the nearest taxi.

"West Seventy-fifth," he told the driver.

Joanna was even more puzzled. That was her address, not the network's.

"What's this all about?" she asked.

The taxi lurched forward. Carter turned to face her. "I'm afraid I'm in love with you," he said.

For only a moment Joanna sat absorbing the shock. But it seemed so perfect, so perfectly *them*, that they would realize their hearts at the same time. Very gently she put her hand to Carter's worried face. "I'm in love with you, too."

His mouth tightened. His chin bunched up.

"This is wrong," he said in a low, desperate voice. "I'm married. I've never been untrue to Blair. I don't play around."

A delicate trembling had overtaken Joanna. It felt like snowflakes, as light as feathers, as electric as kisses, glittering all over her skin, a radiant shimmering sensation that seemed to stem from the spot where her hand touched Carter's face. His beautiful face. She could not believe she was touching him, and something rapturous was released inside her which told her that she had been wanting to touch him like this for a long time.

"Carter," she whispered, "kiss me."

In reply, he turned his face into her hand and closed his eyes and kissed the sensitive hollow of her palm. She studied Carter and saw him, not as coproducer and colleague, but as a man. She saw the sprinkling of boyish freckles across the bridge of his nose and his cheeks. She saw how with his eyes closed his thick lashes brushed his cheeks. Then he opened his eyes and looked at her as she was looking at him, a searching, greedy, naked look that nearly alarmed her with its intensity.

She thought he would kiss her mouth then. Instead, he looked away, but as he did he took her hand in both of his and held it in his lap. "Whatever happens between us, you have to understand, can't be permanent. I won't leave Blair, not ever. That's just not in the realm of possibility. I loved Blair when I married her. In a way I still love her."

Joanna nodded, spellbound, speechless.

"I've always been clear with her," Carter continued, "about what I want in life and how hard I intend to work to get it. Blair's been content to take second place. She's given me a son, and I've given her a luxurious life. I don't want to hurt her."

When he fell silent, Joanna did not speak but merely waited. The pain of hearing Carter speak about his wife was mitigated by the warmth of his hands against hers. Jealousy was only a minor chord in the concerto of emotions playing through her: she was thrilled and even honored by Carter's confidences.

The cab was nearing Riverside Drive. Anxiety rushed through Joanna: would Carter come into her apartment with her? Or would he decide, in spite of the longing that held them both in thrall, to stop this before it went any further? Suddenly all she cared about in the world was this man, and all she wanted was the next hour of her life.

"It's all right," she assured him. "I don't want anything permanent, Carter. I've never wanted marriage or children. God, I could have had all that by now, if I'd wanted. I love my work—you know that. Anything more, anything private between you and me—would be just that. Private." She bit her lip to keep from saying, "I'll take what I can get," but that was how she felt at the moment, desperate for him, ready to promise anything at all, for every atom in her body was humming with joy and desire, every synapse and nerve and cell was begging to be crushed close to Carter, and even her clever, rational, capable mind surrendered before her desire, like a proud tree bowing to the onslaught of a blizzard. If she could have the next hour with him, she would ask for nothing more.

The cab stopped in front of her apartment building.

"Carter, come in with me," Joanna entreated. "Please."

Carter stuffed some bills through the Plexiglas tray and went with Joanna.

She thought—hoped—that once inside, he would embrace her. Instead, he suggested, "Let's have some coffee."

"All right," she replied. "I think I have some instant." Tossing her briefcase on the kitchen counter, she filled a pan with water and turned on the burner. While she was measuring out the spoons of dried coffee grains, she heard Carter walk through her apartment, and then he was there in the kitchen with her, his body seeming enormous in the small room.

"You don't have much furniture," he remarked.

"I know. I've just never had the time to look for any." Tilting her head to look up at him from under her lashes, she added in a soft voice, "I do have a bed."

He was staring at her, entranced. "I've never met anyone

with a place like this. If your viewers could only see your living room!"

"I do a lot of work at home. I never entertain here." She laughed. "I never entertain. I never do anything but work!" She handed him a mug. "I don't cook much, either," she admitted, then proposed, sliding past him to lead the way, "Let's go into the bedroom. It's the only place where we can both sit."

Joanna curled up at the head of the bed, leaning against the wall. Carter settled at the foot. He took a sip of his coffee, flinched, and said, "Too strong. Look, Joanna, I don't know what I'm doing here. I admit I'm confused. I've told you I don't want to hurt Blair, but I also don't want to hurt you." When she began to protest, he shook his head. "Wait. Hear me out. I've never felt as close to anyone in my life as I do to you. I've never felt such companionship. Working with you on the show is just about the best thing in my life. I don't want to endanger that."

Instead of reassuring him, Joanna only nodded. "I understand. I wouldn't want to endanger the show, either."

"For years I've been trying to figure out the appeal that television has for me. It seems that a man could be drawn to sailing or farming or medicine. Those things are *natural.* But television is so artificial. Yet I feel like I was born for it. Joanna, my work is the core of my life."

"I know. It is for me, too."

"I don't know how much I have left to give to anything else, especially to a relationship with someone I respect as much as I respect you." He studied her, his face serious. "I don't think I can subtract my feelings for you from my feelings about my work."

Joanna felt a smile break out over her face. "Carter," she said, leaning toward him, "those are the most romantic words I've ever heard." Setting her mug on the bedside table, she reached out and took Carter's from him and set it on the table, too. "This stuff is undrinkable."

He grinned. "You're right."

Joanna slid down the bed until she sat next to him. "I don't need coffee anyway," she said. "I'm feeling quite wide awake."

"Joanna, we've got to—"

She put her fingers on his mouth. "Sssh." The rush of his breath against her fingers made her nearly moan with desire. "Carter, let's not talk anymore, okay?"

"Okay." He was almost shivering in the warm room.

Joanna kissed him, and Carter drew her against him, and she felt her heart pounding within her and Carter's thundering in his chest. They lay back onto the bed, crosswise, fully clothed, kissing, tasting, exploring, discovering, and then they undressed each other, layer by layer, and came upon the intimate pale surprise of each other's body. They were not adolescents; they did not hurry, but spent the deep hours of the night getting to know one another. When finally they joined together, breast to breast, skin to skin, they discovered to their mutual delight that they were as well suited for each other in pleasure as they were at work.

Joanna sat alone in her office as daylight left the sky, remembering this past year, a period of rich, intense, demanding, rewarding work and love. She thought she had everything. Why was it that now as she sat in her office she felt she had nothing?

Three

$\sim$

$\mathcal{A}$ sharp knock sounded at the office door, startling Joanna out of her reverie.

Sung Chu, one of CVN's custodians, pushed the door open and peeked in. "Oh. Sorry, Ms. Jones. I'll come back later."

"No, no, it's all right," Joanna said, swinging her feet down from her desk. "I'm just leaving, Sung. Come on in." Sliding her feet into her shoes, she glanced around her desk, searching for whatever needed to be dealt with urgently. Folders and cassettes and notes and letters filled her various baskets, but none tempted her. It could all wait.

Sung wheeled in his vacuum cleaner and cart, and Joanna exchanged pleasantries with him as she gathered up her purse and left her office. Gloria's reception area, the long corridor and sleek elevator, seemed unusually empty and quiet, even for this time of day—it was already eight o'clock. Stepping out into the muggy August air, Joanna felt suddenly lonely in the vast sparkling city. She looked up at the sky, which seemed far away and pale with lingering light. As she waited at the curb for a cab, she watched a young couple stroll by, the woman in a sleeveless summer dress nearly entwined like a vine around a lanky, blissful-eyed young man.

She caught a cab to West Seventy-fifth, stopped at a deli for a sandwich and cold drink to take home with her, and headed for her apartment.

"Good evening, Ms. Jones."

"Good evening." Joanna smiled at the uniformed man who held the door open for her; he was a temp, filling in while

Luigi, the permanent doorman, was on vacation with his family.

Everyone in the world was on vacation with his family.

Her apartment was stuffy; the air-conditioning was unreliable in this building. Joanna slipped into a T-shirt and shorts, then went around her apartment, opening windows to the humid night. Sinking onto her bed, she flicked on the TV and spread her sandwich out before her on the bed, using the paper bag as a plate.

Nothing on television held her attention. After a few bites of the sandwich, her hunger disappeared, and she sat cross-legged on her bed in the muggy summer night feeling edgy and discontented until she realized with a jolt that what she really was feeling, for the first time in a long time, was lonely.

Over the past year while she and Carter had been lovers, their work and their lovemaking had intertwined into a profoundly engrossing whole, and Joanna had felt richly satisfied. Carter spent five nights a week at Joanna's apartment; it had been his custom for a long time to spend those nights in the city during the workweek. He had his own telephone line installed at Joanna's; he and Blair spoke every night. When Carter called Blair or Chip from Joanna's bedroom to chat with his son about his braces or a ball game or with his wife about an invitation they'd received to a charity benefit or other scheduling conflicts, Joanna simply went into the bathroom and took a shower, letting the water drown out the sounds of his voice, or into the living room to sort through the boxes of files and materials for the books she was planning to write. Thus she gave Carter privacy and insulated herself from the reality of his marriage.

Oh, there were occasions when she got into a maudlin, overwrought snit of obsession about Carter's loyalties to Blair, but mostly she didn't have time for self-pity or regret— she was busy working at what she loved best with the man she loved. The truth was that Carter was with her more hours of the week than absent. His weekends in Westchester with his family gave her time to lunch with her friends or catch up on her sleep or shopping.

Tory, her best friend, constantly advised Joanna to make a clean break with Carter and find someone else, an unmarried man. But Joanna had no illusions about that. She knew that interesting available men were rare, and furthermore, as she'd ascended in the world of television until she had found her niche here in the starry pinnacle, she understood that more and more men were becoming off limits to her, or would think they were, because she was so successful, and slightly famous, and even a little respected, as well as financially independent. The problem of time also entered in: she lived for her work; few men would be able to accommodate a woman with so little free time or emotional energy.

What she knew of Blair also encouraged Joanna to believe that what she had with Carter was real love, complete and significant, while it was only the facade he shared with Blair. Joanna had met Blair at occasional network parties over the years. She'd been impressed. Blair was beautiful, small-boned, her heart-shaped face framed by a bell of glossy chestnut hair. She moved slowly, as if to an inner music. She was so serene. Joanna could understand how Blair provided the perfect refuge for a man like Carter, who spent most of his life in a network scramble of hurry, hassles, arguments, split-second expensive decisions, noise, furor, disasters, personalities, intrigue. In a perverse way it pleased Joanna that Blair was so lovely; Joanna liked competition and would always prefer to compete with a worthy adversary.

Another source of gratification and even, she'd admit, of a petty pleasure was the fact that Joanna would never in a million years have shown Blair Amberson's residence on *Fabulous Homes*.

The summer after Joanna and Carter became lovers, she had the opportunity to see the Ambersons' home in Westchester when they held a posh lawn party for the network. Joanna had gone with Tory and Tory's husband, John, a network lawyer. The day had been perfectly sunny, and the French doors were open from the house to the garden where an enormous blue-and-white-striped tent had been set up. Tables of drinks and delicacies were set up around the turquoise swimming pool, on the lawn, as well as throughout the house. With a flute of Mumm's in hand, Joanna wandered around, smiling, chatting, and secretly observing with an eagle eye.

The style of the house—French provincial—was not Joanna's favorite. However, the pristine atmosphere was impressive. Each room, like Blair herself, was beautiful, perfect in its proportions, and unutterably calm. No clutter. No frills. No fuss.

That day she'd even seen the bedroom where her lover slept with his wife.

People drifted in and out, upstairs and down, to look at the beautiful house. Joanna decided she needed to use the lavatory on the second floor, and then she walked down the spacious hall and stood just outside the master bedroom, looking in.

She would have gone through Blair's closet and drawers if she could have, but of course she didn't dare, not with all the people coming and going. But where was it? she wondered, the clue, the key, to Blair's soul? The house, master bedroom included, was as tidy and impersonal as a television ad. Luxurious, yes, but bland. Even sterile.

"What you see is what you get." A voice came from over her shoulder.

"Tory! You startled me."

"I thought I'd find you up here snooping around." She sauntered into the room.

"I'm not snooping. I had to use the bathroom and I just passed—"

"I've told you, and you wouldn't believe me. Believe me now? Blair's as deep as lipstick."

"She must have something more. Carter married her."

"She's beautiful. No denying that. Has money of her own, and that probably mattered when they were young. She knows how to present the facade. Blair has *nothing* beneath the facade. The scary part is, she knows it, and likes it that way."

Joanna had turned away from the bedroom, with a glad heart. She and Carter shared so much: passion, an enthusiasm for their work, triumph when shows went well, network gossip, challenging ideas. If all he shared with Blair was this shell of a house, perhaps he should leave her and make a permanent home with Joanna.

Then she'd passed by an open bedroom door. A boy's room, baseball posters on the walls, bats, balls, and mitts on the bedspread, a love-mauled stuffed bear tucked against the pillow. Chip. Blair *would* name her son Chip. Still, the room evoked a person, with desires and dreams—and needs, needs for a whole family, an available father. Joanna did not want to be responsible for taking a father away from a child, not ever. She'd gone silently back down the stairs, into the sunny day. She'd gone smiling, back into the midst of the party.

She'd never asked Carter to leave Blair. She'd never even really wanted him to. Why should she? Her life was full of work and friends and travel and exhaustion as well as his very satisfying love. She was proud of her self-sufficiency.

But on this lovely August evening Joanna didn't want to be self-sufficient. Summer light lingered in the sky and summer sounds drifted up from the streets. Laughter. Singing. The whir and click of roller blades; the excited tap of high heels.

Grabbing up the phone, she dialed Tory's number.

Tory and Joanna had met at a dinner party two years before when they'd been forced to talk with each other by virtue of their placement at the table. Tory was happily married; her life centered on her family. Joanna had just returned from a skiing trip to Vail with a man twelve years younger than she; she was working hard, climbing the ladder of her career. The two women lived very different lives, but their friendship blossomed in spite of that.

At the dinner party, Tory confessed that she'd seen the first few segments of *Fabulous Homes* and thought it was wonderful. Homes were so important, she'd said, and impassionedly she'd told Joanna about the old Victorian house they'd just bought on a bluff in Nantucket. Tory was obsessed with its furnishing and decoration. Joanna asked Tory if she could do a series about decorating the perfect summer house for her new show. Tory agreed; and over the weeks that followed, whenever Tory went to Nantucket, Joanna joined her, taking notes and pictures. Joanna admired Tory's sense of style and her commitment to her family's comfort and pleasure. Tory was fascinated by the way Joanna's mind worked and she respected Joanna's professional achievements. They became close friends.

It was Tory, pleading for the sanctity of the family, who kept Joanna from asking Carter to leave his wife. Joanna should drop Carter, that was Tory's view, Carter was married, and he had a son, and did Joanna really want to be responsible for breaking up a home? But he doesn't love his wife, he loves me, Joanna insisted, and often she wept, and Tory wept in sympathy, and they had gone on arguing that way every time they talked.

The Randalls' housekeeper answered their phone. "No, Ms. Jones," she said, "the Randalls are not here, remember? They're in Nantucket."

"Of course, Lei, thank you."

Joanna hung up the phone, despondent. Of course, the Randalls were on vacation, too. On a family vacation.

Fool! she berated herself. You should have made plans! Stalking into her living room, she flipped through her address book, looking for—what? An acquaintance she could spend the evening with? Irritated, she tossed the book aside. She would read one of the many novels she had stacked in wait. She'd answer some of the letters she'd brought home from her office. She'd—the phone rang. Joanna raced to the bedroom. Was it Carter, calling from the airport to say he already missed her?

"Hi, hon." Tory's warm voice filled the silence.

"Tory! I just called you. Lei answered. I'd forgotten you were in Nantucket. How are you?"

"We're in heaven. It's so beautiful here. It's so luscious, it's paradise. I want you to come to Nantucket."

"Oh, that's sweet, Tory, but I've got so much—"

"Nonsense. It can all wait. It's August, remember? Look, everyone needs a break. Just a little tiny break?"

Joanna considered. In her office, tacked to the huge appointment calendar, was an invitation to an island cocktail party from some people she'd met months before, while taping a show in Austin. Nantucket parties were always good for discovering more potential FH hosts, so she could justify the expense of a flight and a rental car on the network's account . . .

"All right, I'll come!" Joanna decided, and found herself smiling as she said the words.

"Oh, Joanna, what fun!"

"I've got to tie up some loose ends at work tomorrow. Give me a day or two—"

"No. Absolutely not. You'll always find some reason to keep working. I want you to come tomorrow."

"Thursday."

"No. Tomorrow."

"Tomorrow night."

"All right. I'll call Cape and Island Airlines and make the reservation for you."

"Tory, I can—"

"If I do it, I'll know it's done. I'll call you back with the time. Bring a bikini and shorts. No briefcase allowed."

"No briefcase! Tory!"

Tory's response was a throaty, delighted laugh. "Oh, Joanna, it's going to be such fun having you here!"

"I'll be a wreck without my briefcase," Joanna sulked, but secretly she was pleased.

The next day Joanna spent in a frenzy of organization at her office, then hurried home and packed a bag with summer clothes. The glossy art books on houses that Carter had given her were too heavy to cart to the island; she grabbed up some paperback novels.

She slipped a new tape into her answering machine. Shut the windows. Locked her door. At last she was in a taxi to La Guardia. Halfway there, the old cab's air-conditioning broke, causing the squat driver to mutter ceaselessly during the rest of the ride in low, maniacal, rather ominous tones. On the Triboro Bridge, they were held up by a gridlock around a car stopped by an overheated radiator. Finally they arrived at the terminal, where she was immediately ushered onto a plane the size and strength of a toothpaste tube.

Darkness fell as they flew northeast, and coins of light gleamed from the black sky and from the land and occasionally from the water below them. Her fellow passengers chatted about wind surfing and weddings and sunshine and sangria, and Joanna felt her heart lighten.

The moment she stepped off the plane she could tell that it was cooler on this island than the one she'd just left. Above her the sky rose in a starry vault. The air smelled of the sea and roses. Friends and relatives greeted each other with laughter and kisses, and a handsome man wearing white flannels smiled invitingly at Joanna as he ushered his toddling mother from the arrival lounge. Joanna smiled back and pleasure raced through her blood. She felt better already.

"Do you have a convertible?" she asked the clerk at the Hertz counter.

"We surely do. A red Mustang with a white top. How's that?"

"Perfection."

The top was already down on the little car, as if it had been waiting for her. She tossed her bags in the back, settled in, and headed down the long straight road to 'Sconset. She didn't own a car, didn't need to in the city, but she loved driving, and was almost disappointed when finally she pulled up at the Randalls' wide Victorian high on the 'Sconset bluff.

Tory came running out. "You're here! You're really here!"

"God, the air smells like nectar!" Joanna just stood, inhaling great drafts.

"Come in. Get out of those city clothes. I can't believe you're wearing high heels."

"I always wear high heels. I didn't even think—" Joanna followed her friend up the wide steps and into the house.

Tory's husband, John, hugged Joanna warmly. "It's great to have you here."

"Where are Jeremy and Vicki?"

"At the Casino, seeing a movie with some other kids. Is that all the luggage you brought?"

"It's all I need."

"Well, let me show you your room, and change into some shorts. Are you hungry?"

Joanna hesitated. She'd never been one for regular meals. "You know, I think I am. I guess I haven't eaten since breakfast."

"You need a keeper." Tory shook her head in disgust. "Lucky for you we saved some dinner."

So that night Joanna dined on a meal of swordfish and fresh butter and sugar corn on the cob. She ate in shorts and a white T-shirt, her hair tied back, her feet bare. Later, she and Tory strolled along the peaceful village roads, chatting, luxuriating in the fragrance of honeysuckle and wild roses and salt air. After a languorous bath, Joanna slipped between crisp white sheets in the wide comfortable guest room bed. For a while she watched as a capricious ocean breeze made the hems of the starched white curtains lift and dance.

She was so full and content and cool that she fell asleep immediately, only slightly missing Carter.

The next morning she didn't awaken until noon. Her room was full of light; striding to a window, she tossed back a curtain and saw the sparkling expanse of the blue Atlantic. She took a deep breath of fresh air. Then she pulled on shorts and a sports bra and a white T-shirt, brushed her teeth and rubbed sunblock on her fair skin, yanked her long honey-blond hair up into a ponytail, found her sunglasses, and ran barefoot down the stairs.

The air in the kitchen shimmered with sunlight. On the long trestle table, in the great white ironstone bowl of fruit, lay a pink piece of paper covered with Tory's fat, looping handwriting.

> *Joanna,*
> *We're all off bluefishing. We'll be home sometime in the late afternoon. The fridge is loaded, help yourself. The Latherns called to remind you of their cocktail party tonight. Take it easy—that's an order!*
>
> *Love, T.*

Joanna smiled, and choosing a fat purple plum, sank her teeth into it. Sweetness filled her mouth and juice drooled down her chin. Grabbing up a paper towel, she stalked across the kitchen, out through the back porch, and down the long wooden staircase to the beach. The sun-heated unpainted boards warmed the soles of her feet. Heat fell across her shoulders and light flashed against her face. At the bottom of the steps, she turned and struck out for the north. At her left the ocean surged and sang. The world was fresh and cool and gold and blue. She strode along.

She was perhaps twenty yards from the Randalls' property when she realized how fast she was walking—as if she were late for an appointment. "Stop it!" she yelled at herself, right out loud, right there—the group of children playing farther down the beach didn't hear her over the sound of the waves. She sank down onto the sand, stretching her legs, letting as much of her skin as possible make contact with the soothing gritty heat. Wiping her mouth and stuffing the paper towel in her shorts pocket so she wouldn't litter the beach, she ordered herself to relax. She stared out at the vast gleaming, surging water. She rolled the hard plum pit in her hand.

Where was Carter now? Somewhere in Europe. It would be evening. He and Blair would be sipping white wine and looking out at what . . . the Seine? the Rhine? the Grand Canal? For the first time in two years she could not reach her lover if she needed to. She had no idea where he was right now. Would absence make his heart grow fonder? Or would he, during this coming month, find himself getting to know his wife again, and to like her, admire her . . . desire her?

Of course they would make love.

Once Joanna had asked Carter if he and Blair made love often.

He had answered simply, "No."

"Does she mind?"

"I don't think she even realizes, Joanna. She's happy, in her way. She's successful at what she wants to do."

"What is that?"

"Raise a happy child. Keep a beautiful home. Blair's a perfectionist. She needs things to be calm. And all this"— Carter swept his hand over Joanna's body—"this desire . . . it's the antithesis of calm."

But away from her house and its continual demands, living in luxurious hotel rooms in romantic cities, Blair might very well find old habits of desire reviving. Of course she and Carter would make love. And her body would be exciting to him, would be newer, in a way, to Carter than Joanna's was. Husband and wife, their old passion would rekindle, and they would find a new heat and passion between them . . .

Joanna jumped to her feet. Perhaps she'd been wrong to come here. It was true, she was exhausted and overworked; but at least in New York she wasn't stranded in the midst of a perfect family, forced to behold up close and in detail everything she could never have. In New York she could lose herself in work, or office gossip or a new movie or ballet. Tossing her plum pit so far out into the water she couldn't hear its splash, she stormed on down the beach.

About two hours later she returned to the house, slightly dizzy from so much sudden sun and heat. The phone was ringing. She ran the last few steps and dashed across the wide porch and into the cool kitchen to snatch it up. It was her assistant, Gloria, with a problem only Joanna could solve. The Chandlers, who'd been scheduled for filming in October, needed to change the date because of a health problem; could *Fabulous Homes* tape them in the spring? This wasn't a great idea, Joanna told Gloria; the Chandlers lived in a renovated mill on a roaring river in upstate New York; spring was mud season there, which would show murky brown in any window shots; ask them about January, Joanna said. The mill would look picturesque in the snow. And get out their possibles list; whom could they substitute?

Joanna spent most of the afternoon on the phone, cradling it against her shoulder as she and her assistant worked. At some point Joanna pulled a bowl of curried chicken salad from the refrigerator and ate a late lunch. When she finally got off the phone, she had a crick in her neck, so she went to her room and washed her hair and took a long bath, and just as she was wrapping her terry-cloth bathrobe around her, she heard the Randalls come home. She padded down the stairs, leaving wet footprints on the bare wood, to greet them and admire their catch.

All four Randalls were radiant with sunburn, and they smelled of sun and salt and fish. Jeremy displayed a gash he'd put in his thumb while trying to get a fish off the hook.

"Come on, son, I'll show you how to dress these. You, too, Vick." John led his kids to the kitchen and Tory hurried upstairs to shower.

"You're not going to the party?" Joanna asked.

"No. John and I are taking the kids into town for pizza and a movie."

"Which one?"

"*Total Recall.*"

"Better you than me."

"The kids will love it."

"You are such a good mother."

"Damn right."

Joanna went back to her room to dress for the cocktail party, secretly glad it wouldn't be a family affair. She wriggled into a scoop-necked magenta silk dress with a hammered-gold collar that set off her tan and the sun-gilded honey of her hair. Perhaps some elegant eligible man would be there, someone so amazing and sexy that he'd make her forget Carter. Fat chance.

The windows were open in all of the large house, letting sounds drift into Joanna's room: The Indigo Girls whining from Vicki's CD player. The phone ringing. Laughter. Jeremy yelling, "Hey, *Dad!* Where'd you put the charcoal?" John's gruff response. That kid doesn't have a clue, Joanna thought, how his father, a prominent lawyer who makes men in three-piece suits tremble, loves him. The only time she ever saw John Randall completely content was when he was here on Nantucket, in this house, with his family. It was as if everything else was stripped away, revealing the essential man.

Was that how it was for Carter? No, it couldn't be. She knew she satisfied something essential in Carter; she knew he needed her. If she wasn't sure of that, she wasn't sure of anything.

Joanna found she was standing in her room, just staring at a span of blank blue sky framed by white curtains. Looking at her watch, she saw that she was late, and she hurried down the stairs, yelled her goodbyes to the Randalls, and rushed outside to her little rented red convertible. After switching on the ignition, she backed the car out onto the street, then roared off, hurtling left and right like a race car driver along the village byways, past the Sankaty golf course, and finally down along the narrow Polpis Road.

Now the lazy sinuous path made speeding impossible; she had to slow down. She changed the angle of her foot, pulling it back from the accelerator, and accordingly her entire body shifted. She settled more comfortably into the bucket seat. The convertible top was down and the humid evening air drifted around her shoulders like a shawl of mist. The borders of the winding road were thick with wild grasses, Queen Anne's lace, daisies, day lilies. Her shoulders loosened, her thoughts slowed. All the voices cluttering up her head melted and evaporated, and she heard instead the mellow, golden notes of a James Taylor song floating up from the car radio. The sun sent opal streamers across the pale blue sky. It was not yet twilight.

She passed Sesachacha Pond, turned right onto the Quidnet Road, followed it to the crossroad with Squam Road, turned left. This dirt road was deeply rutted and pocked, and she slowed to a crawl between bushes and saplings growing in such lush abundance their branches grazed the car. She could hear birds calling. Rabbits zigzagged foolishly across her path. Braking to a complete halt for a moment, she gazed out at Squam Pond, a watercolorist's dream of thousands of pink mallow roses against blue water and a heavenly green grass. Smiling, she drove on. Her hosts had told her their house was on the ocean side of the road, and had no signpost. She was to turn onto a white gravel road. Coming to one, she did, and went along a driveway so overgrown it was like a green tunnel. Then the view opened up, and there sat the house.

Not her hosts' house. This house was empty. No lights, no cars. Just the house, simple and calm, against the evening sky.

It was a perfectly proportioned two-and-a-half-story gray-shingled house, with five windows on the second floor and two on either side of the blue front door, which was framed by a rose-covered trellis. Two chimneys. A brick walk curving up from the gravel parking area. It was as complete and perfect as a child's drawing of home.

It was not her hosts' home, and she was trespassing, but she had no sense of wrongdoing as she turned off the car's engine and sat in the silence, studying the house. At one end a screened-in porch extended, blanketed in ivy and rose vines. A green wall of privet, untrimmed and shaggy, straggled from the porch to a small garage, providing a shelter from the ocean winds for a weedy, sadly neglected bed of drooping mums and brave rudbeckia daisies.

Joanna got out of the car, closing the door carefully, quietly, and walked across the unkempt lawn and around the side of the house. The lawn extended perhaps twenty feet, then surrendered to the wild thorny tangle of moorland which in turn gave way to the sandy beach that rimmed the placidly rolling Atlantic. The tide was going out, and the sand glistened wetly in the sinking sun.

Joanna looked back at the house. The windows on this side were boarded up; so the house was deserted. What a shame, on such a lovely summer day.

She wanted to linger, but knew she shouldn't, and so she crossed back to the driveway, the slender heels of her shoes sinking into the turf. As she slid back into her car, she had the oddest desire to—oh, it was odd!—say something to the house. To connect with that house. So, feeling strangely very much like herself and not like herself at all, she said, aloud, "I promise I'll be back."

She hadn't planned to say those words. She couldn't imagine why she said them. Shaking her head at her foolishness, she turned her car around and headed back out toward Squam Road. In the rearview she saw the house standing: sturdy, solitary, and proud.

A few hundred feet on, she found the Latherns' residence. Its drive was packed with cars, but Joanna was able to pull her little convertible into a space between a Range Rover and a gorgeous old classic woody station wagon. Sliding out, she took her time approaching the house, studying its unusual architecture, which was gray-shingled, according to the dictates of the Historic District Commission, but otherwise was purely modern, utilizing sharp angles and extreme slopes and lots of shining glass.

She could hear the noise of the party out here. When she was younger, just this moment made her heart beat faster: standing on the threshold, wearing a sexy frock, anticipating any variety of significant encounters with the crowd who gathered inside. Now, more often than not, she found herself girding her figurative loins, as if for some kind of onslaught.

She had met her hosts, Morris and June Lathern, last fall when she featured June's sister and brother-in-law's house in Austin, and now as she entered the house she was glad to find June just inside, standing next to an enormous standing bronze sculpture of summer flowers. All the rooms and even the hall were packed with people.

"I'm so glad you came!" June shouted. She and Morris were lawyers, with their own firm here on Nantucket, and as professional women, June and Joanna had sensed a camaraderie. Joanna also liked June for her height: Joanna at five eight, and as broad-shouldered as she was, often seemed to dwarf other women, and too often caught herself slumping or stooping in a crowd. But Morris and June were tall; Morris was six six and June an even six feet; Joanna felt comfortable with them.

"I turned off on the wrong drive," Joanna informed her hostess. "Coming from 'Sconset. There's the most wonderful storybook house—"

"You must mean the Farthingale house. I think it's on the market. It's got some marvelous old legend connected with it—a treasure, I think. I'll find Bob Hoover, he's in real estate, he can tell you about it. First, let's get you a drink."

There was no hope of hearing each other, so they didn't attempt conversation as they passed through the crowd to the drinks bar that had been set up on the deck of the ocean side of the house. This was an older group, in general, undoubtedly a more conservative one; the men wore Nantucket red slacks and blue blazers, the women, sinfully expensive shapeless silk dresses printed in the geometric blocks in primary colors, making them look like flags of antagonistic nations. As she walked through the room, Joanna could hear the sudden lull in conversation, and then the whispers, as she passed through. And sure enough, by the time she'd been handed a vodka and tonic, here came the first assailants, a short blond husband-and-wife pair who seemed to have been molded from the same plastic as Barbie dolls.

"You're Joanna Jones of *Fabulous Homes,* aren't you?" the wife asked, and not waiting for Joanna to reply, plunged ahead, "I just knew you were. I'm Mindy Whippet and this is my husband, Mark. We own Couturier on Main Street, you must know it, it's the best women's clothing shop on the island."

"I believe I—" Joanna began, but Mindy whipped ahead: "I really do think you should consider doing a segment on our shop. It's terribly clever. The dressing rooms are nothing like ordinary dressing rooms, and the showroom is posh *and* clever. Perhaps—"

"We don't do shops on our show," Joanna replied, smiling as she interrupted the other woman. "We do homes. That's why it's called *Fabulous Homes.*"

"Well, then," Mindy responded, unfazed, "you should do our house. I'm sure you've never seen anything like it. It's a Christian house, you see. Mark and I have an altar in our bedroom and every night before we go to bed we give thanks to God for our good fortune. It would be such a valuable addition to your show. Not to be critical, but you do seem to emphasize the decor of the house and underplay the spiritual ambience of the home—"

Joanna stared at Mindy over her tilted glass as she took a long drink of vodka and tonic. How am I going to get away from this creature? she wondered, but almost before she'd completed her thought, a very tall, extremely handsome man decked out in a buttery linen suit appeared in front of Joanna, and as if by magic, the Whippets melted away.

"May I introduce myself?" He inclined his head in a mock bow. "Claude Clifford, year-round resident and artist. But I often hire myself out as an exorcist for people trapped by the Whippets."

Joanna laughed. "Joanna Jones," she told him, shaking his hand. "They really are terrifying."

"Oh, enough about them, let's talk about you. How do you like my suit?"

Laughing, delighted to be freed from her television role, Joanna walked with her rescuer to a corner of the deck where they could actually hear each other. Claude's dark brown hair was cut in a dramatically styled high spiky crew, accentuating his long, narrow, bony face. He wore a gold ring in his left ear. They discussed his suit, and her dress, and fashion in general, and their hosts and the guests. Claude gossiped with an air of drama and subterfuge that made Joanna lean closer to him, and he gave off an air, almost an incense, of intense sexuality. He was so very handsome he made the evening around him appear more vivid. She felt very comfortable with him, and invigorated.

"What do you know about the Farthingale house?" she asked.

"Oh, not very much, I'm afraid. I live in town and don't get out to the sticks here very much. I know the house has been on the market for years, and there's some slightly juicy legend about it. Some kind of boodle hidden there."

"Really?"

"Mmm. Farthingale was one of those sea captains, demented, you know. Where's Bob Hoover? He knows the scoop." Craning his neck, Claude surveyed the crowd.

"It doesn't matter," Joanna assured him. "I don't want to buy the house. I'm in New York or traveling, I'd never have time to spend there. It just caught my imagination."

And although she met several other people that evening, she never did meet Bob Hoover. When she left the party and drove back down the Squam Road toward Tory's house, she was tempted to turn into the drive of the Farthingale place for one last look, but she refrained. She couldn't possibly buy a house; she wouldn't know what to do with one.

Back at the Randalls', the family was gathered outside on the covered porch, seated around a long table, playing Trivial Pursuit by the light of oil lamps. Joanna was invited to join them, and she did, crunching over fallen chips and nuts as she pulled a bamboo chair up to the table. She added her expertise to John's and Tory's, and they played, the Old Farts against the Young Turks, until almost midnight. As her hosts went off to bed, Joanna's grumbling stomach reminded her she'd had little to eat that night, and she took a plate of lemon meringue pie and a mug of decaf out to the wrap-around porch and snuggled down into the soft cushions of the bamboo sofa, curling her legs up under her. For a long while she ate and stared into the night, which was bright with stars and a sliver of moon, which gave a silver sheen to the expanse of ocean quietly lapping against the beach.

She'd liked Claude enormously and felt comfortable with him, as she did with the Latherns. What would it be like to live here, on this little island, so isolated from the real world?

What would it be like to live in a house with Carter?

That question was taboo. Not to be asked. Not to be even considered. Or dreamed about. Or longed for.

Well, then: what would it be like to have a house of her own? A house would wait for her. Would belong to her. A house would be something permanent in her life.

She sat for a long time on the porch, dreaming, but the next day she flew back to New York, and the rush of work, and before she knew it, September had arrived, and Carter was back, and she returned to her city routines.

Four

—

*W*hen Carter returned from Europe, he demonstrated clearly to Joanna how much he'd missed her, and quickly they resumed their passionate collaboration of love and work.

The next twelve months rippled past Joanna like rich, densely textured tapestries. She had little time for solitary contemplation, and yet oddly enough, not a day went by when she didn't think of the storybook house on the edge of the sea. Its pure lines and forthright air remained with her no matter how many other homes she toured and taped for her television show.

Even the idea of the house grew precious to her, like a private treasure she hoarded away from the sight and judgment of others. On nights when she was lonely, she banished her melancholy with visions of how the house might look inside, how she could live in it—and with whom.

When August rolled around once more, she eagerly accepted Tory's invitation to come to Nantucket. As soon as she rented a car at the airport, she drove directly to Squam. It was late afternoon, a perfect golden day. The house was still there. Still empty. That was a sign, wasn't it? A message?

She knew the house couldn't wait for her forever.

She didn't share her obsession with Tory or Carter, perhaps because it was simply too frail to bear the scrutiny of others. Tory would probably laugh at her. "What would you do with a house, Joanna? Good grief, you haven't even furnished your apartment!"

And Carter? She couldn't predict how he'd react. *Fabulous Homes* was still high in the ratings, but a new show he'd co-produced, a comedy series about two divorced couples, had flopped miserably, and the network was not amused. Pressured by the network, over the past few months Carter had become short-tempered and irritable. Now he was desperately trying to get a new pilot together and the executive producer he was working with had the personality of a wounded shark.

So there hadn't been an opportune moment over the past few months to mention something as frivolous as her infatuation with the house.

Now it was the third month of a new year and something wonderful had happened. Like a lightning bolt, like good luck, Joanna had been struck with a quite realistic dream. On this cold Friday evening as she hurried down the hall and put her key in the lock of her apartment door, she was nearly breathless with hope.

Slamming her door behind her, she flicked on the lights. She raced through her apartment, pulling at her clothes as she went. Outside on West Seventy-fifth, the Friday evening traffic paraded past toward Riverside Drive. Lights flashed, horns honked, brakes screeched, men yelled, and even though the windows were shut against the bitter March cold, the noises and lights penetrated her rooms in a kind of carnival ruckus. Crossing the room in a few impatient strides, she yanked shut the blinds. Curtains would have helped, nice thickly lined curtains; but in the five years she'd lived here she hadn't yet gotten around to having any made.

She had to hurry. Carter said he'd pick her up in an hour, and since she was the one who had asked him—implored him—to give her this evening, she didn't want to keep him waiting.

She stripped off the sleek silk and wool trouser suit she'd worn to work. Tossing it onto her bed, she hurried into the bathroom for a quick shower. Then, wrapped in a towel, she packed. Setting her overnight case on the bed, she approached the chest of drawers in which she kept the apparel for her alternate personality. She took out a new black negligee tarted up with red ribbons, a pair of orange leggings, and a V-necked oversized magenta thigh-length sweater for the trip home on Saturday. A black satin push-up bra, black satin bikini pants. She folded them into the suitcase. There.

Back in the bathroom, the steam from her shower had finally disappeared, clearing the mirror, and she took out one of her makeup bags and set to work, painting her face with skillful exaggeration. Not even on her television show in front of all the cameras did she use this much makeup: blue eye shadow, gold shadow with sparkling flakes for the area beneath her brows, rouge, lipstick, navy mascara.

But it was the wig that made all the difference. Her heavy blond hair slanting down over one eye signaled her identity clearly. When Joanna went out to dinner or to the opera or a play, it was the smooth burnished curtain of hair that caught people's eye, made them look twice, made them stare, then whisper to one another, "It's Joanna Jones." While she rather enjoyed this minor celebrity, she understood how Carter would feel uncomfortable with it. He was afraid a photographer would snap their photo and print a shot of them together at a restaurant or country inn when he'd told Blair he was in the city working. He didn't want to risk that; he asked Joanna to disguise herself when they went out in public together, and she agreed.

First she had tried pulling her hair back into a chignon or a low twist at her neck, but her hair was too heavy, too straight, and immediately began sliding out of place. She decided to go with a wig, and after much experimentation, she'd settled on one of black curls bouncing in a party-girl shag which obscured the strong lines of her face and made her look young and rather cheap. That had led easily to a certain style of dress: flamboyant, alluring, even provocative. Perhaps a bit tacky. Low-cut, high-hemmed, skintight outfits and dangerously high heels. Cheap flashy jewelry.

For a while this disguise had been only a great deal of fun, bringing an element of play into their relationship which hadn't been there before. It made it possible for Joanna and Carter to go out into the city at night, lingering over brandy at a restaurant, or even escaping New York for brief hidden weekends together.

"I can't believe you're doing this," Tory had scolded Joanna. "It's obviously a power play. Carter's not afraid you'll get snapped by a society photographer and Blair will find out. He's just afraid that if you're recognized all the time and he's not, you'll realize you're important and he's not."

"I don't think so, Tory," Joanna disagreed. "In any case, I've promised Carter I'd wear the disguise, especially when we go out of town together for . . . pleasure, instead of work."

Recently Joanna had been surprised and amused and then vaguely disturbed by Carter's response to her disguise: this particular camouflage really excited him sexually. More and more often these days, when they made love, Carter asked Joanna to leave the wig on.

Well, if it made him happy, she'd wear the wig, she'd wear two wigs, she'd cut off her hair, she thought now in a frenzy of abandon. What was a wig now? She pulled it on and adjusted it; in an instant she was transformed. This woman would wear the skimpy scarlet satin dress that made swishy sounds whenever she moved. Joanna did a quick pirouette in front of the mirror to be sure everything was in place. The movement caused her to rush into the kitchen, pull a can of tamales from the cupboard, and stand bending over the kitchen sink, eating them cold as fast as she could. Odd how the hot spices settled her stomach.

If her viewers could see her now, she thought! She knew from her fan mail that the women who watched her show envied her, considering her completely "successful." This year alone she'd been listed in two magazines' polls of the top ten most admired women in America. As she walked through the country's most wonderful houses and interviewed their owners for her weekly television show, she emanated the serene aura of a triumphant woman, content in her life.

Joanna shook her head ruefully at that thought, and the very act of shaking her head set off a current of dizziness through her body. Holding onto the cold porcelain of the sink, she closed her eyes and waited for the nausea to pass. Beads of sweat broke out across her forehead. Bending over, she rested her cheek against the soothing chill of the sink. Outside the window, a few snowflakes swirled down, silver in the light, seeming to disappear into the darkness.

She and Carter had been lovers for over three years. They'd survived production catastrophes and triumphs together. They'd opened their hearts to one another. At this particular moment in time it was true that Carter was not as close to her as he had been, could even be said to be pulling away, but she was certain that was due to his problems with the network. Carter did not carry failure well; it made him cranky.

Which was too bad, when right now she needed him to be loving.

Everything had changed. The world was new to her. She had to change—she was changing with each breath she took—and she had to ask Carter to change also, no matter what pain it caused. Joanna knew that Carter felt little passion for Blair, but profoundly loved his son. But Chip was fifteen, no longer an innocent child. He spent most of his life at camps, and next year would go off to boarding school. Was it really necessary for Carter to keep his home together for Chip's sake? Not any longer. That was what Joanna thought.

Now all she had to do was convince Carter.

Her equilibrium had returned. The silky lining of her red dress whispered against her thighs as Joanna hurried into her bathroom and opened the medicine chest above the sink. It held mostly cosmetics. Joanna prided herself on her excellent good health—she possessed endless energy, and worked through flus that set other people back weeks, and was impatient with her body when it showed any signs of weakness. Uncapping a bottle of Scope, she rinsed her mouth and gargled, returned the bottle to the cupboard, redid her lipstick, and blew a kiss to her reflection in the mirror. She rather looked, she thought, like someone who sang piano bar down in the Village. Grabbing up her fur, gloves, and handbag, she locked up her apartment and hurried down to wait for Carter in the ground-level vestibule.

His dark green convertible Saab slid up the street just a few moments later, and Joanna hurried out, taking care not to slip on the snowy sidewalk. He had to double-park and so she quickly opened the passenger door and got inside, glad for the leathery-smelling heat of the interior. The overhead light showed Carter's face as he turned to greet her: he smiled briefly, but his eyes were icy, and when he turned back to look out the rear window as he nosed the car back into the traffic, his smile faded and his chin jutted out, causing a little bunching fist of flesh just under his mouth which she secretly thought of as his "boxing glove" and which always clearly signaled his mood.

Leaning over, she kissed his cheek. He did not turn his face to meet her mouth with his. Ah, well. Carter never did like it when she asked him for anything, especially not for a meeting on a day that wasn't considered one of "their" days. He did not like change in his routine.

"How are you?" she asked.

He pulled out in front of a cab before replying. The taxi driver leaned on his horn. Shadows and lights flickered over Carter's face from oncoming cars. "Tired. And guilty. I promised Chip I'd come to this game."

She hated it when she had to cajole Carter away from his family, but after she fastened her seat belt, she turned sideways and smoothed the back of her lover's neck. "Sweetie. You do so much for him. You've been home every weekend for months now. You attended all his football games and most of his basketball games. I'm sure he understands."

"I doubt it. As I doubt that you understand how I feel, since you've never had children."

This was like being struck and Joanna flinched but remained silent. She could tell by Carter's tone of voice that he wasn't trying to be cruel; he was only expressing his thoughts in a way that was almost absentminded, for he was also negotiating his way into the heavy traffic that would take them north to Connecticut.

"Did you get a chance to view the New Orleans segment?" she asked. Talking about work usually put Carter in a good mood, or at least into a neutral one, and it did now. As she watched, his facial muscles relaxed and she could almost feel the tension rise from his shoulders like a fog.

"Yeah. The bit about security measures combining esthetics—the wrought-iron railings, the walled garden—that was good."

"I thought you'd like that. In fact, I think it might be worth doing a special mini-segment on just that particular architectural function. It's so prevalent these days."

"In more and more places it's necessary."

She kept their conversation focused on work as they sped up Highway 684 and then along Route 22 to Bedford, New York. The road was slick and treacherous with late winter ice.

The March night around them seemed especially dark. She continued talking, keeping her voice light. She wanted him comfortably relaxed with a drink or two and a hot delicious dinner and a night of lovemaking just within reach before she broached her difficult subject.

The Saab's headlights flared across the stone and clapboard exterior of the eighteenth-century inn. They'd arrived. Carter wove the car through a maze of snowdrifts and finally into a space in the parking lot, then together they made their way along a curving slate path cleared through the snow and lighted by old-fashioned gas lamps. A bitter wind howled, tugging at their coats, while all around them giant evergreens swayed. They hurried into the warmth of the inn, stamping their feet and shaking the snow from their hair. From Carter's hair, from Joanna's wig. A mustachioed maître d' clicked his fingers to summon an underling who took their coats, then he swept before them, ushering them into the dimly lighted wood and leather dining room. He seated them with a flourish, and with a bow presented them with menus. Joanna forced herself to smile graciously. She was as tired as Carter was, and although they'd settled some issues about the next show during the drive up, they'd raised just as many. Part of her wanted to take out her pad of paper and scribble down notes; but the more powerful, primitive part urged her to put all thoughts of work aside.

"A double Dewar's on the rocks," Carter ordered.

"I'll just have club soda," Joanna told the waiter, and she looked quickly at Carter to see what he would say to this, because she almost always ordered margaritas, loving tequila, loving the crystals of salt. Carter was engrossed in the menu.

Their drinks were brought with benevolent speed. Carter tossed back half his Scotch, and almost immediately relaxed. He smiled at Joanna. "I think I'll be barbarian and have the prime rib."

"Good idea," she said. And it was a good idea. Carter was hard on himself, always exercising and watching his diet, and when he let himself go a bit and indulged his senses, a different side of him emerged, a more gentle, tolerant man.

The dining room was almost empty tonight, no doubt because of the difficult weather. Carter looked around: silence, space surrounded him. Leaning back against the high padded booth, he took a deep breath. "This is nice. I'm glad we came. Thanks," he told her, reaching for her hand.

Joanna returned his smile and with her free hand very lightly drew her fingers across his furrowed forehead and down his temple, over his cheek, to rest, light as a kiss, on his mouth. This kind of public affection was rare for them, and she savored it. He held her hand on top of the embossed white linen tablecloth and they looked into each other's eyes, smiling at what they saw there.

When his beeper went off, they both jumped.

"Fuck!" Carter whispered sharply. He rose. "I don't believe it. I'll be right back."

She watched him go off in search of a phone. She was not very concerned. It could be a family emergency, but more likely it was just a network problem; people out on the West Coast had his number and didn't hesitate to beep him whenever they felt the need. She checked her image in her compact and put on more lipstick. She looked fine, she looked just fine, she reassured herself. She would tell him when he sat down at the table again.

But then she saw Carter crossing the room toward her. His face was grim.

He didn't sit down. He hardly paused at the table before turning to leave. "We have to go. It's Chip. There's been an accident. He's in the hospital."

Joanna rose from her seat. "What—"

"Basketball game. Another player tripped him, he slammed his head against the backboard post. That's all I know."

Tossing a twenty on the table, he strode ahead of Joanna, brusquely explaining their hurry to the waiter—"My son's been in an accident"—and headed out the door without waiting to put on his overcoat. Joanna wrapped her fur around her and pulled on her gloves before following. Her wig acted nicely as a hat, keeping her head warm. She hurried outside to find that Carter was already in the car with the engine running. She climbed in and fastened her seat belt.

"I can't believe this happened when I wasn't there. Damn it!" He hit the steering wheel with his fist. "If you hadn't been so insistent—" He let the thought hang in the air as he steered the Saab out onto the road.

"Come on, Carter, be logical. Chip didn't get hurt because you didn't go to the game."

Carter didn't reply. Joanna sighed and stared ahead. The bitter cold crackled like a force field around them as they sped down the road. Snow blanketed the fields on either side of Route 22, and ice gleamed wickedly in the headlights. The world was pure: black and white. Carter's hands, tightly clutching the steering wheel, seemed in the cold lights of the dashboard to be drained of color. His chin was pushed into a boxing glove, his whole face pulled down into an aggressive, angry glare.

She wanted so desperately to soothe him. "Chip will be fine," she said softly.

In response, Carter gunned the motor, just as they approached Highway 684. The Saab hit a patch of ice, sending it into a low-bellied skid. Joanna felt the pull in her thighs and belly, like being on a carnival ride. Centrifugal force slammed her against the door. The double cone of lights from their car illuminated a red pickup truck coming toward them. Joanna watched as the driver, seeing the Saab sliding sideways across both lanes, braked. Pump your brakes, she warned him in an urgent attempt at ESP. But the driver hit his brakes hard, and the pickup skidded, too. The two vehicles drifted ponderously across the road. There was a sensation of weightlessness, then in what seemed a flash of brightness, the collision.

The noise was agonizing as the red pickup and the driver's side of the Saab were molded together into a modernistic sculpture and the door on Carter's side folded in like a bit of aluminum foil. For a moment, instinctively, Joanna's eyes closed as she braced herself.

She felt only a gentle shudder. Her seat belt held her tight. She heard the shock of impact as it resonated through the car and braced herself for a blow, but felt instead only a kind of determined shifting, so that she felt like a creature lifted up and transported to the shore and laid down by a force like an ocean wave. There was a definite flow and ebb to the crash.

When all movement stopped, she opened her eyes and looked down at herself. She was fine. She was intact. Somehow she had come out of this untouched. Her immediate, instinctive reaction was a wash of gratitude. She wondered: was there a message here, a direct communication from Fate? She'd think about that later. Now she was shaking with relief and gratitude.

In the silence, Joanna looked over at Carter. Blood streamed down his face.

Leaning toward him, she asked, "Are you all right?"

"Take off the wig," he moaned.

"What?"

"Take off the wig. The police will be here. If they insist on checking you over at the hospital, it will look awkward if you're wearing the wig. Just be yourself. Tell them we were having a business dinner. Considering the inn for the show."

"Carter, I don't think—"

"Do it!"

"All right, Carter. But are you okay?"

"I can't move my leg."

The temperature was falling inside the car. Snow was already blanketing the windshield, but Joanna was able to see through it well enough to tell that the driver of the pickup truck was collapsed over his steering wheel, not moving.

"I'm getting out. I'm going to see if I can get help," Joanna said.

Carter didn't respond. His head had fallen forward onto his chest.

In her professional guise Joanna had spoken on the phone with Blair many times before, of course, asking to speak to Carter about the show or relaying a message from him when he was in conference, and so after Joanna crawled from the car and stumbled through the snow to the pickup and spotted a CB radio inside next to the unconscious driver, and after she'd pulled her shuddering body up into the cab of the truck, irrationally terrified of the unconscious man next to her, after with shaking hands she figured out how to work the radio and had gotten hold of someone who promised to send the police and an ambulance right out, and after the police had arrived and taken down the necessary information and escorted her to a hospital in the nearby Connecticut town, she called Blair to tell her about the accident. Blair wasn't home, of course, she was in another hospital with Chip, but a friend was at the Ambersons' house, and took the message from

Joanna, and commiserated with her, and also said, "I know this isn't the time or place, but I want to say while I'm speaking to you personally, I tell Blair all the time how lucky she is to know you. I just love your show."

It was a small, pleasant hospital, and it didn't take long for the doctor to check Joanna over and pronounce that except for an understandably elevated blood pressure, she was fine, and free to go home. Carter's leg had been broken and he was already in the operating room. Blair would arrive as soon as she could. There was no reason for Joanna to remain.

It was almost eleven o'clock. Joanna was hungry and exhausted, and she wanted someone to put his arms around her, to say, "Thank God you're all right." She wanted someone to pick her up at the hospital and drive her back into the city and escort her to her lonely apartment and tuck her into bed. And to stay with her, just to be with her, just in case, all through the night.

If not that, then she wanted to be the one who would sit on the scuffed vinyl sofa in the hospital lounge, waiting to hear how Carter was. She wanted the nurses and doctors to reassure and comfort her, to respect her as an integral part of Carter's life. She wanted her claim on him to be acknowledged.

Instead, she had a cab take her back into the city. She'd put the fare on her expense account. After all, Carter had said they were on a business trip.

It was after midnight when she finally unlocked her door and half fell into her apartment. Kicking off her heels, tossing her coat and bag on a chair, she headed directly for the kitchen. She was starving. But of course there was very little to eat in her cupboards or refrigerator—she didn't know much about cooking, didn't have the time. By now as she moved she was weeping steadily, quietly whimpering. She was so cold. She was so hungry. She was so tired. She was so sad. Now she was trembling. Her apartment was always overheated in the winter, but she turned up the thermostat anyway, and started the hot water in her shower, and stripped off her clothes, letting them lie where they fell. She stood under the shower for a long time, leaning against the white tile wall, the hot water washing her tears down her face. Stepping out, she pulled on her terry-cloth robe and the heaviest pair of socks she could find. Shuffling back to the kitchen, she dug out a frost-encumbered box of Sara Lee cinnamon rolls from the freezer, heated them in the microwave, and filled a glass with water—there was nothing except coffee to drink, and she didn't want more coffee. She carried the rolls back to her bedroom, crawled under the covers, and ate them with a sloppy voraciousness that would have irritated Carter. Crumbs fell all over the bedcovers.

Her hunger slightly assuaged, she felt strong enough to listen to the messages that her answering machine's blinking light told her were waiting. She hit the rewind button and then the play, and licked her fingers as she listened.

Who did she think in her wildest hopes would call? Carter? Did she actually think Carter would come out of his anesthetic fog and think to himself, first thing upon awakening, "How is Joanna? Did she get home all right? I need to call her!"?

Of course she couldn't hope for that, and of course there was no message from Carter on the machine.

Gloria's annoyingly efficient voice was first: "Hey, boss lady, you've got some correspondence that needs signing immediately; I'll leave it on your desk for you to get first thing in the morning. Catch ya later."

Beep. "This is Giles Berklow's secretary calling for Joanna Jones. We've finished her taxes. We'll put them in the mail to her unless she wants to pick them up. Let us know. Thanks."

Beep. "Darling, it's Sheila. Now listen. ShinyBowl just called me with a to-die-for offer if you'd only do one little commercial for them. Not glamorous, perhaps, but honey, the money. Call me. Kisses."

Beep. "Joanna, it's Bill Shorter. I'm not too happy with the last show we taped. The lighting was too murky for about two minutes in the children's playroom. Would you come in *immediately* and look at it and see what we could substitute?"

Beep. "It's me again, boss lady. I'm sorry, but the effin' airlines called and the Monday morning flight you were scheduled to take to Charleston has been canceled. You'll have to go Sunday night. Okay? Get back to me."

Beep. "Hello, sweetheart, this is Dot, your personal shopper, and I've found such a collection of suits for you, you'll die with joy. But look, I'm leaving for vacation in a week, so could you call and schedule an appointment for like yesterday? I'd be so grateful. Bye, doll."

Beep. "Ms. Jones, this is the custodial manager of the CVN offices calling. We'll be in to clean your office carpet next Thursday, so could you schedule yourself out of the office that day to give it time to dry? We'd appreciate it."

"My, what a romantic life you lead," Joanna said aloud as her machine trilled to announce the end of the messages. She stabbed the answer button, then slid her empty plate onto the bedside table where it rested amid other used plates, glasses, coffee mugs, pads of paper and pens, layers of dust, her telephone, answering machine, and, barely visible, her alarm clock.

She stared out at her room around her as if seeing it for the first time. She certainly couldn't say her apartment was a nest, a refuge. It was more a way station where she slept, bathed, and changed clothes before rushing back to the network or off to tape a show. When Carter had started spending the night with her with some regularity, she'd bought a king-sized bed and a CD player to put next to the television and VCR along the bedroom wall so they could listen to music, or, more often, look at tapes for *Fabulous Homes.* Because of the way she'd been brought up, she'd never learned the art of collecting *things,* and so she had no porcelain pillboxes or china figurines or antique inkwells, or even the usual jewelry boxes, vases, clocks, goblets, embroidered pillows, crystal perfume atomizers, candlesticks, or any other of the usual objects with which people embellished and enriched their daily lives. She'd never gotten around to getting any furniture for the living room other than a card table and chair on which to stack and sort all the work she took home with her. She kept things in the boxes they were bought in, piled on the wall of shelves in her bedroom and living room, and in the cardboard boxes which she thought worked perfectly well for storing the bags of mail she tried to answer personally, as well as clippings from magazines and newspapers and the copious notes she wrote to herself. In Joanna's mind everything had an order, but Tory had teased Joanna, saying that her living room looked like the back room of a warehouse.

So here she was, particularly unprepared for this moment. Her home was not a refuge, and as she sat with the covers pulled up around her in this rare moment of self-pity, she realized there was nobody to whom she could turn for comfort.

Once she would have called Jake. Jake always listened with an open and concerned mind and gave sound advice. But since Emily's death two years ago, Jake was not himself. He was withdrawn and preoccupied—he was suffering. He did his work, and for the rest, remained isolated behind his screen of grief. Joanna's heart ached for him, and many times during the past two years she'd longed to simply embrace Jake, to hold him against her for a long time in consolation. But he was, after all, her boss, and a man she revered. She wanted to honor his grief. Since Emily's death, Jake engrossed himself in his work, arriving at the office earlier and staying on later than anyone else. He would be asleep now, in the bliss of oblivion; she didn't want to wake him.

It was too late to call Tory. Oh, Tory wouldn't mind; she'd probably even get dressed and rush over, arms loaded with hot bagels and onions and cream cheese—comfort food. But Joanna couldn't call Tory without waking up John, too, and although she knew John was fond of her, Joanna also knew he disapproved of her. Specifically of her affair with Carter. The Randalls were that rare thing, an intact and happy family, and they didn't like seeing other members of the same species endangered. God, when they found out everything, they'd be furious! Joanna moaned aloud at the very thought.

Oh, what was she going to do, what was she going to *do?* Joanna threw back her covers and jumped out of bed. Sliding her feet into slippers, she stalked through the bedroom and into the living room, which at this time of night always glowed an eerie orange from the lights on the street. She went to the window and looked out. Snow was still sifting down, falling onto the black trash bags piled at the curb. An ambulance screamed past. She was exhausted and yet unable to rest; her mind was racing. Things were just too unsettled, too *messy.* She didn't know how she'd gotten to this place, this room so bare and so neglected, necessities unsoftened by any whimsical human touch. To this age, forty years old this year. To this bizarre state of beleaguered loneliness, with so many people wanting bits and pieces of her, and no one wanting all.

It seemed that she had made the wrong decisions at several significant crossroads in her life. Now she was facing the most overwhelming question of all. She knew what the normal, brusque, competent, no-nonsense Joanna would do. But if she had learned anything at all from this dreadful night, perhaps it was to seriously consider her options—all her options. Perhaps she should give up competence and logic and reach for her dreams.

It was time to claim what belonged to her, to take what love had given.

Part Two

Five

~

$\mathcal{A}$ll through the night after the accident, the traffic hummed and whispered like a restless wind. At six it billowed into a powerful storm of noise, rising, around eight-thirty, to a crescendo of horns and squealing brakes.

Joanna woke exhausted and elated. She studied her body carefully: she was nauseous, and groggy from staying up all night, but otherwise healthy and intact.

No blood from anywhere, no bruises.

She didn't think she needed to have a doctor check her over. Her stomach heaved with reassuring authority; she knelt over the toilet and vomited as wretchedly as she had the past three weeks. Then she made her way back to bed and slept.

When she awoke again, it was afternoon. She wanted breakfast food, starches, nursery food, so she called a local bakery and had them deliver juice and milk and a variety of muffins. She sat in bed, eating and scribbling figures on a notepad.

No one called her.

By Sunday she was determined. She knew Nantucket's area code from calling Tory's summer house. Sitting cross-legged on her bed, she dialed.

"Information? I'd like the number for the Robert Hoover Real Estate Agency, please."

She scribbled the number on the notepad on her bedside table, and dialed again. Her heart was thudding with excitement and it plummeted inside her when an answering machine came on with its electronic message. Frustrated, she slammed down the phone. She'd have to wait until Monday to make the appointment, which meant waiting until Tuesday to see the house. Picking up the phone again, she dialed information once more and asked for Bob Hoover's residential phone number. Then she dialed.

A woman answered.

"Could I speak to Mr. Hoover, please?"

"Certainly. Who shall I say is calling?"

She had thought about this. "Ms. Jay Jones."

"He'll be right here."

"This is Bob Hoover. How can I help you?"

"I'm sorry to bother you at home, but I'd like to inquire about a house you have on the market. The Farthingale house." The man was silent. Joanna's heart stopped. "Is it still available?"

"Oh, yes, yes, of course." He seemed bemused.

"Could you tell me the price?"

"Seven hundred ninety-five thousand."

"Wow. That's a lot."

"Actually, that's under its assessed value. It's waterfront property."

"And the house itself? What kind of shape is it in?"

"Well, it's livable—it's got heat, electricity, and so on, but I'll admit it could use some cosmetic work. It's a solid house, though. Substantial. Built over a hundred and fifty years ago by a sea captain, and they built their homes to last."

"When could I see it?"

"When would you like to see it?"

"I'm in New York right now. How about tomorrow afternoon?"

"Tomorrow afternoon?" He cleared his throat. "Of course I could show it to you then, but you know the house won't be at its best. I mean, with this weather. It's a terrific summer house, but—"

"You said it had heat."

"Yes. It does. And it's insulated. But out there in Squam so near the water, it's pretty exposed. I mean only that it won't show to its best advantage, and if you're thinking of it as a summer place, then I'd rather show it to you on a sunny day when you can really appreciate it."

"No, I wouldn't want it as a summer home. I'd want it as my permanent residence."

"Year round, as we say here."

"Right."

"Then by all means let me show it to you tomorrow. I assume you'll be flying in. Can I pick you up at the airport?"

"I'd appreciate that. I have to make my plane reservations . . ."

"Just call my secretary in the morning and let her know what time you'll be arriving and I'll be there to meet you, Ms. Jones." Another pause, and then he said, "Be sure to dress warmly. It's still winter here. So you'll know who I am, I'll be wearing a red down parka."

Some protective instinct made Joanna reply, "I'll be wearing a fur, one that's about the same brown as my hair." She would wear her wig.

Joanna made reservations for a round-trip flight to the island, then she lay back in bed, eyes closed, not quite sleeping, but drifting through a thick mist of memories.

Nantucket had been one of the watering holes in her mother's odd, irresponsible, irrationally optimistic life. Over the course of her childhood Joanna and Erica had been guests in quite a few houses on different parts of the island.

Joanna recalled picking blueberries on the moors in a pink-checked sundress, her fingers stained indigo, the sun hot on her back, birds calling, other children nearby laughing, chasing butterflies.

Running, shrieking with glee, into the cool frothy ocean on a hot August day, hand held tightly by another child.

Picnicking on a blanket while her mother and another woman laughed and talked and stretched their tan slim legs.

Curling up next to her mother in the twin bed they shared in someone's attic, her mother smelling of roses and gin, her mother's tears slipping silently down her face, wetting Joanna's shoulders through her thin nightgown.

Good memories and bad memories, laughter and tears, hope and disappointment, and always, always the houses, with so many rooms, and the clean and shining windows enormous and full of blue and golden light and the kitchens fragrant with cinnamon rolls and berry pies, and the lawns gay with flowers, badminton nets, croquet wickets, wrap-around porches littered with buckets of smelly, salty, decomposing horseshoe crabs or pearly shells, flags snapping smartly in the Fourth of July breeze, swimsuits and striped beach towels flapping from the line by the outdoor shower. The houses were always full of people who dwelt among their families without a thought, who never were outsiders, or lonely, or abashed, or forgotten. More than anywhere else, the families on Nantucket were an enchanted breed.

Perhaps that was why that house, that spot of land, called out to her so powerfully. But Joanna knew she was not being frivolous to succumb to its spell. She'd never been like her mother, drifting on whatever current came her way. She'd always known she would have to take care of herself. And she *had* taken care of herself, at least of the professional side of herself—and the financial side, too; she mustn't forget that. Not every woman at forty can afford to buy a waterfront dream house by herself, but she could, because over the past twenty years she'd squirreled away her money instead of squandering it on frivolities.

Almost as if she'd suspected all along that this day would come, and she would be alone when it came to her.

And what a gift it was that she'd found something that claimed her, that she in turn could claim.

Monday morning Joanna heated up coffee in her microwave as she dialed her office. Her ambitious young assistant answered on the first ring.

"Gloria, listen, I'm not going to make it in today," she said, working hoarseness into her voice.

"You're kidding!"

"I wish I were. I've got a hellish flu."

"Are you sure it's flu? You should check. I mean, I heard about the accident. And I don't think you've been sick in the three years I've worked here." Gloria's voice was eager, smug.

"Listen, Gloria, just take care of things, okay? I have to go. I'm going to throw up." This was not quite a lie; she had, she might again.

"Poor baby. Shall I call you if—"

"No. I'm taking the phone off the hook. Bye." Clicking off,

Joanna threw the portable phone across the room. It landed in a box of papers. Gloria was the smartest, hardest-working assistant Joanna had ever had. She also had the morals of a barracuda. She'd be the last person Joanna would confide in, ever. Joanna thought about that for a moment, about the network and the people she worked with, and then she shook her head and crossed the room to retrieve the phone. Bending over made her stomach heave again, so she just leaned against the wall. It felt like the entire contents of her body and mind were drifting back down into place with the rocking, lilting motion of snowflakes in a paperweight.

When she could open her eyes, she dressed for her trip. She pulled on thick wool trousers and a cashmere sweater and tied a heavy silk scarf around her neck and was so completely warm and cozy she dozed off in the cab on the way to La Guardia.

The island airlines were stuck off all by themselves in a rather temporary-looking little terminal, but she was too hormonally drugged to be nervous during this trip. She was grateful for her fur; it worked like a blanket against the cold, and she sat on the small plane that couldn't quite heat its interior, and leaned her head against the window, taking comfort from the gentle reverberations as the plane hummed its way over Long Island and out to the ocean and Nantucket.

It was another cold, windy March day, but blazingly clear. The tip of Long Island disappeared from her vision, replaced by the vast, glittering, dark blue expanse of the sea. Then, finally, she saw the curving green and brown island, rimmed in golden sand. The plane waltzed liltingly down to the runway and sputtered to a stop. The pilot detached himself from his seat and opened the door that turned into a ramp. Joanna followed the other passengers across the tarmac and into the terminal.

She spotted Bob Hoover immediately; he was the only man not dressed like a carpenter or fisherman. A short, stocky man about her age, he wore a red down parka over a navy-blue blazer and a tie sprinkled with small white outlines of the island. He approached her with a broad smile and shook her hand.

"Ms. Jones? Bob Hoover. How was your flight?"

"Fine, thank you."

"Are you hungry? Would you like a little lunch before we drive out to Squam?"

"No, thanks. I'd like to go on out."

"Of course. My car's outside."

He led the way out of the terminal, across the loading zones to the curb where his Mercedes station wagon waited. Joanna noticed as he drove that his face and hands had the weathered, leathery look of a sailor.

"I thought I might tell you the house's history on the way out," Bob said. Glancing over at her, he added, "In case you didn't know, we're fiends for history here."

"I'd love to hear about it," Joanna told him.

"Great. Well. One hundred and fifty years ago a retired sea captain, Abraham Farthingale, built the house out there on the shore of the Atlantic Ocean. At that time it was considered daft to build a house so far away from town. Although I might add that over fifty years before, about the time of the Revolution, Kezia Coffin built a so-called country estate out at Quaise, one of the harbor's eastern coves, and a long way from the center of the town. But that's another story.

"Anyway, Farthingale was an odd man, proud, secretive, cranky. He didn't care for people, and when he lost part of a leg in a whaling accident, he determined that even though he couldn't go out to sea anymore, nevertheless he'd live as close to it as he could get. He had plenty of money to buy the necessities of life and cart them out into the lonely countryside. He lived the rest of his life out there, seeing only his wife and children. Two sons. When Farthingale died, his family moved back into Nantucket town; they hadn't liked being isolated, and the house had been bitterly cold in the winter." Bob glanced over at Joanna. "Probably still is, at least in the water-side rooms. The wind can be brutal. Even with heat. You should be aware of that."

"Thanks for warning me."

"Okay. Well. Let's see. The house remained in the Farthingale family for seventy-five years, but was seldom lived in for all that time—no one wanted to be stuck out in the sticks. I guess now and then when a newlywed couple was saving up the money for their own place, they'd make do out there. But in the early twentieth century a summer visitor saw the possibilities and bought the house as a vacation home."

"A vacation home, that long ago?"

"Oh, yes. Even before the turn of the century, Nantucket was a tourist resort. In the sixties a family named Baxter bought it from the Farthingales and used it as a summer house for quite a while. Put in heat and a modern kitchen and some other amenities. Like a lot of other people, they started coming down during the fall—it's glorious here then—and then perhaps for Christmas, then early in the spring. Old man Baxter loved the island. When he died, the house passed on to his children, but this last batch of owners, Baxter's grandchildren, prefer the mountains and don't like coming here. At least that's what they say. I have a feeling they'd just rather have the money than the house. Three quarters of a million dollars is a lot of money."

"Yes," Joanna agreed soberly, "it is."

"Still," Bob added, perking up, "you might be the one to find the treasure."

"The treasure?"

They were just turning off the paved Quidnet Road, onto the rough Squam Road. The twigs and branches of the dense bordering thickets were still closed tight against winter, looking sticklike and brittle and gray.

"The treasure," Bob repeated, pronouncing the words as if they felt good in his mouth. "Farthingale found a treasure. Or so he said. It was along the beach he walked daily that he found a chest of gold and jewels, washed up on the sand after one of the many shipwrecks caused by fog and Nantucket's shoals. He brought it home and hid it in his house. At any and all times when he did bless other men with his company, Farthingale boasted of this treasure. A chest of gold and jewels. He promised his sons he'd share it with them, then died before telling them where it was."

"So no one else ever saw the treasure."

"Right. But you see, Nantucket's absolutely surrounded by shoals, and those and the fog and storms have caused plenty of shipwrecks over the years. There are written records of such wrecks and of cargo being strewn all across the beaches to be gathered up by whoever got there first. Clothes, linens, jewelry, money. There were also pirates who sailed these waters, capturing ships coming from England or the Far East, and sometimes after a battle the debris from a sinking ship would wash up on our shores."

"But I would think anyone who owned the house would have searched it thoroughly."

"Of course. Still, it's a large house, an old house. A lot of house to search, four floors, really. Eight fireplaces. Two main staircases, a front for the family, a back for the servants, plus a third down into the basement and a small enclosed staircase leading up to a large attic. The attic itself's broken up into several bedrooms, all with angled ceilings— something could be tucked away up there, under the wide-board floors."

"Oh, the house sounds so wonderful, I can't wait to see it," Joanna exclaimed.

"Well, then, here we are!" Bob replied as he turned off Squam Road onto a wide white pebble drive. It was bordered with slanted, wind-twisted pines, gnarled scrub oak, and wild berry bushes, all so thick and high and overgrown they obscured the sight of the ocean. The wild greenery scratched and skittered along the sides of the Mercedes. Now the shrubs parted, and there was the house, serene and centered against the sea and sky.

It looked as charmingly forthright as it had the first time she saw it, two years before, and again last August when she'd crept down the drive for one brief, clandestine, longing look.

"It's like something from a storybook," Joanna observed.

Bob came around to help her out of the station wagon. "It's a great old house, no doubt about it." They stood side by side, looking up at it. "Its architecture combines the best elements of several periods and philosophies. The plain weathered gray shingles and the basic structural design reflect the Quaker belief in simplicity. But about the time Farthingale built his house, the island was changing and architecture was, too. See the framing of the door?" Approaching the house, he ran his hands over two broad, flat, upright boards on either side of the door. "These are called pilasters, and the board that connects them over the top is called the entablature. You can see how it echoes very simply the structure of a Greek temple. This detail is carried on throughout the house, over the eight fireplaces, although as you'll see, the ones downstairs are more decorative."

"How did Greek Revival get out here?" Joanna asked.

"It all connects up to what was going on at the time. The United States had just come out of the Revolution and then the War of 1812. The people were eager to show in every way, especially in the outward appearance of their homes, that this country had thrown off the English influence and was becoming a strong republic on its own. They wanted to emulate the ancient Greek city-state, which was the birthplace of democracy, so they put up all these sort of miniature Greek temples. As a matter of fact, many of our big beautiful buildings in town—the Atheneum, the Methodist church, the mansions on Main Street—are Greek Revival, and I have to say those buildings are awfully damned elegant." Bob shook his head in admiration, then smiled abashedly. "I'm an amateur historian. Just tell me to shut up when I get carried away."

"No, no, I'm interested in all this, really," Joanna told him, biting her tongue just before she blurted out, "It's my field, actually." He didn't seem to know who she was—not that he should recognize her with the wig on—and she wanted to keep it that way for a while.

"I should be telling you stuff you need to know." Bob stepped back and looked up, pointing at the windows. "Six over six windowpanes. See the ripples? That's the original glass. The good news is that the house hasn't been tampered with very much. You might say that its integrity is complete. That's the bad news, too. Except for the necessary reshinglings over the years, it hasn't been tampered with very much. It hasn't been cared for. It needs a lot of work."

"That doesn't scare me," Joanna told him.

"Okay, then, let's go inside. I came out earlier to turn on the heat, but it's still going to feel chilly. Damp. The way houses do when they've been shut up for a long time." He turned the key in the lock, held the blue door open, and let Joanna pass before him.

Joanna stepped inside. Immediately she was overwhelmed with emotions and, standing very still in the central hall, she gazed around at the sunlight on the burnished wood floors. She heard the gentle hum of the furnace; she smelled wood and dust and sun. The house didn't seem chilly. It seemed welcoming.

She felt she had come home.

"I want to buy this house," she said.

Bob laughed. "You'd better let me show it all to you first." But he waited patiently, letting her look, letting her take her time. They were standing together just inside the front door, at the front of the long central hall from which a wide, graceful staircase wound up to the second floor. Four doors stood open to other rooms.

Another smaller door, no doubt to a closet, opened underneath the staircase. The most compelling view was straight back to the opposite end of the house where tall glass doors framed a view of blazing blue sky above land which sloped to the sea, and Joanna hurried the length of the house to look out.

"One of the best changes the summer owners made was to install those French doors," Bob remarked.

"Yes," Joanna agreed, "I can see that." Three steps led from the doors straight down to a small rectangle of lawn, which in its turn gave way to wild brush, and then the beach and the ocean.

"There should be a deck all along here," Joanna said. She could envision it clearly: blue and white pots of pink geraniums that would be placed at the corners.

"Good idea." Bob waited until Joanna turned from the view, then led her into the large front room, which opened directly onto a room equally large, with its windows full of ocean view. "What we've got on this side of the house are what were called, when the house was built, traditional 'double parlors,' one behind the other. So you can have one large open room, or put a wall in along here and have two good-sized single rooms. You could shut off the ocean-side room— that gets the worst of the wind—and use it only in the summer and save on heating bills if you wanted."

"Oh, it's beautiful," Joanna gasped. The wide-board pine floors, with stain and oil and simple age, had become the color of butterscotch. The walls and ceiling were a gentle cream, marked and soiled enough to need painting. Pewter chandeliers hung from the plaster rosettes in the center of each room, and the two fireplaces were finished off in marble, with the mantels ornamented with beadwork.

She followed Bob across the hall. "Here we have the dining room. This fireplace has a built-in oven and a small closet for kindling beneath. It was once what was known as the keeping room where the family really lived and ate and cooked most of the year. That door leads to what was once the borning room, and is now the kitchen, and was modernized in the sixties. I'll show you the kitchen in a moment, first, this door . . ." Bob stepped from the dining room into a small, low-ceilinged, unheated room, and Joanna joined him. "This little room is what people used to call a wart. It was probably a summer kitchen when the house was built. This century the owners turned it into a screened-in porch. Too bad you're seeing it now when everything's still dead. This room is great in the summer when the vines are blooming all over."

"I can imagine."

Holding the door, he led her back through the dining room and into the only room Joanna didn't appreciate: a kitchen full of avocado appliances, with a linoleum floor and aqua linoleum counters.

"This will have to change drastically," she announced.

Bob tapped the refrigerator door. "The appliances all function until you can get new ones. In here is a nice little half-bathroom." Near the door to the central hall was another, smaller door, and now he opened it, revealing a set of very steep, twisting stairs. "Servants' stairs. They'd come down from the attic this way."

Joanna followed the realtor up the stairs and along the hallway to the large bedroom. "Wow," she said softly, and just leaned against the window, looking out at the panorama of beach, ocean, and sky. Dazzling. This would be her bedroom. The bed here, and a chaise by the window, and she could move it in front of the fireplace in the winter . . . "Does the fireplace work?"

"As far as I know it does. Of course, you'll want it checked out."

She ran her hand over the plain, oiled wide pine board which ran as a panel over the fireplace. It was warm to her touch.

"The Baxters built a nice large bathroom between the two

rooms on this side, but you can always lock this door if you want the bathroom to be strictly for the master suite."

They crossed the hall to another large bedroom with ocean views. This would be her study.

Bob knocked his fingers on an inside wall. "The Baxters put some new walls in up here, to make enough bedrooms for all their children and grandchildren."

"I can see that. I'll have them knocked out. I need a large office." She could envision it as she spoke: walls of shelves here and here—"Could you recommend a good carpenter? And a good electrician?"

"Surely."

"I'll have to have a lot of power in here for my computer, Xerox machine, and fax. This room will be my first priority."

"What kind of work do you do?" Bob asked.

"Oh," Joanna answered, "well, research. For the next year I'll be working on two books, nonfiction, about houses."

Before he could ask more, Joanna turned and went out into the hall and along to the front of the house. The windows in this large bedroom looked out over the driveway and the moors. The ceiling was high and the space was airy, but when it was painted and papered, it would be even brighter.

"No ocean views on this side," Bob pointed out, following her. "However, this room and the other front bedroom will be much easier to keep warm in the winter." He tapped the radiator running under one window. "Great heat, the best, steam heat, and when we go to the basement, I'll show you the furnace. Oil."

She followed Bob up a set of enclosed stairs to the attic, with its several tiny rooms wallpapered in summery flowers, the original pegs on the walls for clothes. The floors up here were unfinished boards, many at least two feet across.

They went down to the basement, and here, too, was a room with beautiful wide-board floors, as well as a fireplace nearly high enough to walk into, a beehive oven built into the bricks, and another, lower, gently arched opening for storing firewood. Here and there large holes gaped in the walls, and brick dust had sifted out onto the floor.

"They probably used this as a summer kitchen." Bob nodded toward one pile of debris. "No doubt places knocked open when someone tried to find Farthingale's treasure."

Moving into other, less finished rooms, he pointed out the oil furnace and the great black oil tank, and the panel of electric fuse boxes, and the water heater. They went outside, walked around the house, looked up at the roof and the trim around the windows, and Joanna saw how much more weathered the wood was on the ocean side of the house. Basically, though, things were in good condition.

Bob locked up the house and drove her into his office in town, and while she drank a cup of hot decaffeinated coffee, he gathered together for her all the listing sheets printed with the details of the house.

It was time for her flight back to New York. The realtor drove her to the airport, and while they waited for the plane to board, he bought her a sandwich. She was ravenously hungry.

"I want to make an offer on this house," Joanna told him as they sat together at a table looking out at the flat paved airstrip. "Should I call you tonight?"

Bob laughed. "I don't think there's any rush. The house has been on the market for years. We've got an exclusive listing, so no one else can get to the owners. Take your time. Think about it. Be sure."

"I am sure," Joanna said.

"Even so, why not sleep on it? Call me in the morning. I'll be in the office, ready to take down all the details."

"I assume the house is available immediately."

"Immediately."

"I'll talk to you tomorrow, then."

"I'll look forward to it."

Joanna smiled. "So will I."

Six

～

$\mathcal{T}$uesday morning Joanna called Bob Hoover and, after the customary discussion, made an offer on the house.

By Wednesday morning the owners had accepted.

In three weeks she would own her own house.

That evening she showered and dressed in a loose-fitting Armani pantsuit and T-shirt and loafers, then hurried out to a nearby Mexican restaurant where with gusto she devoured a pile of nachos deluxe. At seven she took a cab down to the CVN building. She was fairly sure most of the *Fabulous Homes* staff would have left for the day. Certainly Gloria would have gone. She always had a date.

The cab pulled to the curb and she stepped out. A snarling, red-faced, fat woman in a purple coat was intently propelling herself toward the cab in a frenzy to get it before a grim-faced man in a trench coat. As she grabbed for the cab's door, Purple Coat knocked Joanna aside, tripping her in the process.

"God *damn!*" Joanna cursed as she fell. She reached out wildly to prevent herself from hitting the pavement. Trench Coat was close enough to catch her, but he was furious at losing the cab, and only swore under his breath and stalked away. Joanna's elbow hit the curb. Her breath was knocked out of her. The sidewalk flowed with people hurrying in the cold, some of whom cast curious glances her way and rushed on. She pushed herself to her feet and brushed her elbows and stalked toward the network building. It certainly wasn't the first time some random bit of minor violence had occurred; usually she simply chalked it up to life in the city and forgot about it. This time it frightened her and made her resolve even more complete.

After the commotion of traffic and voices, the hush of the empty lobby of the CVN building fell over her like a glass bell. Joanna said hello to the security guard at the front desk and signed in, strode across the glossy marble floor to the bank of elevators, and went to the thirty-seventh floor.

Here the dove-gray walls and charcoal-gray carpet along the narrow hallways combined with overhead track lighting to provide all the warmth and charm of a nuclear submarine at abysmal depth. Gloria had left for the day, thank heavens; Joanna was in no mood for her shiny pertness. Now as she entered the reception area to her office, she noticed—really saw for the first time—the many various touches Gloria had added to brighten what was really a cold and impersonal area. Framed posters of Monet's water lilies hung on the walls; when she first saw them, Joanna had privately been critical of Gloria for having such pedestrian taste. But even though everyone in the world loved water lilies, they were still beautiful, Joanna realized. They added a depth to the room. As did the photographs of Gloria's nieces, nephews, parents, and her cute little dog, Peppy, a white toy poodle. Gloria *would* have a white toy poodle.

A vase of pansies sat on Gloria's desk next to her neat piles of folders. Even her computer was tied up like a present in a green-and-white-plaid ribbon with yellow silk daisies tucked into the bow on top. Gloria decorated her computer to match the season or the holiday. Joanna had thought this a rather dim-witted and even silly thing to do, but now in her nesting mood she saw it differently. It might be cute, but it was also personal; it made this room Gloria's.

In contrast, Joanna saw as she unlocked her office door and entered, flicking on the lights, that her room, this room where she'd worked for five years, had no personality, no sign of what individual worked here. Instead of pictures or posters, charts and graphs and a blackboard and a cork-board and an enormous calendar hung on the walls. Every flat surface was covered not with framed photographs, but with file folders, videocassettes, and working paraphernalia. The most homey area was the space formed by a long leather sofa and two chairs all turned to face a wall of large remote-control television sets with VCRs. The low table in front of them actually did hold coffee from time to time, but more often it held file folders and pads of papers for the notes Joanna made for her shows.

Well, her office might not be charming, but it was organized. Joanna went out into the storage closet off Gloria's reception area, returning with two cardboard file boxes. Pulling her office chair around to face a bank of file cabinets, she sat down and began to transfer from the file cabinets to the boxes all the files about the two books she wanted to do. It didn't take long. On weekends, while Carter was with his family, Joanna had prevented herself from dwelling gloomily on his absence by carefully, even meticulously, organizing the material and writing the outline of the books. Everything was in order. Closing the boxes, she taped them shut and labeled them in large black print. She'd have them mailed to her agent; Sheila could keep them and forward them when Joanna had a new address.

That done, she looked around. What else did she need to take from this room? What else did she want? Rising, she went to her desk and studied it. Odd, but she loved what she saw there; it was all as beautiful to her as a vase of roses. Her in and out boxes, crammed to overflowing with correspondence, memos, materials to be copied. Folders color-coded for different shows. Vouchers to be signed. Letters. Pens, tape, paper clips, a high-tech speakerphone. A computer unadorned by ribbons. Dictionaries, great heavy illustrated books on architecture, furniture, home decoration. Surveying these things filled her with a rich contentment. She ran her hands over the objects and was satisfied. Well, she would be able to replace them all in her study in her house. New pens, dictionaries, folders, equipment. Yum.

She looked at her watch. It was almost eight-thirty, time for her appointment with Jake. She stood a moment in the doorway of her office, memorizing the room as it was now, although she was certain its every molecule was engraved into the plates of her memory.

She would miss her office a million times more than her apartment.

Flicking off the light, she pulled the door shut and locked it. Standing next to Gloria's desk, she studied it a moment, as if memorizing it, then put a hand-addressed sealed envelope in the middle of Gloria's blotter, where she wouldn't fail to see it. Then she turned her back on it and went out to the wall of elevators and up to the forty-fifth floor.

Jake's secretary was gone, but he was there, talking on the telephone; she could hear him shouting. Smiling, she let herself into his office and sat down in a chair facing his desk. He rolled his eyes at her about his conversation, then scribbled on a notepad and punched keys on his computer. She could tell he'd been running his hands through his curly salt-and-pepper hair; it stood out in all directions, making him look like a sixties revolutionary. But he wore a three-piece gray suit hand-tailored just for his stocky, muscular body. Now the jacket was thrown over a chair, his vest unbuttoned, his sleeves rolled up, and his red silk tie yanked down. The top two buttons of his white shirt were undone. He was working hard, he was always working, full speed ahead, top volume.

Finally he slammed down the phone and collapsed into his chair. "You're a sight for sore eyes," he announced. "When I heard about Carter's accident, then heard you were sick, I was afraid you'd gotten injured, too."

"I'm fine, Jake. But I've got some heavy news."

He cocked an eyebrow. "Oh, yeah?"

"Yeah." Joanna rose from her chair and walked across the room to lock the door. When she returned to her seat, she said, "This is all just between you and me. Okay? No one else should know. No one."

"All right, whatever you say."

"I want your word, Jake. Promise me. You won't tell anyone."

"Hey, Joanna. Have I ever *not* kept one of your secrets?"

Joanna just stared at Jake, and soon his expression changed from indignation to puzzlement.

"Okay, I promise. Tell me. What's up? Are you okay?"

"I'm okay, Jake. I'm better than okay." This was the first time she'd shared her news with anyone, and she felt an uncontrollable smile break out across her face. How should she phrase this? She wanted the announcement to be joyous, and elegant, and—

"Good God. You're pregnant!"

Joanna was shocked. "How can you tell?"

Jake shook his head. "That look. Emily used to look that way when she was pregnant. You've never smiled like that before. You are, aren't you? You're pregnant."

"I'm pregnant." She'd said it aloud to her reflection in the mirror a hundred times by now, but this was the first time she'd said it aloud to another person.

Jake was studying her, his dark eyes reading hers. "And you're happy about this."

"Jake, I'm so happy I could burst." To her chagrin, tears welled up in her eyes and overflowed. She clenched her teeth, but her chin quivered like a child's.

"Well, then, good for you. My God, Joanna. Congratulations."

Jake pushed back his chair and came around his desk and as he approached Joanna he said, "Come on. Let me give you a hug."

Overwhelmed and relieved and surprised by this simple, purely positive reaction, Joanna rose to meet Jake, and he enfolded her in his bulky, powerful arms and pressed her against him. She was just his height, so she leaned her head down to rest it on his shoulder and wrapped her arms around him, and they stood like that for a while. Joanna could feel affection, goodwill, and genuine sympathy in Jake's embrace.

"Jake," she whispered, "I'm scared."

"I'm sure you are, honey. That's only natural."

"I'm getting your vest all wet with tears."

"Joanna, you can blow your nose on my shirt collar if it makes you feel better," Jake said gruffly, and that made her break into a laugh, and she pushed herself away from him and wiped her face and smiled while she was still crying.

"Oh, Jake, I'm so happy."

"Come over here and tell me about it." He led her toward his leather sofa. "Want something to drink? A little Evian?"

"Great."

Crossing the room, he opened the cupboard which held a small bar. While he poured their drinks, she blew her nose and composed herself. Then he sat down next to her and said, "Okay. Start at the beginning. I suppose it's Carter's child."

Joanna nodded. "I don't know how it happened. I always use a diaphragm"—here she felt herself blush as if she were a teenager; this was so very private—"but you know I turned forty last month, of course you know, you were at the party. Anyway, I guess I thought I was just so old, or rather I didn't think at all, really. Getting pregnant as a concept had just disappeared out of my mind. But I did feel more and more tired. Really fatigued. I thought it was turning forty. They say it can be a psychologically stressful time. So I didn't worry about it, but then, when I continued to feel so *damned exhausted*—I've been just dragging myself around for the past two months. Did you notice?"

"No. But Gloria mentioned it to me."

"She did?"

"Yeah." Jake's grin was conspiratorial. " 'Joanna's been so preoccupied lately,' " he mimicked in a saccharine falsetto, " 'so sort of *weary* about it all. Do you suppose she's burned-out? I mean, FH is such a great show, I'd hate to see her jeopardize it because she's bored with it.' "

"What a weasel she is!" Joanna exclaimed. "What did you say?"

"I said, 'Gloria, honey, Joanna *is* FH. If she goes down, the show goes down.' "

"Oh, Jake, I love you!"

"As well you should. Now go on."

"Well, after about a month of feeling progressively wretched, I decided that I'd better get checked out. I thought I must have cancer, or chronic fatigue syndrome. Or even that I'd hit menopause a bit early. So I went to a doctor, and he sent me to a radiologist, and then gave me the news. I'm pregnant. With twins."

"Twins!"

"Twins."

"Blow me down."

"The doctor also told me that since I'm so old for a first-time mother, and since these are twins, I need peace and quiet if I'm going to carry them to term. Actually, Jake, he rather lectured me about this. I mean, he thinks there's real risk here."

"So you need some time off from the show."

"Yeah."

They sat in silence a moment, thinking their own thoughts about the ramifications of what she'd just said.

"We've got enough shows in the can for next season," Joanna reminded Jake. "Especially if you reuse some of the specials. Thanksgiving, Christmas, the wedding. We've got lots of calls for repeats for those shows."

"I'm not worried about next season."

"You're worried about the season after that?"

"Right. This is such a good, steady show for us. Doesn't go too high in the ratings, but doesn't ever sink, either. I'd hate to lose it."

"But you won't have to!" Alarmed, Joanna leaned forward. "Jake. I just want a year off. Time to be pregnant, have the babies, establish a home base, get my life in order. Then I'll be back."

"When are they due?"

"The end of October."

Jake looked at her stomach. "Tell me about your plans until then. What does Carter think?"

"Carter doesn't know. And I don't want him to."

"Joanna—"

She held up her hand like a traffic cop. "Stop. Listen to me. I've given a lot of thought about this. You know Carter. You probably know him better than I do, in some ways. He has always told me that he won't leave Blair. Well, he's said Chip, he won't leave Chip, he won't force his son to suffer from a broken home, and I suppose I had hopes that I could change his mind, but after the accident—" Emotion overwhelmed her. Tears choked her throat so she could not speak.

"—after the accident—" Jake prompted softly.

She took a sip of Evian and drew in a shuddering breath. "After the accident, immediately after the crash, Carter didn't even ask if I was okay. All he cared about was getting the story straight so Blair would think we'd been out on business." She couldn't stop the tears. Joanna reached into her purse for a handkerchief and hid her face in it as the tale and her tears poured out. "I had to take a taxi home. Alone."

"Poor kid."

"I thought"—her words rushed out on the torrent of her shame and sorrow and disappointment—"I had *imagined*, I'd worked up in my mind this little fantasy, when I'd tell Carter I was pregnant with his children, and his face would light up with joy, and he'd say oh my darling and take my hand and tell me he'd leave Blair and marry me and we'd float off together to the sound of violins." She blew her nose and wiped her face. "What an idiot I was."

"And now you think it's probably more likely that he'll want you to have an abortion."

"What?" It was like being slapped in the face. Raising her head, Joanna stared across the desk at Jake. Her tears dried up in the heat of her fear. "Oh, Jake," she whispered, shaking her head, "I never thought *that*. I mean, I thought he might not marry me, he might not be happy about it, but—" She sat silent, encountering this new and dreadful possibility.

"Carter's big on control, Joanna. You know that much about him. He'd see these babies as a problem, and a potential for disorder. He'd see them as easily removable elements."

"You're right," Joanna agreed. "I know you are. Oh, God, Jake. Why didn't I realize that myself? I'm such a fool. I had thought—the reason I'm here now—I've decided that I have to disappear for a while, and not let anyone but you know, because I was afraid that if Carter knew I was pregnant, he'd be angry at me, and you know he's such a *force* when he's angry. I was afraid he might cause me to have a miscarriage. I mean, the doctor was awfully definite about the frailty of this pregnancy. He told me I need to avoid stress. And after the accident, I realized that Carter would be so upset about . . . all this . . . that he'd get me all worried and upset, too, and then . . . But I never thought he'd want me to have an abortion."

"Well, I could be wrong."

"No, you're right, I know you are. You're absolutely right." As anger, defiance, and pride sparked within her, she felt her old energies revive. "Thank God I came in and talked with you, Jake. Now I'm more than ever determined to get away from here."

"Where are you going?"

"If I tell you, will you keep it a secret?"

"Of course."

"I'm buying a house in Nantucket."

Jake threw back his head and laughed. "You're buying a house in Nantucket. Your doctor tells you to avoid stress, so you go off and buy a house." He rose from his chair. "I'm having a drink on that." Jake returned to the bar and added a splash of Scotch to his Evian.

"It's the house of my dreams, Jake. It's a beautiful house, it's a treasure. And I know plenty of people on the island, it's not like I'm going someplace totally foreign to live among strangers. It's got lots of room, and I'm going to work on two books while I'm waiting for the babies. I've already spoken to Sheila about this—she's been trying to get me to finish the books for ages. If I get them finished in time for publication next year, they should bridge the gap and keep my name in front of people until I can get back to FH."

"Sounds like you've got things under control." Jake's smile was affectionate.

"I think actually I do. But I need your help." Reaching into her briefcase, Joanna took out a letter she'd written on her FH stationery, addressed to Jake. She handed it to him. As Jake scanned it, the words she'd written tracked through her mind.

Dear Jake,

Certain recent events have convinced me that I need to change my life completely. I've decided to go away for a while. Don't try to find me. You won't be able to. I feel the need to make a clean break with my past and I'm telling no one where I'm going. Don't worry. I'm happy with my decision. I ask you to trust me on this.

I've left enough new episodes of FH to carry you through next year, if you run the holiday shows again— we've got lots of letters asking us to repeat. I intend to return to work sometime next year, early enough to put together a new season of Fabulous Homes, *and I'll be doing some groundwork on that in my new location. In the meantime, I'm working on two books which already have contracts and which will come out in time to give FH a boost.*

Please say goodbye for me to everyone else.

Affectionately, Joanna.

When Jake had finished reading her letter, he raised his head to look at her. Joanna said, "You can say you found it on your desk."

"All right. But what are you telling Carter?"

"Nothing. You can show him the letter. That will be all he needs to know."

Jake was silent a moment, thinking.

"Even Carter," Joanna pointed out, "self-absorbed as he is, will eventually remember how he treated me during the accident. He'll think I was so—hurt, angry, shocked—by him that I decided I had to break it off with him, and the only way I could break it off would be to get out of range of his powerful charms." Joanna smiled ruefully. "Which is not untrue."

"What about all your fan mail?"

"I've written a note telling Gloria to forward it to my agent. I'm going to give Sheila my address—and instructions to give it to no one else."

"And Tory?"

"I *will* tell *her*. She'll be glad for me. She knows I've wanted children. And she'll be glad I'm breaking off with Carter. She'll find it very easy to thwart Carter's attempts to find me—if he even tries." Restless at that thought, Joanna stirred in her chair, snapping shut the lid of her briefcase. "So that's it. I'd better go. I've got a lot to do."

"What about your apartment?"

"I'll contact a rental agency. Let someone rent it for the year. It won't take me long to pack up my personal possessions, and I'll have movers come for them. Or maybe just UPS. I don't know. These are things I've got to take care of."

"When do you think you'll actually be in your house?"

Joanna stood up. "As soon as possible."

Jake rose, too, and walked with Joanna across his office. Snapping off the lock, he opened the door, then turned and studied her face. "It's a remarkable thing you're doing, kid. But then you're a remarkable woman."

Once more Joanna flushed helplessly with emotion that rushed tears into her eyes. "Jake, I'll miss you. Will you come visit me when I'm settled?"

"Sure." Reaching out, he pulled her against him and hugged her again. He kissed her ear, then gently released her. "You'll be fine. You'll be just fine. And you know you can call me if you need me. Anytime, day or night."

"Thanks, Jake." Now that the moment was here, she was finding it hard to leave.

"Hey. We'll be talking about next season's FH before you know it."

"You're right."

"You'll be back here so fast you won't know you were gone."

"I know. I know."

"Take care of those babies," Jake admonished her. "Eat right. No booze. Plenty of rest."

Joanna smiled. "Okay, Jake." Forcing herself away from him, she set off, walking through his secretary's office and out into the hall.

The elevator doors slid open with a whisper almost the moment she pressed the down button. She stepped inside, punched the button for the lobby, and leaned back in the corner. She was so exhausted and revved up that even this elevator car with its walls of gorgeous swirled wooden grain and its shining brass handrails felt intimate to her. Its hum and tremble as it carried her down forty-five floors was comforting; she knew its vibrations and sounds as thoroughly as if it were a kind of gentle, docile, ever-willing creature, a mixture of machine and beast. On the back wall just above the brass rail was a Z-shaped scratch in the veneer which Joanna smiled at every time she saw it: it had come from the buckle of her trench coat digging into the wood one night when Carter in his passion had pressed Joanna against the wall and himself against her. She ran her fingers over it; just feeling the narrow furrow made her body flush with lust.

Oh, she'd been happy at the network. She'd been happy working here, meeting Carter secretly, planning to meet him secretly. She'd been happy in this damned elevator, every single time she rode it, wondering if the door would open and Carter would step in. Then his eyes would meet hers. If other people were in the car, he'd only nod and say, "Joanna," in greeting, but the sexual electricity that flashed between them would exhilarate her for hours.

With a ping, the elevator stopped and the doors opened onto the vast quiet lobby. She stepped out. No looking back, she told herself. No regrets. She crossed the wide lobby and went out into the night.

Seven

⌒

At six-thirty on a bright May morning, Joanna boarded a plane destined from La Guardia to Nantucket. The air was fresh and clear. As the plane flew steadily northeast, Joanna looked down to see clearly the long speckled brown and green strip of Long Island, or the very bright, deep blue ocean.

But suddenly ribbons of mist were curling past her window, then the plane entered a thick mass of white. It circled and rose and fell, then turned, defeated, away from the bank of fog and toward the mainland and the Hyannis airport.

Once the plane landed on the runway, the pilot assured them with boyish optimism that they'd take off again as soon as word was radioed that the fog had lifted. The other passengers chatted and read; Joanna half dozed against the window. Finally they were all ushered off the plane and into the small terminal to wait for an announcement of improved visibility from the Nantucket airport. They waited. Free coffee in Styrofoam cups was available, but Joanna didn't drink it. She sat in a plastic chair. She strolled around the room. She waited. She studied posters of endangered wildflowers on the cape and islands. The flight from Hyannis to Nantucket took only twenty minutes; the ferry two hours and fifteen minutes; but when after an hour the fog still hadn't lifted, Joanna took a taxi to the steamship authority and boarded the nine-fifteen ferry.

Riding the ferry was like dreaming, Joanna thought as she leaned on the white rail looking out at the dancing water. A light breeze ruffled the curls of her wig against her cheeks and fluttered the hem of her gauzy cotton skirt gently against her legs. Everything in sight was haloed with the reflected brilliance of bright sun on radiant water.

She had an appointment at one o'clock with Bob Hoover; her lawyer, June Lathern; the sellers' lawyer, Ernest Reilly; and the bank representative in charge of mortgages. Over the past six weeks all the necessary paperwork had been taken care of except for these final acts: signing over the money, signing the mortgage papers, signing the deed. Soon she would hold in her hand the keys to her very own house. After the legalities were taken care of, Bob was going to take her out to Rainbow Motors to buy a four-wheel-drive vehicle, and still later she had an appointment at her house with Doug Snow, the carpenter Bob had recommended. June had asked her to have dinner and spend tonight at their place and Joanna had accepted.

Now the boat moved beyond the final tip of land and into the open ocean. It began to rock back and forth in a slow, gentle, irresistible rhythm, and Joanna felt the nausea, which had been lessening over the past few days, rise in response to the ocean's swells. Bracing herself with her hand, she went back into the cabin and found the blue booth she'd marked for herself with her overnight bag and pale blue duster. She sat down and looked around.

This boat was named the *Eagle*. A strange name, she thought, for an oceangoing vessel. Why hadn't it been named the *Whale* or the *Dolphin* or at least the *Gull* or the *Petrel*? The main, enclosed lounge was the size of a small auditorium, broken into two separate areas by a central compartment with rest rooms and a snack bar. The low ceiling might have been oppressive were it not for the large sliding windows spanning the entire boat, the soothing cream of the walls, and the bright blue of the vinyl-covered benches and booths, which came only to shoulder level, giving a spacious air to the room. Her booth was large enough to seat four, two on each side of a white table, and as she looked around, she saw other passengers busy writing letters, or eating a late breakfast, or playing cards. Several dogs were on board: a Dalmatian with a red collar, a black Lab with a blue checkered bandanna around his neck, and a curly-haired yellow mutt being nuzzled on the lap of a curly-haired blond woman.

At the booth behind her, three women in jeans and sweat-shirts and sneakers had settled in, spreading their belongings around them in a temporary nest: purses, shopping bags, coffee, doughnuts, paper napkins, magazines. Now a fourth woman, casually dressed, approached them.

"Did you have to spend the night, too?" she asked, and Joanna couldn't help overhearing their conversation; the back of the booth was so low she could have rested her head on the shoulder of the woman seated behind her. She took out her notebook and studied her list, but the conversation next to her was lively and loud. All four women, she came to understand, were islanders who had flown off from Nantucket to go outlet shopping for a day. Their trip had been inspired by a special one-day round-trip airfare, but the plane they were scheduled on, the last plane at night, was grounded by fog and they'd had to spend the night at the local Hyannis Regency. They weren't too upset, because they got to eat at McDonald's—a rare treat—and see a movie on a big screen. They began to describe their shopping finds, and Joanna filtered out their conversation and let her eyes roam the room for more exotic entertainment.

She found it in the sight of a young man leaning against a wall. He'd obviously just bought himself a cup of coffee and was on his way back to his seat but had been waylaid by three young women who pressed against him, flirting, smiling, chattering, nearly giddy in his presence. Joanna stared; he didn't notice. Probably he was used to it. He was exceptionally handsome in a bronzed, muscular, dense, teen idol way. His shaggy hair was blond, his eyes a dreamy blue, and his nose had that broken-while-scoring-a-touchdown look that accentuated the symmetry of his other features. A gold earring glittered from one ear. Beneath his white T-shirt his shoulders were wide and powerful, and long sturdy thigh muscles bulged beneath the worn, straining denim of his jeans. As he talked to his admirers, he seemed kind, or at least impartial, smiling at them all, laughing in an easy way. Maybe he was stupid, Joanna thought, or shallow, but he seemed completely fortunate, a radiant and healthy young man.

She amused herself by imagining his life. He was a golden boy, she decided, like all the golden boys who had never dated her in the various high schools she'd attended. They'd always looked her over, checked her out, but couldn't figure her out, and after all, neither could she. She didn't know how long she'd stay in any one school or even how long she'd live in any one place, and so she'd kept to herself mostly, finding friends in books and her daydreams. While these young men, athletic, popular, humorous, and smart enough to hold down a good B-minus average when they tried—and they did try, because they hated to disappoint people—these young men strode through the halls of the high schools like the young gods they were. It hadn't changed since she was in high school. It would never change. There would always be these lucky ones, envied and liked by the guys, lusted after, dreamed of by the girls.

His eyes met hers. She looked away, embarrassed to be caught staring. The boat was really rolling now. Looking around the room, Joanna noticed that quite a few of her fellow travelers had stretched out on the long blue benches, purses tucked beneath their heads as pillows, paperback books tented over their eyes to block out the light. It seemed such an intimate thing to do, to sleep out in public, and yet— Joanna put her purse on the bench against the wall and lay down, tugging her blue duster over her like a blanket. The boat rocked like a cradle. She fell at once into a blissful sleep.

She awoke feeling refreshed and oddly alert.

". . . Farthingale house . . ."

The words floated past her, above her, almost visible. The women in the booth next to hers were talking.

"Who?"

"Won't say. Hoover can be like that."

"It will be in the paper when they print deed transfers."

"I wonder if she's rich."

"Of course she's rich! She'd have to be to buy the Farthingale house!" This woman's voice was high and shrill and Joanna envisioned a shrew in human clothes, tiny hands with long tiny pointed fingers resting on tiny hips.

"Yeah, and what do you bet *she'll* be the one to find the treasure. Not an islander who could really use it, but one more rich tourist."

"I can't believe you still get riled up about the treasure. I don't think there's any such thing!" This woman's voice was rough and cracked, perhaps with age or smoke or whiskey—Joanna couldn't see. She lay on her side on the blue bench, eyes closed, feeling trapped yet excited by the conversation.

"Of course there is!" Shrew Woman insisted. "Read your history books! Those old whaling captains brought back things we can only dream of. Think of the silver on the name-plates and door handles of the Three Bricks. Or the china in the Hadwen House."

"The Farthingales searched. The Baxters searched. My father knew old Mr. Baxter and they talked about it. Old Mr. Baxter spoke to Bertram Farthingale, who had been a baby when Captain Farthingale was still alive, and he said the old captain was determined that no one should find it. He didn't think anyone deserved it."

"What a nasty old man."

"True, but he built a beautiful house on a beautiful spot. I wouldn't mind living in the Farthingale house."

"Too cold for me out there. She'll have her hands full keeping the place heated."

"You keep saying she. Where's the he?"

"Isn't one from what I've heard."

"A woman all alone in that big old house? Surely not."

"That's what Corinne said, and her daughter is Ronnette's best friend, and Ronnette is Bob Hoover's secretary."

"Well, I think that's queer," Shrew Woman proclaimed. "A woman wanting to live all alone out there."

"Just because you're such a busybody doesn't mean everyone else is," Whiskey Voice replied.

"Shove over. We're almost there. I need to use the ladies'."

The conversation ended with a great rustling as the four women packed up their gear and headed off to the rest room. Joanna sat up, stretched, then went out on deck to watch the boat enter the harbor. The ferry, rounding Brant Point, sounded its horn. As the island and its village came into view, it seemed to wrap around the ferry, to welcome it with open arms.

When she'd ascertained that her traveling companions had returned to their booth, she went to the rest room herself. As she washed her hands and combed her hair, she studied herself in the mirror. Her hair was covered by the damned black wig. She'd determined to do whatever she could for the next few weeks to keep her identity unknown so that word of her presence on the island wouldn't get back to Carter. Over the past six weeks as she'd negotiated and organized the move, she had avoided talking to him. Or perhaps he had avoided talking to her. She knew from Jake that Carter was pent up in the hospital, immobilized by necessary traction for the multiple fractures in his leg, but he'd had his staff set up a working office for him in his hospital room. He had access to more than one phone from his bed. And he hadn't called Joanna. He might be waiting for her to get the number from his staff and call him; certainly she should call him about the show. It was the longest time in five years they'd gone without talking to each other, and Joanna felt this terribly. But her longing for him was balanced out by the urgency she felt to keep her pregnancy secret, safe.

It was reassuring to know that Bob Hoover wasn't gossiping about her. She'd had to send every legal document but her birth certificate to the Nantucket Bank to apply for the mortgage, and she'd opened an account there. It was good to know she could count on the bank as well. Of course they had patrons far wealthier than she, so they must have a policy on discretion, but she could understand the temptations of gossip in any small community.

Today she didn't think she looked like the Joanna Jones of television. Her New York clothes were always tailored, but now her garments flowed, not simply as a change in attitude but also as camouflage over her increasingly large belly. She was amazed at how fast she was growing. Now she slipped on dark glasses, tucking the stems under the dark curls of the wig. Sliding the long strap of her leather briefcase over her shoulder, she blew a kiss at herself in the mirror and went back out on deck to watch the ferry draw into its berth.

All the windows now were beaded with drops from the fog which still hung over the island. The air was white, and where the sun managed to break through, it glistened with silver. It was chillier here than on the mainland, and she turned up the collar of her duster and held it closed at the neck. Down below on the wharf people wearing a variety of raincoats and sweaters awaited the boat, waving and calling. A straggling line of people waited behind a rope onshore to board the outgoing boat. Leaning on the railing, she watched the crew swinging the gangplank up and fastening it with chains and ropes. Other arriving passengers came out of the closed cabin, passed behind her and down the stairs to the deck. She could hear the group of women chattering away, but she didn't turn to look at them, not wanting to draw their eyes to hers. And she didn't want to think of anyone else. She wanted to savor this moment. When the line of people moved, she joined it at the end, going down the stairs, across the deck, down the slanted ramp which trembled beneath her feet. She had arrived.

Bob Hoover was waiting for her. He drove her to the bank, where she sat at a long table with two lawyers and the bank's vice-president, signing a multitude of papers, sliding them smoothly back and forth across the shining top of the mahogany table. She said very little and held her normally expressive face blank. The entire procedure took less than an hour.

It didn't take as long to buy her new Jeep. Bob drove her out to meet the salesman with whom she'd already spoken on the phone, and he had waiting for her the vehicle she'd ordered: a Jeep Grand Cherokee Limited, Quadratrac, with leather seats and a compact disc player. It was a dark navy-blue color with a caramel and navy interior.

"This is about as big as some apartments I've lived in—and better equipped!" she told Bob as she sat behind the steering wheel.

He was standing outside, looking at her, and now he remarked: "You look good in it. It suits you."

"It does?" Such an opinion amazed her. She'd never thought about how she looked in a car—she'd never been much interested in them. During her college days she'd been forced to buy and maintain a malevolent old Chevy, but once she moved to New York, she hadn't owned a car, hadn't felt the need for one. So many things in her life were changing.

As she wrote out the check for thirty thousand dollars, she silently congratulated herself once more for having lived so frugally. Bob escorted her to and through the maze of buying automobile insurance and getting plates from the motor vehicles registry at the town hall. When those legalities were taken care of, and she had the keys of her Jeep in her hand and even more papers in her briefcase, the realtor asked, "Is there anything else you'd like to do today? Anything I can help you with?"

"Thanks, I don't think so. I'm eager to get out to the house. My house."

They were standing in the parking lot of Rainbow Motors, which was at the same end of the island as the airport, and as they spoke, a plane flew low over them toward the runway. Now the fog had lifted; the late afternoon was sunny.

Looking up at the plane, Joanna remarked, "Perhaps my luggage has arrived. I'll drive over to the airport and see. Then I'm on my way home!"

"Would you like me to come help you with your luggage or out to open up the house—*your* house?"

"Thanks, but I'd rather be alone." She smiled, wanting not to seem rude.

"Doug Snow plans to meet you there about five."

"Good."

"And you're set for dinner and a place to spend the night?"

"I'll be at the Latherns'."

"My wife and I would like to have you over for dinner this week. Give you a list of the best shops, that sort of thing. Tell you about the town."

"I'd like that. The phone company is supposed to hook my line up today. Why don't I call later on?"

"Great." Bob shook her hand firmly. "It's been good doing business with you. I wish you the best of luck in your new home. And if there's anything you need, anything I can do, just call."

"Thanks."

"Uh, one more thing." He looked slightly abashed. Joanna thought she knew what was coming.

"I don't want to intrude, but are you *the* Joanna Jones? Of the *Fabulous Homes* television show?"

She smiled. "Yes. But I'd rather no one knew. For a while. Privacy and quiet are necessary to my health."

"I understand," Bob told her. "Mum's the word."

"Mum's the word indeed," she agreed, feeling her face flush with an uncontrollable joy.

Climbing into her Jeep, whose door shut with a satisfying thud, she turned the key in the ignition and began to drive.

It took only a few minutes to reach the airport. Her luggage had arrived. She carried her two bags out to the car and tucked them into the back of her Jeep. Driving out to Squam, she noticed how the yards, farms, and the gently rolling moors were laced with the delicate green of spring. The fog had entirely disappeared.

Turning off onto the narrow Quidnet Road, she wound her way toward the ocean, made another left turn, and slowed to a gentle bounce down the unpaved, rutted Squam Road.

She was almost there.

She was almost home.

At last she came to the winding pebble drive. The bushes scraped the sides of the Jeep; *her* bushes, she realized. She'd have them cut back. And here was the house, solid and abiding, framed by blue sky and sea.

Joanna turned off the engine and sat in the sunny silence, breathing deeply of the clean, salt-scented air. She looked and looked. All this was now hers.

She jumped down from her Jeep, walked up the winding brick walk, and stood at her front door. Painted and weathered to a perfect Nantucket blue, it needed a nice brass knocker, she decided. She would put that at the top of her list of things to buy. Already the trellised roses were leafing out. Birds flew singing across the blue sky. The sun was warm on her shoulders. She wished she had a bottle of champagne to crack against the front stoop in a celebratory gesture.

Bob had given her a ring of keys: front door, back door, shed, and several old-fashioned heavy F-shaped keys meant for various inner doors. Joanna put one of the keys into the lock, pushed the door open, stepped inside.

She stood quietly in the front hall, looking around. The air was warm, dusty, still. Joanna walked the length of her house and threw open the French doors to the fresh May air. Taking off her wig, she stuffed it into her briefcase and ran her hands through her hair: ah, that felt better!

Then she walked through her house. Through the gracious parlors, the outdated kitchen, the elegant dining room. The screened-in porch was still cold; the sun couldn't get in through the ivy vines. She went up the front stairs and through the bedrooms.

What matters most in your home? That was one of the

questions Joanna asked the people she interviewed. Location, some said, or a sense of style, or a living room with enough space for two grand pianos. The answer was always different. The answer was perhaps inexplicable. Who could say just what combination of wood and glass shaped just so in the neutral air would refresh and comfort the heart? Some people can describe it and have it built; others must find it. Does one love a home because of the way the light comes through the windows or because of the view one has standing at those windows looking out? As she walked through all the rooms of her house, taking her time, running her hand over the burled wood of the newel post, along the fireplace mantels, leaning against windows as she took in the view, she knew that what mattered most to her was a home for her children.

She knew exactly what kind of home she wanted these babies, her children, to have: this paradise. They could tumble on the lawn and build sand castles on the beach. They could ride their tricycles down the drive without fear of traffic. They would sleep in rooms as familiar to them as their own bodies, they would find their way through the house on a dark night without stumbling into unfamiliar doors. Perhaps there would be ponies; there was enough land. Certainly there would be dogs and cats, and she and her children would grow their own cherry tomatoes, and berries they could pick. They would have separate, private bedrooms, with shelves of toys and books, and there would be a playroom, too, for the rainy days.

A red pickup truck rumbled down the drive. Joanna hurried to the front door.

"Ms. Jones? Doug Snow."

"Hello. Come in."

Joanna held the door open, and as the carpenter entered, she looked him over. He was just her height and slender in a compact, intense way. He looked a bit like a cowboy in a plaid flannel shirt, jeans, work boots, but he had a beard and a long mustache that gave him more of a folksinger air. When he took off his cap, she saw how his short, shaggy blond hair was mixed with white and gray, like his beard, and as they stood talking, she studied the lines on his face and judged him to be somewhere in his forties. He wasn't exactly handsome—his dark blue eyes were too small and deeply set, his nose too large and crooked—but he had a definite presence.

She felt it as she walked through the house with him, describing what she wanted to have done. He listened carefully, asking occasional questions, and she had the sense that he was serious about his work.

"Why are there glass panes at the top of all these doors?" Joanna asked.

"Those are called lights, and there are two theories about them: first, that with all the fires burning in the various rooms, it was a way to check on how a fire was doing without opening the door, or to spot a fire that might have broken out of the fireplace and caught on the rug and so on. The other theory is more fun: it was a way to keep courting couples from having too much privacy."

"Really!" Joanna was amused.

"Oh, you'd be surprised at how prudish the old-timers were. There's even a law on the Commonwealth of Massachusetts books prohibiting a husband from kissing his wife on a Sunday."

"Things have certainly changed, thank God," Joanna observed.

"This is a nice touch," Doug pointed out, running his hand over the dark wood handrail as it spiraled and curved around into an open pedestal at the base of the stairs. "It's called a volute. It's also here—" He traced the scrolling wooden trim decorating the base of each step along the bottom of the staircase. "A definite Greek Revival touch; from the Ionic and Corinthian capitals that topped their columns."

Joanna ran her fingers over the design. "Elegant."

"One of nature's best designs, as a matter of fact," Doug said. "It will be a pleasure to refinish it."

Privately Joanna felt reassured: this carpenter really was familiar with old houses and their architectural details; she could trust him.

"Someone's painted over the wallpaper here," Doug observed, running his hand over the wall ascending from the first floor to the second, pointing out spots where the wallpaper bubbled and bulged. "It'll have to be stripped."

"You can do that?"

"Sure." Peeling back a section already loose, he murmured, "Several layers here. Who knows how many." Smiling, he looked at Joanna. "These old houses hold lots of secrets."

It took perhaps an hour to go through the house, and they agreed on a general working estimate to be adjusted as the renovations progressed, and a date on which he'd begin—he had some other work to finish up—then they shook hands and he left.

Joanna shut the front door and simply stood a moment in the front hall. So much had to be done. Still, the basic house was solid, fine, and richly burnished by the years. Children had been raised here. For a moment she imagined another woman descending the stairs, Mrs. Farthingale, lifting her long skirts with one hand, carefully holding onto the banister with the other, protecting the child she carried.

There had once been graciousness and beauty here, and there would be again, Joanna would see to that. She was ready to spend enormous amounts of time and energy and money on the restoration of this house.

Now she was tired. It was just after six o'clock and still light out, but the quality of the light had changed. The sky was a pale, icy blue, and although Joanna had closed the French doors earlier, the house still felt cool. She didn't turn on the heat; she couldn't stay here tonight. Regretfully she left her house, locking the door behind her, and, taking her overnight bag from the Jeep, walked down the road to the Latherns'.

Eight

⁓

The next morning, Joanna summoned her courage and went to the doctor's appointment she'd scheduled. Although Gardner Adams was new to the island, he'd already developed a reputation for insight and sensitivity. Tory, Bob Hoover, and the Latherns had all spoken highly of him, and so here she was, in the waiting room of his office at the Nantucket Cottage Hospital.

The concept of a family physician had never been part of Joanna's life. She had been an unusually healthy child, which was fortunate, because any sickness on her part was inconvenient for her mother and annoying to her father's girlfriends. The treatment for any illness had been a day in bed, with aspirin and 7-Up if necessary. Her mother's theory was that whatever it was, it would eventually pass, so there was no point in encouraging malingering with little treats like breakfast in bed. This was one thing on which her parents actually agreed. Her father believed that doctors were helpful only in cases of emergency and disaster—and for voluntary cosmetic surgery, of course; otherwise the body would take care of itself. And luckily Joanna's body had.

Her only childhood medical memory was of standing in line in some high school gymnasium waiting to take from a small white paper cup her dose of polio booster. When she was nineteen, she went to her university's health clinic for her first gynecological exam—and her first prescription of birth control pills. When she met Carter, she saw a doctor to have a diaphragm fitted. And that was pretty much it until the doctor in New York told her she was pregnant.

So she wasn't used to strangers analyzing her body; or rather she was used to their scrutiny, their judgment about the way her body looked, but this kind of judgment was new and unsettling. When the doctor in New York had told her she was old for a first pregnancy, she'd almost apologized.

Now she sat with a clipboard in her hand, filling out a long and complicated form about her medical history. She had no problem with the questions about any previous conditions she might have, but the section on her parents' health stopped her cold.

Had her father or mother had a history of diabetes or heart disease or high blood pressure? She didn't know. And she could not ask. Her father had died first, of a heart attack at seventy. He had been jogging with his current girlfriend, a young woman of twenty-nine named Twana, who had been the one to call Joanna, the one to arrange the cremation and dispensation of ashes, the one who wept at the lonely— Twana called it "intimate"—service. Had he had heart problems before? Twana had been living with him for a long time—six months—and didn't mention any. Joanna's mother had died a less abrupt and much more difficult death of cirrhosis of the liver but, vain to the last, hadn't called her daughter to tell her until the very end. She hadn't wanted Joanna to see her looking so unpleasant. By the time word reached Joanna and she'd rearranged her schedule and flown down to Sarasota, her mother was in a coma. Clearly Erica had died of drinking too much. There was no space for that on the form.

She had no brothers or sisters. She didn't even have any cousins. All at once Joanna was overwhelmed with the realization of her solitary state in the world and of the consequences of this for her children. If they showed signs of some illness, there would be no way to trace it back through their genetic line—but worse than that, Joanna thought, these children would have no grandparents. No aunts or uncles or cousins. Her parents were dead and she had no access to Carter's. No one else would be especially entranced by her children, or especially pleased even to see them arrive on this earth. She was flooded with sorrow. Resting her elbows on her clipboard, she buried her face in her hands, pressing them against her face to hold back tears.

"Ms. Jones?" She looked up to see a nurse standing in the doorway, a clipboard in her hand.

Joanna nodded, then rose and followed her. She was weighed, then ushered into an examination room. The nurse's name was Cindy, according to the tag on her breast pocket, and Joanna couldn't help but reflect how it suited this woman, who was around Joanna's age, but plump and rosy, all smiles and floral perfume. They chatted easily together as Cindy instructed Joanna on the use of the paper cup for the urine sample and took Joanna's blood pressure and then gently drew some blood. Then she left Joanna to change into a paper gown and wait, perched on the high examination table, for the doctor. As she waited, she felt the beginnings of anxiety percolate within her. All this—the high table, the technical instruments, the folder waiting on the counter—was new to her, and mysterious.

But when Gardner Adams entered, Joanna was startled out of her anxiety into a new flurry of emotions. He was so young! The Latherns had told her he was young, but she thought that meant he was her age, in his forties. This man was somewhere in his early thirties. And he was intensely attractive: tall, lanky, long-boned, slender, with curly brown hair and dazzling green-yellow eyes. She could feel her nipples tense and the hair on her arms rise in an immediate, instinctive, sexual response. Horrified, she clutched her paper gown at the neckline and changed her posture, sagging at the shoulders, sinking down into her pelvis, pushing her pregnant belly out before her in defense.

"Joanna Jones? Gardner Adams." Standing just in front of her, he held out his hand. "How are you?"

"I'm waiting for you to tell me," Joanna quipped, shaking his hand. It was warm, firm, large, and his handshake was brisk and definite. No-nonsense, confident. "I'll bet everyone says that," she added.

He smiled and nodded. "Quite a few." Crossing the small room, he picked up her chart, and as he scanned it, Joanna studied him. He looked like a runner, with his high-top Reeboks and long, supple, all-of-a-piece movements. He smelled of antiseptic and mint. He radiated good health, and his long hands and the back of his neck were rosy and clean. But one of the buttons on his shirt collar had come undone, and the collar pointed up at his chin in a crisp white triangle. He seemed unaware of this. When he turned to look at her, his gaze was steady, intelligent, and calm.

"Let's take a look. Could you lie back on the table?"

The New York gynecologist had been in his sixties, portly, bald, and weary. Because his examination had been made with bored, automatic movements, Joanna had disconnected her mind from her body, numbing her senses as much as possible. She'd thought of the next FH show. She'd effectively removed herself from any emotional response.

But as Gardner Adams moved his hands over the mound of her belly, pausing here and there to palpate with his gentle fingers, Joanna was completely anchored in the room. Gardner Adams was interested in her pregnancy, and a variety of expressions played over his face as he explored her, seeming to listen with his fingertips, murmuring to himself, and nodding with satisfaction.

"Good," he said, his face inches away from her belly. "Good. You're doing well."

His touch was so gentle, so courteous, that the knowledge came to Joanna that her body was important, at once fragile and powerful. Remarkable. Worthy of respect. Tears welled into her eyes and a hot flush of blood swept over her face and neck and chest, and for a few radiant moments she felt the responsibility and privilege of being a woman carrying babies in her body.

"Twins," he said, straightening up. "You'll be busy."

"Is everything okay?"

"Fine." He folded his stethoscope. "I'll let you get dressed, then I'll be back to see if you have any questions."

He left the room. Joanna rose, pulled on her clothes, and sat in a chair by the desk.

He returned, pulled a chair around to face her, and opened her folder. From behind him the sun filtered in through the venetian blinds, causing a kind of angelic aura around his body.

"Looking at your chart, I'd put your due date in late October. A Halloween baby. You're about fourteen weeks along right now." He paused. "Your blood pressure is a little high. Nothing to alarm you, but something to be aware of. I'd like you to cut out salt completely. Be sure you take some nice long slow walks every day. Every day. And take naps. You don't smoke, do you? Or drink?"

"No."

"Good. Because we don't want to elevate your blood pressure any more than it is. You're clear on that?"

She nodded.

"Good. That's very important." He stared at her steadily for a moment, as if to impress the warning on her. "Do you have any questions? Any concerns?"

"Well . . . only that I've gotten so big so soon."

"This is common with twins," he assured her. "Nothing to worry about, and there's not much you can do about it. Don't try to diet. You need nourishment for these babies. Watch what you eat—stay away from fats and, as I said, salts. Eat lots of fish and fresh fruit and vegetables. That should be easy for you at this time of year. Anything else?"

She'd been meeting his eyes, fascinated by how calm he was, how determined and serious. Looking down as she searched her thoughts for any other questions, she noticed that his socks didn't match. One was a navy and white argyle; the other plain gray. She bit her lip, holding back a sudden fit of giggles.

"I'm a bit of an emotional powder keg," she confessed. "Tears, laughter, anger . . . I never know what's going to hit me for no reason at all."

"That's to be expected with pregnancy. It might calm down over the next few months." He smiled. "Then again, it might not. You've got a lot to be emotional about, lots of physiological changes taking place in your body."

"I've got a lot of changes taking place everywhere," Joanna murmured.

"Really?" He was rising to take his leave; instead he sat back down and looked at her intently. "Good changes?"

He seemed so concerned she felt almost guilty. "Well, yes, good changes, but major ones. I'm moving here from New York. And I'm leaving a job I like a lot."

"Do you have a supportive partner?"

For a moment she didn't understand what he meant. Then, smiling ruefully, she admitted, "No. No partner at all. But I do have good friends here."

He leaned forward, as if to impress on her the weight of

his words. His gaze was calm and steady. "It sounds to me as if you're going through a lot all at one time. Simply being pregnant with twins is a major feat in itself. You have to take care of yourself. Your mind as well as your body. According to your chart, you have no relatives. Will you be able to afford help toward the end of your pregnancy, and then after the birth of your twins?"

"Yes." She felt her face flush. "Money won't be a problem."

"That's good, then. That will make things much easier. I'd advise you to buy some good books on pregnancy and childbirth, especially about twins, and also decide if you want natural childbirth, and if you do, think of who you might ask to be your partner. See if you can't find a friend to share this experience with you." His smile was very sweet. "You'll need a friend."

Joanna was warm with affection for Gardner Adams; she felt at once like his mother and his daughter. "All right."

"And call anytime if you have any questions or worries. Don't be embarrassed by the smallest thing. You shouldn't let yourself be anxious."

"All right. Thank you."

He rose then, handing her a slip. "You can get dressed now. Please give this to the receptionist. And make an appointment for a month from now. Good luck."

Joanna sat for a few moments after the physician left the room, almost palpably absorbing Gardner Adams' warmth, as if a nimbus of light had been left shining in the air. Looking around the room again, this time she saw past the medical equipment to the pictures on the walls. Framed with blue or pink, often hand-lettered and decorated with bows and ribbons and rattles, were photographs of babies Gardner Adams had delivered. Most of the pictures had a smiling mother and father leaning around the baby in a kind of completed circle with the baby as the hub.

As she dressed she thought of other photos: those of Chip that Carter carried in his wallet. The framed photos Jake kept on his desk of Emily and his grown sons—and even one of his golden retriever, Bucky. The walls covered with photo collages Tory had made of her family on various trips and holidays. The albums all her friends had of the years of their lives as their children grew from babies toward adulthood.

She had a few photographs of her parents as children, and even one of her as a baby in her mother's arms with her father standing proudly nearby. But her mother hadn't had the time or inclination for keeping albums, and they would only have been a bother during her many moves. The few photographs she did keep were tossed loosely in the bottom of a shoe box Erica had used to carry old costume jewelry she couldn't bring herself to throw away.

Who would be in the picture with her and her twins when they were born in October? Anyone? Feeling rather dismal, Joanna dressed and left the examination room.

Doug Snow was completing another job and couldn't start work at her place for about a month. Joanna had moved out of New York, but she had things to do before she could settle into her house—things to buy. She flew to Boston, rented a car, and treated herself to a month-long shopping spree throughout New England. She drove up into Maine and New Hampshire and Vermont and paid extravagant prices for the plainest old pine pieces to be shipped to Nantucket. She stayed at charming guesthouses in small country towns, dining at quaint little inns, tasting the arrival of spring in the tender asparagus, juicy lamb, delicate berries served over ice cream. She took a room at the Ritz Carlton in Boston for a week while searching out and buying a new queen-sized pale oak bed with four square posters, a gauzy canopy, and the best mattress money could buy. She bought Royal Worcester china for everyday, Limoges for dinner parties. She bought a coffeemaker, a toaster, a microwave, damask tablecloths and napkins, sterling silverware, delicate champagne flutes. She sat for hours comparing swatches of fabric for drapes.

During that month as she drove from town to town, she was content with her own company. Her mother had trained her early on to amuse herself, and waiting for Carter to find time to be with her had also sharpened her self-sufficiency. When she was lonely, she called Tory and talked to her for hours about her treasures. But she wasn't often lonely. At night in hotel rooms she made lists and drawings and diagrams, envisioning where the furniture should go in each room of her house. When she couldn't bear to think of home furnishings for one more moment, she went to a movie—a real luxury in her life, for during the five years of FH, she'd been really too frantically busy to have time for movies. Sometimes she simply stayed in her hotel room and watched a movie on television.

She tried not to mind being cut off from the network and all its accompanying news. She assured herself she didn't need to worry about competition now; the end of spring and all of the summer were fallow months for television. Everyone knew better than to challenge sunshine and warm weather, so it was almost certain that any show that would rival hers would premiere in September. Still, she bought *Interview* and *Variety* and *Premiere* and *TV Guide,* searching for any signs of possible competition. It was funny how even the old, familiar titles of *Designing Women* and *This Old House* always caused her heart to lurch with dread. Her audience was devoted, but not large; she couldn't bear to lose anyone to an imitation show on another network. But she still held the field to herself. She thought.

Just to be certain, to put herself at ease, she spent a morning with her charge card and the telephone, subscribing to the National Academy of Television Arts and Sciences newsletter and magazine, to the *International Journal of Satellite Communications*, and to *TV Executive Daily,* as well as a few other trade newspapers and periodicals. That simple task demonstrated to her with startling clarity how much of the tedious paperwork Gloria had done for her. She would miss her even more, Joanna realized, when all those publications started arriving at her house. Gloria had always scanned and excerpted them for her, clipping out and highlighting anything significant. Now she'd have to plow through it all herself.

What she missed even more was the inside network gossip. She made a note to ask Jake to have the network newsletter mailed to her on Nantucket; but what she really needed was a spy to pass along the early-warning rumors. Many times during the month of May Joanna reached for a phone, intending to call Dhon; but always she withdrew her hand. Dr. Adams' careful voice admonished her: if she wanted to carry these babies to term, she had to watch her blood pressure. Dhon existed in a state of permanent frenzy. She had to rest, to relax. That meant forgetting about the network and her show for the next few months.

Once she made up her mind, she discovered it was easier to do than she'd anticipated. She was finishing the fourth month of her pregnancy and the nausea had dissipated. In its place her wise hormones generated a kind of soothing honey in her blood, a delicious languor. She didn't feel her usual drive to accomplish things, to get on with it all. She wasn't anxious or hurried or pressured or worried—she was lazy. Her stomach was quite swollen now. Because she carried twins, she looked much further along than she was. One day she bought an entire new wardrobe of maternity clothes. And comfortable shoes—ah, the exquisite pleasure of comfortable shoes! She'd always worn very high heels at the network, wanting to appear sexy and powerful at any and every moment, but now she dropped her standards and her arches and wore Rockports and Reeboks and moccasins.

The last purchases she made before she flew back to Nantucket were twelve enormous photograph albums, a red leather diary, and a compact, very clever video camera. She'd come up with a brilliant idea: she'd keep a record, a diary, of the renovation of her house, complete with videos of each stage of the work. Perhaps when she returned to the network, she would do a segment, or several segments, on Joanna Jones' own fabulous home.

On the first day of June, Joanna moved into her house. It was a brilliant spring day, sunny and not yet humid or hot. As ungainly delivery trucks rumbled into her driveway, the local cable company installed a satellite dish. The cost was high—around thirty-five hundred dollars—but she couldn't imagine life without television; she would have paid anything. The dish, small, black, and fairly unobtrusive amid the tangle of brush, was brought in and a trench dug in the ground to the house to hide the cables. When the work was completed, she had around one hundred and fifty channels available on her new forty-five-inch RCA stereo projection television. Just in case she couldn't find anything she liked, she added a VCR. All that was tax deductible.

After the movers and their trucks had rumbled away, leaving her alone at last, Joanna went through her house, putting snowy sheets on her bed, hanging thick soft towels in her bathroom, plugging in her telephones and television and toaster.

The spring evening filled the house with a pastel light; she didn't realize how late it was until an ache in her back caused her to check her watch. Almost nine o'clock. No wonder she was exhausted!

She made herself a drink of cranberry juice mixed with sparkling water and went out the French doors at the back of the house. The moment she sat down, the dew on the steps soaked through her jeans. It was a misty spring evening, the far horizon and the near edges of her property blurred with drifting fog. She thought of moving to a drier spot, but now that she'd relaxed, she was too tired to move, and it was so warm that even damp she wasn't cold.

The absolute silence was bliss. There was no wind, and the house was far enough away from the ocean so that when the water was calm like this, she couldn't hear its rhythmic lapping. Even the birds had settled down for the night. A rabbit ventured forth from the wild moor side, froze at the sight of Joanna, then hurried off down under the *Rosa rugosa* that ran to the sea.

She had never known such silence, such peace.

It was not a thrilling sunset. The silver light slowly drained from all the air, like water sinking through sand, taking the shine with it, leaving the surface gritty and dull. It was wonderfully tranquil, and enveloping. She felt not apart from nature, a human speck goggling at a spectacle, but part of nature, part of everything, as if she were a figure in a pointillist painting, the dots of her body blurring into those of the landscape.

Oh, she was getting very kharmic in her old age, she thought, and smiled at herself. She raised her long blue cotton sweater and placed her hands gently against her belly. She could relax at last.

Did Carter wonder where she was? Did he miss her? Was he sad?

She forced Carter from her thoughts.

Joanna sat on the wide steps of her home, leaning back on her elbows on the step behind her, looking into the darkness.

This was the first time in all her life she'd ever been alone, outdoors, in such an isolated spot at night. She was not afraid. All color had drained from the landscape. Sky and sea, all the outside, was dark. Joanna felt her lighted house rise behind her, sound and safe, like a ship carrying her into the deep unknown.

Nine

～

*J*oanna was just sipping her first cup of boring herbal tea when she heard the crunch of tires on gravel and then a knock. The carpenters were here.

"Good morning," she said, opening the door.

"Morning," Doug Snow replied. Today he wore jeans and a worn khaki work shirt washed to an appealing softness; the sleeves were rolled up over his strong, muscular forearms. "Ms. Jones, this is my son, Todd. He'll work with me."

"Hello, Todd." Joanna smiled, remembering at once where she'd seen this gorgeous blond male before—on the ferry ride over, surrounded by girls. Of course. Like father, like son. She shook his hand.

"I thought we'd start to work on those rooms upstairs you want made into a study," Doug told her.

"Perfect," Joanna said. "If you'd like coffee first—"

"No, thanks. We've had breakfast. We'll just bring our stuff in."

"I'm planning to go through the house with a video camera," Joanna told them. "Take a series of before and after shots. I hope you won't mind if I come in with the camera while you're working. I'll keep out of your way."

"No problem," Doug replied, and turned and went out the door. Todd followed.

For a while Joanna just leaned against the living room door, watching as the Snows carried their sledgehammers and power tools and sawhorses through the wide central hall and up the stairs. They were careful not to scrape the walls as they went, and they moved calmly, but the sight of the muscles and sinews bunched and swollen under their shirts as they labored and the sound of their breathing as it quickened and deepened had a brute carnality that stirred Joanna. Even their footsteps as they moved in the room above her head fell hard and explosively on her ears, like hammerblows. She was surprised and slightly dismayed at the strength of her reactions but also excited and apprehensive. She was causing real and concrete changes to take place in this old, dignified home. The sense of responsibility was rather daunting.

Deciding to use her nervous tension to fuel her own work, she dug the new camcorder out of its box, stuck in a fresh cassette, and hurried back upstairs. Quickly she panned around the walls of the two boxy bedrooms the Snows would change into one. Then she went through the house, shooting everywhere except the boring basement.

Finished with the first round of taping, she labeled the cassette and went through the dining room and out onto the screened porch, where she'd set up a temporary study. She'd put an ad for a cook/housekeeper in the local newspapers, which came out once a week. Today was the first day her ad would run and she brought out her cordless phone so she could wait for calls about the ad while she began sorting through her papers. Sinking onto the fresh blue-and-white striped cushions of a new white wicker chair, she opened the first box, lifted out a sheaf of folders, then suddenly stopped. She looked around. She was wearing sneakers, baggy white cotton pants with an elastic waist, and an oversized blue denim work shirt that fell nearly to her knees. The air was perfumed from the flowers curling on the screens, and she could hear birds singing. What a way to work!

Forcing herself to stop gloating, she reminded herself that she needed to concentrate if she was to have both books done before the babies arrived. She had contracts and advances for both: a chatty, informal book compiled from questions about houses from her viewers and her detailed, illustrated replies, and a glossy coffee-table picture book entitled *Joanna Jones' Favorite Fabulous Homes.* She had to choose the photos and elaborate with anecdotes and accompanying remarks. The books would come out in conjunction with the return of her new, streamlined, improved show a year from this fall.

She would start with the question-and-answer book. Over

the years, Joanna had collected bags and boxes of letters from viewers, and with the idea of these books in mind, she'd diligently separated and coordinated each viewer letter, her response, and related notes and clippings in variously colored file folders. Now she geared up her computer and began to type in a list of topics derived from the letters to see if she could arrange her book in topical categories. There had to be some clever way to organize this mass of information.

She felt a presence near her and looked up. A young woman was standing in the shadowy doorway between the dining room and the screened porch.

"Yes?"

"I'm sorry if I startled you. The front door was open. I knocked . . . I've come about the ad for cook/housekeeper."

"But I put only the phone number in!" Joanna said, surprised.

The young woman half turned away. "I'm sorry. I wanted to be the first to apply."

"No, wait. It's all right. Just tell me: how did you know where I live?"

The young woman peeked up at her from under long, thick lashes. "On this island . . . you know where the new people are."

"Of course. Well, come in. Sit down." Joanna studied the newcomer as she stepped down into the light.

Her hair was jet-black, almost iridescent in the sunlight, pulled back in a thick long braid. Her skin was a smooth café au lait, and her eyes were black. She was of medium height, terribly composed, and oddly dressed in a simple blue cotton frock several sizes too large for her, probably worn in an attempt to hide her large rounded bosom and swelling hips. While not fat, the girl was voluptuous; even her arms curved dramatically from thin wrists to plump elbows. Perching on the edge of a chair, she folded her hands neatly in her lap and waited for Joanna to speak.

Joanna smiled. "What's your name?"

"Madaket Brown."

"Madaket. That's an unusual name."

The young woman nodded. "I know. My mother was named Cisco. My family loves Nantucket, so we're named after beaches." She drew in a deep breath. "I should tell you right off that they call me Mad Kate."

"Why?"

"Because my parents were wild, and they died young. I lived with my grandmother, and I dropped out of school at sixteen. I like to walk in the rain. I like to walk on the beach in storms."

"And that's all?"

The girl dropped her eyes to her hands, then looked up at Joanna again. "I don't hang out with the kids my age. That makes them mad, so they call me names. And I'm part black and part Wampanoag Indian. I'm different."

"And you're beautiful."

Madaket looked shocked, even alarmed. "I don't date," she announced.

"Well, no wonder they call you Mad Kate! All men assume you're crazy if you don't want to go out with them!" Joanna said, and was pleased to see a smile steal over the other woman's face. "Do you have any work experience?"

"Yes. I've worked all year for two years now for Marge and Harry Coffin, who run the bakery on Orange Street. That's from four-thirty in the morning till about noon. In the summer I've worked as a chambermaid in several hotels. They'll all give me good references."

"Have you done any baby-sitting?"

"Yes. A lot." She reached into the small backpack she carried over one arm and handed Joanna a sheaf of papers, bringing a light mist of herbal-sweet air as she moved. "I've written down the names and phone numbers of all the people I've worked for in the past five years."

Joanna skimmed them: letters of recommendation from the Coffins, from the Jared Coffin House and the Harbor House and the Four Chimneys, and from five families she'd baby-sat for.

"These look good. Why would you want to change jobs?"

"I've been at the bakery for a long time. It just seems like the right time to move on."

"How old are you?"

"Nineteen."

"Are you planning to go to college?"

"No."

"That's good. I mean, for me. I want someone who will work into the fall, who can stay on for a year. I'm going to have babies. Twins. I'm going to need help."

"I like children."

"So when they call you Mad Kate, it's not because you're crazy."

"I'm not crazy." The young woman smiled. "I'm not even mad."

"Well, Madaket," Joanna said, leaning back in her chair and sighing, "you can see the size of this house. I'm having work done on it, and gradually I'll get it furnished. I'm working on some books, which will take up all my time, and as I said in the ad, I need a housekeeper and a cook. Do you think you could handle the job?"

"I know I could."

"I'll pay very well, but in return I need to know you will work a full year. I can't be left with two babies and no help."

"I'd work for the full year. Or more."

"Don't you want to travel, at least to leave the island?"

"Never."

"How did you get out here, by the way?"

"I rode my bike."

"Such a long distance!"

"Not for me. I bike everywhere."

"Well, this would be a problem, you see. I need someone who can drive. To get groceries and the dry cleaning, that sort of thing."

"I can drive. I just don't own a car."

"Um." Joanna nodded, musing. Madaket was not at all the kind of person she'd summoned up in her imagination. She'd wanted someone sturdy and rather dull, who wouldn't sap any of Joanna's energies with the dramas of her own life. She'd had too many of that sort as secretaries. But Madaket was an appealing young woman, and Joanna could envision her easily running up and down the stairs and through the large house while older women might only trudge. Her youth had strength and agility, and yet she also had an odd grandmotherly air about her—her full body made her look comfortable and comforting.

"Wouldn't you be bored out here, working for only one person?"

"I'm never bored."

This girl kept surprising Joanna. She was so genuine.

"I want to interview other applicants. But you are the first, and I won't forget that. What's your phone number?"

"I don't have a phone. I'll put down the Coffin Bakery. You can always leave a message for me there." Madaket bent to print the number in clear firm numerals.

"I'll definitely call you, one way or the other," Joanna said.

"Thank you. Oh, and I brought you something." Madaket reached into her backpack. "An introduction to our island. I make jams and jellies out of the island berries every fall. My grandmother did it as a cottage industry sort of thing, and I helped her, until she died."

She put her gift on the desk: two small glass jars of jam, which gleamed rosily in the sunlight. Beach plum jam and rose hip jelly.

"Rose hips are good for you," she said solemnly. "When you're pregnant. They're full of vitamin C."

"I'll remember that," Joanna told her. "Thank you."

The girl bit her lip, nodded, and nearly curtsied in a quick little shiver before turning and hurrying away.

Joanna waited until she was gone, then opened the rose hip jelly and stuck a finger in. The taste was delicate, tarter than she would have thought, and unusual.

Joanna worked steadily after that, engrossed in the letters from viewers and their questions. And warmed by the compliments they gave her about her show. It really was a good series. She typed entries into her computer for a category in her book entitled "Creative Solutions," with pictures and articles about dormers and mood-enhancing colors and patterns and mirrors to reflect light and add a sense of space—all the tips she'd given people on how to improve a room. Her stomach growled fiercely. Stretching, she realized she was stiff, and hungry, so she rose and with her mind still mostly on her work, walked through the dining room and into the kitchen. Absentmindedly she opened the refrigerator and studied the contents: skim milk, orange juice, lettuce, a grapefruit and a melon, a bag of carrots. Not much to make a lunch out of, even combined with the food in the cupboards: a box of spaghetti and a loaf of whole-wheat bread. She'd never been one for cooking large meals, and now she realized what a luxury it had been to be able to dash out for a pastrami sandwich or a bowl of curried rice or take-out sushi or a luscious Cobb's salad. Why hadn't she bought more food yesterday, for heaven's sake? Well, she hadn't had time, more deliverymen had come with her furniture and she'd been overwhelmed with giving directions and unpacking and settling in. She flipped open the phone book. No take-out places listed. Not that anyone would come out this far anyway. Too bad she didn't already have an assistant, one she could send out for something. She drifted toward the front of her house and looked out the dining room window. Doug and Todd Snow sat on the bed of their truck, eating, open lunch pails and thermoses beside them on the lowered tailgate. Even from here she could see that their sandwiches were thick. She licked her lips. Her stomach rumbled again.

"All right." She spoke aloud. "Calm down. I'm going to get you some food." Where was her purse? Not on the screened-in porch. She went up the stairs. It wasn't in her bedroom. It was in her dressing room. Living in a big house could be complicated, she could tell already. She hurried back down and out the front door.

The Snows' red pickup was parked next to her Jeep. Doug was sitting with his back against the side of the truck, one leg stretched out onto the tailgate and the other angled up so that his arm hung lazily over it, elbow resting on knee. Sunlight flecked his blond hair and beard and mustache with gold lights.

"I'm going into town," she told the men. "Groceries."

"Give us a yell when you get back. We'll carry them in for you," Doug said, and he smiled a lazy smile.

"All right. Thanks." Joanna returned his smile, feeling slightly flushed as she did, and with a rush of completely unanticipated pleasure she remembered a day years ago when she was a freshman at a new high school and a cute boy wearing a letter jacket told her he'd meet her after school and carry her books home. Mystified by the power of this memory—for the boy had walked her home only once, and never talked to her again—she climbed into her Jeep, started her engine, and headed down the driveway for town.

She went to Finast, where she filled the back of the Jeep

with groceries, including an array of microwavable food. As she drove home, she gobbled her makeshift lunch—a hunk of cheddar, some breadsticks, an apple. Now she'd be able to get right back to work. You could waste a lot of time on this island if you weren't carefully organized. She was glad she was finding this out early. She had a lot to learn.

When she returned to her house, the Snowmen thumped back and forth across the wooden floors, carrying in the groceries, and Joanna unpacked them and put them away in her cupboards. As she worked in their company, she felt blithely domestic. Doug whistled a sweet, clear, slightly melancholy tune, and the sound played over Joanna's senses like a spring breeze, alluring, tempting. Something within her lifted its head. It would be very easy, she realized, to indulge in a fantasy about Doug Snow.

The day grew more and more overcast, and she was grateful, because it didn't coax her out to the beach, away from her piles of paper. She worked steadily, organizing her materials, stopping occasionally to take phone calls and schedule interviews with prospective housekeepers.

At five o'clock, she went up the wide staircase to the two large rooms on the right, where the Snows were breaking through a wall that separated two bedrooms. All afternoon the house had resounded with blows from sledgehammers and screams from saws, and now most of the wall was down. The air of the room was still gritty with plaster dust and a few floor studs stood, but Joanna could see how the room would look. A middle bedroom caught between front and back, with only two windows on one side, had now been opened up to the bedroom that looked out over the ocean. She was pleased. She would eventually have a spacious study.

Leaning against the doorway, she gazed around the room, surreptitiously studying her workers as well. Todd was sweeping up nails and plaster dust and bits of wood. Around his forehead he'd tied a batik bandanna, which served to hold his shoulder-length blond hair in place. He was taller than his father, and larger, bulkier, but his father looked the more powerful of the two. There was an air of restraint in each of the older man's movements, a sense of suppressed strength. As if he felt her eyes upon him, Doug looked up, smiling his slow smile.

"You got a lot accomplished!" Joanna said.

Todd only nodded in reply, but Doug, pulling an orange extension cord into a tidy loop in his rough, tanned hands as he talked, said, "Yeah, we got further than I thought. We had to do it carefully. You never know with these old walls. This one wasn't load-bearing."

Simply for the sake of conversation, Joanna asked lightly, "Did you find any treasure?"

Todd kept sweeping but his eyes went to his father and then to Joanna. His father cocked an eyebrow at Joanna. "How did you hear about the treasure?"

"Bob Hoover told me."

"Wouldn't find it in this wall," Doug said. "This wall's only about fifty years old. The treasure was here with the original house."

"So you know about it."

"Everybody who lives here any length of time has heard about it. I was born on Nantucket, and I expect to die without ever seeing it found."

"Don't you think it exists?"

Doug shrugged. "It's all the same to me."

As Todd emptied a dustpan full of debris into a large plastic trash barrel, he casually volunteered, "I saw Madaket Brown out here this morning."

"That's right. She came out to apply for the job of housekeeper. Do you know her?"

Todd hesitated. "Sort of."

Joanna waited for some elaboration, but the young man only went back to his sweeping. His father said, "Madaket's an island girl. She's all right. She's had a tough life. Her parents caused a lot of trouble in their time."

"Oh?"

"They were both pretty wild. And her grandmother's a little on the odd side. Or was. She just died. Madaket's living alone with a dog and a cat out in a shack. They call her Mad Kate, you know."

"Why?"

"Oh, well. She's different. She keeps to herself. She got the name about three years ago when we had a hurricane, or almost a hurricane. Winds of one hundred miles an hour, and rain, and Madaket went out walking in it. She certainly looked mad, her hair loose and flipping around her in that wind. She could have been killed by a flying branch. And she shows up barefoot in the middle of the night on the beach in the winter, that sort of thing."

"Would she be a good housekeeper?" Joanna asked.

"Far as I know. She's hardworking."

Todd picked up the full trash barrel. "I'm going to take this down to the truck, Dad, then I'm ready to go."

"I'll be right with you," Doug told his son, then turned back to Joanna. "I wouldn't hesitate to recommend the girl." He paused, studying Joanna, then asked, "I don't mean to pry, but do you have some friends on this island? People who can advise you? Who'll help you out? 'Cause I can't help but notice that you're alone."

"A few. Mostly summer people," Joanna admitted.

"Well, look, if you ever need anything, feel free to call me. Okay?"

Moved by his concern and his simple, genuine offer, Joanna flushed. "Okay. Thank you."

He nodded, then approached her, and for a moment her breath caught in her throat. Was he going to touch her?

He only walked by her, slipping sideways past her through the doorway. "Anytime. Day or night. I mean it." She could almost feel his breath on her skin. "See you tomorrow."

"Yes. See you tomorrow."

Doug went back down the stairs and out the door, slamming it behind him. Joanna walked slowly to the front of the house and looked out the window at the red pickup truck as it went off down the driveway and out of her sight. Tory had told her to go slow with the island people. She'd warned her that they weren't an easy bunch to get to know, and they resented newcomers trying to move into their lives. But Doug Snow couldn't be any nicer.

She went back to the kitchen to put a potato in the oven for dinner. She'd have it with a nice healthy filet mignon, and fresh lettuce and asparagus from a roadside stand. Her taste buds cried out for a glass of wine, but she mixed cranberry juice and seltzer. She was all alone, and it was very pleasant.

Over the next two days, she interviewed six women. Two were college students who could only work until the end of the summer, one was a frail elderly lady, and the other three were middle-aged women with families and worries and no energy left for charm.

Sunday morning, Joanna drifted gently up from sleep to find her room filled with a pearly light. The carpenters wouldn't come today. Pulling on a robe, she slid her feet into slippers and went down the stairs, through the long hall, and out the French doors into the warm day. The uncut grass dropped cool beads of water on her feet and against her ankles as she walked through the small yard, down the path through the brambles, and onto the beach.

A white mist rose from the ocean, caused by the warm spring air against water still cold from winter. Just above the horizon, a creamy sun gleamed behind vaporous clouds. The tide lapped calmly against the shore. Except for the occasional cry of a gull, the silence was complete.

So different from morning in the city.

Sinking down on the sand, Joanna stared out at the glittering blue and let her thoughts drift.

She wondered what it was like at CVN these days. She'd been gone two months now. They'd be over the shock. They'd be rallying. It would be business as usual: phones would ring and Jake would do five things at once and Dhon would fret and Gloria would *tap, tap, tap* on her determined little feet, taking charge. Taking over?

Gloria. Gloria was the most efficient assistant Joanna had ever had, and the most treacherous. Joanna certainly didn't miss her.

Dhon had really been fond of Joanna, as she was of him. Right now what she missed most about him was his wonderful sense of humor and his talent of mimicry. But he was such a gossip; if he knew where she was, he'd be unable to resist telling everyone else.

Carter, Jake, Bill . . . oh, they'd all do fine without her, and the network would flourish; Joanna's disappearance would be only the sudden brief flash of a minuscule star exploding in the network's spangled cosmos. Her absence would first, briefly, be considered a problem—but quickly it would become an opportunity. Hordes of writers with new ideas and bright young women with perfect skin and limitless energy would crowd in to fill her absence, and in the rush of it all she'd be forgotten.

Her heart knocked and blood surged in her ears at that thought. A cold rose of panic bloomed within her chest.

She didn't want to be forgotten! She didn't want to be displaced, replaced. But a year was a long span in network chronology. It would require diligence and imagination to stretch out the new shows she'd taped over the next season, and suddenly Joanna realized how much she was counting on Jake's faith in her and his own steadfast determination to protect her from both the powers above her and those below her to see that her slot was filled with her own work instead of being preempted.

She had to trust Jake, especially Jake, who would be faced with the task of explaining her absence to the network brass in a way that would make it seem advantageous to them. Jake could do it. Carter would take his lead from Jake; no matter what he personally thought or felt, he would be sure to stay on Jake's good side.

She pushed herself up off the sand. Perhaps she should phone someone. Gloria or Dhon. Just to remind them that her absence was temporary.

But no. She couldn't do that. Mustn't. Her blood surged in her ears. She sank back onto the beach and forced herself to take deep breaths. Until the babies were born, she needed to remain hidden, and quiet. There would be plenty of time after their birth at the end of October for her to get back in touch with the network. There was plenty of time.

She could tell by the way the blood pulsed just beneath her skin that all this worry about the network wasn't good for her, was causing her blood pressure to rise—exactly what she had to avoid. If she wanted these babies, she had to relax. Now.

Monday morning the carpenters returned. Joanna was glad to see them. There was something reassuringly companionable about the sound of their voices and their footsteps as they moved above her on the second floor. She resolved to buy a CD player and some CDs. Immediately. And when Pat Hoover called to invite her to dinner, she accepted with alacrity.

Ten

$\sim$

*W*ednesday night Joanna was perfectly content. She'd beavered away and accomplished a lot on the organization of her books this morning, and then she'd spent the afternoon relaxing as she skimmed through the pile of professional newspapers and magazines and journals which had been arriving in the mail. Nothing she came across seemed the slightest threat to her show.

More exciting than that was the movement she'd felt in her belly while she'd sat, feet up, reading. She'd caught her breath, and stared at her stomach, and focused, and yes, there it had been again, a definite stirring of life within her.

"Oh, babies," she'd said in tones of soft awe, and gently she'd stroked her abdomen. "Hello."

Just now it had seemed a great luxury and pleasure to step outside her house, lock its door, and stroll at her own leisure to her waiting Jeep. She started the ignition and slipped in an Enya CD. Music of her own choosing filled the air as Joanna drove from the country into the town and along Nantucket's charming side streets.

The posted speed limit was twenty-five miles an hour, and the roads were narrow and winding, forcing her to drive slowly and giving her the opportunity to appreciate what she passed: houses with their doors and windows open to the summer air, window boxes spilling with flowers, families playing croquet, a boy and girl strolling, arms entwined, a little old lady garbed in a flowered dress, pearls, and sneakers out walking her Jack Russell terrier. How different this was from rushing out to Lexington Avenue, waving for a cab, hoping the driver spoke English and wasn't stoned, then being tossed around inside the cab like a die in a cup as she was carried at erratic speeds to her destination—and keeping guard at every moment to be sure the driver was headed in the right direction.

Oh, she was headed in the right direction now. She had liked Bob Hoover, so it was possible she'd like his wife; perhaps she'd have a friend on the island, someone who actually lived rather than only vacationed here. She pulled into the drive of the Hoovers' Main Street residence. A massive brick Federal, it rose foursquare and proud, its windows shining. She knocked on the door, and Bob answered it, looking nautical, as always, with his Nantucket red trousers and navy blazer and ruddy face. The room he ushered her into was impeccably furnished in antiques, the walls covered with glowing oils and watercolors.

His wife crossed the room, heels sinking into the deep pile of her white carpet, to take Joanna's hand. She was slender, with the erect posture and graceful movements of one who has long studied ballet. She wore a simple black silk dress accented with an emerald brooch which brought out the green of her eyes. Her long hair was elaborately coiled at the back of her head, and the threads of silver among the black glittered.

"Hello, Joanna. I'm so glad you came. Bob has told me so much about you."

"Thank you for inviting me," Joanna replied. They smiled at each other with the instant and instinctive sympathy of attractive, confident women.

"You know Morris and June."

"Oh, yes. Actually, they're responsible for my being here. Two years ago I was on the way to a party at their house and I accidentally turned on the wrong driveway—and found my house."

She smiled with affection at the Latherns and was pleased when June rose and kissed her cheek. "Not to mention I was her lawyer when she bought the house." Both the Latherns were tall and big-boned and athletic, always nearly humming with a kind of eager and barely suppressed energy. They looked more like brother and sister than husband and wife.

Claude Clifford was there, too, wearing a melon-colored ultra suede jacket over a rose-colored silk shirt. He greeted Joanna with a theatrical bow: "We meet again!"

Bob asked, "What can I get you to drink? We're having vodka tonics."

"Just seltzer, please," Joanna told him.

They sank into their various chairs and sofas. As Bob handed Joanna her drink, he looked steadily at her face and remarked, "This is the first time I've seen you without a wig. Your real hair suits you."

"A wig?" Claude's eyes lit up. "You wear a wig?"

"I left my television show rather abruptly," Joanna explained. "No one in New York knows where I am, and I'd like to keep it that way for a while."

"How deliciously Gothic!" Claude exclaimed.

"So you mustn't tell a soul that Joanna's on the island, Claude. *Really.*" Pat looked sternly at Claude.

"Darling, cross my heart!"

"Also," Joanna continued, "I've acquired a bit of celebrity because of *Fabulous Homes* and I'm just very tired of it. I want to be a normal person. I want to walk into a coffee shop or a bookstore without people judging me. Staring." As she spoke, she covertly checked to be sure the oversized linen jacket she wore covered her bulging middle. No need to explain that yet.

"Then you're in the right place," June assured her. "We get all kinds of celebrities here: politicians, millionaires, movie stars."

"The ones who mean it when they say they don't want to be photographed or recognized," her husband added.

"Couldn't recognize them if you tried," Claude sniffed. "They all dress like ditchdiggers and cleaning women. No glamour. It's awful."

"Now, Claude. You can go somewhere else if you need glamour." Morris turned to Joanna. "We moved here from New York five years ago because we wanted some tranquillity—"

"—and we haven't regretted it a minute!" June finished her husband's sentence and they nodded at each other in perfect synchronicity.

Pat leaned toward Joanna. "How are you settling in?"

"Well, so far. Things are chaotic, but that's to be expected. It's so beautiful out there. Every time I look out a window, I'm amazed."

"If you ever feel lonely, don't forget we're nearby," June told her.

"We can't see your house from ours because of the lay of the land and the trees, but we're always there," added Morris.

"Oh, please," Claude protested. "You two are always flying off to New York."

"You do manage to have the best of both worlds," Pat reminded the Latherns.

"And the Snows? How are they working out?" Bob asked.

"Very well, so far," Joanna began, but June interrupted to ask, "Are they civil?"

"What June means," her husband interjected, "is that the Snows, like a lot of the native island people, have a bit of a chip on their shoulders. They tend to blame anything negative in their lives on what they call the year-round summer people."

A maid in a black dress appeared discreetly in the doorway, signaling Pat, who in turn said, "Shall we go in?"

The dining room, an opulent peach and gold chamber, gleamed in the light from the elaborate chandelier suspended over a long mahogany table. They sat down to a first course of steamed littlenecks and mussels in a wine broth, and for a few moments the only words spoken were murmurs of appreciation.

Then Bob picked up the thread of conversation. "You can't blame Doug for being bitter." He turned to explain to Joanna. "The past few years have played havoc with a lot of people. For a few years we had a real estate boom. Like the rest of the country. It seemed like property values were going to climb eternally. Of course you know what happened. Here as well as in what we call the real world. Doug Snow was one of those who had bad luck. He sold off the piece of land and house he'd inherited when his parents died: a nice bit of property but nothing too exciting. Probably made two hundred thousand tops on it. Just enough of a profit that they could buy as an investment—with a whopping loan from the bank—an old summer house in Dionis. Water views. Architect-designed, but needed work. They invested a lot of money and time in the place, fixing it up for summer people, and right in the middle of it all the bottom fell out of the market. I believe Snow paid something like three hundred thousand for the place. Thought he and Todd could fix it up and sell it for six hundred thousand, *easily*. Instead, he had to sell it for under two hundred, because he couldn't keep up with the mortgage payments, and he still owes money to the bank, and he never gained back the cost of all the work and time and materials they put into the house."

"What a shame," Joanna said.

"It's a common story, unfortunately," Morris told her. "It happened to a lot of people here. Of course, some others made fortunes selling their family homes. It was just the luck of the draw."

"Still, that family does tend to take it out on others," June observed. "Helen Snow does housecleaning, a perfectly honorable profession as well as a fairly enjoyable one, I'd imagine, given the luxurious houses there are to clean around here. Not to mention what she charges: sixteen dollars an hour. She thinks she's too good for her job. She acts like dethroned royalty. Very standoffish."

"Well, Todd and Doug seem perfectly nice," Joanna said. "Quiet but pleasant."

"I wouldn't be surprised if they weren't hoping to come across Farthingale's treasure out there," Morris remarked.

June nodded her agreement. "That would just be like them."

The maid removed their shallow plates of broth and the bowls of discarded shells, and brought in the main course: grilled salmon with pear chutney, fresh asparagus, saffron rice. Bob went around the table pouring wine.

"Ah, yes, the treasure," Joanna sighed. "Is there really any substance to it?"

"Oh, my dear, of course," Claude replied. "Don't you know, there've been dozens of shipwrecks on this island over the past few hundred years. Why, there's an entire book devoted only to Nantucket shipwrecks!"

"Mmm," Pat agreed, wiping her lips with her damask napkin before going on. "The Nantucket shoals have caused many wrecks. And the fog. Terrible storms which drove ships up on the beach."

"But were there fortunes in them?" Joanna asked.

"Yes, actually, in many. Families coming from England or the Continent to live in the New World brought the family's jewels with them. As well as gold coin. And of course there were the wars, and pirates. There are accounts of vessels wrecked along the very coast where you live, and the entire cargo of linens and foodstuffs—boxes of tea, of spices—and silver and gold as well, all strewn up and down the shore. The islanders could run out and take their pick."

"Quite a few houses here have been built with the wood washed up from shipwrecks," Bob added.

"Really." Joanna thought a moment. "That's a little— eerie, isn't it?"

"Darling, just think of it as recycling!" Claude laughed.

"Claude found a treasure in his house," Bob said.

"Oh, really?" Joanna looked at Claude.

"Really. My house is very old. Seventeen ninety. Tiny, low ceilings, some of the windows held together with wooden pegs instead of nails. You should come see it."

"I'd love to," Joanna replied.

"It's a dream," June said, and at the same time Morris said, "It's a jewel."

"Thank you, darlings. Joanna, have you ever heard of an Indian room?"

"No. Tell me."

"In many of the early houses, a small space was built into the chimney flu in which to hide silverware and other goodies from Indians."

"Nantucket never had problems with Indians, I feel honor bound to point out," Bob interjected. "The term came over from the mainland."

"So when I was having work done on my fireplace—you know, they drive a sort of long tube down your chimney and pour concrete in all around, and *voilà,* a new flu?—but before then, they had to put in a new damper, and they found it, up inside the chimney behind some loose bricks: a little hideaway, and inside were some tortoiseshell combs with beads glued on, and a gold locket with a curl of hair inside— so romantic I could have died!"

"*And* a tea set of English silver, complete with sugar tongs," Bob reminded him.

"Yes. I hate to mention it. That's the one thing I sold, for the money, you know, so I could fix up my little place. But I *did* donate the combs and the locket to the Historical Association."

"Is that the group who sets rules for the way houses are built and added onto?" Joanna asked.

"No," June answered, and Morris continued, "That's the Historic District Commission."

"We're all *very big* on history here," Claude informed Joanna.

"Claude, don't be snide," Pat scolded.

"Do you know about the Quakers, Joanna?" June asked. "You might be interested. We still have Quaker meetings here. One of the main tenets of the Quakers was the belief in the intellectual and spiritual equality of men and women."

"Equality and simplicity," Morris elaborated. "Their ideals are the inspiration for Nantucket's unique beauty."

"Oh, please," Claude protested, waving his hands. "The Quakers were nuts. They banned dancing and playing cards—good God! They weren't even allowed to wear buttons on their clothes! Buttons! They thought buttons were the inventions of the devil!"

"Still, Claude, you can't discount them entirely. Think of Lucretia Coffin Mott. She was one of the first abolitionists, and when she traveled the country making her speeches, her husband went with her and sat onstage holding her bonnet! Can you imagine that today? We've done nothing but go backwards since then!" Pat's voice rose in argument.

The maid removed the dinner plates and set a crisp salad before them. The discussion continued and Joanna watched, amused and surprised by the way the others were caught up in the relation of the past and the present. When the maid brought in blue and white Spode dessert plates laden with homemade strawberry shortcake, everyone stopped to savor the treat, and then Pat turned the conversation back to Joanna.

"Have you found a housekeeper?"

"Oh, yes," Joanna replied. "I wanted to ask you about someone. Madaket Brown."

A sudden silence fell across the table.

Then Claude said, "Really! You're all too dramatic. Joanna, Madaket Brown is a fine young woman. Thoroughly grand."

"Yes," Pat agreed. "Claude is right. Madaket is all right. Perhaps a little reclusive. But nice. And hardworking. She has to be, to survive."

"I don't know," June mused, her brow furrowed. "These days they're saying that genes carry on certain traits, and her parents were definitely trouble."

"Now we're coming to the gossip," Claude whispered theatrically to Joanna.

"Scoff if you will, but it's a fact: Dan Brown sold drugs." Morris announced.

"And Cisco was—promiscuous," June added.

"Cisco was Madaket's mother," Pat informed Joanna. Taking a sip of wine, she leaned back in her chair. "Madaket's parents were both gorgeous, and wild. They caused a lot of commotion on this island. They both had exotic looks—well, they should, they're part everything: Irish Catholic, early Puritan, Portuguese sailor, black. Even a strain of old Nantucket Indian blood. Dan Brown, Madaket's father, ran the stable on Madaket Road. He was magic with animals."

"And with women," Morris added grudgingly.

"And with women." Pat nodded at Morris. "Half the women on the island took riding lessons when Dan worked there. When he was about twenty-five, he married a young girl named Cisco. She was a real beauty. Her mother, Irene, was a nice enough woman. Sort of weird, with her herbs and stuff. I think the Indian strain must have come through Irene and Cisco. For a while Dan and Cisco were inseparable. You could feel their passion for each other if you were just standing in the room with them. They used to be seen walking in the woods in the middle of the night. Then they had Madaket, and I don't know what happened. Perhaps Dan was worried about supporting his family."

"Perhaps he was worried about supporting his habit," Morris said dryly.

"You don't know that he did drugs," Claude pointed out.

"Please," Morris protested, "we know that he sold drugs."

Morris turned to Joanna. "Dan was arrested with cocaine and heroin on him. About fifteen years ago, when Madaket was still a toddler. He was tried, sent to prison, did some time, came back, and continued to be trouble."

"Every kind of trouble," June continued, picking up the thread of her husband's tale. "Drunkenness. Fighting. Stealing. Breaking and entering."

"He never carried a gun," Claude reminded them.

"Oh, well, that makes him a saint!" June shot back.

"He was so handsome," Pat sighed. "Such a waste."

"Where is he now?" Joanna asked.

"Six feet under," Morris quipped. "To make a long and exceptionally turbulent story short, when Madaket was about five, Dan ran off with someone else's wife. They both died in a car accident on the mainland. They were drunk; Dan was driving. Madaket and Cisco moved in with the grandmother, Irene. Cisco worked as a chambermaid, and she slept around like a real little tramp for years. Then she got pregnant and died in childbirth. The baby died, too. I think that was hard on Madaket. She was only twelve. She'd been a cheerrful child until then, even though she was already shunned by a lot of parents. Not that you could blame the mothers when Madaket's mother had been sleeping with their husbands."

"Madaket lived with her grandmother, Irene," Bob continued. "When she was sixteen she dropped out of high school and went to work. She must be eighteen, nineteen now. Still lives in the awful little rented shack she shared with her grandmother. She's always been a loner. Never dated, never hung around with the island girls. Just worked, and helped her grandmother pick berries for jams, and mooned around barefoot on the moors, and rode that bike of hers. You can see her everywhere on that bike. That's how she got the name Mad Kate. She loves bad weather. In the worst storm you'll see her out biking furiously toward the moors, pedaling like mad against the wind, totally in her own world."

"It's a little spooky," June said.

"You wonder what's going on behind those deep black eyes," Morris agreed.

"And then she's got that rather disturbing body," June added. "She should lose some weight."

"Come on!" Claude protested. "That child is effing gorgeous! She's a walking Reubens. Just looking at her makes me wish I were of the typical persuasion!"

"I think she must be terribly lonely," Pat said musingly. "No friends her age. No friends at all, really. No wonder she acts half-wild. I think you're all being dreadfully unfair. She hasn't done a single thing wrong. It's unjust to blame a child for the parents' sins." Turning to Joanna, Pat concluded, "I don't see any reason in the world why she couldn't be a good housekeeper. She's got loads of energy, and she's young and strong."

"I don't know," June protested. "I just don't trust these island people."

"Please," Claude objected, leaning forward, "give us a break. The island people! Darling, it's the summer people who are serious crooks. They've bought their waterfront million-dollar homes with money they've embezzled from savings and loans or nursing homes or whatever misguided state of which they're a government official. All the men can do is sail a boat on a calm day and all the women can do is lie down for plastic surgery or a quick—"

"Claudie," Pat admonished softly, patting his hand.

"Sorry. I get all riled up, I know. But honestly, now, June, can you name one single thing that Madaket's done wrong?"

June pursed her mouth. "No, Claude, I can't. She's just so quiet and secretive. She passes right on by me on the street without saying hello, after all these years."

"Perhaps she's shy," Joanna suggested.

"Perhaps. But don't forget that the islanders have their own kind of snobbery," June insisted. "And I think the girl's got to be weird, coming from that family. But other than that," she relented, "I really can't say anything bad about her."

"My advice is, Joanna, get a young woman," Pat said. "I've hired older women who couldn't carry the vacuum cleaner up the stairs or even see the dust through their glasses."

For coffee they moved back into the living room, and Joanna took the opportunity to stretch. She walked around the large room, studying the paintings.

"You have so many lovely things," she told Pat.

"She should, dear, she owns an art gallery," Claude informed her, coming to stand next to her.

"Really?"

Pat nodded. "On Main Street. The Hoover Gallery."

"I'll have to come in. I don't have a single decent picture. Well," Joanna laughed, "I only barely have any furniture."

"Pat has divine taste," Claude said. "And she travels all the time, the lucky thing, to London, Paris, Venice, and Florence. She knows *everything* that's happening in the art world."

"I don't really need to travel to do that," Pat told Joanna. "We have an amazing artists' colony right here. Artists move here from all over the world because of the light. Something about the way the moisture in the air diffuses the light. And of course, in the summer we have so many people from all over the world who know good art and can afford to buy it."

Joanna paused before a painting which was like a whirlwind of blossoms: vivid greens, delphinium blues, intense violets. "Now this, I love. I think this must be what flowers look like to bees. Such passion, yet captured, held still."

"Ah, there you are, Claude, that should lift you out of your depression," June said.

Joanna turned.

"Claude did that," Pat informed Joanna, and she hugged Claude, who looked toward the ceiling in great discomfort.

"You painted that?" Joanna asked. "Do you have others like that? Could I come see your work? Are you exhibited in Pat's gallery?"

Claude made a choking noise, gasped: "Throat!" and left the room.

"Is he all right?" Joanna glanced around the room. No one was rushing after him. "Did he swallow something the wrong way?"

"No, no, don't worry, sit down here with us," June said, patting the sofa cushion next to her. "Claude is the world's most clever conversationalist until you talk about his work, then he becomes absolutely tongue-tied."

"He's tremendously talented," Morris said, "but just as tremendously insecure about his work."

"I didn't mean to embarrass him—" Joanna began, but Pat said, "No, no, you didn't embarrass him. You probably made his day. His week, his month! And don't worry. I do exhibit his work, and I'll show it to you anytime. He's very much in demand."

When Claude returned to the room, they were all involved in a discussion of world events, and he slipped back into his place in the group with ease.

When the party broke up, Joanna was pleasantly fatigued, and as she drove back to Squam, she followed the Latherns, who left at the same time she did. She steered her Jeep along behind the red lights of their Isuzu, her thoughts still back in the Hoovers' house: she'd liked Pat a lot. And Claude. It had been a good evening.

The night was darker, thicker, out in the country. She slowed to a crawl on the rutted Squam Road. The Latherns turned into their driveway, tooting a light staccato farewell. When at the end of her long driveway she saw her house waiting, with the porch lights shining like beacons, she laughed aloud with pleasure. The air when she stepped out into it was damp and chilly and full of reverberant rustlings from the bushes. She hurried inside.

Tucked away in bed that night, her thoughts wandered restlessly from the work the Snows were doing on her house to the dinner party and most often to Madaket. She imagined the young woman lying alone in her bed, dreaming of riding her bike through a howling storm, her braid undone, her hair flying behind her like a stormy cape. Madaket, who said she was never bored. Madaket, whose parents had deserted her. Madaket, whom some people didn't trust, because she could be alone. Something in Joanna responded deeply, instinctively, to the young woman. She felt both like her and very different. But putting emotions aside, it was simply true that Madaket was the best candidate for housekeeper.

She decided to call Madaket Brown the next morning, to tell her she was hired.

Eleven

◦

On a sunny day during the second week of June, Joanna made an awkward exit from her Jeep while up on the front porch of her Victorian summer house on the bluff in 'Sconset, Tory waited, smiling.

"Tory, come here a moment," Joanna called out. "I want you to meet someone."

Tory walked down to the lawn and Madaket stepped out of the car.

Joanna introduced them. "Tory, my best old friend, meet Madaket, my new right hand."

The two women smiled and shook hands. Together they were like night and day: Tory was tiny and dainty and slender, with the pale blue eyes and white-blond hair of her Icelandic ancestry. She wore brief white jogging shorts, a white T-shirt, and sandals, and she didn't look old enough to have any children, let alone two adolescents. Standing next to her, Madaket seemed the older. Certainly she was larger. She was as tall as Joanna, and broad through the bosom and hips, and though Joanna had come to suspect the young woman had a small waist, she couldn't know for sure because of the loose dresses Madaket wore. Tory looked very contemporary, very urban; Madaket could have arrived directly from an isolated village in the last decade of the last century. She had the look of a Victorian mill worker about her with her solid black work boots and her simple dark print cotton dress falling almost to her ankles and her hair pulled back in a braid with tendrils and curls and strands escaping romantically about her pretty face. Tory, as always, had on perfect makeup, so expertly applied it looked natural. Her lips were shell-pink. Beside her, Madaket, who wore no makeup at all, was naturally flamboyant, with eyes so black and intense and almond-shaped and long-lashed they flashed like coals catching fire, and the skin on her full rosy lips had an odd violet tint and around her eyes it was almost blue.

Madaket was polite but shy, and Tory tried to put her at ease.

"What a beautiful summer dress you're wearing. It's just the thing I see in the Tweeds catalogs. My daughter would die for it. Where did you get it?"

"At the thrift shop. It's a secondhand store in town."

"Of course, thrift shops are the best places to find marvelous old clothes. Well, I'm so glad Joanna has you to help her," Tory said. "She's hopeless when it comes to running a home."

"Hey, wait a minute!" Joanna protested, laughing. "I'm an expert on homes."

Tory waggled her eyebrows at Madaket. "Just mark my words."

"All right," Madaket replied. Getting back into the car, she said to Joanna, "I'll be back to pick you up in two or three hours."

"Don't hurry," Joanna told her.

"And drive carefully," Tory admonished. "The tourists are crabby these days."

Once Madaket had driven away, Tory turned to embrace Joanna.

"I can't believe you're so pregnant!" she said, gently touching Joanna's belly. "And you own a complete and entire house! Come in and tell me all about it."

Wrapping her arm around Joanna's shoulder, Tory led her friend up the steps and through her spacious house and out to the shady covered porch. As she stood with Tory, gazing at the expanse of dappled-blue Atlantic, Joanna felt happy, both relaxed and excited—it was so good being with Tory again, and she wanted to tell her everything at once.

Joanna settled into a chair. "Where are the kids? How was the trip?"

"Hair-raising. Jeremy's got his license and insisted on driving most of the way, with Vicki grumbling that she should be allowed to drive, too. Here, I made you a nice nonalcoholic fruit drink."

Tory had furnished this house wittily, in what she called British Pukka, with lots of airy Indian and Pakistani touches. The porch furniture was bamboo with lime-green cushions. Chinese wind chimes tinkled. Round glass tables supported by fake, highly detailed elephant legs held small painted porcelain rice bowls filled with chocolates and nuts. At the far end of the porch stood the battered old table and chairs where the Randall family had played raucous games of Monopoly or Clue or Trivial Pursuit by the light of the glass hurricane lanterns. It was all comfortably worn and familiar. Joanna leaned back on a chaise and accepted a tall glass adorned with a pleated paper umbrella and a straw.

"Thanks. Wow. I'd forgotten how magnificent your view is. So much more dramatic than mine."

"Yeah, but there's no access to the beach here unless you want to throw yourself over the edge of the cliff and free-fall. But I do love it. Joanna, you look absolutely radiant. How do you feel?"

"Wonderful. I'm disgustingly happy and healthy. I've never been better in my life. I love my house. I love having a house. I love being pregnant. I love Nantucket."

"Don't you miss Carter?"

"Of course." Joanna paused, reflected, took a deep breath. "But all this"—she put her hands on her belly—"was never part of any plan or promise between the two of us."

"I know. Still, I worry about you trying to raise two children without a father."

"I can do it. Lots of women—"

"Oh, I know, I know, but it's hard. Without someone to help you love and protect them, to love and protect you. I'm afraid you haven't considered the long lonely nights when both babies will be sick and you'll be sick and—"

"—and then I'll call you," Joanna laughed. "But I'll have help. Don't be so gloomy! Remember, Tory, I'm a woman who was sure she'd have neither husband nor children. I've already adjusted to a lot of, well, not losses, but absences. Being pregnant is such an unexpected miracle."

"Yeah," Tory mused, "I remember. Hormonal heaven. And they're so sweet as babies and so fascinating and adorable, and so loving." Her face grew solemn. "It's really hard now that Jeremy and Vicki are growing up. They're secretive. They don't want me to hug them, or even be seen with them. I miss them. The little ones."

"From what I've heard, Tory," Joanna said consolingly, "all teenagers disown their parents at a certain stage in their lives."

"I know. Still, I envy you. You're at the fun stage. Hey, tell me about your house. When can I see it?"

"Everything's in chaos, but come over anytime, as soon as you can. I can't wait for you to see it. I've got a father-son carpenter team knocking out a wall between two upstairs bedrooms so I can have a larger study. They've got to patch the walls, repair the woodwork, and paint the room. While they're fixing up my study, I'm working on the screened-in porch. Sorting stuff, organizing materials for two books. Justin Karnes at DBP's given me an advance. He wants them as soon as possible."

"Does he know where you are?"

"Nope. I told him my agent will send chapters along to him as I finish them. He can always leave messages for me at Sheila's office."

"Such subterfuge! Such drama!" Tory teased.

"You know how everyone talks in New York. Or Carter could go charm Justin's secretary into digging up my home address. I just didn't want to take the chance. I want Carter to feel that all roads are blocked off. No access. Dead end."

"Do you have a secretary here?"

"No. But, thank God, I've got Madaket. She's only worked for me for three days now, and I don't know how I lived without her. She's energetic and polite and wonderfully self-starting. I don't have to make a detailed list of things for her to do. I just said, you're the housekeeper. She cooked dinner for me last night—grilled monkfish, rice, fresh asparagus. And strawberry shortcake. It was a feast."

"You're going to get fat."

"Are you kidding? I'm already fat! But Madaket watches my diet more carefully than I would. She's big on fresh fish and fruits and veggies."

"I'm glad she knows what she's doing."

"Me, too." Joanna hesitated, then confessed, "I've had a

checkup with the obstetrician here. He says I need to be careful about salt and so on. It looks like my blood pressure's getting high."

"Oh, Joanna, how worrisome. That can cause real problems."

"I know. Especially with twins."

"You just have to force yourself to rest a lot," Tory insisted. "You can't run around like a madwoman the way you usually do, working night and day."

"That's why I've moved here, where it's peaceful and quiet. I'm trying hard, Tory. I've read all the books. I'm doing all I can." To her chagrin, tears flooded her eyes.

Tory leaned forward and stroked Joanna's hand. "Honey, you'll be all right. I'm sure you will be."

For another hour they lay back in their bamboo chairs, sipped their drinks, talked about pregnancy and babies. Joanna was at the stage where she wanted to know everything, in graphic detail, about the way babies grew in utero, and were born, and were nursed and cared for, and Tory was glad to oblige, confessing that such memories were balm to her soul.

A horn sounded outside: Madaket returning with the Jeep full of groceries. Together Tory and Joanna made their way through the cool, shadowy rooms of the old Victorian house and out to the front porch.

"I'll be right down," Joanna called to Madaket. Turning to Tory, she embraced her, saying, "I'm so glad you're here." Then, halfway down the steps, Joanna turned and looked back up at her friend. "By the way, I didn't get a chance to ask—have you seen anyone from the network? Jake or Dhon or—anyone?"

Tory laughed. "Now, where would I see them?"

"Oh, at a party, perhaps . . ."

Tory shook her head. "Shame on you. No, Joanna, I have not seen anyone from the network, and especially I haven't seen Carter. He hasn't called me to ask where you are. He hasn't called John; John would tell me if he had. I haven't seen Jake, either. He's the only one I'd run into at parties, you know. Now come on. Remember what the doctors have said. Forget about them all. You've got to relax."

"I know, I know," Joanna grumbled. Turning away from

Tory, she made her way down the rest of the front steps.

"Take care of yourself," Tory called cheerfully. "Everyone in New York is doing just fine without you!"

"That's what I'm afraid of," Joanna said to herself, and she was in a quiet and thoughtful mood as Madaket drove her home.

That evening, after the Snowmen rode off in their red pickup, after Madaket biked away, Joanna went for a solitary walk—or rather, she thought, a waddle—along the beach. The day had been full and busy, and she was cheered by Madaket's presence and by Tory's arrival on the island, yet tonight she was melancholy.

She missed Carter. Terribly. She thought of him on first awakening and on lying down to sleep. Because of her hormones, her appreciation of the world was intense, and every moment of the day she encountered tastes or sights she longed to share with him.

She missed his voice, his warmth, his elegance, the sparks of their collaboration. She missed his body. Even though she'd done everything she knew to keep her life here secret, whenever she heard the phone ring, her heart leapt with the hope that it would be Carter calling. Every afternoon as she strolled down her driveway to take the day's mail from the box at the road, she hoped she'd find a letter from him.

Yet she would not call him, or write him, and she knew she had to stop wanting him. She understood how the power of her longing was serving to blur reality, and she reminded herself that Carter was a man who always got his way. She wasn't certain that even now she could withstand the force of his displeasure.

These days when Joanna walked down the main street of Nantucket, she saw tourist families together, young sweet-looking men barely out of their teens with babies strapped to their chests in little canvas knapsacks. She saw couples walking together, mother holding one child's hand, father holding another child's hand, all of them eating ice cream cones. She saw a bearded professorial type seated on a park bench with a tiny baby in his arms. He fed the baby from a bottle while his wife, inside a woman's clothing shop, tried on garments, posing in the doorway for his approval. Couples like this made tears come into Joanna's eyes and she wondered for the millionth time if what she was doing was right.

But what was right?

Had it been *right* for her parents to have a child when neither was capable of having a home? She certainly hadn't had the perfect family, a daddy holding one hand, a mommy holding the other, and yet she'd turned out reasonably well.

So she tried not to think of Carter, and instead to concentrate on her work and her beautiful house.

"You'll have to be patient," Joanna told Madaket when she hired her. "And flexible. With all this work on the house, it's bound to be chaotic." But Joanna discovered that her life quickly fell into a comfortable pattern. Five days a week Madaket biked out, arriving at the house at eight o'clock, in time to fix breakfast for Joanna. Madaket joined her for coffee as they discussed the day's schedule, then Joanna went onto the screened porch and spent the morning working on her books. Madaket cleaned house and cooked, the Snowmen hammered and painted and plastered away upstairs. After the lunch Madaket brought out on a tray, Joanna walked along the beach for an hour, returning for a catnap. Then she resumed work on her books until the hammering stopped and everyone left and she could relax in the still of the evening, eating at her leisure whatever Madaket had prepared for dinner. Still later, she talked with Tory on the phone, or often simply sat on the screened porch, looking out at the light playing on the water, sometimes listening to a classical CD, sometimes reading, sometimes only daydreaming, until, very early, perhaps at only ten o'clock, she climbed the stairs and went to bed, falling asleep instantly. She felt perfectly safe alone in her huge old house. It seemed to accept her and all the changes gratefully, holding the warmth of the day in its rooms at night, receiving light from the moon and stars in its deepest corners.

Joanna liked having Madaket in the house. The young woman was quiet; she was quick. Obviously she was trying hard to please. Unlike Joanna's city assistants, she wasn't argumentative or pushy or strung out over her current lover or her landlord. In fact, she never talked about herself at all.

Often as she worked she hummed under her breath, and when she came or left the room, a fragrance of herbs and spices drifted through.

The first morning, as they went over the plans for the day, Madaket stood in front of Joanna, hands folded decorously in front of her, but this respectful, rather servile attitude bothered Joanna, and she said, "Oh, Madaket. Sit down," and gestured to the other side of the kitchen table. "I can't think with you standing there like a little soldier at attention. Help yourself to a cup of coffee, and join me. And please, speak up if you have some thoughts. I need all the advice I can get!"

"Oh, I think you're doing everything perfectly," Madaket replied, but a few mornings later she surprised Joanna by taking the initiative. "Which cupboard do you want me to stack the plates in? And the canned goods? And the staples?"

"Why do we need staples in the kitchen?" Joanna asked, truly dumbfounded. "I have plenty in my box of office supplies."

Madaket's mouth twitched. "Not those kinds of staples. Cooking staples. Flour. Sugar. Baking powder. Those kinds of staples."

"Oh, God, I'm an imbecile! Well, does it matter? I mean, are there rules for this sort of thing? Guidelines? Does someone anywhere care? There are so many cupboards. Look, why don't you decide?"

"I'd love to," Madaket replied eagerly. And as Joanna sat on the screened porch, reading through her files to the hum of her computer, she heard through the doors from the porch to the dining room and the dining room to the kitchen the companionable sounds of Madaket singing to herself punctuated by the pleasant, orderly tap of plates and cans being set down on wood.

The next day, when Madaket brought Joanna her second cup of decaffeinated coffee, she paused, then said, "Joanna, could I suggest something?"

Joanna turned in her chair. "Of course."

They were on the screened porch. It was a cool, rainy day, and the rain drummed on the roof. The windows, thick with dripping vines, enclosed the room in a humid, fragrant green. Joanna had turned on the overhead light as well as the standing lamp, and the cool blue radiant lake of her computer screen gleamed. Madaket's hands were behind her back and she stood very straight, as if at attention.

"I don't mean to be rude," Madaket began, licking her lips, and then, taking a deep breath, she forced it all out: "but you see, you don't have much cooking equipment. It limits what I can make for you."

Joanna shrugged. "I told you I was new to all this household stuff. All right, Madaket, sit down. Please. Now tell me. What else should I have?"

Madaket settled on the edge of a wicker rocker and leaned forward. "Loaf pans, and then I could make bread. I make delicious bread. A set of measuring cups and spoons. A Cuisinart. Cookie sheets. Pie pans so I could make you quiches or fruit pies. An electric mixer. A large breadboard. Decent knives. Slotted spoons. Wooden spoons. Some nice big pottery mixing bowls. Shall I go on?"

"You mean there's more?" At Madaket's affirmative nod, Joanna sighed. "You poor thing, what have you been using to cook with?"

Madaket grinned. "It's been a challenge. You do have lovely china and crystal and silver, but you've neglected to buy the basics. If you'd like, we could go in together and select things."

Joanna leaned back in her chair and considered. She imagined them together in the housewares department of Marine Home Center, debating over teakettles, and her immediate reaction was definite. She'd be bored to death. She always had been bored to death with kitchen paraphernalia, and it seemed she hadn't changed. She wanted to spend her time on the architecture of her books, constructing a complete and satisfying thing from words and photographs and images and questions and answers, and so she asked Madaket, "Do you think you could buy everything yourself?"

"Yes, of course. But—"

"It's just that I'm worried about getting these books done before the babies get here. And my energy is limited, and besides, Madaket, I can't pretend, I just don't know a thing about food except how to eat it and I guess I don't really want to learn. I'd be grateful if you'd just go buy everything you need. I trust your experience and taste. Buy the best quality, that's my only qualification. Okay?"

"Okay," Madaket answered. Her eyes were bright. "This is going to be fun. And oh, you'll be amazed at what I'll be able to make for you!"

The young woman was practically wriggling, puppylike, in her eagerness. Joanna found it endearing that anyone could get so worked up over kitchen equipment. "Well, let me give you a blank check. Go now, why don't you. Never mind about the breakfast dishes. They'll wait."

"No, no, I'll do those first. Then everything will be clean and in place when I come back." Madaket jumped up, then turned back. "Perhaps you should give me two checks. Then I can run into town and buy some fresh Bartlett's lettuces and veggies."

"Yes, you do that."

Madaket flew off. Joanna bent over her papers.

Three hours later Madaket returned, glowing. Joanna lost count of the trips Madaket made through the central hall from the Jeep to the kitchen. At last Madaket appeared in front of Joanna, breathless. "Would you like to see it all?"

"Not now, thanks. I'm sure you bought great stuff."

"Here's the receipt. I know it's a lot of money, but you needed so much—"

"That's fine, Madaket. That's great. Thanks for doing it."

"Well, I'll fix you a nice lunch, then I'll unpack it and wash it all and put it away." She sounded as happy about the prospect as if she were going to a party.

The following day the gentle rains surrendered to a true summer storm. Wind howled and shook the windows. Raindrops as hard as marbles were thrown against the house, their staccato clatter competing with the more general buzz of the Snows working on the second floor. Joanna had Madaket carry her files into the dining room, and she sat at one end of her long pine table, working intently, until the seductive dark aroma of chocolate came curling around her like a crook. Dropping her pen, she went into the kitchen. Madaket was bending over the oven, taking out a pan of brownies.

"My mouth is watering." Joanna reached out her hand.

Madaket tapped it lightly. "Don't touch. You'll burn yourself. They need to cool a bit before I can cut them."

"Oh, all right, but I hope they cool fast." Joanna went back to the dining room and her work.

When Madaket finally came in to Joanna, bearing a plate of brownies and a glass of skim milk, she asked, "Would you mind if I took a plate up to Todd and his father?"

Around a mouthful of warm, melting chocolate, Joanna replied, "Of course not. It would be cruel not to, with this aroma wafting through the house. They must be salivating like mad. Oh, Madaket, this is ambrosia." She sipped some milk, then stretched and yawned. "I'll come up with you. I need to move this old body, and anyway, I'd like to see how far along they've gotten. Here, I'll carry the plate. You bring along some glasses of milk."

On the second floor they found both men in the center of what was now a long, open room. Splintered boards and nails were scattered all over the floor and plaster dust coated the room and the men as well. Both men had stripped down to white T-shirts and jeans, and over their chests and backs the white cotton was nearly transparent from perspiration. Her city senses were snagged by the fresh, brute, stimulating scents of sawdust and sweat in the air. Doug straightened up, turned, and hitched up his jeans, which were riding low on his narrow hips. Joanna was suddenly stunned with lust at the sight of the two muscular, very physical men. She had to clear her throat to speak.

"We thought you might like to take a break. Madaket just made these brownies."

With his forearm, Todd wiped sweat off his forehead. "Great. Thanks."

He approached Joanna and accepted the plate from her, then turned to Madaket and took a glass of milk. Joanna saw Madaket's face as Todd approached her: the young woman's black eyes scanned his face briefly, intently, greedily, a living camera snapping a shot to keep forever. Then she dropped her eyes. But when Doug Snow reached out to receive his glass of milk from her hand, Madaket did not raise her eyes, but stood paralyzed, and when the older man said, "Thanks," her nod of reply was so abrupt it looked as if she had flinched.

"Well," Joanna exclaimed, "you've gotten the wall down. It's going to be a good-sized room."

"We'll need to redo the floor and the ceiling," Doug pointed out, indicating the rough, jagged parallel lines left from the wall.

Joanna talked to him a bit more about the work he would do, or rather listened to him, nodding in what she hoped was an intelligent fashion. Really, she was thinking: what's going on? Did this man emit sexual electromagnetic currents to which her pregnancy had tuned her sensitive body? For as Doug gestured, Joanna found herself captivated by the track of sweat through the white dust that had sifted onto the curly, ash-colored hairs on his taut, powerful arm. The veins stood out on his arms and hands, and his hands were abraded and swollen; his flesh would not feel soft like her flesh, but hard and rough. When he moved, his long, lean, solid thighs swelled within the fabric of his jeans. Doug's strength was physical, and physically obvious in his every movement, unlike that of the men she'd worked with every day at the network whose strength was in their minds. They used the cut and expense of the fabric that hid their bodies to indicate their power.

She came out of her trance to realize that Madaket had already gone down the stairs. Todd was leaning against the window, looking out at the rain while he ate.

"I'll leave you to your work," Joanna said, "and get back to my own. It seems like you're getting a lot accomplished in a short time. Thanks."

When she returned to the first floor, she found Madaket in the kitchen washing up the bowls and pans. Joanna took another brownie and leaned on the counter companionably.

"Don't tell anyone, but I find both those men really sexy," she confessed to Madaket in a low voice.

Madaket's black gaze flashed over Joanna's face then back down into the sink of soapy water. "Mr. Snow, too?" she asked.

"Mr. Snow especially. He's got such an aura of intensity about him. I find him terribly interesting."

Madaket smiled grimly. "I find him frightening."

"Doug Snow, frightening?"

"Yes." Stacking the final pan in the drainer and pulling out the sink plug, Madaket turned to dry her hands on a dish towel.

"How odd, I don't get that feeling. I mean, Doug is shorter than Todd and slighter. And older. Todd's bigger and has that rebellious teen idol look about him."

Madaket bent over with a whisk broom and a dustpan just then, so Joanna could not see the young woman's face when she said, "If Todd were a rebel, do you think he'd be working for his father?"

"You mean he wanted to do something else?"

"Oh, I don't mean he's ever talked to me about this personally. We know each other because we both grew up here, but I certainly don't run with his crowd, but everyone has heard, everyone knows—Todd was a great football player, and he's smart. He could have gotten an athletic scholarship to college, perhaps even an academic one. But his father didn't want him going off to college. Didn't want him to leave the island. Wanted him to work with him. And that's what Todd's doing."

"You like Todd, don't you?"

Madaket put things away in the broom closet and closed the door. Turning, she looked directly at Joanna and, smiling, answered, "Everyone likes Todd."

"And Doug?"

The light left her face. "I don't know. I know he didn't like my father—at all—and consequently I'm sure he doesn't think much of me. Perhaps he suspects—I mean, I know this is impossible and sounds egotistical of me even to say it—but I think Mr. Snow thinks I might, oh, seduce Todd somehow and make him marry me or something." The young woman's hands flew up to cover her face. "I probably shouldn't have said that. I'm embarrassed to have said that. But I want you to understand why I get so—*stupid*—around Mr. Snow. I know he's never liked me. I know he's suspicious of me."

"I think you misjudge him, Madaket. In fact, Doug Snow spoke very highly of you the day you came out to apply for the job. He said you were hardworking; he recommended you highly."

"Really?" Madaket looked surprised.

"Really. He didn't have one negative thing to say about you." Joanna waited a moment to let her disclosure sink in. "I suggest you give him a chance. But anyway, Madaket, I like you, and if Doug Snow ever says anything against you,

BELONGING ~ 151

I'll just tell him to mind his own business and go back to his boards. Okay?"

"Okay." Madaket smiled shyly at Joanna. "I'd better go finish vacuuming now."

Madaket went off, and Joanna returned to the dining room, holding her brownie in one hand while she took up her pen with the other. She bent over her work, intending to concentrate on the letter from Dahlia Martin in Virginia, who wanted to turn a former stable into a recreation/game room and connect it to the kitchen of the main house and needed clever ideas about how to best utilize the necessary twenty feet of space. Joanna had several suggestions and sketches, but for the moment she was preoccupied with thoughts of Doug and Todd and Madaket.

Was Doug Snow really frightening? Certainly he was intense. That perhaps would be enough to intimidate a young woman; Joanna had to remember that Madaket was still an adolescent, and Doug Snow was old enough to be her father. Perhaps any paternal authority figure was frightening to her. She remembered how long it had taken her to feel comfortable with any older person in authority when she first started working at the network.

The crucial point was that Doug Snow behaved with civility toward Madaket. Joanna didn't foresee problems arising from them all working in the house together.

Except, she thought, and she sighed and ran her hands over her belly, whatever problems her own conscience gave her for the foolish and secretly delicious lust she felt for Doug Snow.

Twelve

~

*J*oanna was constantly amazed by the light. So much light, such a variety: the spacious, generous, steady gold of day; the shadowy, textured, flickering luminescence during a storm; the dramatic, silvery, blue-tinged intensity of a starry night. When the moon was full, the entire world seemed to expand. One night she walked along the beach all by herself under a full white moon. The sky was indigo, the air and sand were lavender, and the ocean was a shivering sheet of radiance.

She'd never cared much for light before. It had always been something to work with, or against, as she and her crew tried to set up shots in which the right objects would be spotlighted and the wrong ones obscured. For years she'd dashed into the network before light and out after dark, unfazed. She hadn't had time to pay attention to something as trivial as the weather. Personally, she'd thought of strong sunlight as a kind of enemy who provoked wrinkles and skin cancer on her face as well as perspiration stains on her clothes. In her New York apartment, her kitchen and bathroom had been illuminated only by fluorescent lights, so that day and night were the same. The studios at the network were similarly windowless.

Now it seemed to her that every steady beam of sunlight carried with it a kind of tranquilizing force. She could hardly pass by any especially sunny spot without wanting to curl up in it and snooze like a cat. Her pregnancy, of course. She was always drowsy in the honeyed light of day.

Somehow this was all mysteriously connected with her new ability to be alone. She enjoyed the sounds of Madaket and Todd and Doug coming and going in her house; she liked lunching with Tory and was delighted by her growing friendship with Pat. But she'd discovered within her a surprising capacity for solitude. In the evenings she could sit on the chaise on the screened porch, listening to the birds and the insects, gazing at the way the light filtered through the leaves on the screens, or walk along the beach, watching the setting sun throw sequins on the waves, or even sit curled up on her sofa in the living room, staring at a patch of blue sky as it gradually, silently deepened into indigo. So much as an hour could slide by. She sat in a blissful daze, growing her babies. She imagined herself as a kind of basic creature; she fancied herself connected at last with all sorts of things, other people, animals, plants, with even the light itself.

June deepened into true summer. She was fully in her fifth month of pregnancy. She'd already gained thirty pounds. Her babies were growing.

Every morning she'd lie in bed on awakening, just staring at the sky, half dreaming, feeling her babies move inside her with little stirring, turning movements. It felt the way a stone skipping over water looked: there—there—there. She put her hands on her belly and felt the skipping movement on both the right and the left.

"Hello in there," she said. "This is your mother with the morning weather report. Too bad you can't see it, it's a glorious day. We'll be having orange juice and blueberry muffins for breakfast; Madaket's bringing some out fresh from town."

Was she fooling herself to think the babies fluttered in response to her voice? She tried to envision them inside her, curled up in their wet chamber, growing.

In early June Gardner Adams had offered her the opportunity to have amniocentesis done; she had decided against it. After discussing it carefully with the obstetrician, they'd concluded that the one percent chance of spontaneous abortion from amniocentesis, as well as the attendant emotional upheaval often caused by the procedure and the period of waiting, was in this case worth avoiding. If, Gardner pointed out, something was found to be wrong with one of the babies, the sheer grief and guilt and turbulence of deciding whether or not to attempt a "selective birth" might be enough to cause a spontaneous abortion of both babies.

But even if the procedure were to go perfectly, Joanna felt an instinctive aversion to too much knowledge about her babies. Perhaps she was being superstitious, primitive, naive, but it seemed that Nature or Fate or simple Accident had given her these children, this family of hers, and she knew and felt that it was absolutely right, the right time, even the right number. Two babies. An entire and complete family.

Dr. Adams had also told her that with either ultrasound or amniocentesis they could detect the sex of the babies. No, thanks, she'd said. She didn't want to be deprived of the excitement of the news at birth, and just being pregnant was exciting enough for now. Secretly she believed that the babies were a boy and a girl.

Joanna was stirring her first cup of decaf of the day when Doug ambled in smelling of salt air and sunshine. He held out a package wrapped in brown paper.

"Like bluefish?"

"I've never had it."

"Try it. Madaket will know how to cook it. I caught it this morning."

"This morning?" She looked at her wrist; her watch read exactly eight o'clock.

He smiled his lazy, sensual, seductive smile. "Some of us get up earlier than others." With a nod, he sauntered off and up the stairs to work.

Often when he came down to refill his mug from the fresh pot of coffee Madaket kept hot on the stove, he'd stick his head out through the dining room door and ask, "How're you doin' today?"

"I'm getting stiff from hunching over this computer."

"Well, why not come on up and help us out? We'll loosen you up a bit."

His comments, and hers, too, it seemed, were very lightly laced with sexual innuendo; but perhaps that was only her perception. She doubted that he found her an irresistibly sexual object in her increasingly large tops.

Occasionally all four of them enjoyed moments of congenial conversation, especially over town gossip; then Madaket and Doug and Todd all vied to describe the particular characters in colorful detail to Joanna. It seemed a special source of joy to the three natives when Donald Trump's yacht was unable to enter Nantucket's harbor because it drew too much water.

One especially lovely morning the sun was so bright and the air so fresh that Joanna couldn't bear to stay tucked away inside with her paperwork. She went off in search of Madaket and found her out in the driveway, slamming shut the rear door of the Jeep.

"What are you up to?" Joanna asked.

Madaket rested her foot on the rear bumper and bent forward to retie her work boot, her long black hair, pulled back in a ponytail today, falling over her shoulder. She wore a blue cotton dress which rather resembled a child's pinafore: loose and falling nearly to her ankle, it buttoned down the back and had deep patch pockets on the skirt. As Madaket moved, the lines of her very adult body were traced out in silhouette by the sunlight. She had a lovely, full-bodied, deeply sexual figure, with broad hips and enormous breasts swelling out over a slender waist. No wonder she wore loose-fitting dresses. Men would stare at her otherwise, would think her very body an invitation.

"I'm taking another pile of junk out to the dump. I have to go through town on the way. Need anything?"

"Just a break. I'm restless. I'll ride out with you."

"To the dump?" Madaket looked amused.

"Sure. I've never been to the town dump. As a matter of fact, I've never been to any dump. If I'm going to live here, I ought to know how to find it."

"Okay," Madaket agreed. "Hop in."

With the windows rolled down and the radio tuned to an oldies station, Joanna and Madaket drove through the green countryside. Overhead, the sky was a delicate hydrangea blue. At the rotary Madaket turned left, taking the route past Finast and then up the hill past the windmill to the Madaket Road. Along the curving residential streets, people knelt at work in their flower beds. Farther out on the Madaket Road, rugosa roses spilled over white fences and horses nibbled new grass, their coats gleaming in the sun. As the Jeep drew near the dump, they had joined a line of trucks filled with grass cuttings and old brush.

"Everyone's working outdoors today," Madaket remarked. They turned into the landfill drive and stopped by the booth. The supervisor directed them to the great hill of refuse where giant backloaders scooped dirt over the trash and seagulls swooped screaming by the hundreds, looking for food. Madaket got out and dragged and tossed their load into the pile, then slammed shut the Jeep and drove back toward the main road.

"What's that?" Joanna asked, pointing to a cement island between the entrance and exit lanes.

"That's where you sort your recyclable bottles."

"And that?" Joanna pointed to an odd area where used furniture and damaged appliances stood forlorn under the sun.

"That's the take-it-or-leave-it pile. If you've got something that's not good enough to sell but not bad enough to destroy, something someone might be able to use, you leave it there. Anyone can leave stuff, anyone can take it."

"What happens if no one takes a piece?"

"I guess it gets tossed in the trash heap."

"Slow down. Stop. I want to get out and look."

Joanna dropped from the Jeep and walked over to the fenced-in lot. She'd never seen anything quite like it before, but then never before in her life had she seen this side of home ownership. It seemed such a melancholy, heartbreaking thing: all these objects, solid and once valuable, abandoned under the sun. A three-legged table leaned on a perfectly sturdy wooden chair with the cane torn in the seat. An open box overflowed with pink-and-white-checked curtains which once had billowed starchily at someone's kitchen window. Joanna was filled with a sudden pity.

"Joanna?" Madaket came up behind her.

"Look at that!" Joanna exclaimed. Stepping over a crooked push lawn mower and a stained rolled rug, she picked up a picture frame. "This is a perfectly good frame!"

"Joanna, it's come apart at two corners, and the glass is cracked."

"Well, we can replace the glass and glue the corners together and clean it up and repaint it and it will be as good as new. It's beveled wood, Madaket."

"Joanna, you can buy a much nicer frame in town."

"Of course I can. That's not the point. Why should this be destroyed? Just because the original owner doesn't want it doesn't mean it should just be tossed away!"

"Well, of course if you want it, if you think you'll use it, take it," Madaket told her.

So they put the frame in the back of the Jeep and took it home. Later that week during the long evenings when Joanna was alone, she worked on the frame in the kitchen, washing it, scrubbing out the crevice in the beveling with a tooth-brush, gluing it together, and finally painting it a shining, clean, navy blue. She was so pleased with it when she was fin-ished that she hung it on the kitchen wall even though she hadn't yet found a picture to put inside. After that day, she made an outing at least once a week with Madaket to sort through the take-it-or-leave-it pile to see if anything else needed rescuing. She liked having projects which didn't in-volve sitting at the computer in the evening.

Tory often asked Joanna to join her at movies or lectures or art exhibits in town or shopping for clothes. But their lives ran on different rhythms. Tory had houseguests almost all the time, and her children had houseguests. With so many peo-ple in her house to feed and wash and entertain, Tory had brought up from New York her maid, a tiny, shy, older Viet-namese woman named Lei, who crept noiselessly around the house doing her chores. Lei did not enjoy conversation, and hated the beach and the sun; but Joanna had been present when Tory said, "Lei, how would you like a nice big color television in your bedroom?" Lei had smiled beatifically, and after that Tory kept the maid supplied with soap opera tabloids and boxes of soft-centered chocolate candies, and in return Lei adored Tory.

"Perhaps Madaket would like to meet Lei," Tory sug-gested one day.

"I can't imagine why," Joanna responded. "They have nothing in common."

"Darling, they have everything in common. They're both maids. You know, like *Upstairs, Downstairs*."

"This isn't Victorian England, and we don't have a Victorian class system, or at least those of us who are enlightened don't!" Joanna snapped.

"I'm not trying to insult your little housekeeper," Tory said in a soothing voice. "God forbid. I just thought they might enjoy each other's company."

"Why? Lei must be twenty years older than Madaket, at least!"

"But they're both in domestic service, Joanna. I'm serious. Madaket might know things about the best way to cook fish or something. But if you don't think it's a good idea, let's drop it. You really should watch yourself. Getting angry so easily can't be good for your blood pressure."

Had Tory always been so irritating, Joanna wondered privately, or was her pregnancy making her irrational? She listened with barely concealed boredom when Tory called to describe her endless rounds of fishing and sailing and golf and tennis, with cocktail parties every night and dinners for sixteen at pricey restaurants. When Joanna was invited along, she always politely refused. Tory's group was too noisy and boisterous. Joanna needed peace and quiet. She was gestating like a primitive creature, needing only to be.

"I understand how you feel," Tory said to Joanna one afternoon. They were on Joanna's screened-in porch. Joanna was leaning on her chaise with her feet up, and Tory was seated nearby in a wicker rocker. "Still, it's not good for you to be cooped up all the time. You need exercise."

"I do exercise. I walk on the beach every night. And just walking around this huge house, up and down the stairs— Doug said just the other day—"

"That's another thing." Tory rose, pulled her chair around to face Joanna, and leaned close to her, almost whispering. "You need to get out of the house more often. If you only could realize how many times you've said to me recently: Todd said. Or Doug said. Or Madaket said. Joanna, don't you know that it's really not, oh, I don't know—*appropriate*—for your employees to become your society."

Joanna laughed. "Oh, come on. I see other people all the time. I had dinner at the Latherns' the other night. And I was at Pat Hoover's gallery opening last week. Besides," she continued, more seriously and defensively, "my main interest at the moment is in my house, and no one knows more about it now than the Snows and Madaket. I'd much rather talk to them than make small talk with people I don't know at some superficial cocktail party." Seeing Tory's expression darken ominously, Joanna confessed frivolously, half joking, wanting to lighten the mood, "Furthermore, I haven't seen a male anywhere else on the island as sexy as Doug Snow."

"You think Doug Snow is sexy?"

"Yes. Don't you think so? He's got a sort of rough, tough, Rolling Stone, Marlboro Man look about him."

"I guess I can see what you mean. But—"

It was so pleasurable, talking about Doug, it warmed Joanna all over. "When I told Madaket, she was shocked. She thinks he's—"

"You told Madaket you think Doug Snow is sexy?" Tory nearly rose out of her chair. "What a stupid thing to do!" Now Tory was really angry.

"What on earth's the matter?"

"Joanna, don't be naive. These island people tell each other everything."

"Tory—"

"Haven't I told you? Hasn't everyone told you? It really is them against us on this island. No matter how nice they appear on the surface, the island people hate us for being rich summer folk."

"I think you're wrong, Tory, at least about Madaket. She's—"

"She's your *help,* Joanna, and that's all. Don't make the mistake of treating her like a friend or a companion. And for God's sake stop talking about Doug Snow being sexy! For one thing, he's married."

"Well, I know that, Tory. But a man can be married and still sexy." Once again Joanna tried to lighten the atmosphere. "I mean, I can look, can't I?"

"*Can* you? I don't know. Can you just look? You didn't just *look* at Carter."

Joanna felt her face flush as if she'd been slapped. "Tory, give me a break, will you?"

Tory's mouth tightened to a thin line. For a few moments she sat in silence. When she spoke again, her voice was controlled. "I'm sorry, Joanna. It's just that I worry about you so. You're doing so many erratic things. Going to such extremes. Buying a house, not just a house, but such a big old house that needs so much work. Getting yourself so isolated out here on this island. Running around wearing a wig. Having babies all by yourself. I just don't feel you're behaving responsibly."

Joanna responded heatedly. "Tory, not everyone can have the perfect family the perfect way. Not everyone can afford a house on Nantucket just for the summer. Not everyone gets to marry the person she loves. Not everyone would consider owning a house, writing two books, and having babies instead of aborting them irresponsible."

"I *never* suggested you should have an abortion!" Tory snapped.

"Then you can't criticize me for 'having them all by myself.' In fact, Tory, I don't think you have the right to criticize me at all!"

"I never approved of your affair with Carter."

"I know you didn't. And if it makes you feel better, I'm not having it with him anymore!" Joanna smiled at her own wit, but Tory only looked exasperated.

"I'll say it again, Joanna. I'm just worried about you. I know you're happy about these babies, and so I'll try to be happy for you. And you know I'll always be ready to help you at any time. But in the meantime, will you please try to be more—circumspect? Stop talking about carpenters being sexy. Stop confiding in your cleaning lady."

"Madaket's more than my cleaning lady."

"Are you sure she should be?"

"Whyever shouldn't she be? Are there rules about this sort of thing?"

"Don't be so cavalier, Joanna. You really shouldn't trust the natives. They certainly don't trust you."

"Look, Tory, I suppose I should be grateful for your concern. Obviously, you've been connected to this island longer than I have. And I will agree to stop talking about Doug being sexy. I suppose being so fat and pregnant makes me think I can say silly things and get away with them. I mean, it's not like I intend to act on my feelings. But as far as Madaket goes—I really like her. I like her about as much as anyone I've ever met. I trust her. I enjoy being with her. And

I'm not going to weaken that by any kind of suspicion. Besides, as I said, she doesn't like Doug Snow. She wouldn't tell him anything."

"Yes, but she might tell someone else who would tell him."

"From what I hear, she wouldn't. She's a loner."

"Well, I'd find that worrisome if I were you. Why doesn't she have any friends?"

"Oh, for heaven's sake, Tory!" Joanna exploded. "If she has friends, you think she's a gossip, and if she doesn't, you think she's odd."

"I've had so many maids and nannies over the years, and so many difficult experiences. I'm just trying to protect you."

"I don't need your protection. I just want your friendship. Come on, Tory. At least trust me. I'm an intelligent person."

Tory just glared at Joanna from her pale blue icy eyes. "Just say you'll keep what I've said in mind."

"All right. I will. Now, can we talk about something pleasant?"

Tory let out a loud, exasperated breath. "Okay. Truce. What shall we talk about?"

"How about the treasures I've been finding at the dump?" Joanna suggested mischievously.

"The dump." Tory groaned and shook her head. "I don't know what's to become of you."

Two days later Joanna woke to discover the temperature had fallen radically. The sky hung low and gray and the wind whipped the delicate bushes into a frantic dancing. Far out, ocean waves surged and sank in great agitation, hurrying to dash themselves upon the shore.

Dressed in a sweater and thick socks for warmth, she worked on the porch all day. The Snows were painting the walls and woodwork in the large upstairs room, and she told them she had to avoid it because the smells of paint and turpentine could be dangerous to her pregnancy. And she was glad to keep away. Her conversation with Tory had left her feeling foolish every time she saw Doug.

At five the Snowmen left for the day, pounding down the stairs, bringing with them the scent of sawdust and turpentine. As they ran out to the truck, it was just beginning to sprinkle. Joanna found Madaket in the kitchen, tossing a huge salad with a garlic dressing. A pot of stew simmered on the stove and a pan of homemade corn bread cooled on a trivet.

"God, this smells good!" Joanna cried. "Madaket, you're a genius! This is the perfect thing to eat on a day like today."

"I made a fresh apple pie, too, and brought out vanilla Häagen-Dazs," Madaket told her, smiling shyly.

Joanna leaned over the stove, greedily inhaling. "Look," she said. "You've made far too much for one person. Stay and eat dinner with me."

"Oh, I can't," Madaket began, but just then, with a tearing sound, the sky broke open, spilling its burden of rain out. It fell in torrents against the windows with an incessant pounding sound.

"Now you have to," Joanna said. "You can't possibly ride a bike in this weather."

Madaket stood still in the middle of the kitchen, looking out the window. She was wearing her usual outfit: work boots and a loose flowered cotton dress; today she'd pulled over it a fisherman's knit sweater against the cold. Her heavy braid gleamed like carved ebony, lustrous against the creamy woven wool.

"Come on," Joanna cajoled. "I'd really enjoy your company, Madaket. It makes me melancholy, eating alone night after night. Especially on a night like this."

Madaket contemplated the night. Rain streamed down.

"All right," she said softly. "I'll stay." She looked down at her hands, as if wondering where to put them.

"Great!" Joanna said. "I know what we'll do. Let's eat in the dining room, by candlelight! I haven't eaten in there yet. It's too big for one person."

"The dining room is awfully—" Madaket hesitated, searching for the correct word.

"Formal? I know. But one thing I've learned doing my show is that there is no *one* way to use any room. Just because it's furnished with expensive antiques doesn't mean it should never be used. Just the opposite, I think. I mean, what is beauty for? I'll set the table, you bring in the food."

Keeping up a running line of chatter to put Madaket at her ease, Joanna went into the dining room and took a snowy white damask cloth and two napkins from the sideboard, the silver from the rosewood box, the china from the corner cupboard. She lit white tapers on either side of a vase of peonies and phlox, then the tall, dark green candles twisting up from the silver candlesticks on either side of the fireplace mantel. Between them stood an antique clock with the sun, moon, and stars smiling from its silvered face. It didn't run—it was one of Joanna's treasures from the dump—but it looked as if it belonged in the dining room, as if it had stood in this particular spot for decades. On the spur of the moment, Joanna turned off the electric light in the chandelier and wall sconces.

"Isn't it romantic!" she said to Madaket as the girl came into the room. "My first meal in my own dining room! Isn't my china beautiful?"

Madaket set the stew in its tureen on the table. "Yes," she agreed wistfully. "I've never seen such a beautiful table."

Joanna saw how hesitant the young woman was in her movements. She sat at the table almost paralyzed until Joanna put her napkin in her lap; then Makadet did the same. "Shall I?" Joanna said, gesturing to the stew, and she served everything, the salad on the salad plate, the stew in the bowl. "I've heard that in England when a group of adults meet each other for tea, the person who decides to pour asks, 'Shall I be Mother?' I wonder if they really do that. I wonder if someone says that when the group is entirely male." She spoke lightly, with a smile. Madaket smiled in return and waited until Joanna had taken the first bite until she lifted her fork to eat.

In her work, Joanna had learned to draw people out by asking about their strengths and their loves, and so as they ate, she asked Madaket about her cooking skills. Madaket talked about the island's bounty—mussels on the jetties, berries on the moors, bluefish at Surfside—and by the time she cut into the warm apple pie, she spoke more easily about her grandmother, who'd taught her to cook.

"You're lucky you had your grandmother to teach you things," Joanna said. "I never knew my grandparents. God, I hardly knew my parents." She felt Makadet's eyes on her, waiting, reluctant to pry. "My parents were divorced very early in my life. I grew up sort of on the road with my mother. I was mostly an encumbrance when she was visiting her friends. Or I was shoved onto one of my father's girlfriends, who as you can imagine were not prepared for a child in the house."

"Really?" Madaket was fascinated right out of her shyness. She leaned forward. "That's hard to believe."

"Why?"

Madaket shrugged, drew back into herself, embarrassed to have made such a personal remark.

"No, really, Madaket, tell me. I'm curious. You can't hurt my feelings. Lord, think about what I just said—it would take more than your remark to hurt my tough old feelings!"

Joanna felt the young woman's eyes on her, judging.

"It's just that you seem like one of the ones who . . . belong," Madaket confessed.

Joanna nodded. "I know what you mean. But it's an act. I've really led a rather makeshift life. Always envying those with a home and a family . . . which is undoubtedly why my show is called *Fabulous Homes.* To me, all homes are fabulous."

As she talked, Joanna felt the other woman's keen interest like a scent in the air. She could see how still Madaket was keeping herself, as if trying not to disturb Joanna's mood. Madaket was not resting back in the chair, arms crossed, or leaning on her elbows on the table in the posture of a listener relaxing into a long tale, but rather she was leaning forward from the waist, as if she expected something to come toward her at any moment, and she wanted to be prepared to hear it clearly.

She has not had many of these nights, Joanna thought. She has not exchanged many secrets with women.

Joanna relaxed in her chair. "When my mother took me with her to visit her friends, she always warned me not to fuss or call attention to myself. You remember that old 'children should be seen but not heard' adage? That was definitely my mother's motto. She'd say to friends, 'Oh, don't worry about Joanna. She can sleep on the floor or curl up in a chair.' And often I did."

"What happened when you stayed with your father?" Madaket asked.

"I never stayed with just my father. I always stayed with him and one of his girlfriends, at the woman's home. The women tried to be nice, and I think some actually liked me, even enjoyed me. But mostly I could tell that my suitcase full of all my stuff—you know, clothes and toothpaste and books and dirty laundry—always presented a problem to those women. It ruined the glamour of their apartments. Usually I had to sleep on the living room sofa. I spoiled their decor." Joanna went quiet, leaning her chin on her hands, remembering, considering those difficult days and nights. "Some of the women had such cold eyes. Phony smiles. 'Oh, what a little doll!' they'd say, and all the time their eyes were like knives."

"That's terrible." Madaket looked genuinely shaken.

Joanna roused herself. "Oh, it wasn't all bad. I got to travel a lot. I'm sure I've seen every major city in this country." Joanna poured herself another cup of decaf. "My parents have both . . . 'gone aloft,' as a friend says."

Madaket smiled at the euphemism. "Mine, too."

"Do you miss them?"

Madaket looked down at her hands. "I miss my grandmother. I miss my parents—the way you miss a hurricane. They were exciting to be with, but they made people so mad. They made each other mad. They were always fighting. Sometimes hitting. Always leaving each other." Madaket looked at Joanna, looked away. "Always leaving me."

"Did you, um, did they have a home? I mean a house or an apartment here on the island?"

"Sometimes. One summer we all lived in the stable where my father worked. We slept in the hayloft and washed from a bucket."

"You're kidding!" Joanna said.

"No. And it was wonderful." Madaket lifted her head, suddenly looked years younger. "I loved it. The barn cats and the farm dog, an old mutt named Penny, used to sleep with me. The hay smelled so sweet, and in the morning I could lie on my back and watch the dust motes float in the sunlight. I liked going to sleep with the sounds of all the animals around. I always thought it would be nice to be part of a family with brothers and sisters."

"I know what you mean. I liked visiting people who had children my age, especially girls. The boys seldom even talked to me, but sometimes the girls were nice. Some girls had twin beds in their rooms and I got to sleep in one of the beds. Then I'd pretend it was my room and the girl was my sister."

"The worst times were when we slept in the car," Madaket admitted. "I've never told anyone that we did that, but you— you can probably understand. My father would come home drunk, or offend the landlord's wife, or get in a fight with my mother and make a lot of noise, throwing things, and suddenly we'd be tossed out. We never had any money, and sometimes my grandmother told my parents she washed her hands of them, she wouldn't help, and so they wouldn't take me to her house, and I had to sleep in the backseat with my mother. Then sometimes the police found us, if Dad hadn't parked the car far enough out of town, and that was always awful . . ." Madaket suddenly stopped talking and, pushing back her chair, began to remove the dessert plates.

"Are you okay, Madaket?" Joanna asked gently.

"Oh, sure," Madaket replied with a little shrug. "I just realized it's getting late." She disappeared into the kitchen, bearing the dishes with her.

Joanna waited in silence. The spell of intimacy was broken, and she didn't want to force herself on Madaket. Clearly the young woman had memories that would make her own childhood seem idyllic, and just as clearly Madaket couldn't handle remembering it all at once. Joanna shivered.

When Madaket came back into the dining room, Joanna rose, saying, "I'll help you with the dishes."

"No, please, Joanna. I'll take care of all this. You need to rest."

Joanna was tired, and the thought of merely going up the stairs was daunting. She always slept well when it rained. She crossed the room and looked out the window. Rain was streaming, thundering down.

"Look, Madaket, it's foolish for you to even think of going home in this weather. Why not spend the night here?"

Madaket, on her way to the kitchen, paused with dishes in her hands. "I have to go home. My animals have to be fed, and poor Wolf needs to be let out."

"Are you sure? Very well, then, but take the car. I won't have you trying to ride your bike in this. You'd catch pneumonia. And you'd never get anywhere anyway, not in this rain. The Squam Road will be all mud."

"If I take the car, you'll be all alone out here without transportation. And I'm used to riding my bike in bad weather."

Madaket's reluctance both irritated and amused Joanna. They were two of a kind, she thought, although superficially they looked entirely different, Madaket dark and voluptuous and quick, Joanna so fair and big-boned and big-bellied. They'd turned self-sufficiency into a religion, a doctrine by which they ruled their lives.

"Suit yourself," Joanna decided, and walked down the long hallway and up the stairs to her bedroom.

Looking out the window, she saw only darkness until, in the distance, lightning struck, forking across the blackness, illuminating the rain like a net of sequins glittering against the glass. Joanna grabbed up a sweater and pulled it around her shoulders. She went into the bathroom to prepare for bed, but suddenly, almost without thinking, she strode back out of her bedroom and down the back stairs to the kitchen.

She threw open the door. Madaket was at the sink, carefully washing the china. She looked over her shoulder at Joanna, who stopped at the bottom step.

"Oh, for Christ's sake, Madaket, if you must go out in this wretched weather, take the goddamned car! If you don't I won't be able to sleep. The keys are on the hook by the back door. All right?"

Madaket smiled. "All right," she said.

Joanna turned and stomped back up the stairs to bed.

Thirteen

~

*O*ne rainy late June evening Joanna was stretched out on her living room sofa, wrapped up in an afghan, watching a video, when lights flashed over the front of her house and the crackle of driveway gravel announced a visitor. Going to a window, she peered out: it was Tory, in a strapless silk sarong. She looked as lithe as an adolescent as she ran through the downpour and through the door Joanna held open.

Shaking droplets of water from her shaggy white-blond hair, Tory shivered. "I was just coming home from a party in town and thought I'd drop in. Am I interrupting anything?"

"Not at all. I'm just watching a video. Here, put this sweatshirt on. You look frozen."

"Thanks. This weather! Have you ever seen temperature change as quickly as it does here? I was dying of the heat earlier today. Mmm, this feels good." Her words were muffled as she pulled the navy-blue sweatshirt over her head. It fell almost to her knees. She curtsied, pulling out the hem of her sarong as if it were a gown. "What the best-dressed islander wears." She kicked off her high-heeled sandals.

"Where's John?"

"In New York. Working. He's taken on a tremendous workload this summer. I'm concerned. And a little pissed off, frankly. He knows how important it is for him to spend some time here with me and the kids."

"Want some tea?"

"I'd love some."

They walked together back to the kitchen. Joanna put the kettle on and they sat at the long pine table.

"Whose party?"

"The Scofields up on the cliff. You don't know them. They're nice but boring, and their party was nice but *really* boring. But I just had a great idea."

"Have a date-nut bar." Joanna unwrapped a plate. "Madaket made them."

"Yum," Tory said. "My dinner was canapés at the party. This can be my dessert. Listen, do you know who George Mullen is?"

"The zillionaire?"

"Right. He's got a yacht as big as this house, and he's sailing up from Newport on the Fourth of July weekend, and he's throwing an enormous party on the Fourth, and we're invited. This is delicious."

"We?" Joanna poured the tea, placed a mug in front of Tory, and lazily set the milk carton on the table next to the sugar bowl.

"John and I actually, but John's not here, so you can be my date. Mullen won't know. I've been to several of his parties and haven't even met the man. His private secretary does all the official greeting. Please go with me. The food is out of this world, and every glamorous person you can think of will be there. It'll be fun."

"I'll have to wear my wig."

"Fine."

"And I won't be able to stay as late as you'll want to. I just get tired earlier than you do."

"We'll leave after the fireworks, okay?"

"Okay." Tory hugged Joanna. "I'm so glad you're going to do something fun with me. I've missed larking around with you."

"Me, too," Joanna answered, hugging her friend.

At eight-thirty on the Fourth of July, Joanna reluctantly slipped her swollen feet into low-heeled evening sandals. Taking up her shawl and gold mesh bag, she made her way down the stairs just as Tory honked from the driveway.

"You look amazing," she exclaimed as she slid into Tory's Range Rover. Tory was sheathed in what appeared to be a slip of cloth the color of aluminum foil and the thickness of a sheet of phyllo dough.

"I feel great!" Tory said. "And you look pretty, too."

Joanna looked down at her turquoise-swathed girth. "Just as long as I don't look like Joanna Jones, I'm happy."

"If I didn't know who you were, I wouldn't recognize you," Tory assured her. "It's not just the wig. It's also your face—you've gotten sort of chubby-cheeked with your pregnancy."

"Thanks so much."

"This is going to be a great party. I feel it in my bones."

Joanna smiled at Tory's excitement. It seemed such a youthful emotion: excitement over a party. As if she thought something marvelous could happen tonight.

The enormous yacht rode the water all gleaming white, chrome, and silver, with flags flying and sonar cups angled to the sun. It looked like a city from the future that had just dropped into the harbor. Joanna and Tory walked down Old South Wharf, past the quaint, tiny fishermen's shacks now doing service as boutiques and galleries, and along the weathered plank boardwalk to the slip at the end. Here crew in natty gold-braid-trimmed uniforms stood in attendance to help the two women across the ramp and onto the main deck. Laughter and conversation and whoops of gaiety enveloped them as they made their way through the teak-paneled stateroom to the stern deck of the boat. A bar was set up here, and a raw bar, and a linen-covered table of delicacies: a mountain of peeled shrimp on crushed ice in a crystal bowl, caviar surrounded by sliced lemon and toast, a plate of almonds coated with silver leaf.

Joanna took a flute of sparkling water, Tory took one of champagne, and together they made their way through the crowd and up the stairs to the top deck. Tory spotted their host, so surrounded by guests that when she pointed him out to Joanna, all Joanna could see was an occasional glimpse of silver hair or navy blazer. Leaning on the railing, they looked out at the panorama of harbor and village and sky, then down to the deck below where clusters of people gathered and regrouped like multicolored chips in a turning kaleidoscope.

"There's Claude. Walking up the ramp," Joanna said. "And the Latherns."

"Shall we go back down?"

"No, they'll come up. Let's wait here."

"Want to sit for a while?"

"Yes." Joanna lowered herself onto a deck chair. "Go on, Tory, make the rounds. I'll be perfectly happy right here looking at the view."

"All right. If I see Claude or the Latherns, I'll send them your way. I'm going to try to say hello to Mullen."

Tory went off. Joanna planted her feet firmly on the floor and relaxed. She studied the other guests: there was a lot of expensive and awfully gaudy jewelry here; this group was a little more flashy than the usual Nantucket crowd. She heard the elaborate, multisyllabic music of Italian being spoken, and after a while a gaggle of gorgeous, emaciated revelers swanked by speaking French. No one stopped to speak to her. People looked at her, then looked away. She was only an anonymous pregnant woman.

Joanna kept a half-smiling, bemused look on her face, insisting to her private self that she must take advantage of this unusual chance simply to sit and observe. Always before, at a party of this caliber, she would have been unable to detach from her professional self. She'd have cruised this crowd, searching out likely candidates, practically interviewing people about their homes, looking for something new and different for her show. She would have been very charming. And because Carter and his wife, Blair, were often at the same party, she would have also been flirtatious, enticing the best-looking eligible man in the room with every word and gesture, trying to drive Carter wild with jealousy.

Now she could be serene. Instead, she felt insulted on behalf of both her private and her disguised selves. Was the woman people saw now as they leaned on the railings or strolled across the deck not worthy of someone's interest? Did people think that because she was pregnant she was therefore boring?

She couldn't blame them if they did think that. Now she remembered vividly all the times she'd gone out of her way to avoid pregnant women, assuming that their bovine physicality indicated minds equally softened and dulled.

But more than that, worse than that: was the Joanna Jones of *Fabulous Homes* really so easy to disguise, to overlook, to forget? She felt her cheeks flush with anger at the thought and her fingertips and lips went cold as she contemplated the extreme consequences of this possibility. Someone else could do her show. She could be replaced. Her heart knocked in her throat.

She must stop this, this flooding panic. She forced herself to return to the moment, this Fourth of July.

Beneath them the yacht shuddered deeply as its motors churned into life. They pulled away from the dock and headed out of the harbor and around the jetties, passing sailboats and smaller yachts waiting for the fireworks. Immediately it was cooler, as the sea breeze rushed against their skin. Scarves and skirts fluttered and the movement of the ship caused the sinking sun to flash sparks of light off the passengers' jewelry in a Morse code of wealth. They anchored far out from Jetties Beach, where throngs of people were gathering on the sand and in the dunes.

"Hello, Joanna. What a surprise." Suddenly Jake stood next to her, casually garbed in deck shoes, blue jeans, white polo shirt, black linen jacket. He had recently acquired a tan which set off his dark eyes and hair and the flash of his white teeth as he laughed.

Joanna gaped. "Jake! What are you doing here?"

He bent to kiss her cheek and she inhaled the scent of gin and spice. "George invited me. I motored up here with him from Newport yesterday. What are you doing here? I didn't know you knew George."

"I don't. Tory knows him. She brought me. How nice to see you! Please sit down."

Jake pulled a deck chair close to Joanna's and sank into it. "How are you?" His dark eyes were warm.

"I'm great. Enormous but great. How are you?"

"To tell you the honest truth, Joanna, I think I've been working too hard."

She laughed at this, throwing her head back so hard in her delight that her wig almost flew off. "It's about time you realized it! Have you taken a day off in the past two years?"

"I don't think I have. I've worked most nights, too, one way or another." His face grew somber and Joanna knew he was thinking of his wife's death.

"It was what you needed to do at the time," she reminded him.

"I know. Now I'm trying to see if I've entirely lost the knack of having fun."

"And have you?"

"It seems to be returning. If I can't enjoy myself on this pleasure craft, I'm a doomed man. Want to see my cabin?"

"I'd love to."

For the next hour Jake escorted her through the boat, showing her the various guest rooms with their private baths and walls of burnished rare woods. Opulent touches throughout proclaimed Mullen's wealth. In the dining room hung a glittering crystal chandelier whose prisms must have tinkled crazily in a rolling sea. The main lounge sported a glowing masterpiece of Turkish carpet. Large, thick, sensual Steuben glass sculptures of seals and whales and naked women graced the curving bank of wood housing the entertainment center.

"The message seems to be that he's rich enough not to care if all these treasures are ruined by a storm at sea," Joanna said.

"Well, yes, George does have trouble spending his money," Jake agreed. "But he's a good sort at heart. Gives a whopping amount to charities."

When she'd seen it all, Joanna and Jake stood a moment in the narrow teak passageway, cozily buffered from the noise of the party on the deck above them.

"Jake," Joanna ventured casually, "how's the network?"

"From hell. A whirling vortex of confusion, frustration, and egotistical maniacs."

Joanna grinned. "That good, huh?"

"That good. We've got a great fall lineup going. The California division wants to see us ease away from anything directed to people under twenty-five, and that's giving us a whole new perspective."

"*Fabulous Homes* is targeted to people above twenty-five," Joanna reminded him. "Way above twenty-five, or at least with incomes and interests of professional, accomplished, mature—"

"Hey, honey," Jake interrupted her. "You don't have to sell me."

"I'm just—" Joanna urgently needed to finish her thought, but Jake put his hand on her cheek, sliding it beneath the false curls, and she felt the coolness of his hard palm on her skin and realized her face was burning.

"It's okay," Jake said. "It's all right, Joanna. Don't worry. I won't let them take the show off the air. We've got it under control."

"Carter—"

"I told Carter I'd deal with it. He's working on some new projects."

"Gloria?"

"Gloria's working with me to slot in a few of the best old shows among the new. I'm watching her."

The wave of anxiety ebbed within her. Joanna leaned against the wall. "Do you miss me?" she asked, tilting her head coquettishly, trying to seem playful about this immensely important question.

"We all miss you like hell," Jake told her. His hand was still on her face; the wide, hard tips of his fingers were gently caressing her cheek. Such sensuality . . .

"Do you think Carter—"

Jake shook his head once, impatiently. Removing his hand, he stepped away from her. "Joanna, I don't talk to Carter about his personal life at all. We had one brief and extremely businesslike conversation about how to deal with FH in your absence, and that was it. I don't know what Carter thinks, and frankly, I'm not interested. Let's go on back up."

Joanna agreed meekly. "Yes, all right."

They returned to the upper deck, where Jake settled Joanna back in a chair then went off to fetch her more seltzer. People were crowding up on deck in anticipation of the fireworks. Suddenly Tory appeared from the crush, with Claude and Morris and June in tow.

"Darling!" Claude whispered, bending to kiss Joanna. "I never would have recognized you! This must be the wicked wig!"

Jake knew me, Joanna thought, and thank God for that.

Jake returned, and Tory greeted him with cries of surprise and then she and Joanna introduced him to their Nantucket friends. As they talked, darkness fell. The water rippled away from them like black satin while on the shore buds of light bloomed and dipped as the fireworks show got under way. With a shrill whistle, the first display rocketed through the sky and burst above them into a fluorescent flower.

"Can you stand?" Jake asked. "There's a better view from the rails. Here, lean on me." Joanna joined the crowd, exclaiming in delight as the multicolored fireworks streaked across the sky. The big yacht rocked gently in the black water. The fresh salt air, the explosions of color, the cries of pleasure, the scent of champagne, and the solid comfort of Jake's arm as he supported her combined to make Joanna sentimental. She felt certain that tonight something was beginning. Perhaps it was only the beginning of the Nantucket summer season, but romance and the possibility of rapture floated in the air like the ribbons of light that burst, full of magic, in the night sky.

When the yacht finally headed back to the harbor, Joanna went back inside the cabin to sit where it was warm. Stewards were handing out coffee and she was glad for it.

"Well, there she goes, folks," Tory teased. "She's fading on us."

"As well she deserves to do," June declared.

"Come on, Cinderella," Tory said. "I promised I'd drive you home when you got tired."

"Let me help you." Taking Joanna's arm, Jake carefully escorted her down the ramp and off the boat. The darkness of night fell around them as they stood together on the wharf.

Joanna stared at Jake, as if trying to fill up her eyes and her soul. "It is so good to see you again. How long will you be here? Can you come see my house?"

"Not this time, I'm sorry to say. We're leaving tomorrow for Maine. Another time. I promise." Jake leaned forward and hugged Joanna against him. "Take care of yourself, honey," he said softly. She felt his breath against her cheek. His embrace was invitingly warm against the cool night air.

"You, too, Jake," Joanna replied. She put her hands on his shoulders. His body felt solid, strong.

They looked at one another.

"Joanna—" Quickly Jake bent his face toward hers and kissed her full and hard on the lips.

"Is that you over there?" Tory called out. "It's so dark here I can't see a thing." Detaching herself from a group of friends, she approached Joanna and Jake, who pulled away from one another.

Joanna wondered if Jake felt as suddenly shy as she did. "Oh, Jake, I wish—" She shook her head in confusion, not certain what she meant.

"I'll be seeing you, kid," Jake said.

Tory, high on good spirits from the evening, grabbed Joanna's arm. "It's okay, Jake, I've got the old girl now."

"Well, take care of her," Jake said gruffly. Relinquishing Joanna, he nodded brusquely, then turned and strode up the ramp and back onto the yacht.

As they rode back toward the east end of the island and their homes, Tory said, "See? I told you it would do you good to come to this party! Wasn't it wonderful?"

"Tory, it was amazing," Joanna said. Closing her eyes, she leaned her head back against the seat. The air, sweet and silken as honey, slipped past her as they drove through the night.

Saturday afternoon the Snowmen quit work early. They shut off their screaming saws, swept up the sawdust, packed their gear into the red pickup, and tore away toward town. In the sudden silence, Joanna stood at the front of the house, looking out the living room window at the white dust settling back down onto the drive. She rubbed her lower back. She'd worked hard today and accomplished a lot.

"I guess I'm off, too," Madaket called. "Unless there's anything you need."

Joanna turned. The young woman was standing in the front hall tying a red bandanna around her braided hair. The air around her was vibrant with sunlight.

"What a wonderful job of housekeeping you're doing," Joanna remarked. "Look how the floors gleam. The baseboards are so clean. Even the corners are shining."

"Thanks. I like working in this house."

"So. What are you doing tonight?"

Madaket's eyes lit up. "I'll work in my garden. Then when it's dark, take Wolf for a long walk. And you?"

"I might see a movie with Pat."

"Well. Have fun."

"You, too."

Still Madaket remained in the hall. Meticulously she repositioned one pink-tipped white peony in its bouquet in a blue and white vase on the hall table. Joanna waited.

"I was wondering"—Madaket paused, then plunged ahead—"do you have plans for tomorrow?"

Surprised, Joanna answered, "Not really. Why?"

"Would you like to . . ." Madaket stooped to pick a bit of dust off her sneaker. "I thought maybe you'd enjoy seeing a place I go. An outdoors place," she concluded awkwardly.

"Why, I'd love to do that, Madaket. What a great idea. I know so little of the island. Shall I pack a picnic lunch?"

"All right, if you'd like, that would be nice." Obviously encouraged by Joanna's response, Madaket ventured, ". . . if you could pick me up in the Jeep, I could bring Wolf along. That is, if you wouldn't mind a dog in the car. Wolf's clean and well mannered."

"I'm sure he is. I'd love to meet him. I'll pick you both up."

They agreed on a time—ten, early enough for Joanna to drive into the Hub and buy a *Times* before they were sold out, late enough to let her have a nice morning lie-in. Then Madaket left. Joanna stood at the open door of her house, watching the young woman pedal away, the sun gleaming off the chrome of the bike.

Sunday morning Joanna and Madaket pulled up at the small red Trustees of Reservations gatehouse. Wolf, a shaggy shepherd-mutt mix, sat happily in the backseat, his head hanging out the window, tongue lolling.

"It costs forty dollars for a sticker each year," Madaket informed Joanna, "but it's worth it. You can drive out to Coatue and Great Point from here. Todd and Doug are probably out there casting for bluefish right now."

While Joanna wrote a check, Madaket let the air out of the tires. Then they were off, slowly rolling past the very civilized cottages and main building of the Wauwinet Inn. The road curved, became a track in the sand cutting through the narrow stretch of land between the Atlantic Ocean and the inner harbor. On their right, sand dunes lined with private summer cottages rose to a crest, obscuring the sight of the Atlantic just on the other side. On their left, the land sloped to the curving beach and the calm, dark blue harbor waters. A few hundred yards out a speedboat sparkled while behind it a water-skier skimmed over the waves. Boardwalks lay between the road and the beach to protect bare legs from the razor-sharp beach grass, which was spotted and tangled and woven with white daisies and pink roses and also with rampant, maliciously glistening poison ivy. Far to their left the sleekly trimmed lawn of the Wauwinet Inn sloped to the water.

Madaket slowed the Jeep to a crawl over the sandy road which gave way and sank beneath the wheels, giving the passengers a drifting, swaying feeling.

"Do you know who Wauwinet was?" Madaket asked.

"I don't. Tell me."

"Wauwinet was an Indian sachem. There's sort of a romantic story about his daughter. Would you like to hear it?"

"Sure."

Madaket stopped the Jeep, pushed a button and a lever, and it hummed into four-wheel drive. "In the 1600s two tribes of Algonquin Indians lived on Nantucket. They were always fighting over territory. Wauwinet was the sachem of the eastern tribe. His daughter Wonoma knew how to use medicinal herbs and plants and had a reputation as a healer, a kind of nurse. One day someone from the enemy village on the west came to say that Autopscot, the tribe's young sachem, implored her to come help his people who were stricken by a devastating pestilence. He promised that she would be safe. She went, and tended the sick, and she and Autopscot fell in love. They wanted to marry. But Wauwinet knew her father would object, so when she returned to her own tribe, she kept silent, waiting for the right time to tell him."

As she spoke, Madaket steered the Jeep along the ruts of sand, turned left, and stopped, letting the engine idle as they looked out over a field of delicate green grass separating a bright blue saltwater lagoon from the strip of sandy beach and the far dark sweep of harbor water. "Look!" Madaket pointed. A white bird curved in elegant stillness in the lagoon. "An egret. They like it here."

"He's beautiful," Joanna said quietly.

The Wauwinet Inn was now far off to their left. Madaket continued her tale. "One day some braves from Autopscot's tribe hunted on Wauwinet's land. Trespassing, a serious crime. Because of this, Wauwinet's tribe decided to go to war. But the night before they were to attack, Wonoma sneaked out of her father's village and paddled across this harbor and then ran, her way lighted by moonlight, all the way to Miacomet, where Autopscot's tribe lived. She told her lover about her father's plans. Autopscot hurried to Wauwinet to hold an audience before the fighting could begin. Autopscot told Wauwinet he would punish the men who had trespassed on Wauwinet's land, and then told him that he loved Wonoma and wanted to marry her. This would unite the tribes. And so there was a truce and a royal marriage."

"What a lovely story. Sort of an American Romeo and Juliet with a happy ending," Joanna said.

"Right." Sunshine poured through the windows and across the seats. "They say that since then there have been no wars on the island."

"Didn't the Indians fight with the white settlers?"

"Actually, no. The Indians sold their land to the first settlers, and they lived together in peace. Gradually the Indian population died off from smallpox and alcoholism and other white men's disease." Madaket steered the Jeep along a rough narrow path between the lagoon and a long rise of land forested with rugged evergreens.

"That's too bad," Joanna remarked, looking out at the stretch of untamed landscape.

"Mmm," Madaket agreed somberly, and for a moment they were quiet in contemplation of the past. Then Madaket said in a wry tone, "Now, of course, we've got the ongoing wars between the year-rounders and the wealthy summer people."

"Would you really call them wars?"

"Some people would." The Jeep hit a spot of soft sand and bucked and stalled. Madaket turned her attention to maneuvering back onto the track. Joanna grabbed onto the handhold built into the door. "Hang on. We're almost there," Madaket assured her.

At last the road emptied them onto the long stretch of beach. Madaket stopped the Jeep and turned off the engine. For a moment both women sat in silence, soaking in the intense, relaxing warmth, gazing out in an almost stuporous pleasure at the sunlight on the water. But Wolf whined, then barked sharply, and so they stirred, opened their doors, and stepped out onto the sand.

"I'll carry the cooler," Madaket said. "Can you manage the towels?"

"Sure." Joanna followed Madaket to the water's edge and spread the striped beach towels, which fluttered in the breeze. For a moment they both bustled around domestically, perfecting their temporary nest, holding down the towels with the ice bucket and cooler and beach umbrella and Joanna's woven bag full of sunblock and lip balm and hairbrush and scarf. Wolf raced down to the water, then dug furiously in the sand.

"Want to go for a little walk before we eat?" Madaket asked.

"All right."

"The place I want to show you isn't far away. I don't think many people know about it." As she spoke, Madaket turned eagerly away from the harbor, heading inland toward the scrubby forest. Wolf bounded after her, and Joanna followed, her feet sinking awkwardly into the soft sand. "Don't take your shoes off just yet," Madaket instructed. "We might hit poison ivy." Madaket was barefoot herself, and wore a long white cotton man's shirt opened over an old-fashioned one-piece black swimsuit which could scarcely contain her substantial breasts and rounded hips.

An overgrown path cut up a sandy incline into a grove of gnarled and twisted cedars and pines. Stepping out of the sunshine, Joanna had the sensation, as surely as stepping over a threshold and through a door, of entering a room. Leaves and twigs and needles and branches wove overhead in a rich canopy and fell like tapestried walls to the ground, bathing the air in a dreamy green glow. Deeper in, the silence grew so complete that even the steady susurration of the water against shore dimmed, then disappeared. Sunlight hung like banners in the shade. Ferns, grasses, and glossy-leafed bushes laced the air, now and then prickling Joanna's legs. The modern world seemed far away, its troubles insignificant in this mysterious, ancient place.

Madaket stopped before a silver-barked tree, certainly one of the larger trees Joanna had seen on the island. Perhaps it was three or four trees grown together, for its thick trunk was deeply grooved, and just at shoulder height its base radiated out into many branches which stretched and turned with the flexible grace of a many-armed Hindu goddess, forming several natural seats and cubbyholes just right for human bodies.

Resting her hand affectionately on the rough bark, Madaket said, "This is what I wanted to show you. This is one of my favorite places on the island. I don't think many other people even know it's here."

"It's peaceful here." Joanna looked around. "A good place for daydreaming, I think."

"Yes. That's what I do here," Madaket admitted quietly.

"And what do you dream about?"

"The Indians. Sometimes I imagine I can hear them, feel the ground pounding under their running feet, hear the rustle of the leaves and grasses as they pass. I think I would smell them before I see them. They would have such natural, *vivid* smells—sweat, of course, and animal oils used to smooth their hair and protect their skin, and the crisp grassy odor of the mats they wove and wore for clothing, and the leather thongs, and the clean earth on their bodies, like the ground tilled in spring, fresh, yet powerful, and salt dried on their skin from the sea. And I would hear them calling to each other. And laughing. They laugh a lot, especially now in the summer."

"God, Madaket, you're giving me chills! I can almost see them!"

"I like to imagine them, an entire tribe, and especially one family. I like to pretend that family is my family. My ancestors." Madaket's voice was wistful. "I like to imagine a girl, my age, who would have been my sister. If I had been alive then. Or, perhaps, we'll meet in another time."

Suddenly something came crashing through the woods, making as much noise as a bear, and then Wolf broke through the brush, vines caught in his coat, trailing over his tail to the ground like ribbons.

"Wolf, you fool, you gave me a heart attack!" Joanna cried, relieved. "Madaket, I've got to get out of here. I need daylight!"

With Wolf circling them and barking happily, the two women walked back out into the sun. Returning to their towels, they carefully oiled themselves with sunblock, then unpacked the picnic lunch: green grapes, whole-wheat crackers with various cheeses, slices of carrots and peppers and celery. A healthful meal—except for Madaket's dark chocolate brownies, which Joanna brought for dessert. She hadn't forgotten Wolf. She laid out on a Tupperware lid a gourmet assortment of cold cuts. True to his name, Wolf swallowed them in one gulp, then lay with piteous longing watching Joanna and Madaket eat.

They stretched out on their towels then, and rested, half dozing in the sultry heat. Joanna liked the way the warm sand beneath her could be scooped and molded to fit her body as she lay on her side.

At some point she fell asleep, waking to find that Madaket had covered her with a beach towel to prevent burning. The sun was lower now, less direct, but the day was hotly silent, as if muted by heat. Joanna sat drinking a bottle of Perrier, and then she and Madaket set off beachcombing, walking ankle-deep in the cool water, stopping at the discovery of an especially remarkable shell. Here and there the tide had deposited the dark brown, menacing, tanklike shells of the horseshoe crab.

"Those are perfect animals," Madaket told Joanna, pointing.

"The horseshoe crab?"

"Yes. We learned this in science. This creature has existed exactly as it is for billions of years. Its design works. Unlike human beings, who must be at the beginning of their evolution."

"At least we're prettier," Joanna said.

"Not to a horseshoe crab," Madaket retorted.

They strolled south, occasionally walking on spongy humps of dried eel grass, which felt pleasantly cool to the soles of their feet. Pink and white roses speckled the grassy dunes and perfumed the air. Seagulls swooped low over the water while farther down, a flock of tiny sandpipers scurried worriedly back and forth over the damp sand, seemingly involved in a neurotic search for something they'd lost. An older couple sat close together, staring out at the water, arms linked, their hair and smiles gleaming white against the leathery tan of their skin. Joanna and Madaket turned and walked north, retracing their footsteps in the sand.

"I don't think I've ever known such quiet," Joanna remarked. "Not ever in my life."

"It's a luxury, isn't it?" Madaket said. "One of the greatest luxuries of all."

"Luxury?" Joanna contemplated the idea, then agreed, "Yes. I suppose you're right."

Finally they gathered up their paraphernalia and headed home, even though the sky was alluring with its pearly streaks of high, fair-weather cloud. Joanna was so relaxed she was almost comatose, and even though she knew she should learn how to use the air pump at the main road to fill the tires back to their proper air pressure, she was simply too tired to move.

"Look, Madaket, just drop me at home, drive yourself home, and bring the Jeep back tomorrow when you come out. I'm too blissed out to drive."

"You'll be okay out here without a car?"

"I'll be fine. I'll just lie on the sofa. I feel about as evolved as a clam."

Madaket laughed, then looked anxious. "Shall I come in and fix you some dinner?"

"Of course not. It's your day off. I can fend for myself. God, Madaket, what a perfect day. Thank you."

In her house Joanna emptied out the hamper and shook sand from the beach towels. That done, she showered, then stretched out on her bed in her terry-cloth robe. She had a glossy new novel waiting for her on the bedside table, but all at once in the early twilight she was lonely.

It had been a lovely, perfect summer day, and she was glad she'd gotten to know more of Madaket's world, but what sustained Madaket would not sustain Joanna. She needed more than trees and daydreams.

Although her daydreams had been pretty interesting lately. Jake's kiss had stirred her deeply, roused her curiosity, and made her hungry for more . . . yet thinking of that kiss, Jake's warmth and intensity, caused Joanna's heart to trip and pound. Her face flushed, her fingers went numb. Not good. Not good for her pregnancy, and foolish besides, to indulge herself in schoolgirl fantasies. Jake was a kind man. He was fond of her. That was all.

But she could not stop thinking of him.

Perhaps it was only that she missed the network so much.

Impulsively she picked up the phone and dialed Dhon's home number, which sprang complete into her mind.

"Happy birthday, Mr. President." Today Dhon had the breathy tones of a fake Marilyn Monroe on his answering machine tape. "So sorry I can't talk to you now, but I'm in a nice, warm, wet, perfumy bubble bath. Wish you were with me. I'd let you pop my bubbles. Leave me a message and you know what I'll do."

Abruptly the beep shrilled against her ear. Joanna put down the receiver. The very act of almost talking to Dhon had started her blood racing. Her mind churned with confusion. She loved Dhon, she missed him, she was dying to hear how he was and to get all the New York gossip—but Dhon was so seductive. It would take him no time at all to find out where she was, and how she was, and why she was there. With the best of intentions, he'd spill out every secret he knew, and some he only suspected.

And with the best of intentions, he'd rush to work the next day to gush out to everyone at the network anything Joanna divulged to him.

She felt caught between two worlds and a part of neither. The network glittered dangerously in one direction; the silence of the summer dark lay emptily in the other.

Pushing herself up and swinging her feet to the floor, Joanna headed for her study. She'd do some work on her books; that would settle her down.

But a wave of nausea struck her. At the same time a bolt of pain hammered across her forehead and flashing lights sparked before her eyes. Sinking back onto the bed, she closed her eyes and just sat, holding on.

The message from her body was clear and direct. When the headache subsided, she carefully lowered herself back onto the pillows. Now the flashing lights dimmed, but in their place blinked words from the books she'd read on pregnancy:

Preeclampsia. Toxemia. A rise in blood pressure. Symptoms: Headache, nausea, flashing lights, vomiting. More likely if you are pregnant with twins or over forty. Danger to the babies: premature labor. Birth before the babies are mature enough to survive. Danger to the mother: convulsions. A possible state of coma. Treatment: bed rest.

Joanna forced herself to be still. She kept her thoughts on the summer day, the sunshine, the drugging heat, the expanse of sparkling water. She could feel her blood pressure falling. Only four more months, she told herself. She could make herself behave for four more months. Then she would have her babies.

Fourteen

~

*J*oanna sat on the edge of the examining table. She'd just dressed after having her July checkup, and with a polite knock, Gardner Adams opened the door and returned to the room. He looked worried. Her heart skipped a beat.

"What is it?" she asked.

"I'm concerned about your blood pressure." He leaned against the counter, folded his arms over his chest, and looked at Joanna. Backlit by the window behind him, he seemed, with his glowing halo of sandy hair, slightly angelic. "Let's talk about this a little, okay?"

"Okay."

"Have you chosen a birth partner?"

Joanna flushed. "No. Not yet."

"Are you living alone?"

"Yes. Well, sort of—although it doesn't seem like it. Doug and Todd Snow are at the house six days a week, eight to five, doing major and necessary renovations. Also, I have a young woman, Madaket Brown, who comes in every day to help with the housework and the cooking."

"She cooks for you?"

"Most meals, yes."

"I'd like to talk to her."

"All right. She's out in the waiting room. I have to have her drive me everywhere these days—I've gotten so big."

"How many days a week does she cook for you?"

"Five. And leaves casseroles and so on for me for the weekend."

"And you say she takes care of the housework?"

"Yes. I'm rushing to finish up two books."

"*Two* books." He sounded as if he were passing judgment. "Are you getting sufficient rest?"

"I think so."

"Do you have any extra worries, added pressures, since we last talked?"

Joanna shook her head. "Not really. I'm very excited about these babies. I'm really happier than I've been before in my life."

Gardner's smile seemed affectionate. "That's good. Let's go talk to your cook."

Reaching over, he took her by the arm and helped her down from the table, then opened the door and ushered her out along the corridor to the reception room, where Madaket sat thumbing through a magazine. Today she was wearing a pale coral dress printed all over with tiny violets, and her long black hair was held back by a coral ribbon. When she saw the physician in his white coat and stethoscope approaching with Joanna, she jumped up, alarmed. Her black eyes flew to Joanna's face.

"It's all right," Joanna hastened to assure her. "Madaket, this is Dr. Adams."

"Gardner," the doctor said, holding out his hand.

Madaket shook his hand. "Hello."

"Joanna tells me you cook for her, and I'd like to talk to you about this a moment. Perhaps she's told you: she's got a bit of a problem with blood pressure. High blood pressure is common with twins, but it can lead to serious difficulties, and we want to prevent those. I just wanted to be sure you know you should keep salt away from your employer."

"Yes. I've got her on a salt-free diet."

"Good. Also, be sure she gets plenty of rest. Bed rest. Not lying flat, but well propped up on pillows."

"I wonder—could I fix her some herbal teas?"

"What kind of herbs?"

"Bearberry leaves, from the moors, carefully picked and washed, then soaked in brandy, then brewed in boiling water. Sweetened. Bearberry is a natural diuretic."

"I wouldn't want it soaked in brandy or any alcohol. Not for a pregnant woman."

"All right. No brandy." Madaket thought a moment. "I'll

mix the bearberry leaves with dandelion and peppermint leaves."

"Where did you hear about the properties of bearberry?" Gardner asked.

"It's my grandmother's recipe. Her grandmother's actually."

"Sounds like it couldn't hurt and it could help. Along with other measures, such as watching salt intake and enforcing rest." Gardner smiled at Madaket and, leaning toward her, confided in a low voice, "My feeling is that you'll have to be a bit of a policeman with our patient."

"Please!" Joanna protested. "You have no idea how much I want these babies."

"Then take good care of yourself," he admonished, reverting to his more formal self. "See if you can cut down on stress. Perhaps you could even try to finish only one book instead of two. Shorten your workday. Break it up into nap periods." Gardner turned back to Madaket. "I'll leave her in your hands."

Joanna and Madaket were in the parking lot, just getting into the Jeep, when to their surprise a side door of the Nantucket Cottage Hospital opened and Gardner Adams came out, walking so briskly his white lab coat flew out behind him and his stethoscope flapped against his chest. He came to the passenger side and leaned in the window. The sunlight blazed through his curly hair.

"Joanna. You live out on Squam Road, right?"

"Right."

"Look. I live out there, too. I think I'll start coming by a few times a week to check your blood pressure. No, no"—he patted her arm—"I'm not trying to frighten you. I just want to keep an eye on it, and there's no reason for you to make the trip into town, especially in this heat." He looked across the Jeep at Madaket. "You'll be there? You can answer the door?"

"I'm there between eight and five."

"Good. See you later. Oh, and could you save me a bit of your tea? I'd like to taste it."

"Sure."

"Great. See you." He streaked back toward the hospital.

"How unusual," Joanna said when Gardner Adams had gone inside the building.

"For most doctors, I suppose, but I've heard he's especially sympathetic," Madaket replied. "The Coffins were talking about him. He's supposed to be good, too." She started the engine and steered the Jeep out of the lot, around the corner, and toward town along Pleasant Street. "So now you're meeting Tory for lunch?"

"Right. At the Boarding House."

"What time should I pick you up?"

Joanna looked at her watch. "Two o'clock. I'm meeting her at twelve-thirty, or I thought I was. We'll be late with all the traffic!" she cried, as they joined a sluggish line of cars creeping toward Main Street. "What's going on?"

"It's overcast. Looks like rain. People can't go to the beach."

"I've heard for years that the whole atmosphere of the town changes between the winter and summer months, but this is the first time I've noticed it. God! Look at that!" Joanna shook her head as a father on a bike wavered out in front of a car, while the baby wobbled, fragile head helmetless, in the seat on the back of the bike.

"Our fire chief said in the newspaper that the tourists think Nantucket's a theme park. Not real, so they're free from all the laws of the real world. They think they're immortal here," Madaket told Joanna.

"How many tourists are there?"

"According to records, seven thousand people live here in January. Forty thousand in August."

"It must drive the natives mad."

"Well, yes. It also gives them a living. July and August are the busiest tourist months. Most of our businesses make more than half their yearly income then. I know the Coffins are always overwhelmed and exhausted by the time Labor Day comes. You should see the grocery stores. There are lines to get in the lines."

"It's worth it to be here," Joanna told Madaket as they briefly double-parked on Federal Street. With effort she pried herself out of the Jeep. "See you at two!"

Crossing the street to the restaurant where Tory sat waiting at an umbrella table, Joanna, in a pale pink float which fell loosely about her as she glided along, felt large and help-lessly spectacular. But no one turned to stare. Had her television fans forgotten her already? Perhaps her large-brimmed straw hat and sunglasses were disguise enough.

Tory looked fresh and summery. She wore loose white cotton and sipped a strawberry daiquiri. As Joanna slid into a chair across from her, Tory remarked, "I don't think I've seen you in town before without that awful wig. You look great."

"Thanks. I just hope I don't run into anyone I know."

"Why not?"

"Well, because of Carter."

Tory stared at Joanna levelly. "Do you really think it matters now?"

Her words pierced like a splinter. Joanna waited until the waitress had taken their order, then demanded, "What do you mean?"

Tory's eyes searched Joanna's face, and finding something there that made her sad, leaned forward and put her hand on Joanna's arm. "I'm sorry, honey. I didn't mean to be abrupt, but I've been meaning to talk to you about this . . . Joanna, I think that if Carter wanted to find you, he would have found you by now. It's been almost four months."

Joanna looked silently at her friend. When she could steady her voice, she replied softly, "I suppose you're right, Tory. I guess I just haven't wanted to give up all hope." She smoothed her napkin over her lap, working for self-control, but when she looked up at Tory, her eyes filled with tears for the second time that day. "Shit," she whispered sharply, and stabbed her sunglasses back up her nose, closer to her eyes. "I've become an absolute faucet!"

Tory continued to stroke Joanna's hand. "I'm so sorry, Joanna. I'm so sorry. I didn't mean to be unkind."

"I know you didn't, Tory."

"Tell me. How are the babies?"

That brought a smile back to Joanna's face. "Gardner Adams said they're perfect. My blood pressure's on the high side, so I have to cut out salt." As the waitress set their salads before them, she added, "Just think: I'm sitting here eating for three!"

"You look like it, too. You're growing so fast I can never remember your due date."

"Late October, early November. Which reminds me." Joanna put down her fork and folded her hands in her lap. This was a momentous moment for her; she wanted it to be memorable. She was asking a favor, but she was also, in a way, honoring Tory. Clearing her throat, she said, "I'd like you to be my birth partner."

With her fork, Tory pushed aside a cucumber and speared a bit of marinated avocado. "Sorry, hon, I can't."

Joanna was stunned. Tory had always praised birth as the ultimate moment in a woman's life; Joanna assumed Tory would be thrilled to share it with her. "Why not?"

"You know Jeremy starts boarding school this fall. I promised his coach I'd be a soccer mom—help transport the kids to games and all that, and I'm going to be on the fundraising committee for Vicki's school. I'll be up in Connecticut all fall." She glanced at Joanna. "Are you okay?"

Joanna had to take off her sunglasses to wipe away tears. "I'm all right. Just surprised. I thought—I was counting on you—"

"Joanna, you know I'm happy for you. You know I'll do anything I can to help. But you also know my family always comes first with me. Always has, always will." She leaned forward again to pat Joanna's hand. "Once you have your children, you'll understand."

For the rest of the lunch, Joanna listened while Tory discussed the plans for the new sports facility at Vicki's school. She had planned to do a number of errands after lunch, but when Madaket arrived with the Jeep at two, Joanna was so weary she told the young woman simply to drive back to the house. She needed to lie down and rest.

"Are you okay?" Madaket asked.

"Just tired. Very tired."

"Put your seat back," Madaket suggested.

"Good idea." Joanna pressed the electric button and her seat slowly reclined. She lay back. That was better. She took deep breaths. The Jeep quietly rolled away from the town and along the winding road to Wauwinet. Shadows and sunlight trailed over her eyelids like scarves of indigo and gold chiffon, and with it memories drifted across her thoughts. Suddenly she remembered—no, it was more of a reliving—riding in the car with her mother at the wheel when she was small. The breath, perfume, gentle movements of another woman caused a kind of radiance from her which made Joanna feel protected and cherished, and also terribly female, and glad to be so. When she was young, riding like this as her mother traveled from one friend's home to another's, she was aware of a sense of excitement, an eager hope for all that lay ahead, an awareness of myriad possibilities and a desire to be prepared for them. That was something, Joanna realized, to be grateful for. If her mother had not been good at making a home, she had been wonderful at making journeys.

"We're here," Madaket announced, and she turned off the engine.

"I'm almost asleep," Joanna yawned. "I think I'll go on up to bed. Oh, no, I'd forgotten the Snows would still be here," she moaned.

"They'll be downstairs."

"I know. But they'll be making so much noise."

"Well, they can change their plans, or take a break. Your health has first priority," Madaket said.

Joanna's study was finished now, one spacious, clean, light-filled room. Yesterday the Snows had carried all her equipment and her boxes of files out of the sunroom and up to her new study. Today they started work downstairs. Tory, Madaket, the Hoovers, had all advised her to have a room off the kitchen where the babies could be as messy as they wanted. Joanna wanted the Snows to close up the door between the dining room and screened-in porch and to open up a door between the kitchen and the porch, then to turn the screened-in porch into an insulated room she could use year round as a playroom.

She'd hoped they'd do the noisiest of their work today, but as she and Madaket entered the house, they found it quiet, simmering with summer silence.

"I'm going on up to nap," Joanna told Madaket.

"Have a good rest," Madaket replied.

The heat had made her feet swell. Joanna kicked her espadrilles off and lethargically climbed the stairs in her bare feet.

As she approached the top step, Doug Snow came out of

her bedroom and to the head of the stairs so quickly she almost stumbled backward.

"Doug!"

His face showed concern. "Are you okay? I thought you were going to be out all day."

"I felt too hot and tired. I need to lie down."

"Here. Let me help you."

Before she could reply, Doug came down the three steps between them and put his arm around her, pulling her close to him. The scent and feel of his masculine presence overwhelmed her for a moment, making her feel even weaker. She sagged against him. His arm and chest were hard and warm. She was almost exactly as tall as he was. Against her plump, soft, female body, she sensed clearly the bone and sinew and muscles and gristle of his maleness as he enclosed her. The contrast excited her. Blood surged to her face.

"If you don't mind, I'd like to show you something in the study," Doug said.

"All right." It was all she could do to reply. An old sensual hunger was spreading through her, and it felt delicious.

Keeping his arm around her, he helped her up the last three stairs, across the wide landing, and into the study. There it was, her beautiful room, with its long work counters and gleaming computer, fax machine, printer, copier, file cabinets, telephone . . . and in front of her state-of-the-art typing chair, a footstool with walnut legs and base and a blue silk cushion.

"I took the liberty of making that for you. I've seen you working, and it seems to me you'd be a little more comfortable with your feet up. It'd be good for you, too, I think."

Tears rushed into her eyes.

"Doug, how thoughtful! Thank you!"

At her tears, his face darkened with embarrassment. Although he kept his arm around her, supporting her, he moved his body just slightly away, or contracted somehow, withdrawing into himself.

"It just seemed sensible," he said gruffly.

She could almost feel his breath when he spoke. She could kiss his cheek, she thought. That would not be unreasonable. A kiss of gratitude. This man had thought of her. He had thought of her at night, when he was away from this house and his job. He cared about her comfort. Measuring, cutting, sanding the wood, rubbing his hands over the legs to smooth them with oil, he had thought of her.

"My wife bought the silk cushion," Doug said. "I asked her to choose it. I wouldn't know what to get."

She looked away, now embarrassed by her own thoughts, and at the footstool. "Please thank your wife for me. The cushion's beautiful."

A movement caught her eye. She turned slightly to look, and her body pressed more tightly against Doug's arm. Todd was standing in the hallway. Something sparked between the three of them, a small shock of discomfort and even alarm. The scent of guilt drifted around them.

"Dad."

Doug didn't release his hold on Joanna. "I'll be right down."

Todd thundered down the stairs, his large feet in their heavy work boots making a *clomp, clomp, clomp* noise on the wood. Joanna had had them pull the stained, shaggy runner off days ago, and now she had to decide whether to buy a new runner for the stairs or to have them sanded and stained.

"I guess I'll have to have a new carpet put on the stairs to muffle the noise so people won't wake the babies," Joanna murmured, partly thinking aloud and also trying to hide the pleasure she felt as she stood pressed against Doug's body.

"I'll help you into your bedroom," Doug said.

"Thanks."

She leaned against him as he led her into her bedroom and gently lowered her into a sitting position on the bed.

"I'm as big as a walrus and I find it about as easy to navigate," Joanna remarked, trying to dull the intensity of the moment, trying to say in code: I'm pregnant, I'm unattractive, therefore don't think I'm having sexual feelings about you.

"I'll get back to work," Doug replied, and nodding curtly, he left the room and clomped down the stairs.

Joanna sat on the edge of her bed, letting her thoughts settle. Something else was stirring within her—no, not lust, not grateful surprise at the footstool, either. Something . . .

The sounds of the footsteps down the stairs.

Why hadn't she heard Todd coming up the stairs?

What were the men doing here on the second floor today?

She had been coming up the stairs, and Doug had come out of her bedroom. His appearance had startled her, but his approach, his arm around her, his nearness, had driven all questions out of her mind. Now they buzzed around her.

What had Doug Snow been doing in her bedroom?

She looked around her room. Madaket kept it clean. She vacuumed, dusted, straightened, polished the windows and mirrors to a sparkling sheen. But Joanna kept it messy. Piles of books, magazines, notes to herself, pens, catalogs, were scattered on every surface. On her bureau stood a large velvet-lined jewelry box, open now, exposing a tangle of costume jewelry.

Rising, Joanna crossed the room and, leaning against her open closet door, looked around from this perspective. She'd had Todd and Doug build a cabinet for her small metal safe into the wall of drawers and cabinets in her study and she'd told them, casually, without even thinking about it, that she kept all her real jewelry in there rather than in her bedroom. Todd wouldn't come in here to steal costume jewelry.

Her clothes hung in an orderly row along the rod in the closet.

But when she turned on the overhead light, she saw, at the far end, several boxes of shoes tumbled over each other, spilling out a high-heeled black silk pump and a rhinestoned red sandal.

They'd been in her closet. They'd been in her closet because they thought she'd be out all afternoon, and when they heard her coming up the stairs, Doug had rushed out to stall her while Todd had tried to put things back in place.

But why would they be in her closet?

She had to know.

With her heart beating a rapid tattoo against her chest, Joanna descended the stairs. She found Doug and Todd and Madaket gathered around the rough, jagged opening broken between the kitchen and the screened-in porch. The largest bits of debris had been picked up and two giant rubber trash barrels stood next to the kitchen wall, overflowing with torn wallpaper and bits of splintered wood and plaster.

"—not in your way," Todd was saying to Madaket, who was staring at him, entranced. Todd stopped in midsentence and all three turned to look at Joanna as she entered the room.

"Joanna! Are you all right?" Madaket asked.

"I'm fine, Madaket. Doug, please tell me: what were you and Todd doing in my room? In my closet?" She kept her voice low and reasonable.

Madaket gasped. Todd looked at his father. Doug's face slowly turned a deep red, but when he spoke, his voice was steady, and he seemed more angry than embarrassed.

"Todd and I were checking the wall between your bedroom and the front bedroom. Sometimes people build hiding places into walls. We can usually tell by knocking on the walls how deep and solid they are."

"I see. You were looking for the treasure." Joanna looked straight at Doug, who did not look away. He wasn't uncomfortable as he coolly stared at her. If anything, he was enjoying himself.

"Sometimes things are hidden behind walls," he told her, and he seemed to be making a double entendre. He was not quite insolent. His dark blue eyes glittered.

"And you found—?"

"Nothing. The wall's regular. Solid. Nothing unusual."

"So you won't be needing to go into my bedroom again."

"Right."

Still he stared at her. She waited one beat, two, for him to apologize, but he said nothing else and finally she simply turned, left the room, walked through the hall, climbed the stairs. She was glad she'd long ago learned the tactical value of silence. It often did more than a million of the best-chosen words to intimidate or discompose. But Doug obviously knew this himself.

Back in her bedroom she sank onto her bed without taking off her clothes. Her heart was calming now, but the adrenaline which had rushed through her as she confronted Doug and Todd was still in her system. Her hands shook, and her breathing was irregular.

It made sense that they were looking for the treasure, she decided. She believed him. But it was clear to her that now she'd have to make some rules about her house, and about the treasure—whose it was, who had the right to search for it. Her thoughts raced from Doug to Tory to Carter, all of whom, she felt, in a welling up of self-pity, had betrayed her in their various ways. Finally, exhausted, she fell asleep.

She awoke several hours later, refreshed, and went downstairs to find everyone gone. Madaket had left a cold pasta and vegetable salad in the refrigerator for her, along with a rhubarb-strawberry pie. Joanna sat on her back steps, eating, looking out at the water, wishing the deck were built. The wind was rising, skipping waves across the ocean's surface, teasing the hem of her dress and tugging at her hair. Her thoughts skipped and tumbled. Finally she went back inside, put her dishes in the sink, then walked from room to room, turning lights on as she entered, standing quietly in each room, looking around, opening herself to any and all sensations. The past remained here in the long cracks running through the plaster like a trail of years, in the scarred wood of the stairs or the bubbles in the glass in the windows, in the way the worn floors rolled. But she felt no ghost here, no animus, no lingering spirit. She felt safe in all these rooms, and only slightly lonely. Languidly, frivolously, she tapped on an attic wall. Of all the walls in the house, these had been the least changed over the years. Many of them were still unstained rough wood. Tapping as she went along, she listened for some slight change that would draw her attention, but she couldn't perceive any difference in sound.

Which was fine. She didn't need any treasure, any jewels or gold. Leaning on a windowsill, she looked down over her property—three acres, she'd been told, but the boundary lines were not defined by a fence or hedge, and so from this vantage point it seemed the world was hers: lawn and moors and beach and ocean, all cast in velvety amethyst shadows by the falling night. Her babies languorously kicked inside her. *She* was a house hiding treasures, and that was all that mattered.

Turning off lights as she went, she returned to the second floor and prepared for bed. The wind played around the house with a high, girlish, breathless chatter, and as Joanna stretched out in bed, she decided it was a Monet wind tonight, lily pads fluttering on the surface of a bright pond. She put her hands on her belly and felt her children move within her. Easily, once again she fell asleep.

* * *

The next night she and Tory went to a Neil Simon play at Bennett Hall, a small theater in a modest building attached to the grand old white Congregational Church. The theater was small, seating only about a hundred people, and theatergoers had to be seated off the main central aisle, so that those being escorted to their seats became a kind of preshow entertainment.

Joanna took an aisle seat because of her bulk. She and Tory had just settled into their chairs and were opening their programs when Tory nudged Joanna's arm.

"Would you look at that!" Tory whispered sotto voce.

Joanna swept her eyes around the room and saw Gardner Adams enter with a woman who clung to him with long magenta fingernails.

"She doesn't seem his type at all," Joanna told Tory.

She sensed someone's gaze on her and, looking up, saw Pat Hoover, who sat with Bob on the other side of the aisle and a few rows up. Their eyes met, they smiled, their eyebrows raised, very slightly they shook their heads in mutual wonder. Of all the women in the world whom the handsome physician could have chosen, this was the one?

Gardner and his date sat down, or rather Gardner sat, and his date arranged herself ostentatiously around him, encompassing as much of his body as she could while at the same time positioning her hand so that she could enjoy the flashes of her brilliant engagement ring.

"I just can't believe it," Tory whispered, pretending to study her program. "I've met him at a few parties and functions, and he's adorable, a real sweetie. How in the world did he get hooked up with her?"

Gardner's date—his fiancée, it seemed—could not have been any less an island type if she'd landed directly from the moon. Her bleached blond hair was styled and sprayed and backcombed; her dress dripped great clots of rhinestone, and her earrings were as big as teacups.

The theater filled. Murmurs rose in the air like a kind of humming, the lights dimmed, and the curtain was raised. The show on the stage began.

At intermission most of the crowd strolled out for the light refreshments sold in the lobby or into the mild misty night for fresh air. Tory and Joanna joined the throng.

"Oh!" Tory exclaimed. "That's it!"

"That's what?" Joanna asked.

"Sssh. Don't look. Come over here under the tree."

Puzzled, Joanna followed Tory out onto the brick walk and across the lawn so that they stood in shadow looking back at the people illuminated by the light from the lobby windows.

"Don't look now," Tory whispered, "but the reason Gardner is with that horror has just become crystal-clear. She must be Dr. Sandler's daughter."

"Dr. Sandler?"

"Horatio Sandler, our old obstetrician and gynecologist. He's practiced on the island for about a hundred years. Everyone loves him. Worships him. That one, the tall one with the white hair."

As Tory spoke, Joanna scanned the crowd until her eyes caught on the figure of a stunningly attractive man standing with Gardner Adams and the blonde. At least six feet six inches tall, and all bones, garbed in expensive old perfectly fitted tweed worn down to a silky suppleness, the old man hunched forward, absorbed in his daughter's chatter. He had a head of hair as full and dazzlingly white as a snowdrift, and a smile that sparkled in the night. Joanna could see how much the dreadful blonde resembled her father: she was tall and slender and gorgeous, in her rather electrifying way. But while Dr. Sandler seemed to radiate warmth—particles of light really did seem to glimmer around his body—his daughter seemed to crackle with darkness.

Pat and Bob Hoover crossed the lawn to join Tory and Joanna.

"Who'd have thunk it?" Pat said. "Gardner Adams and Tiffany Sandler."

"Tiffany?"

"Tiffany. Horatio is without a doubt the most wonderful, lovely, gifted man on the planet. He's saved so many lives, and so many babies' lives, and his hands are magic. But his daughter is a stupid bitch."

Joanna laughed in surprise. "Does she live on Nantucket?"

"Oh, no. She's a stockbroker in New York."

"But if she's planning to marry Gardner—"

"—then either she'll have to move here or Gardner will have to move there. And I've always heard that Gardner wanted to take over Horatio's practice. Be the island's family doctor. I don't know where Blondie fits in. What a mystery."

"Gardner is going to deliver my babies," Joanna said. "He's awfully nice, and calm, and intelligent. I *thought* he was intuitive."

"Love makes even the smartest man blind," Bob said.

"He can't love her!" Pat protested. "It's her father he loves. And the daydream of marrying the king's daughter and inheriting the throne."

Another couple, an architect and a schoolteacher, joined their small group. Now they all formed a small circle, leaning in toward the middle to talk with one another, and as they spoke, Joanna flashed back on her days as a girl standing alone on the playground of one of the many schools she found herself moved to throughout her childhood. How she'd envied groups like this, friends gathered together, leaning just slightly forward into a circle of easy fellowship. She'd dreamed of belonging, just like this. Here, under the stars on an early summer night, she felt that she belonged, felt she was part of a group she could call her own.

Fifteen

～

$\mathcal{M}$onday afternoon Joanna lay on the long white couch
in her living room while Gardner Adams took her pulse and
blood pressure. She was cranky. Her sleep was troubled by
the August humidity, which coated everything with a slimy
dampness. Her sheets stuck to her skin. Her body was enormous and heavy and cumbersome. When she awoke, she
showered, then rested on her bed, feeling like some wallow-
ing great sea mammal as she lifted the heavy globes of her
breasts in order to pat talcum powder against her sweating
midriff. A dark line divided the mound of her belly in half;
her thighs were swollen with the weight of her body.

But her children were coming alive to her. They were becoming individuals. The twin on the right was rowdy, strong,
and active, kicking, hiccuping, and punching. One tiny heel
continually jabbed Joanna in the rib cage, under her right
breast, as if trying to make more room. The twin on the left
was more sedate. His movements were blunt and rolling; he
seemed to stretch his body and arch his back. Joanna thought
of the twin on the left as the Swimmer, content and intro-
spective; the twin on the right she called the Chorus Girl,
bored with her small space, eager to get out and start dancing.

Joanna wished they could be born now. She felt so sorry
for them, all squashed up against one another inside her.
Certainly her own activities were limited. She couldn't even
drive anymore. Her bulk would not fit behind a steering
wheel.

With one brisk movement, Gardner undid the black cuff

on her upper arm. As he folded his equipment, he asked, "Have you been having headaches or vomiting?"

She thought a moment. "No."

"Vision problems?" His clear yellow-green eyes were intense as he watched for her reply. He would not be an easy person to lie to.

"No."

"Swelling?"

"Yes. My feet."

"I don't think we've got anything to be alarmed about, but your blood pressure doesn't make me happy. We want you to carry these babies to term. I want you to have a serious amount of complete bed rest. My best guess is that if you don't do that, you'll end up in the hospital."

Joanna reached out an entreating hand. "Gardner, is it that bad?"

He patted her hand. "Don't be alarmed. My point precisely is that it's not dangerous, but it could be. Tell me, how are you coming on those books?"

"I'm almost done."

"Almost means—?"

"Another two weeks of work, a month at the most."

"Have you chosen a birth partner?"

"No. Well, I did, I asked my friend Tory, but she won't be here."

"How about a sister?"

"I have no siblings."

"Another close friend?"

Briefly she thought of June Lathern; no. June was too formal, too reserved for the naked intimacies of childbirth. And Pat Hoover was very kind and perhaps would one day be a close friend, but they'd only met in May. "I don't know. I have to think about it."

Madaket was standing in the doorway, watching, and now she crossed the room and, coming around behind the sofa, stood with her hands on Joanna's shoulders, protectively. Today she wore a cotton dress of a pale topaz color, almost exactly the color of her skin. She was darkly luminous and strong yet soft, and Joanna was grateful for her touch.

"Is there anything I can do?"

Gardner looked up at her. "Could you live here?"

Madaket paused, then replied, "I have animals. A dog, a cat . . ."

Gardner looked back at Joanna. "Are you allergic to animals?"

"No. I love animals. At least I think I do. I've never had any of my own." She smiled. "Wolf is wonderful. I'd love to have him around."

Gardner was folding his stethoscope and blood pressure kit into his black bag. "Don't forget, after your babies are born, you'll need help at night as well as day."

"That's right. We agreed you'd work for me for at least a year, Madaket. Oh, do move in!" Joanna reached up and covered Madaket's hand with hers. Madaket squeezed her shoulders in reply. "You could make yourself a suite of rooms on the third floor. Your animals could have run of the house. You could give up your other place and you wouldn't have to worry about paying rent."

"Could I have some time to think about it?" Madaket's voice was low with indecision.

"What else is there to think about?"

"I'd hate to leave the garden at my house. My grandmother started it, and we tended it together for years. The house isn't much, but the little plot of land with it is very good. Good soil. It gets lots of sun."

Joanna waved her hand impatiently. "There's plenty of land right outside!" she reminded Madaket.

"Yes. But building a garden takes time. If I give up my little rented house, I'm giving up all those years of enriching the soil. I know Mr. Sherman would rent it out to other people. Who knows what they'd do with it. It would all change."

Joanna closed her eyes, admonishing herself to be patient. Caring about gardens was not something she was used to. Her mother's friends had gone in for swimming pools with cabanas and drink carts. Perhaps a pot of petunias or geraniums for color. Her father's girlfriends had lived in town houses or apartments, only occasionally bringing in cut flowers to brighten the room.

"Gardens are part of my life," Madaket continued. "My grandmother knew everything about plants and nutrition and health. We made teas and tonics and sachets, using what we'd grown without any pesticides or fertilizer other than compost. We've worked on the garden for years."

"So leaving the garden would be a real farewell to your grandmother."

"It would also be a real farewell to the soil we built up and the plants we nurtured."

"Well, Madaket, I intend to stay here for years. I can envision keeping you on here for years. I won't be able to raise twins and work without help. You and I certainly seem compatible. I can't offer you complete security, but I can promise you a few years of stability." Joanna twisted around on the sofa and, looking up at Madaket, clasped her hand and pleaded, "Madaket, please do it! I can't tell you how I worry about this fall. The babies will come at the end of October, and I'll be here all alone, and you'll be struggling along in foul weather on that bike. I'll go crazy!"

Madaket chewed her lip a moment, then decided: "All right. I'll do it."

"Great!" Gardner announced, slapping his hands on his thighs and pushing back his chair. Joanna noticed, when he stood, that his cotton chinos were slightly too short for him; he must have washed and dried them himself, and shrunk them. Why didn't his horrible fiancée, Tiffany, tell him to send them to a laundry? She could also advise him to get a haircut; his curly sunny hair was beginning to resemble a shrub. "I'll go along now. I'll stop back by in a few days to check you."

"Thanks, Gardner," Joanna said, but when Madaket returned from seeing the doctor to the door, she complained, "I feel like a biological specimen!"

Madaket laughed. "You *are* a biological specimen. You're an older primipara with twins."

"I'm what?"

"An older primipara with twins. That's what Dr. Adams said you are."

"How delightful," Joanna groaned. To her surprise, she began to cry.

"You're not as depressed as you think you are," Madaket assured her. "Water retention does this, causes you to—"

"Oh, shut up, Madaket!" Joanna snapped.

Madaket sent a sympathetic smile her way. "I'll go make you some nice iced herbal tea."

* * *

Some days it would be true summer, hot and sparkling and dry. Suddenly, often within hours, the weather would change. Low clouds would roll in with dramatic swiftness and thunderous rain would fall. A Van Gogh wind would howl and moan around the house. For stretches of time it would be dreary and cold, not like summer, not like any season at all.

Doug brought her flowers. The first time, he arrived with a loose bouquet of white daisies and purple phlox in his arms. The fragile lace of the blossoms set off in startling contrast the masculine strength quiescent within his roughened hands.

"These are for you," he said, bowing slightly as he presented them to her.

"They're lovely," Joanna told him. "Thank you." Although they were not particularly fragrant flowers, she bent her head over them, hiding her face. The petals quivered against her skin lightly, like the sense of sexual attraction flickering against her senses.

"They're from my wife," Doug informed her. "She loves flowers, can't grow enough of them."

"Thank her for me, please. I love fresh flowers."

Another time he brought her scarlet poppies, so exotic and flamboyant and erotic they seemed a kind of declaration.

"How beautiful!" Joanna exclaimed. She was standing just inside her study door, and Doug stood near her in the shadows of the hall. "Thank your wife for me."

"These aren't from my wife. She had to give all her cut flowers to the church this week."

"Oh?"

"These are just from me. I bought them for you. You said you like fresh flowers."

The color of the poppies was so intense it seemed to burn her cheeks. "You shouldn't have—"

"I like to do it. I like to give you flowers."

Joanna met his eyes and read a challenge there. She realized he meant her to interpret his words in any way she liked. His nearness, his boldness, took her breath away.

Footsteps sounded on the stairs. Madaket was coming up to put the clean linens in the cupboard.

"I'll get back to work," Doug said, and nodded and went off down the stairs.

What did this mean? What was she to do? She couldn't believe Doug Snow was helplessly attracted to her, especially in her ballooning form. Perhaps he was being only nice. Still, the insinuation of the gift sent the same rich, intense, physical pleasure through her as the poppies themselves.

With Madaket's help, Joanna crossed the hall each morning to work in her new study. It was bliss—a beautiful room complete with worktables to hold her piles of papers, a state-of-the-art computer and printer, a small copy machine, and an electronic typewriter. She'd had a half-moon window installed at the ocean end of the room, and she found herself often just staring out the window, dazzled by the dancing light.

Madaket moved into the house, bringing two other powerful presences with her, the dog Wolf, and Bitch the cat. Both animals looked like their names, but only the cat acted like hers. Wolf, shaggy and huge and dangerous-looking though he was, spent his days yearning for love. If Madaket was around, he was at her side; when she was gone, he hurried to be with Joanna, wherever she was. Wolf had blue eyes and a multicolored coat. Bitch was all black, with green eyes. She was furious at being moved, furious in general. She hid in the house, coming out only at night to eat the food they'd set on a shelf of the sideboard where Wolf, even standing, could not reach. She would not make friends with Joanna, but eyed her with disdain. If Joanna entered a room to find Bitch sleeping on a cushion in the sun, Bitch would awaken immediately and streak from the room, in spite of Joanna's most appealing entreaties.

Madaket had chosen a bedroom in the attic, a small room with a wonderful long window looking out at the ocean. Long before Madaket even considered moving in, Joanna had bought furniture and linens for the room and attic bathroom and decorated the stairwell and rooms with paintings she'd adopted from the dump and lovingly rejuvenated. Now she offered to buy anything else Madaket needed—a standing mirror, a desk? But Madaket said she was happy with everything just the way it was. Joanna had purposely refrained from watching when Madaket carried her things from the Jeep into the house and up to the attic, but she was aware of how quickly the work was done; Madaket didn't own much. She didn't want to appear to pry, and yet she finally gave in to her curiosity and climbed the stairs. Standing in the doorway to Madaket's room, she looked in. Madaket was transferring a stack of white T-shirts from a cardboard box into a bureau of bleached pine which matched the headboard, bedside table, and chair. The lines of the furniture were clean, almost stark, a basic style Joanna had assumed Madaket would like.

"How's it going?"

"Great!" Madaket answered. "What a wonderful view!"

"There is a radiator in here, but I'm afraid it still might be hard to keep warm in the winter. Especially when it's windy."

"That's all right. I'm used to that."

"Where did you get that lamp?" Joanna asked, surprised.

"Do you like it?" Madaket crossed the small room to caress an elaborately beautiful lamp: the bottom was a cast-metal statue of a voluptuous woman whose flower-twined hair wrapped around her body, covering her breasts and pubic area. The woman's arms were raised, stretching high up above her head, disappearing beneath the blue and red stained-glass shade capped by a cast-metal finial. Her feet were surrounded by flowers.

"It's fabulous," Joanna replied. She knelt to inspect it. "Looks Art Deco."

"I bought it at an art dealer's a few years ago. It used up most of my savings. But I don't buy much. That lamp and that painting."

Joanna looked at the oil Madaket had hung just where her eyes would fall on it when she lay in bed. It was an impressionistic scene of the ocean at night. The water was dark, the waves spangled with silver moonlight. A round moon slid out from the cover of a frothy cloud.

"What beautiful things you have," Joanna murmured. She caught herself from adding that such sensuality surprised her.

"Well, they're all I have," Madaket confessed. "The house we rented came furnished. The stuff wasn't very high quality, to put it mildly. My grandmother and I didn't have a lot

of things people considered necessities—we bought our sheets
and blankets at the Second Shop, for example. Found our
rugs at tag sales. Bought most of our clothes there, too, for
that matter. You'd be surprised what good things you can
find there."

"Tory raves about your beautiful dresses."

Madaket laughed. "They're really just old housedresses,
the sort of thing people brought to the Second Shop when
their grandmothers died." Her eyes fell. "I've always known
my grandmother wouldn't be able to leave me any money,
and my parents of course didn't leave anything, so I guess this
is just my way of providing myself with heirlooms."

"You're very wise, Madaket. Really. I'm impressed. I wish
I'd thought to do that when I was your age."

Madaket smiled shyly, ducking her head in pleased embarrassment. Joanna continued to look at the room, realizing how with those two pieces Madaket had made the room
her own.

Later, with Joanna's permission, Madaket put boxes of glass
jars and jam-making pots and utensils in the butler's pantry.
Her herbs gleamed greenly on the windowsill. From the moment she moved in, she used every free moment to work outside on an open plot of moorland away from the house and
ocean in preparation for a garden.

Joanna loved the sound of Madaket and her animals coming and going. Their various footsteps, Wolf's eager barks,
Madaket's gentle admonitions to the animals, all blurred together into a soothing and distant music, like water running
over rocks. The evenings were more companionable with
Madaket around. They ate together, discussing recipes, their
day, the news, and took long slow walks on the beach, watching the sun set. At night they sat together in the library reading, or watched videos or played cards. Madaket was knitting
blankets for the babies.

Joanna sometimes talked about Carter to Madaket, and
then pleasurable memories flowed through her like honey,
but just as often Joanna would be jolted by the remembrance
of Carter's temper, his arrogance, his moods, and she'd shake
her head in wonder at what she'd settled for.

She said nothing to Madaket about Jake. What could she

say? He had kissed her on the Fourth of July. He had looked handsome, and slightly younger, as if the strain of grief had eased somewhat. She could close her eyes and remember the way his hand had so gently touched her cheek as they stood in the cabin of George Mullen's yacht. A touch, a kiss, a starry summer's night . . . a recipe for daydreams. But she mustn't make too much of it; besides, now was the time to concentrate on her babies.

One morning shortly after Madaket moved in, as Joanna was working in her study, a large cry sounded in the air. Seconds later, Todd came thundering up the steps two at a time.

"Joanna! We've found something!"

She swiveled in her typing chair. Todd ran into her room. Wolf was at his heels, barking at Todd's excitement, racing in circles around Todd's ankles.

"What do you mean?"

"In the kitchen! In the floor! Dad and I were pulling up that awful old linoleum, and we found a trapdoor! Come on! I'll show you!"

Madaket appeared in the doorway then, her hands covered with gardening soil. "What's going on? I heard shouting."

Todd whirled toward Madaket. "Dad and I found a trapdoor in the sunroom. I bet it leads to the treasure."

Joanna waited for Madaket, usually reasonable at most times, to glance over at her with gentle scorn. It was such a boyish thing, Joanna thought, to think he'd found a treasure. But Madaket's eyes remained on Todd's face as he talked.

"We had all the linoleum up, and then we started prying up some damaged wood, bits and pieces, that looked like they'd been just nailed down any old way—"

Joanna interrupted. "If you'll help me, I'd like to come down and see it."

"Of course." Instantly Madaket came to Joanna's side and, wrapping an arm around her just under her shoulders, supported her as they made their way down the stairs and into the kitchen. They found Doug standing inside the space they'd broken open between the kitchen and sunporch.

"We didn't want to proceed any further without your permission." Doug spoke as if he were the voice of reason, but his dark blue eyes were intense with excitement.

The floor of the screened porch had been covered with an unattractive green linoleum, which Joanna had in turn covered with various pastel dhurrie rugs. Now the rugs, rolled and tied, lay in a corner. The linoleum had been ripped up in jagged pieces and stacked in piles along the perimeter of the room, waiting for the Snowmen to take them to the dump. The final layer of subflooring consisted of old boards, wide and splintered and warped. Underneath all that was hard-packed dirt. The carpenters had laid down sheets of plywood to walk on as they prepared a level underlay for the playroom.

In the middle of the screened-in porch, surrounded by the plywood, a section of the original floor of rough, unstained boards was exposed. Here a small wooden trapdoor with a frayed leather handle was disclosed, dirt demarcating its edges.

"We haven't pulled it up yet. We're going to now. Okay?" Doug looked at Joanna.

She nodded but felt compelled to warn softly, "It might be only another way into the basement."

"No," Doug responded instantly. "The basement runs under the kitchen, the hall, the two front parlors, and the dining room. Todd and I have already searched for any kind of opening in this direction. All along this side there are no openings. No doors. No way to get through. The basement walls are brick and mortar."

"So let's go!" Todd urged.

Bending over, Doug took hold of the frayed leather handle and pulled. At first it didn't give, and Joanna thought it might be somehow attached from underneath, but suddenly with a creak one side of the door parted, and as bits of dirt slid downward with a rustling sound, the door came up.

There were no hinges. It was just a large rough square of wood, which Doug laid aside. They looked down into a dark wood-framed hole barely two feet square.

"We need a flashlight."

"I'll get it," Madaket said. In an instant she found one in a kitchen drawer and handed it to Doug, who immediately aimed the light downward. A rough wooden ladder led into a dark pit.

"There's a room down there. Probably a cool cellar for the original house. They kept vegetables there during the winter."

"It could even be Indian," Madaket offered, almost whispering. "The Indians who lived on the island before the white settlers came made themselves dugouts, sort of caves dug into the ground for protection against the wind. This could be that sort of thing."

Joanna leaned as far forward as she could over her belly. She could see only darkness. Madaket crowded close to the men, bending over to peer down.

Todd asked, "Can I go down?"

"All right," Joanna said. "But be careful."

Todd took the flashlight from his father, tested the first step for soundness, and began to descend.

Joanna sat watching as Todd's taut body disappeared into the opening, first his long blue-jeaned legs, then his muscular torso, and with a twist, his wide shoulders. Then they saw the top of his head, his thick blond hair.

"It's a room," he called up. "Just a small room. Brick walls. There's a hole in one—hey!"

They could see the darkness parted by his flashing light.

"I'm coming down!" Madaket announced. She squeezed herself into the opening. A few minutes later, she said, "Wow."

"What is it?" Joanna called.

After a few seconds of frustrating silence, Todd spoke. "The damnedest thing. It looks as if there was a tunnel from this room. It's pretty much filled in now, sand has sifted through the rough wooden beams—Dad, which way's the ocean? I've lost my bearings down here."

"Over here." Doug stamped on the floor.

"Right. Then this would lead toward the ocean."

"They always said there was smuggling going on."

"There's an old crate down here, too," Madaket called. "But it's empty. No lid or anything. Just an empty wooden box."

"There's something in the tunnel," Todd muttered.

"What is it?" Doug Snow called.

For a few moments Joanna and Doug waited in silence.

"I have to . . . I need a shovel. Or a . . ."

". . . a wooden spoon would do," Madaket said. "Mr. Snow, could you get a big wooden spoon from the drawer on the right of the stove?"

Doug got it and leaned down to hand it to Madaket.

More waiting. They heard digging sounds.

"It's a little chest!"

"Bring it up!" Doug ordered.

Madaket and Todd came up. Specks of sand glistened from their hair and clothing and shoes. Madaket put the box on the center of the kitchen table and they all gathered around to stare down at it, as if waiting for it to speak. It was a small chest, only about ten inches long and five high, made of iron with brass reinforcing the corners. The hinges were wrought-iron. The flat lock was brass.

"Open it," Joanna said.

Todd tried to pull the lid up. "It's locked."

"We'll have to break it open," Madaket decided. "We'll never find a key that fits."

Todd looked at Joanna. "What do you say?"

"I hate to break it if there's another way to get in," Joanna said.

Todd grabbed up the box and shook it. They all heard the muffled rattle.

"Listen!" he said triumphantly. "Something's in there."

"Please open it, Joanna!" Madaket pleaded.

"All right. Todd—see if you can do it carefully."

Todd took a screwdriver off his tool belt and gently inserted it into the lock. He turned and twisted, but nothing happened. Running his screwdriver around the edge where the lid fit down onto the body of the chest, he searched for a space. He found one, dug in, drew the screwdriver along toward the lock. He pried upward. The lip of the lid bent back, but the lock didn't give.

"Hell," Doug said. "I'm getting my wire cutters."

He went out to his truck and returned with a tool with long rubber-covered handles. He forced the blade between the lid and the box. In only seconds the lock was cut.

His son pulled back the lid, which made a rusty, rasping noise. Inside the box was a small pouch of dark muslin.

"Here." Doug handed the pouch to Joanna. "Whatever it is, it's yours."

The pouch was simply closed by a drawstring around the mouth. Joanna pulled the strings and tipped two large stones into her hand.

"Rubies," she said.

In the bright flat kitchen light, the stones glittered like capsules of red wine against Joanna's skin. They were cut in rough ovals. Joanna handed them to Doug, who held one stone between thumb and forefinger up to the light and squinted, studying.

"I can't judge gemstones," he said. "Possibly they're only garnets."

"Possibly," Joanna said.

"But maybe they're rubies, Joanna." Todd took them from his father and turned them in his hand. "And you know, if those were down there, maybe there are more."

"Maybe we've found the treasure," Doug said, awe coarsening his voice. The wine-red color of the rubies seemed to glow on his face.

"It is an important discovery," Madaket told her. "This could be a whole chapter of Nantucket history. We should tell the Nantucket Historical Association."

"Oh, Lord," Joanna moaned. "I'm really not up to all of this. I mean, buried treasure—if this gets out, the press will be camping outside my door—no, they'll be pounding on my door day and night, wanting to get in and take photos of the trapdoor and the cellar. I'll never have any peace." She felt weak and nauseated, and reached out a hand to steady herself.

At once Madaket was by her side. "Are you all right?"

"I'm not sure . . ."

"Here, Joanna." Doug placed a chair behind her, and he and Madaket helped her sit down.

Joanna ran her hands over her face, taking deep breaths and collecting her thoughts. "Look, Doug, Todd. I'll make a deal with you. Let me have these babies before we go public about finding these stones. I'll—I'll give you one of the stones if you'll do that."

"That's not necessary!" Madaket protested, indignant. "That's not even reasonable." In a calm but determined voice, she said to Todd, "Give them to me. I'll put them in Joanna's safe with her other jewelry."

"Who died and made you queen?" Todd demanded, his face flushed with anger.

Madaket answered calmly. "Joanna's in a delicate condition right now. When she's had some time to think about it, we'll see if she wants to give the stones away."

"She's right, son," Doug said. "Give Madaket the stones."

Reluctantly Todd held out his hand, watching the gems as Madaket took them and slipped them into the muslin pouch, and put the pouch in the metal box, and slammed the lid down.

Madaket bent over Joanna. "You're trembling. Your blood sugar must be low. You need to have some lunch."

"That's all right, Madaket. I'm not hungry." Joanna sat with her eyes closed. She heard Todd and Doug walk out onto the sunporch, where they conversed in low tones, then the sound of boots on wood resounded as Todd thumped down into the cool cellar, his father right behind him.

"Can that room collapse?" Joanna asked without opening her eyes.

"I don't think there's any danger of that," Madaket answered. "It's all brick, and the wall broken open by the tunnel exposes a layer of stone behind the brick. I'm sure it's a strong foundation."

"What's the tunnel like?"

"I didn't see much of it. Only two or three feet. It's been framed in wood, but it looked to me as if most of it had caved in." She set a drink before Joanna. "Here. Drink this."

But she had no thirst, no appetite. She felt weak, exhausted, overwhelmed. "I think I need to rest before I eat anything."

Madaket was at her side. Putting her hand on Joanna's shoulder, she lifted the glass to Joanna's lips, and as if speaking to a child, coaxed, "Just a sip."

Joanna drank some of the cool, sweetened herbal tea and immediately felt better. The Snows thudded back up the cellar steps and into the kitchen.

Todd stepped in front of her, the veins of his hands bulging as he fought for control, hands clenched at his sides. "Joanna. Miss Jones. Would you please give me permission to explore the rest of the tunnel?"

Joanna looked at Todd. He looked tremendously handsome now that he'd dropped the sullen mask from his face. His dark blue eyes glittered.

"Is it safe?" she asked.

"I wouldn't take any risks," he replied.

"I don't know. We have no idea how old the tunnel is or what shape it's in. The land is all sand, it could easily fill in on you—"

"I've looked at it," Doug intervened. "I don't think there's any danger."

"I'll help him," Madaket interjected. "I'll go down with him and help."

"Absolutely not!" Joanna cried. "That's all I need, for one of you to get killed under my house!"

"All right, all right, we'll talk about it later," Madaket quickly conceded. "Let's get you up to bed. Then I'll bring you some lunch."

Joanna was not unaware of the look Madaket shot Todd, but she had no energy left to use for confrontations. Madaket supported almost all her weight as she climbed the stairs, but her feet were so swollen that she nearly wept with the effort.

Upstairs she sank gratefully into her chaise by the window. She closed her eyes. She heard Madaket pad across the hall into her study and return.

"There. I locked the little box with the bag of stones in your safe," Madaket said. "We'll deal with this all tomorrow."

"I don't mean to spoil your fun." Joanna spoke with her eyes closed.

"Joanna, I wouldn't call this fun," Madaket admonished gently. "Not to the Snows and me, at least. You shouldn't treat it lightly. It will set you apart from those of us who love this island and its history."

Joanna opened her eyes and looked at the young woman. "Madaket. I promise that after I've rested I'll listen to you. Now let me rest."

How she wished Jake were here to help her think this through! The old professional side of her longed to put this all on record, even on videotape; a discovery like this could be the focus of an entire show.

Suddenly the nausea flared up, swamping her, pulling her into a vortex of discomfort. Her vision blurred. The message was clear. If she wanted to carry these babies to term, she had to rest.

Sixteen

~

$\mathcal{T}$he evening after they discovered the rubies, Madaket drove Joanna to a dinner party at the Hoovers'.

"My dear!" Pat exclaimed when she opened the door. "How can you even walk?"

"Pat, it's going to get worse before it gets better. I'm only in my sixth month."

"Dear Lord. I wasn't this big at nine months. Come in and let's get you seated before you fall forward on your face."

Joanna wasn't sure she felt well enough to enjoy the party, but when she entered Pat's beautiful living room and saw the cluster of people assembled there, and when they came rushing over to greet her and to offer her drinks and canapés, she was glad she had come. Claude was there in a gorgeous burnt-sienna silk suit she would have loved to own herself; June and Morris were there, standing side by side, finishing each other's sentences, nodding simultaneously; and Gardner and Tiffany were there.

Gardner looked tired, harassed, and jumpy. He wore a beeper on his belt and had dark circles under his eyes and he still had a piece of tissue stuck to a spot on his neck where he'd cut himself shaving. His shirt was wrinkled and the cuff of a trouser leg was unraveling. Tiffany, on the other hand, twinkled like a Christmas tree as she tossed her sparkling golden curls and flashed her engagement ring with every sentence. Her body-hugging leopard-print spandex dress was something Joanna might have worn during one of her clandestine nights of disguise with Carter. Joanna sank onto a sofa, joining Tory and Claude and Tiffany.

"Don't imagine you'll be wearing a dress like that anytime soon," Tory murmured so only Joanna could hear.

"Or anytime in the rest of my life," Joanna replied.

"Tiffany, you look very Marla Maples tonight," Claude said.

"Oh, thank you!" Tiffany cooed. "I just feel so like celebrationy, I guess."

"And why is that?" Claude asked.

"Well . . ." Tiffany leaned forward. "Don't tell a soul, but I've convinced Gardner to move back to the real world."

"Child, whyever would you want to do that?"

"Oh, Claude, don't be dense. You can't think I'd really be able to live here in the winter. I would like *die* of boredom."

"I hope Gardner will be here through October," Joanna said, slightly alarmed.

Tiffany looked at her. "Why?"

"Because she's going to have twins and Gardner's her doctor," Tory snapped.

"Well, the hospital does have other doctors," Tiffany countered, her voice rising defensively. "This is just the thing I mean, anyway," she continued. "All these people thinking Gardner is theirs somehow. I said, Gardner, now look. Think of yourself as a kind of technician. Say a television repairman. People don't have to, like, *bond* with some guy just because he fixed their TV."

All heads swiveled toward Gardner to see what his response would be, but he was intensely involved with a scallop wrapped in bacon on a toothpick. Conversation stopped. Joanna's eyes swept the room.

Claude smoothly picked up the dropped thread of conviviality. "Yes, I can see that's one way of looking at any profession." Eyes twinkling mischievously, he leaned forward and asked, "What do you, like, do? I mean, for a, like, profession."

Tiffany scrutinized him a moment, suspicious, then tossed her glittering curls and said, "I don't *do* anything, Claude. I want to spend my life taking care of Gardner and seeing that we both have some fun. Instead of being at the beck and call of everyone else. Before we get too *old*." With a meaningful flash of eyes at Tory and Joanna, she finished: "Excuse me. I want to powder my nose." She rose in one lithe movement and on gloriously sleek long legs strode out of the room, her leopard spots undulating all over her.

Morris asked Bob about an expensive piece of real estate which had just sold and the discussion rose, surrounding Gardner so completely that Claude and Tory and Joanna, seated near one another, could gossip without the others hearing.

"What a little terror!" Claude whispered, rolling his eyes.

"I wonder what her father thinks of her now," Tory said.

"He adores her. I've watched them together. But poor Gardner. He looks like she's literally chewed on the man." He flicked his wrist and waggled his eyebrows. "Not that I wouldn't mind doing that myself."

"Claude, mind your manners!" Tory said reprovingly.

Joanna sat smiling, pretending to listen to their banter but with her thoughts in a turmoil. She'd intended to ask the group their advice about how to deal with the business of the rubies, but Tiffany's announcement drove all other thoughts out of her head.

Gardner couldn't leave the island! The thought of entrusting her body and its precious cargo to a stranger was terrifying. She would have to ask him point-blank, during the evening, when he planned to leave, or rather, if he planned to stay through her delivery.

Pat called them into dinner and Joanna was helped up from the sofa and delicately ensconced in her dining room chair, where she oohed and aahed with everyone over the artistic arrangement of the flowers and the food, but she was trembling inside. The conversation washed around her. She nodded and smiled and worried, until over the salad Claude leaned forward and said, "Gardner, I hear you'll be leaving us soon."

Gardner flinched. A hunted look passed over his handsome young face.

"Well, ah, um, it's not definite exactly," Gardner began, but his fiancée cut in sharply.

"Oh, it is, too." Looking defiantly around the table, Tiffany announced, "I have to live in the real world."

"It's um, uh . . ." Gardner struggled for words, finally took a big sip of wine, and promptly dissolved into a coughing fit.

"Traitor," June accused, glaring at Gardner and, whipping her gaze toward Tiffany, pleaded, "Darling, couldn't you get a pied-à-terre in New York and leave Gardner here? I don't think we can manage without him."

"Of course you can!" Tiffany retorted. "And I'll tell you something. I'll tell you all something! I'm not going to live my life sharing my husband with you. I grew up without a father and—"

"Tiffany," June said reprovingly, "you had a perfectly wonderful father."

"No! *You* had a perfectly wonderful physician! My father was never there for me. What do you think happened when I was the star little pony in my ballet recital? Do you think he came? And saw me? And told me how beautiful I was? No. He got called in to deliver some damned woman's baby. And that's what happened over and over again all through my life. He couldn't take me to the father-daughter dinner at my high school. Hell, he didn't even see me graduate from high school!"

Joanna watched Tiffany. She was very beautiful with rage flushing her face, making her glow and shimmer even more, and as she tossed her curls and nearly shuddered with indignation, she fairly burned with anger. But at the other end of the table, Gardner sat looking purely miserable. He wasn't staring at his beloved with awe at her beauty but rather sinking into himself, as if his very chest and the heart within were collapsing.

When Tiffany finally stopped to drink some wine, Joanna leaned toward her. "I can understand," she began, intending to confide that her father had also been a doctor.

But Tiffany snapped her head, tossing her curls back, and glaring at Joanna, interrupted: "No one can possibly understand."

The maid entered then to ask people whether they'd like coffee, decaf, or tea with their dessert, which would be cherries jubilee, and as the guests concentrated on this, the little miasma of fury that had settled over the table lifted off and floated away into the night air.

"She's selfish and self-absorbed and young," Joanna whispered to Tory, "but beautiful. And passionate."

"Yes," Tory agreed. "I can see why Gardner loves her. But

God, if any two people in the world ever seemed incompatible, it's those two. Look at him, Joanna. She's going to eat him alive."

"Tory, are you and John racing tomorrow?" Morris directed his calm gaze at Tory, and the conversation shifted to sailing.

Except for an occasional disdainful sniff, Tiffany remained quiet, pouting, for the rest of the evening. Joanna sat back in her chair and enjoyed a few bites of the very sweet dessert. Her stomach was so crushed in on itself by the burgeoning bodies of her babies that she could scarcely work up any kind of appetite. At several points during the conversation Joanna opened her mouth to mention the discovery of the room beneath her house, and the rubies hidden in the room, but each time she changed her mind, closed her mouth, let the others speak. She had no energy left for what would be a turbulent discussion. And there had already been enough drama at the table for one night.

They adjourned into the living room for after-dinner drinks. Joanna sipped on clear seltzer and tried to stay awake. At ten-thirty Pat called, "Joanna, your ride's here," and Joanna rose awkwardly and kissed her hosts goodbye and said goodbye to everyone and lumbered toward the front door where Madaket waited.

"Did you have a good time?" Madaket asked. She steered the Jeep along the narrow lanes toward Main Street, which was wide and shadow-swept and flickering with people strolling and laughing and gazing in shop windows under the swaying canopy of summery lavish-leafed trees.

"Umm." Joanna yawned and stretched and scratched her belly in blissful abandonment. "But I'm exhausted. Oh, God, these cobblestones."

"I thought you'd like to hear the street musicians." Madaket slowed the Jeep. Music drifted in on the warm air from a folk guitarist, a saxophone player, and a bizarre overwrought young man who played "Feelings" on his violin to the taped accompaniment of a synthesized orchestra.

Streetlights flared and dimmed across the windshield as they turned down Orange Street. Joanna trailed her hand out the window in the lake of cool night air.

"I'm beginning to feel a bit decadent," Joanna admitted,

"with you chauffeuring me everywhere. I feel like . . . some old depraved Roman empress. Next I'll be nagging at you to peel the grapes."

Madaket laughed. "I don't think you know what decadence is."

"Oh, and you do."

"Well, I've worked in some pretty decadent homes on this island."

"Such as?"

"Three years ago I worked as a cook for a family who had rented a house on the Cliff for a month. Forty thousand dollars for the month of July. The wife was there only three days, the husband only one. But their children were there the entire time; the son was nineteen and the daughter was seventeen. The wife had compiled a complete set of menus for three meals a day for the entire month. Lots of fresh fish, fresh vegetables, fresh fruit. Lots of homemade desserts and whole-wheat breads. The decadent part was that—never mind that at nineteen and seventeen people should be capable of fixing their own meals—the daughter was anorexic and ate only about three chocolate chips that month. The son had a lot of friends and mostly they drank and ate pizza and vomited."

"God! Did you tell the woman?"

"I told her secretary. I felt it was such a terrible waste of food. But the secretary said the woman insisted that I make decent meals available in case her children were hungry, and that if I didn't, she'd find someone else who would. Every now and then the secretary would stop by the kitchen to be sure I was doing my job, and the woman had sent one of her maids over to keep the house clean, and I suspected the maid was reporting on me, too. So that entire month I cooked three nutritious, delectable meals a day, and set them on the table, and waited for a while, then threw all that beautiful food away."

"I don't believe it."

"Believe it. There's another woman on the island, a terribly wealthy woman, who hates to wait for trees and shrubs to grow and bloom, so she hires a landscaping company to plant full, flowering bushes in her garden, and when she's tired of looking at them, she has the landscaper dig them up and take them to the dump. But before they go to the dump, the landscapers have to sever the plants from the roots—while she watches. She's afraid that someone else might take them from the dump and plant them in their own yard. She buys them with her money and she wants no one else to have those plants."

Joanna had been listening with her eyes closed. Now she opened them and looked over at Madaket to see her expression. "Does all this make you angry? Resentful? Jealous?"

Madaket considered. "I'm sorry about the plants and food. I regret the waste. But I pity the people. I think they must be so lonely, cut off from the important things."

"But, Madaket, they have so much. You have so little."

Madaket shook her head. "No. I have so much. You'll see after you've lived here for a year. After you've had the seasons on the island. Each day here is like a treasure. And somehow, you get to keep it. It stays with you. A wealth in your soul."

Joanna searched the young woman's face as she spoke and saw there a soft radiance that fairly glowed off her. "You are lucky," she agreed. "To love someplace so much."

"You will, too," Madaket assured her, "after you've lived here awhile."

After a few moments of companionable silence, Madaket asked, "Have you thought any more about the tunnel?"

"Not really. Oh, I don't know, Madaket. I really don't know."

"We would only explore it. Look around. Anything we found we'd bring to you."

"It's not that. Not the matter of possession. It's more a matter of—anxiety, I guess. What if the tunnel caved in? I can't get down there to see it and judge myself."

"We wouldn't do anything stupid."

"I know, but, Madaket, I couldn't bear it if anything happened to you."

Joanna spoke honestly, but she meant it in a selfish way, and so she was surprised when Madaket replied in a choked, hushed voice, "Oh, Joanna. I didn't know that."

Joanna turned to look at the young woman who was driving very seriously now, looking very determined and blinking back tears. The summer heat and humidity had made some of Madaket's black hair escape from the braid and it twined and curled down around her face in glossy ringlets. Her profile was proud and beautiful, the strong cheekbones and wide nose and enormous deep dark eyes all struck into sharp relief by the shadowy light. Beneath her cotton dress, her huge bosom heaved with repressed emotion, and Madaket looked like a goddess, a dark goddess of earth and fecundity and nature and night: a goddess for the proud and fiercely alone. Joanna realized with a shock that this was probably the first time, or one of the first few times, that Madaket had heard concern for her expressed.

"You and Todd seem to be getting along very well these days," Joanna said, wanting to make Madaket happy.

It worked. Madaket's lips lifted in a spontaneous, irrepressible smile. "I know. We talk a lot. We're getting to know each other. He's really very nice. And he really wants to explore the tunnel."

"Is this so important to you, Madaket?"

"Yes. Very."

"Why? Do you actually think you'll find treasure?"

"Joanna, we already did find something! You should have those stones valued. But it's not the treasure. It's the knowing. The discovery."

"But what if you find more? What will happen to my precious peace and quiet, my privacy? What there is left of it."

"Joanna, we've known about the rubies, or whatever they are, for twenty-four hours now. We would have talked about it right away if we were going to. But we haven't told anyone. Your peace and quiet haven't been disturbed. You should trust us."

Joanna shifted in the seat, leaning her weight against the door. She was irritated by a strange tension stirring within her. She realized that she wanted Madaket to have her own way simply because it would make Madaket happy. She wanted that almost as much as she wanted to have *her* own way. It was unsettling to be pulled by contrasting desires.

"I do trust you, Madaket." They were in the dark open countryside now. No more streaks of streetlights. Deep silence rolled in the air. She took a deep breath. "All right, Madaket. You and Todd can explore the tunnel."

Madaket laughed, a pleased light laugh. It filled Joanna with delight.

Seventeen

~

*E*very warm September evening after dark had fallen, a flash of lights broke over the front of the house, and the red pickup truck crackled over the gravel and stopped. Todd entered the front door without knocking—they all agreed it was simpler if he did—and Wolf fell all over himself in a flurry of legs and fur getting down to greet him. Madaket followed more slowly, first checking to be sure Joanna was comfortable and had everything she needed for the night.

Equipped with battery-powered lights and spades and shovels, and taking down wood for bracing, the two young people climbed down the rickety steps into the root cellar. They'd formed a plan about how they'd go about their search, and they had discussed it thoroughly with Joanna. Carefully they scooped sand into buckets, poured the sand in a pile in a corner of the cellar, and made arches of wood to support the roof and walls in the tunnel. They told Joanna their work was hot, boring, and dirty. So far they'd found nothing but sand.

When Madaket came up to bring Joanna her warm milk and nighttime snack, she'd have grains of sand glistening like bits of opals in her black hair. Often Todd came up to Joanna's bedroom, too, appealingly awkward in his jeans and heavy work boots. Not wanting to get any of Joanna's furniture sandy, he'd just sprawl on the floor, back against the wall. Wolf would throw himself on top of Todd, and there they'd sit, two especially successful strains of male animal, in Joanna's very feminine room.

* * *

Joanna called Morris Lathern one day and told him she had a legal question. She would pay for his advice, and she wanted his promise of complete confidentiality.

"If any treasure is found in my house, in the attics or under the ground or anywhere on my land, to whom does it legally belong?" she asked.

Morris answered: "To you. Without a doubt. If it were something belonging to the former owner, which they might have accidentally left behind, then there might be a question. But if you're talking about something that's been hiding away there for over a hundred years, then whatever it is, it's your property by law."

"Don't turn Madaket into your husband," Tory advised Joanna one sunny day as they walked together down Main Street.

"What!" Joanna was shocked.

"I mean, don't rely on her too much. Don't invest too much emotionally. Bottom line, she's your employee, you're her boss. The way you've got her living there, you act as if she's family. But that's not fair to her, Joanna. She's only nineteen. She can't live here the rest of her life. She's got to grow up and get married or have a career, have a life of her own. You've got to know she'll leave you. You mustn't get too dependent on her."

"Oh, for heaven's sake, Tory." As they walked into the Espresso Cafe, Joanna was irritated, unsettled by her friend's remarks.

"You go on out and get a table in the shade. I'll get the drinks," Tory suggested.

"All right. I want an iced decaf cappuccino." Joanna stepped out onto the sunny patio and settled at a table near a tub spilling with pink begonias.

Tory soon joined her, a white mug in each hand. Sinking into her chair, she continued, "Well, I worry about you. I just don't want you to become too dependent on Madaket."

"Look, Tory, it's not as if I have a choice. Gardner told me I have to take care. I need full-time help. Madaket's my employee but also, thank heavens, I really like her. She's agreed to be here for the next year. What's wrong with that?"

"Nothing's wrong with that, except that since she's living in your house, it will be easy to get the roles confused. Between employee and friend, I mean. I don't want you to get hurt when she takes off next year."

"Who says she's taking off next year?"

"Joanna, don't be so touchy! No one's saying that. We're talking in circles. I mean only that she *might* take off next year. She's not your family. Don't count on her to care for you. She's with you because you're paying her."

"I guess no one would stay with me otherwise," Joanna snapped. She had intended to mention the discovery of the rubies and the cellar and the tunnel; she'd intended to let it all spill out in one rush of eagerness and anxiety. But Tory leaned back in her chair and regaled Joanna with descriptions of the clothes she'd bought for Vicki for school on their latest shopping tour. Joanna let all thoughts of the hidden treasure sink back into the shadows of her mind. Without asking she knew what Tory would say.

Early in September, Pat's gallery held a private champagne opening for the painter Wallace Stark. This was a grand occasion, admittance by personal invitation only.

"You've got to go," Tory lectured Joanna. "Stark is probably the most famous painter in America and he never shows up in public. John and I bought a Wallace Stark oil fifteen years ago, when it had cost only fifty thousand dollars. Now that he's in his seventies and producing little, it's worth ten times as much. He's a real character, and one who's not going to be on this earth much longer. You'll never get this chance again."

"I know," Joanna said, "but, Tory, it's just so hard for me to get around these days."

"Oh, Joanna, wait till you have your twins! Then you'll really know what it is to be tied down. Come on. One last party."

Joanna smiled abashedly. "I already gave my two invitations to Madaket. I just can't go, Tory."

"Well, I've got two, one for me and one for John, and he's going to be in New York, so you can be my date. It's settled. I won't take no for an answer."

When the night of the party came, Madaket helped Joanna

into her familiar turquoise silk tent, and brushed her hair, and helped her down the stairs and out to the driveway and into Tory's car. Wolf whined at their side; he'd adopted Joanna and didn't like it when she left the house.

"Now, you're coming, too, right, Madaket?" Joanna asked as the young woman gently and firmly closed the car door. "I know you don't like snobs, but this is a different kind of affair. A once-in-a-lifetime occasion."

Madaket nodded. "I'm coming. I just have to change."

"Promise?"

"Promise."

"Are you bringing a friend?"

Madaket smiled. "Yes."

"Enough chat, ladies, I don't want to miss a minute," Tory said, and started the engine and drove out of the driveway and down the Squam Road and along into town. The night was breezy and mild, with just a bit of crispness in the air.

"Look, Tory," Joanna said, pointing to her high wide stomach, which bulged here and there as the twins moved inside her.

Tory laughed. "It looks like your babies are dancing."

"Practicing karate is more like it. Ooh! They can really kick."

"How's your blood pressure?"

"Gardner says I'm in a holding pattern. Not getting any better but not getting any worse."

"You're counting down now. Only two more months."

Joanna groaned. "Each day seems like a month, Tory. I feel so helpless. So vast and vulnerable."

"That will all change soon enough," Tory replied offhandedly, not really interested. "Here we are." She double-parked the car on the side of Main Street. "I'll let you out. Wait for me on the bench. I'll find a parking spot and we can go in together. And try not to talk about the babies *all* the time, okay?"

"Tory!" Affronted, Joanna searched her mind for a proper riposte, but Tory demanded impatiently, "Joanna, would you get out? I'm holding up traffic."

Joanna negotiated her way from the car and across the cobblestones to the brick sidewalk. Sighing gratefully, she

sank onto a bench to wait for Tory. It was a lovely evening.
The sidewalks weren't as crowded or noisy, and as she
scanned the long block of shopfronts, she fancied that the
stores, full of lights and luxuries and people, were a kind of
theater and she was here in the dark audience, watching.
Then Tory came and, taking Joanna by the elbow, helped her
stand, and together they made their way into Pat's art gallery
and became a part of that particular play.

The gallery was crushed with people, the air rich with
laughter and perfume. At the bar Tory took a glass of champagne, Joanna one of Perrier, and they slowly made their way
around the room, looking at the newest, vast, lush, Wallace
Stark paintings.

"I could eat them," Joanna sighed.

"You could eat anything," Tory told her.

"I think he's bordering on the decadent," whined a voice
in the crowd.

The paintings were classical, pictures of nudes reclining in
various poses on tapestry-covered beds, among hanging bro-
cades, silver chalices, sly furry pets, enormous bowls overflowing with ripe fruit.

"I have to sit down," Joanna told Tory after about fifteen
minutes. "I'm sorry, but my ankles—"

"Fine. I'll cruise."

Joanna found a chair and sank into it with gratitude. The
pictures were overwhelmingly sensual. She craved Carter.
No, she craved anyone at all who would cover her mouth in
a kiss. Stark's art brought back to her powerfully the sensuality she'd almost forgotten.

She saw Madaket enter. With Todd.

Joanna stared, hypnotized. Madaket wore a full, ankle-
length, flowing, Gypsyish skirt of red, embroidered with gold
and purple and green, and a green velvet vest which swelled
and clung over her remarkable bodice, the top cut just low
enough to show the deep cleft of her heavy breasts, the buttons tight enough to display her small waist and flat stomach. She'd let her hair free of its restraining braid and it
curled and spiraled around her head while against it her gold
hoop earrings glittered. On her feet were sandals, the laces
crisscrossing around her ankles. She wore no makeup, but her
face was radiant with pride and pleasure and she looked like

a priestess or goddess, some magnificent female force representing all nationalities; she could be Indian or African or South American or Mediterranean or Mexican.

Beside her, Todd shone, too. He was her match, her complement, with his golden hair and dazzling blue eyes and tanned skin. He wore jeans, a white T-shirt, and a black blazer; the gold earring was no more bright than his young skin and eyes and white strong teeth.

Madaket moved through the room like a princess, her expression haughty. But when she looked up at Todd, her face softened with such sexual yearning that Todd always swayed toward her, and sometimes even bent to whisper in her ear, touching her shoulder slowly with his hand.

"Oh, dear," Joanna said under her breath.

She didn't want Madaket to find her sitting there staring, so she pushed herself up off her chair and made her way around the room, pausing to study Stark's paintings. Soon Madaket and Todd approached her.

"These paintings are wonderful, aren't they?" Madaket said. She glowed with happiness; she could have been looking at Mickey Mouse cartoons and found them wonderful.

"You are what's wonderful," Joanna said. "Madaket. You look absolutely amazing." Seeing that she'd embarrassed the young woman, she said to Todd, "And you don't look too shabby yourself."

"Thanks," Todd said easily, and continued earnestly, "And thanks for giving Madaket the invitation. Carpenters don't often get invited to this sort of thing."

"My pleasure," Joanna replied.

"Hello, everyone," Tory said, joining them. "Hi, Todd. Madaket, you're looking fabulous."

"Thank you." Madaket was very dignified as she looked back at Tory.

"My dear young woman, how I would like to paint you."

They all turned to look at a short, round, old dumpling of a man who had suddenly approached them and stood next to Madaket, staring up at her.

"Hello, everyone," Pat said smoothly, quickly easing herself next to the stubby little gnome. "I'd like you all to meet Wallace Stark."

As Pat introduced them one by one, the painter extended

his short arm with its strong, plump, cool hand, and looked at their faces, his little piggy brown eyes alight with interest. There he was, the great master, America's artistic pride, as rotund and likable as Humpty-Dumpty.

"Mr. Stark," Tory said, "I own one of your paintings. I bought it several years ago. I love it."

"Thank you," Stark said, nodding his head in such a long and courteous bow Joanna thought he might topple forward. Instead, he raised his head and looked at Madaket. "I'm doing a commission now. But if I get back to this island anytime soon, I would like to paint you. You are an avatar."

"Wallace, I'm sorry to interrupt," Pat said, gently steering the painter toward a pair of summer people with money etched in the impatient set of their clenched jaws, "but I'd like you to meet some collectors—" She led him off.

Tory leaned toward Madaket. "An avatar is a god appearing on earth in bodily form," she whispered.

Madaket smiled. "I know."

"You do? Really?" Tory's tone and look were skeptical.

"I didn't finish high school, but I've always read a lot," Madaket told her politely.

Tory was discomfited. "Well, good for you. And congratulations on getting such a compliment from such an esthete." She turned slowly toward Joanna. "Excuse me. I'm going to get another drink. Want some more Perrier?"

"Please." Joanna handed Tory her glass.

"I don't think Tory likes me," Madaket said.

"She's just jealous," Todd told her. "Every woman in this room is jealous of you."

Madaket pressed her lips together in an attempt to hide her smile; it was obvious to Joanna that Todd's compliment had touched her in a way that no one else's, not even Wallace Stark's, could. My God, Joanna realized, Madaket's in love.

Why this made her anxious she didn't know, but just at that moment someone elbowed her in the back; someone else stepped on her foot. The clamor of voices, punctuated with shrieks of laughter, the press and nudge of bodies, the smoky air, reminded her of New York. Reminded her of all the parties she'd attended, going alone, drunk on the thrill of seeing Carter there alone, too; the two of them would stand a good two feet apart, as stiff and formal as business colleagues should be, while their eyes and their skin and their lips and their bodies called and responded to each other on an invisible electric frequency of lust. Oh, Carter. Carter. Flushing, overheated, suddenly struck dead center in her heart with grief, Joanna struggled through the mob to the open doorway and stood there inhaling great drafts of fresh air.

"Joanna. Are you okay?" Suddenly Madaket was there, forehead wrinkled with concern.

"I'm fine," Joanna answered, then reached out to rest on Madaket's arm, and confessed, "Actually I'm tired. I need some fresh air. I'll just sit out here on the bench until Tory's ready to go home."

"Would you like me to get Tory?"

"No, no. She's having a good time. And you should, too. I need to just sit for a while and be pregnant. Catch my breath."

"Let me just help you to the bench," Madaket insisted, and Joanna gratefully leaned on the young woman as she made her cumbersome way across the sidewalk to the wooden seats ringing the strong old maple tree canopying the wide street.

"I'll stay with you awhile."

They sat in companionable silence watching the people pass up and down Main Street. There were few children at this hour and many lovers. So many couples holding hands strolled along, pausing to gaze dreamily in at the window displays, leaning together in rapt discussion. A bearded young man stood in front of a jewelry shop, playing an acoustic guitar and singing of love. Through the lighted windows of the gallery, Joanna and Madaket could see as clearly as if onstage the guests drinking champagne and looking at Wallace Stark's paintings and laughing and talking, and they saw how Todd, as young and handsome and dashing as a movie star, was approached over and over again by women who smiled and gestured at a painting and began a conversation with him.

Madaket laughed. "Isn't he handsome!"

"He really is," Joanna agreed.

"There you are!" Tory squeezed herself between the crush

of people and out the door to the sidewalk. "I've been looking for you. God, it's a sauna in there. Are you okay,
Joanna?"

"I'm fine. Just tired of standing."

"I am, too. Let's go." Tory looked at Madaket. "You'd
better get back in there before someone steals your beau."

"Oh," Madaket said, shaking her head, "Todd's not my
beau. I just asked him to come along because Joanna gave
me two tickets and I thought he'd enjoy it."

"He's enjoying it, all right," Tory declared, and the three
women turned to see Todd engrossed in conversation with a
stunning blond.

"Um," Madaket said, obviously discomfited, "maybe I'll
just wait out here."

"Nonsense, Madaket, go back in," Joanna urged. "You
know Todd's bored to death talking to those city creatures."

Madaket flashed Joanna a quick smile of gratitude.
"Thanks. See you later?"

"I'll probably be asleep when you get home. I'll see you tomorrow."

Madaket went back inside, disappearing into a crowd of
noise and people, and Tory went off to get her car and pulled
up in front of the gallery a few minutes later to pick Joanna
up. For a few moments the two friends were quiet, absorbing the soothing sounds of the summer night as they drove
back out of town. Then desultorily they discussed the party
and Wallace Stark's paintings.

"Joanna," Tory asked, "have you thought about what
you're going to do when they're sleeping together?"

"What do you mean?"

"I mean, what are you going to do when Todd starts sleeping with Madaket? Are you prepared to lie in bed listening
to the bedsprings squeak overhead in the attic, and to hear
Todd come clomping down the stairs in the morning, ready
for work?"

"I don't know that that's going to happen, and Madaket
certainly doesn't."

"Oh, please," Tory scoffed. "Anyone with two eyes—"

"Tory, look. I've got enough on my mind without worry-
ing over some figment of your imagination."

"I'm only trying to help you be prepared . . ."

Joanna reached over and flicked on the radio. "Let's have some music. It's such a nice night."

They rode the rest of the way home together peacefully, soothed by a radio concert of Brahms.

Eighteen

~

Toward the end of September, Joanna finished both manuscripts. By this point she was practically immobilized by her girth, and because she couldn't go to him, her editor, Justin Karnes, offered to fly up from New York to discuss them with her.

"I wish I could give him a dinner party," Joanna moaned one night as Madaket was brushing her hair.

"Why can't you?" Madaket asked in a sensible tone of voice.

"Because I can't do any damned thing except lie here and gestate!" Joanna whined.

Madaket kept brushing with long, even strokes. "Well, I can do all the work, Joanna. All you have to do is tell me whom you want invited and what you want served."

Eyes closed, Joanna mulled it over. Finally she said, "Are you in love with Todd?"

Madaket laughed in response. "What does that have to do with giving a dinner party?"

"Nothing. I just thought I might catch you off guard."

"There are lots of delicious fresh apples these days. I could make you a fabulous fall meal."

"Are you sleeping with Todd?"

"Joanna!"

"Ouch!" Joanna's eyes flew open as Madaket gave the hairbrush a stiff yank through her hair.

"Well, it's not your business whether I'm sleeping with Todd or not."

"Yes, it is. I need you. I'm going to need you desperately.

I don't want you falling in love and getting pregnant and getting married."

Madaket shook her head solemnly. "No fear of that."

"Oh, Madaket." Joanna reached up and covered the young woman's hand with her own. Holding it firmly, she said, "Seriously, Madaket. If you ever need any advice, or help, about any of that stuff—contraception and all that—please ask. I won't joke about it. It can be confusing. Love can be terribly confusing."

"Thank you. And I will ask," Madaket replied shyly. Her voice fell to a whisper. "But there's no need to yet. He hasn't even tried to kiss me."

Seeing the shadow of sadness darken Madaket's face, Joanna patted her hand briskly and changed the subject. "All right. Back to the dinner party. What's our menu going to be?"

Justin arrived from New York, checked into an inn, and drove out every day for a week to work on the manuscripts with Joanna. He was delighted with her work and predicted good sales for both books. He planned to fly back to the city on Saturday morning, after the dinner party Joanna was giving in his honor on Friday night.

Friday she spent the entire day in bed, resting, luxuriating in the delicious aromas wafting up the stairs from the kitchen. Late in the afternoon Madaket helped her dress in a comfortable tent of white accented by a choker and earrings of diamonds and topazes that Carter had given her one Christmas. Madaket had asked Joanna if she would hire Todd for the evening to help in the kitchen with the heavy work and the cleaning up; Todd would be glad to do it since they couldn't work on their explorations in the cellar that night. Joanna agreed and that evening Todd drove home with his father after work, returning by himself, smelling fresh and clean and spicy. His blond hair was damp and slick. He wore clean, tight jeans and a sleeveless black T-shirt that gave him a dangerous air, but as he helped Joanna down the stairs and into the living room, he could not have been more gentle. With his arm wrapped around her back, just at her waist—or rather, where once her waist had been—he steadily supported her as they walked.

"This is so embarrassing," Joanna said.

"I know what you mean," Todd replied, easing her down a step. "I tore a ligament in football one year and had to hop everywhere on crutches."

He settled her in a wing chair, and Madaket handed her an icy glass of lemon tea, and Joanna sat in state while Todd played butler, opening the door and showing people into the living room. The Hoovers had been invited and they brought Joanna's editor from his inn in town. Joanna introduced Justin to the Latherns, and Tory and John and Gardner, and Claude. They arrived full of good cheer and bonhomie, for the summer was over and the best season of all had arrived, when the September days were warm and lush and hushed and golden and the nights clear and full of stars.

They all came but one. Gardner was the last guest to arrive and he entered alone.

"Where's Tiffany?" Joanna asked as Gardner bent to kiss her cheek.

Gardner looked both embarrassed and relieved. "Right now, a few thousand feet above the Atlantic Ocean."

Conversation stopped. Everyone looked at Gardner, and he held out his hands as if to show them all they were empty and announced: "The engagement is off."

"Gardner! What happened?" It was Pat asking for everyone.

He smiled self-deprecatingly and sank onto the sofa and, leaning elbows on knees, clasped his hands in front of him. "It just didn't work out. It's all right. It was a mutual decision."

"But why?" June pressed.

Gardner grinned. "Why? Let's just say I wanted to become the father she's always wanted to rebel against."

"Darling," Claude exclaimed, "are you shattered?"

"Not at all. Please, everyone, there's no need to worry or feel bad. I feel fine." He blushed. "I probably shouldn't say it, but actually I feel great."

"I never did think she was your type," Pat confessed.

"But it's so hard to know!" June cried. "I mean, they say opposites attract but then you're supposed to have mutual interests."

Morris leaned forward, tamping tobacco into his pipe as

he spoke. "So, Gardner, before we try to solve the mysteries of romantic love, tell us, why is Tiffany over the ocean? I've heard of being over the moon with joy, but never the ocean. Is there something I've missed?"

Gardner laughed. "Tiffany's flying to Europe with a friend for a few months."

"And you're staying on the island?" Joanna asked, holding her breath.

"Yes. Of course." His joking facade fell away. "I don't know why it is, because I didn't grow up here, but I feel as if I belong here. I hope I never have to move off."

Madaket had come into the room during the conversation, and as she bent toward Gardner with her platter of caviar on creamed cheese and toast, she smiled at his words.

"You know what I'm talking about, Madaket, don't you?" he asked.

She nodded. "Yes. I know."

"It is the strangest thing about this island," Morris observed. "I swear, sometimes it seems to me that people get chosen by the island rather than the other way round."

"What a remarkable thought, dear," June said, turning to him in surprise.

"Perhaps that explains why there are so many artistic souls here," Claude interjected. "I'm sure we must have more than the normal share per capita of artists, musicians, magicians, actors. You know, I sometimes fancy that all these visions of beauty, of the fine things accomplished, incorporate themselves into the very air and somehow make the island more beautiful."

Justin laughed drily. "Manhattan island's got its share of artists, and it's not exactly increasing in beauty."

"Sorry, Claude," John agreed, "your theory's a little too dreamy for me."

"If you were in the real estate business, Claude," Bob added, "you'd think more realistically. The wealthiest people, who buy the largest and most beautiful plots of land, are hardly artistic. They want nothing more than to divide the land and sell it off for profit. If you think spiritual output affects the atmosphere, then I'd say it's a wonder that the land stays as beautiful as it does."

John nodded. "Every year there are more condoms scattered on the moors and candy bar wrappers scattered on the beach."

"Oh, John," Tory said softly, putting her hand on his knee as if to gently restrain him.

But he persevered, "This island is headed for trouble. No matter how much you romanticize the relationship between population and territory, the facts are that the people are continuing the process they began two hundred years ago of destroying the island environment."

"Well, that's a little strong," Morris protested.

"Excuse me," Madaket said from the doorway. "If you could continue your discussion in the dining room, dinner is ready."

Everyone rose and passed through the hallway and into the room Madaket had made especially beautiful for the evening. The long mahogany table was decorated with autumn leaves, berries, and nuts in a brass bowl, and tall orange tapers burned on the table and fireplace mantel and sideboard, bathing the room in a gentle, generous light. The wine Madaket poured into the crystal glasses looked like light turned liquid. A heated conversation continued as Madaket brought out creamy clam chowder, and poached salmon with fresh berry chutney, and a salad of her own lettuces. The dessert was a triumph: Indian pudding baked in a pumpkin, served with cinnamon whipped cream.

Madaket and Todd both served, and poured the red or white wines and the dessert champagne. As the evening deepened, Joanna leaned back in her chair and simply watched and listened. Outside, the wind was rising, weaving around the house in arabesques, singing against the corners of the house. Occasionally the candle flames flared sideways, as if blown by an invisible gust. The room smelled of salt air, pumpkin, cinnamon, and coffee. The cheeks of her guests were hollowed deeply in the candlelight, and the liquid of their eyes glowed against the pallor of their skin. Todd and Madaket were the most in shadow, and as they came near to serve and faded away into the darkness, Joanna saw how Madaket looked at Todd. Everything was there at once: the need, the passion, the adoration, the sexual craving—so painfully strong that Joanna had to look away. She had loved

Carter in just that way. She put her hands on her stomach.
Well, and she was glad.

She drank no alcohol, but by the end of the evening, it
seemed as if she had. Her vision blurred at the edges, and a
slight headache tightened itself across her forehead, pushing
in at her temples. It was all she could do to make her way
across the hall into the living room, where her guests gathered for after-dinner brandies and more conversation. Supported by the arms of the wing chair, she sat nodding and
smiling vaguely at everyone, too exhausted to keep track of
what was actually being said. She thought her guests would
never leave. When finally they did, Madaket helped her up
the stairs and into bed.

"Todd and I are going to clean up, but we'll work quietly,"
Madaket said.

"You could hold a dance and I wouldn't know," Joanna
groaned, sliding gratefully between the covers.

She fell asleep at once. Her sleep was deep and matted and
dreamless and suddenly she awoke, racked with thirst. The
night was black, the house dark and quiet. She wanted more
than water, she needed juice, orange juice, gallons of it. Slipping out of bed, she padded across her bedroom and out
into the hall, the floor pleasantly cool to the soles of her feet.
It seemed simply too long a detour to walk all the way to the
front of the hall and down the wide front staircase, and so,
holding on tightly to the railing, she began to descend the
steep back staircase directly to the kitchen.

Voices stopped her. Madaket. Todd.

She started to push the door open to the kitchen, but then
the blurred music of their talk clarified into words.

"What would you do if you suddenly had the money?"
Todd asked.

Madaket answered at once. "Buy a piece of land and build
a house."

"Me, too." Todd sounded young and less cynical than
usual. "It's not impossible. That we'd find treasure here.
Think of the *Andrea Doria*. Can I have another beer?"

"Sure." The refrigerator door was opened and closed.
"Here."

"Thanks. Look, Abraham Farthingale said there was treasure in this house. No one's ever found it. Dad and I have

checked every wall or floor of this house and found nothing strange. It's got to be down in the cellar."

"Yes, but even if we do find anything else, it won't be ours, Todd."

"Come on, Madaket. Joanna's generous. Hell, she should be. She's rich. I bet she'd let us have some part of it, just a little part. That's all we'd need." Todd lowered his voice. "Besides, if we do find more jewels lying down there, what's to stop us from slipping one or two into our pockets?"

"Todd, that would be stealing."

"From whom? Joanna? Why should she get it all, she already has more than she needs. If it's there in the sand, it should belong to whoever finds it."

Joanna heard movements, chairs creaking, clothing shifting. Now Todd was almost whispering. Joanna had to strain to hear. She wished the door were a one-way mirror.

"We could change our lives."

"I won't steal from Joanna."

"Madaket, get off it. You're just the freaking hired help here, even if you do call her Joanna instead of Miss Jones. Just because you live here, that only makes you the live-in housekeeper. You know how the summer people are." Todd minced in a falsetto: "I've just got to have a live-in. Any other kind of help is just *too* unreliable!"

"Joanna's not like that."

"Don't fool yourself. She's not going to give you anything more than your pay. What's happened with the rubies *we* found? She hasn't mentioned them. We go down in the sand, getting all dirty, working at night. Whose island is this anyway? Hers, just because she came along and wrote a check?"

"I don't know why the devil is always depicted with dark hair and eyes, Todd Snow." Madaket's voice was fondly scolding.

"Madaket. You're so beautiful."

"Todd. Don't."

"Madaket. Get real. It's you and me, against the rest of them. Think about it. You know I'm right."

"Todd—"

"Your skin is so smooth."

"Don't, Todd."

"I could make you happy, Madaket. I could love you."

A long silence pulled at Joanna's senses. Then, whispers, whimpers, low sounds with only one interpretation. Then a scuffle.

"Go home, Todd. I'm going to bed."

"Let me come with you."

"No."

Madaket's voice came near the door to the back stairs, and Joanna, wanting not to be caught eavesdropping, pushed herself up and awkwardly hurried back up to the second floor. She paused at the top, heart thudding. She heard Todd say, "Madaket. Just think about what I said. At least think about me."

Joanna couldn't hear Madaket's reply.

Nearly running, Joanna reached her bedroom and collapsed onto her bed. She simply sat for a while, letting her heart slow down, catching her breath. She was still thirsty. She drank the entire glass of water from her bedside table, then lay down on her side and, wrapping her arms protectively around her babies, stared out into the darkened room. After a long time she heard the light whispering of Madaket's feet as she climbed the stairs from the first floor and then went on up into the attic. Still later, she heard Madaket hurry on tiptoe down the stairs and out into the waiting night.

Nineteen

When Joanna awoke the next morning, it was after eleven. She had a persistent, heavy headache, and she felt swollen all over, her bones like twigs encased in numbed cushions of flesh.

Madaket peered in the open door.

"You're awake!" She approached Joanna's bed. "Would you like some coffee? Or juice?"

"Please. I feel terrible."

Madaket went off and came back a short while later with a breakfast tray. Joanna had managed to get to the bathroom and even to brush her teeth, but changing from her wrinkled gown was impossible.

"Drink this," Madaket said. "It will help." While Joanna obeyed, she said, "I went into town this morning and took Justin to the airport. He said to tell you goodbye and to thank you for the party."

"The dinner was great, Madaket. Thanks."

Madaket peered at Joanna. "You really don't feel well, do you?"

"I had trouble sleeping last night."

"Did I wake you up when I went out?" Madaket looked worried.

"No," Joanna lied.

"I try to be quiet. I love being outside at night, especially this time of year. The air is like crystal."

"I don't think I'll get up today. I think I'll try to sleep."

"Good. First you really should drink this orange juice. Gardner said—"

"I know what Gardner said!" Joanna snapped, and feeling churlish and at the same time saintly for repressing the anger which was welling up inside her, she grabbed up the glass of juice and drank it so rapidly some spilled down her chin and onto her gown.

"Let me help you change gowns," Madaket offered, and leaned forward, but Joanna waved her away.

"Never mind. I can sleep in a soiled gown. What does it matter?" She closed her eyes and lay back against her pillows.

Madaket took the tray and went away. A short while later she quietly returned, and Joanna could hear the ice tinkling in the pitcher Madaket set on the table next to her, but she didn't open her eyes.

All day long, Joanna drowsed on and off, trying to rid herself of an incessant, heavy headache. She felt anxious and unhappy, and couldn't seem to separate her emotions from her physical discomforts. Vaguely she heard the Snowmen working down in the sunroom. Gnawing, staccato pains of hunger began to counterpoint the deeper black pooling drum of nausea.

"Joanna?"

"Mmm?" She opened her eyes to find Madaket kneeling next to the bed. "What time is it?"

"About three o'clock."

Wolf was right beside Madaket, trembling and whimpering. Joanna pushed up onto her elbows. "What's wrong?"

"Someone's here to see you," Madaket whispered.

"Well, who is it?" Joanna threw the covers back and stretched.

Madaket rose and pulled Joanna to her feet. "It's a man," she said. "You'll probably want to comb your hair."

"Why, Madaket, your hands are freezing!" Joanna exclaimed. "What's going on? Who is it?"

"He said his name is Carter Amberson."

Joanna clutched Madaket's arm. "You're kidding."

"No."

"Oh, God, oh, Madaket! He came!" Her heart raced with joy.

"He doesn't look happy," Madaket warned her.

"He never does," Joanna replied, smiling. "Help me up."

Joy had spontaneously ignited sparklers of energy inside her and she rose from her bed and hurried into the bathroom to wash her face and brush her hair. "Get my long red sweater," she told Madaket. Sliding onto the bench in front of her dressing table, she grabbed up a brush and powder and lipstick and set to work.

Madaket stood behind her, watching. "He said he's in a hurry. He's got a plane to catch."

Joanna laughed. "If he's gone to the trouble of finding me, he's not going to rush off. That's just Carter's way of making sure you understand how important he is. There. I look as good as I can, don't you think?" She smiled, triumphant.

"You look beautiful. I'll help you down the stairs."

"Great. And then—come back up and tidy my bedroom."

"Joanna—"

"Put clean sheets on the bed. The ivory set."

"Joanna, I really think—"

But they had started their descent, and both women went silent as they saw Carter. Pacing the front hall in his herringbone overcoat, a glossy leather briefcase clutched in his hand, he looked as if he were waiting to board a shuttle. At the sound of Joanna's steps, he turned and stood watching as she descended, leaning heavily on Madaket. His eyes shone fiercely cold and as blue as an arctic sea. He didn't speak until Joanna reached the final step and the hallway. Then he said, "Hello, Joanna." He didn't move to kiss or touch her. The bunched fist of flesh she'd privately called his boxing glove protruded from his chin, a sure sign that he was angry, and ready for a fight. He was not here, then, for romantic reasons. Joanna took a deep breath.

"Hello, Carter. Thanks, Madaket. Shall we go into the living room? Would you like a drink?"

"No. Thank you." Carter followed Joanna. Madaket flew back up the stairs.

Joanna sank into an easy chair and gestured to Carter to do the same. "Won't you take off your coat?"

"No. I'm not going to be here very long." He sat on the edge of the sofa across from her.

"Oh?" She was trying hard not to break into a wide smile of sheer pleasure at the sight of this man she had loved so much, and still loved so deeply. She'd forgotten how handsome he was, how shining, like a creature more angelic than human. Finally he'd found her. "How did you find out where I was?"

"The Kaufmans saw you over Labor Day weekend. Joanna, I think you owe me some kind of explanation."

"I think you're looking at the explanation, Carter."

"You're pregnant."

"With twins."

"They're mine?"

"Of course!"

"Why didn't you tell me?"

Joanna dropped her eyes. "I thought you'd want me to have an abortion."

"You were right. I would have."

That hurt. She flashed her eyes back up at his face. "Why are you here, Carter?"

"I wanted to see if the rumors were true. Which, obviously, they are. And I wanted to get some things clear with you."

"What things?"

"I want it understood that I will not claim these children. They will have no access to my money or any claim to my estate. They—"

"Carter, for Christ's sake!" Joanna exploded, leaning forward in her chair. "What is your problem? What do you think I've been doing for the past few months, following you around on my knees?"

"I think you've been playing a game," Carter replied icily. "I just wanted to be certain you know I'm not playing it with you."

They stared at each other in silence. But Joanna had seen this expression on Carter's face so many times before. He had found her, had come to her; she couldn't believe she couldn't break through to him.

"Carter. Love. Don't worry. I have no intention of asking you for anything. I have no intention of asking you to leave Blair. I—"

"Joanna, I've left Blair. I thought you knew."

Her heart leapt with joy. "Oh, darling!"

"I'm going to marry Gloria."

His words came like a kick in her abdomen. For a moment

she couldn't speak. When her breath came back, she said, forcing herself to speak lightly, "Gloria Breck? Why, Carter, she's just a child!"

"On the contrary, Joanna, she's a capable and ambitious young woman."

Joanna stared into Carter's eyes and saw that he was serious. Her heart twisted. "Well, then, congratulations."

He responded with a brusque, irritated nod. "So you see why I want to be sure we understand each other."

"Yes." Now she wanted only not to humiliate herself further.

"I did not want these babies conceived. I do not want them born."

"Fine. I'm not asking—"

"When they are born, I don't want to see them or know anything about them. I don't care if they're male or female or hermaphrodite Siamese twins."

"Really, Carter, there's no need to be cruel—"

"I don't want my name on their birth certificates. I don't want them to know anything about me. I don't want them to know my name."

"Carter, I didn't ever intend—"

"I don't care if they live or die. They have nothing to do with me."

"Stop it!" She wanted to be dignified, but she was trembling. "That's enough!"

"I think you should go now." Madaket was standing in the door, Wolf close by her side, his lips curled, his teeth bared, small growls rumbling in his throat.

Carter stood, a great shadow looming over Joanna. "I mean it, Joanna. Everything I said."

"Yes, I know you do, Carter." Joanna raised her head to look at him, letting her anger and sorrow show clearly on her face. Carter looked down at her, his face unreadable. Then he walked off. Joanna heard the front door open and close, heard the spatter of gravel as the car roared off.

"Are you all right, Joanna?" Madaket came quietly into the room.

"Yes. I just need to be alone awhile, please."

"Can I get you anything to drink?"

"No. No, thank you, Madaket."

"I'll just be in the kitchen, then."

Joanna leaned back in her chair and closed her eyes. Her head ached horribly. She'd never imagined anything like this. She'd imagined herself alone, having left Carter, and she'd imagined herself and Carter reunited—oh, she'd imagined that in so many different ways. But this! Well, of course she'd been a fool not to prepare for this. She knew Carter always liked to have the last word. She should have known he would not let her be the one to leave him.

But Gloria Breck.

Carter was leaving his wife for Gloria Breck.

That manipulative, phony little twit.

She realized her hands were strangling the arms of the chair. Her body felt almost rigid with anger and grief. She wanted to throw things. She wanted to howl.

After a while, she pushed herself up from the chair and with great effort made her way into the hall. She pulled on a coat and scarf and mittens. "Madaket," she called, "I'm going out for a walk."

She stepped out the French doors. The brilliant late September afternoon shocked her, almost assaulted her with its sharp clear beauty. Today the world seemed such a profoundly clear and beautiful thing, and she felt ugly and muddled and ill and useless within it. Conflicting desires tore at her. She needed to lie down. She wanted to run.

Picking her way through the prickly *Rosa rugosa,* now speckled with red rose hips, she made her way to the beach. The sunlight on the dancing dark blue ocean, the capricious wind, all seemed particularly intense and Joanna realized that this was because she was in a crisis now, at one of those climaxes of life when everything becomes intensely real and vivid. She would always remember this day.

Far out at sea a fishing boat bobbed, its masts and shrouds flashing like a code, the sun glancing off at such a low angle that sometimes the boat seemed to disappear from sight. It could be an illusion, the boat, just as Carter's love had been an illusion. Joanna had been a fool—or had been fooled. For in her deepest heart she'd believed that the love between her and Carter was real and would never vanish. Even though she'd never admitted it to herself, the entire time she was running away from Carter, she secretly thought he was going to find her. Claim her. She'd believed he would be the one person in all her life who would say: you belong to me. I belong to you. Now she walked down the beach toward the water, illusionless, in defeat, and achingly alone.

Far out on the water the fishing boat rose and fell on the waves, flickering and vanishing in the bright light as the huge white sun sank lower on the horizon. It made her dizzy to watch the rocking boat. Really, she was in terrible pain, terrible, terrible pain, pain of such intimacy she was ashamed. Sinking to her knees, she wailed, and toppled over, a great useless balloon of a thing. Her cries were lost in the roar of the surf.

How long she lay in the sand she didn't know, but when she looked up, the sun was lower; the fishing boat was really gone. It was colder. She was still in pain. She tried to push herself up and an arrow of agony shot through her body, and she yelped like a wounded beast.

"Oh, no," she whispered. "Oh, body, *no.*" For something was wrong. Something was going on, and the pain was relentless.

"Madaket!"

She didn't think she could stand. She knew she had to get back to the house. She tried to crawl.

"Madaket!"

Between flashes of pain she inched her way up the beach, away from the ocean's roar.

"Madaket!"

This could not be happening to her. She had been so careful, so prepared. She was healthy, she'd taken good care of herself—the pain folded her in on herself relentlessly, and she collapsed on the sand, moaning, her arms hugging her belly. When it retreated, sinking back like a tide, she lifted her head and yelled as loudly as she could.

"Madaket!"

Wolf came running down the beach, wagging his tail, whimpering, eyes fraught with worry.

"Get Madaket," Joanna begged.

Finally she saw Madaket running down the path to her, her black hair flying up behind her like wings. Madaket sank to her knees, cradling Joanna's head in her arms. "I'm here.

I'm going to call the doctor. You'll be all right." But there were tears in her eyes. Then everything went dark.

She opened her eyes to see Gardner and Madaket and Wolf all crowded around her. A blanket had been thrown over her, and the satin trim brushed her chin. Beneath her the sand was gritty and cool. The sun was almost gone. She felt her belly contract with the mute stony hardness of a shelled creature.

"Gardner! What's happening?" she asked.

"You've started labor," Gardner told her. Gently he massaged her hands. The last of the light seemed to catch in his blond curls, giving him a halo. He smelled of mint. "An ambulance is on the way."

"My babies—"

"They'll be okay. Don't worry."

"But it's too early!"

"I know. But we can slow it down. Maybe stop it."

"Gardner—" she implored in a whisper, and he bent close to her. "I'm afraid."

"Don't be. I'm here."

"The ambulance," Madaket cried, and Joanna heard the sand rasp as Madaket spurted up the path to the drive. A few minutes later she returned with two young men.

Gardner rose. "Joanna, they're here with the stretcher. Relax. They know what they're doing."

With a gentle, professional speed, Joanna was lifted onto the stretcher. Closing her eyes against a wave of pain, she inhaled a potpourri of good male odors: garlic, beer, sweat, clean clothes, soap. Normal, healthy life. They strapped her in. Madaket took one hand and Gardner took the other.

"Oh, Madaket," Joanna moaned. "I hurt."

Madaket looked at Gardner. "Can't you do anything?"

"We need to get her into the hospital. Then we'll see."

Joanna felt herself being carried like some sort of pagan flesh offering through the fresh air, Wolf circling the group and whining, the last streaks of sunlight dimming above her. With Gardner and Madaket holding her hands, her terror faded into a quiet anxiety. Her stomach hardened, seeming to rise to a point, and she felt staked down by it, the hub of an inexorable wheel.

As she was slid into the ambulance, she was so frightened

she cried out. "Gardner, can Madaket ride with me?"

"She'll follow in the Jeep. I'll be with you, Joanna." Gardner stepped into the mechanical cave. The door slammed with a metallic finality. A light flicked on above her, exposing a cargo of instruments, masks, canisters, and rubber hoses.

"I hate all this," she said.

Gardner held her hands. "It's new to you, that's all. And this stuff is all just necessary equipment." He stopped talking to time her contraction, then launched into an anecdote. "The first twins I ever delivered . . ."

Joanna listened to Gardner, not really hearing him, but comforted by his presence. He was trying to assuage her fears, and she was grateful to him. They arrived at the hospital; she could tell by the lights and the way the ambulance slowed. Joanna's heart skidded with a sudden fear. The back doors of the ambulance opened. She grasped Gardner's hands.

"I'm so frightened," she whispered.

"You'll be fine," he told her. He shouted orders to the ambulance attendants. Then he stepped back and Joanna was lifted out into the night.

In the hospital, for at least an hour, people fussed over her helpless body, taking off her clothes, draping her in a hospital gown, poking and pricking her, squeezing cold gel on her belly. Madaket had been asked to wait in the hall; and from time to time Joanna could see her black hair as she hovered near the doorway.

Gardner returned to the room, garbed in white. He stood at the end of her bed, talking in a low voice to the nurses. He bent over Joanna and listened to her belly, felt her pulse. His hands were strong and clean and efficient.

"How do you feel?" he asked.

"Like the bride of Frankenstein," Joanna told him, glaring down at the number of tubes and attachments protruding from her body.

Gardner smiled and perched on the side of her bed. "Here's the situation. You're in preterm labor, but we're getting that under control. That IV in your left arm is Terbutaline, which will slow and we hope stop your labor. But it will also make you feel a little jittery, and it will speed up your pulse, so if you notice that, don't worry. We've also injected you with be-tamethasone, which will help your babies' lungs mature."

"—my babies—"

"—are both all right. We're going to keep the fetal moni-tor on you so we can chart their heartbeats. We've got two strong heartbeats, so your babies are just fine. But your blood pressure's high and you've got a little toxemia, so we need to keep an eye on that. We took some blood so we can check on some things, and we're running a test to check for protein in your urine. You've got a catheter in right now. For the next day or so, I want you to have complete bed rest. And no food, in case you end up going into labor anyway. That IV on your left arm is just sugar water and saline to keep your system in shape."

"Are my babies in danger?"

"I don't think so. But we want to give them every extra day we can to develop before they're born. The best thing you can do for them now is just to rest."

"Can Madaket stay with me?"

"Would you like that?"

"Yes. I wouldn't feel so alone here."

"All right, then. We'll put her down as your closest rela-tive. And of course if you need anything, or feel anything that worries you, just press this button."

"How long will I be in here?"

Gardner shrugged. "We'll see. A few days to start with until we're sure everything's under control. We'll take it a day at a time. For now, the best thing you can do is rest."

Joanna dutifully closed her eyes. She heard Madaket come into the room, and when the young woman pulled a chair close to the bed and sank into it, Joanna breathed a sigh of relief and sank into sleep.

Twenty

*J*oanna lay flat on her back in her hospital room, wired and monitored and charted like some sort of volcanic mound about to erupt. The tubes, needles, IV bags, and all the other shining technological apparatus of lifesaving frightened her at first, yet soon became oddly comforting, reminding her of the cables, meters, microphones, and equipment used in taping *Fabulous Homes.* The hard part for her was simply lying there, a thing, helpless as she drifted in her fate.

During the first five days of her stay, friends came often to visit, Pat or June or Claude, bringing with them fresh air and flowers, but her reaction to even those gentle excitements caused her blood pressure to rise and the nurses to fuss and scowl. Madaket's presence seemed to soothe her, or at least not to elevate her monitors, so Madaket stayed in the room almost constantly, slipping home to tend the animals when June or Pat came in. Madaket read to her, brushed her hair, or sometimes only sat next to her, watching television. When Joanna woke at night, she found it a great comfort and companionship that Madaket was always there, sleeping on a cot provided by the hospital. When Joanna opened her eyes and looked at Madaket's sleeping form, the young woman would awaken, too, immediately alert, concerned.

"Joanna, are you all right?" Her eyes would gleam in the dark.

"I'm fine," Joanna would answer, and they'd both snuggle back into their covers. Madaket would fall back asleep. Joanna could hear the soft rustle of her breathing.

Quietly Joanna would run her hands over her abdomen.

The Chorus Girl would kick and the Swimmer roll in reply. Sometimes she envisioned the future: her babies toddling on the beach, the ocean rippling and gleaming in front of them, her perfect house rising behind them like a shield. The Chorus Girl would be a handful: rebellious, difficult, energetic, and obstinate. She would like to dress up in Joanna's clothes, pretending she was a queen. The Swimmer would be tranquil and poetic, a musical child. He would play with miniature knights and dragons, castles and steeds; he would play piano and baseball and he would swim in the water like a dolphin. Together the three of them would learn to sail.

Many hours Joanna simply slept, but in the long deep center of the nights she found herself awake, and after reassuring Madaket, and watching Madaket fall back asleep, Joanna would lie staring at the moon-yellow glow of light levitating over the clean swirled linoleum floor of the hallway. She closed her eyes when the nurses came in on their rounds, not wanting to worry them or obligate them to stay to chat with her, and often as these women came near her to check a monitor or tuck in a bit of blanket, the whispering puff of air, scented with perfume and clean womanly flesh, and the exquisitely light sense of an intelligent presence and of concerned, concentrated caring would pass over her just like the gentle brushing of the sleeve of her mother's quilted peach-hued satin robe had so long ago. Then she would remember being very young, and physically small, so little that her mother could carry her, and did carry her, up the stairs of strange houses and into strange bedrooms. In those days Joanna was allowed to begin her night's sleep in her mother's bed, her face pressed into the familiar scent and feel of her mother's nightgown. Later her mother would come up and move Joanna to another bed, sometimes one in the same room, sometimes in another room, and then she would gently tuck Joanna in with much the same tender vigilance that these nurses showed. Had her own mother loved her with the ferocity Joanna felt for these unborn babies? She must have, Joanna decided, to give up her figure and its seductive powers for nine months and then to take her with her everywhere she traveled.

She had never stayed with her father when she was very small, only when she was a big girl, seven or eight, and by then they were unaccustomed to each other's presence and touch and always slightly embarrassed and even wary of each other. Her father had not been a demonstrative man. When after an absence of nine months he greeted her as she stepped off a plane in New York, he never reached for her or hugged her. He said only, "Hello, Joanna. How nice to see you again."

Some of his girlfriends were friendly, some were even maternal toward Joanna, but by then Joanna knew better than to let herself grow fond of any of her father's women. He was never with any one for very long, and it took all of Joanna's emotional resources simply to keep up with the turbulence of her mother's life. She always arrived at her father's new place stunned and exhausted, with no reserves left over for investing emotions in women she would know only briefly in her life. The later women complained to Joanna's father that Joanna was cold; Joanna heard what they said as she pretended to sleep, curled in a guest room or on a pull-out sofa. "She's always been that way," her father replied, and at first this made Joanna want to rise up from her temporary bed, wrap a blanket around her like a protective cape, and rush in to confront her father and force him to take back his words. She was not cold! She had never been cold! In her heart she boiled with emotions, anger and love and fear and longing, oh, such a deep wide tearing desire to have her father just once in his life look down at her and say, "My daughter. My beautiful child."

She never confronted her father. She knew too well in advance that nothing would be gained. She knew this because she'd overheard so many scenes very much like the one about which she fantasized played out between her father and one of his furiously frustrated women. "What do you want?" they would cry, or "What can I do?" "Must you go out tonight?" was the first sign; when Joanna heard a woman ask her father that, and heard her father reply with scarcely smothered fury, "I'm sorry, but I do have to meet with the hospital administrator, I never have time during the day, I'm always seeing patients or operating, if this is too difficult for you, I'll simply have to move out, I've never lied to you, I've always told you my work must come first with me—these people, if you could only see these poor damaged people, faces scarred by fire or birth, you wouldn't begrudge me a few hours by myself in a hospital conference room with a bunch of bald-headed old bureaucrats." "He's lying," Joanna wanted to say to the woman; "he's meeting someone else, a nurse perhaps, or a former patient, believe me, I know." But she would never tell on her father. What good would it have done? She would instead be especially agreeable when her father's woman offered to take her out to a movie or shopping. She would tell the woman how pretty she was.

Joanna had known that her father was an unusual man, a man with an enormous ego and voracious sexual needs. She knew other men stayed married and faithful; she saw these men occasionally; some were married to her mother's friends. But she didn't count on having such a man, a man both faithful and desirable, appear in her life. She had vowed to herself at an early age not to make the mistake of expecting such a miracle to happen to her.

Although Joanna had slept with men before Carter, and had even been fond of or infatuated with some of them, not until Carter had she felt that deep pull and tug of connection which she thought was love. Sometimes as they lay together in bed, legs entwined, bodies joined at the groin, lips swollen with kissing and wet with saliva, hands locked, every finger interlaced, they would look in each other's eyes with such honesty and shamelessness that Joanna would feel that the two of them were one, one radiant creature, joined eternally, two halves of a whole. This proud, profoundly intimate, certain love flowed in a warm dazzling liquid rush through her veins and into the smallest, most secret places of her body and soul.

Had it been false? Did Carter's present rejection of all they had together obliterate the past?

No. The world moved on, and love between two people was after all only another kind of activity within the world. The sea might wash over a rock, but that did not mean that the rock had not once been there, was not somehow still deeply there, however hidden by salt water. Her parents had not loved each other long, but they had loved each other once, and here she was. Carter did not love her now, but he had loved her once, she believed that, and here were these living children within her. And she was strong enough to go ahead, to love her children, to be, all by herself, enough for them. She would not let the present cold cancel out past heat—the process could be reversed, she could bring warmth to what had once been chilled and shadowed. Had she not spent the past few months restoring the luster and life and dignity to her house? All by herself she'd found and paid for and restored that wonderful house, and she would inhabit it with her babies, she would live there in the present, and plan and look toward the future, and that was more than sufficient, that was everything. Time and death and darkness would eventually come for them all and dark moments and despair would wash over them as it did in the lives of all people, but she would live with her babies in her house, in their shelter, in their rock, and when the black tide of life swept over them, she would pull shut the curtains and light a fire and read her children stories, until the dark retreated and she could open her curtains and open her windows and once again let in fresh air and light.

Now as she lay in the hospital, feeling beneath the dome of her body her babies move, but move less than usual, feeling her blood pressure rise with worry, she thought endlessly about these things. Her thoughts ran incessantly, engraving themselves into her very heart. As her babies moved within the vault of her body, she determined to be faithful to these children in a way her parents had never been faithful to her. She would love these babies, she would endure for them. She would close her eyes and hold very still so that the nausea would not well up within her. She would not, and did not, tell Gardner that she was growing daily more nauseated, that she could not swallow food but dumped it down the toilet or into flower vases, that she often felt faint and dizzy even when lying down. She willed herself to be all right. She demanded of herself, she demanded of the universe, that these two babies, so little to ask after all, in a world overpopulated with children, that these two babies live and thrive and be born out of her body and into her arms and her life.

Sometimes she heard from down the hall, which in the Nantucket Cottage Hospital was not very long, the cries of a woman in labor, and then the chillingly eerie and beautiful wail of a newborn babe. Sometimes then she would shake with desire and fear and Madaket would put down her book and approach her bed and lean over and hug Joanna, whispering in her ear, "You'll be all right. Your babies will be all right."

One afternoon a nurse entered, checked Joanna, and left quickly, her mouth grim. A few minutes later Gardner came in. Swiftly he examined Joanna and the monitors, then took her hand and said, "Okay, Joanna, here's the situation. We're going to do a C-section now." As he spoke, Madaket rose and came to take Joanna's other hand. "We're concerned because the heart tone of one of your babies is dropping."

"What does that mean?" Joanna asked.

"It means a baby's in danger."

Her heart thumped. "Will they be okay?"

"I hope so, Joanna. We'll do our best."

"Can Madaket come in with me? Please? Gardner, I'm afraid."

Gardner looked at Madaket. "All right. Go find the nurse. She'll give you some scrubs."

Things began to blur. Joanna was lifted onto a gurney, wheeled into the operating room, and moved onto a table under a bright light. Soft-voiced strangers helped her to sit, and steadied her with her legs hanging down and her head slumping forward as they administered the spinal. She tried not to imagine the intrusion of the needle into her delicate core. Her mouth filled with bile, and jagged clouds of black and gray pressed against her eyes.

Madaket came in, the dark brilliance of her eyes framed by the green cap and face mask. She put her hands on Joanna's shoulders, smiling, saying, "Isn't this exciting! You're about to meet your babies!" But Joanna could sense the tension in the room.

With Madaket's help, they lowered Joanna back down onto the table. The anesthetist pierced her vein. An icy numbness spread up her legs and through her belly. Gardner worked with quick, certain movements, his blue eyes dark with concentration. A draped section was placed between her breasts and her belly, shielding her from the sight of her abdomen being cut into and pulled apart so that the babies could be lifted out. Something deep inside seemed to tug at her heart.

She couldn't help but sense that something was wrong. Her heart turned inside out with fear. Then the electric power seemed to fail, for the lights flared and dimmed, and appeared to be falling toward her. She called out to Madaket, "What's happening?" but realized that her sounds didn't form coherent words. Madaket disappeared. Faces clothed in white bent over her. Jets of icy cold spurted through her hands and feet. Her throat sucked at her mouth, pulling it down. Just before her eyes rolled back in her head, she understood that she was going into convulsions.

"Joanna."

Faces floated at her from thick clouds.

"Joanna. Can you talk to us?"

Her eyelids were heavy. The world whirled at her with dizzying speed. She was afraid she was going to vomit. She felt sick. She wanted only to sleep.

"Joanna. Hi."

As the room swam into view, she realized that it was night, for through the window the sky showed black. She couldn't imagine how she'd slept so soundly in a room blazing with so much white light. Even the people gathered around her seemed to be iridescent, flickering. Madaket was there, and a strange nurse, and Gardner. And a shadow, a dark blur, like a blot in the air.

"My babies?"

She spoke before she thought, and as she spoke, she looked down. She was tucked quite tidily into soft blankets and so she imagined rather than saw her body, sliced and stapled, bathed and bandaged. She was in pain, she was groggy, and there were still IVs in her arms.

But where were her babies?

"Hold out your arms."

She did as directed. A nurse folded pillows beneath her arms to support them. Gardner handed her a small soft bundle.

Inside the blankets, a small rosy face gleamed. Two dark blue eyes looked up at her with an expression of infinite calm. The baby's tiny fists rested beneath its chin, and as Joanna studied it, the baby stretched its limbs in a long, languorous, fluid movement, then nestled against Joanna, its serene face turning toward Joanna's breast.

"Meet your son," Gardner said.

Tears flooded Joanna's eyes. "It's the Swimmer!" she said. "Oh, isn't he perfect!"

"He is. Four pounds eight ounces. A healthy size. He'll need a little time in the incubator before you take him home. He's a preemie and needs to build up his lungs. But other than that, he's a healthy baby."

Joanna looked up at Gardner. "And where—?"

She saw the tears well in Madaket's eyes and didn't need to finish the sentence.

"She didn't make it, Joanna," he said. "I'm sorry. There was nothing we could do. The umbilical cord was around her neck."

"It was a girl?"

"Yes."

"It was the Chorus Girl!" Joanna cried. "Oh, no!"

"I'm sorry. She was stillborn."

"Can I see her?"

Gardner nodded. A nurse left the room. Another nurse took the Swimmer from Joanna. The nurse returned with a bundle and handed it to Joanna. Opening the blankets, she looked in to see a perfect baby, tiny, exquisite, lovely, and blue.

"Her color is off because when the cord was wrapped around her neck, she was deprived of oxygen," a nurse informed her.

"That was why she was kicking so," Joanna said. "She was trying to change positions—but there was no more room—"

"There are many different reasons for this," Gardner said. "It's something we can't control."

Joanna wrapped her hand around the Chorus Girl's fist. It was cold, hard, a little ridged stone. But she could not stop looking at the baby, as if the warmth of her love, and the sheer enormity of her longing, would make the baby come back to life. Pulling back the blankets, she saw that the nurses had dressed the baby in a white cotton sleeper, and that human gesture, of garbing the stillborn child for its few moments on earth, twisted Joanna's heart.

She closed her eyes. Let this not be real. Let it all go back to yesterday. Please.

"Your little boy's fussing a bit. Would you like to try nursing him?" the nurse asked.

"Not yet. I'm still—" She stroked the pale cold face. She bent her head and nestled her warm cheek against the tiny lifeless perfect head.

"Joanna. You need to take care of your baby now." Gardner reached out to remove Joanna's dead daughter from her arms.

"No. Not yet."

"Joanna, you can see her again. But your little boy needs you now."

"No," Joanna insisted. "I want to keep her." She clutched the baby against her, and for a moment was overcome with a rushing flood of longing to have this baby, her little girl, back inside her again, safe, alive, kicking. Peering up at Gardner and Madaket, she recognized concern in their eyes.

"You can give her a name," the nurse said. "For the birth certificate."

"Thank you," Joanna said. Somehow, oddly, that helped. She surrendered her daughter to Gardner, who accepted the baby as carefully, cradling the little head in his hand, as if she were alive, as if it mattered if her tiny neck wobbled.

As the Swimmer was settled back in her arms, a cold and numbing despair wrapped around her heart. This was the wrong child to live, she thought, I would have liked the Chorus Girl better. I wanted a daughter. What will I do with a son?—then she hated herself for such thoughts and tried to shut them away from her consciousness.

"What are you going to name your baby?" Gardner asked.

Joanna shook her head. "I don't know."

Madaket came next to the bed and put her finger into the diminutive fist. "He's so beautiful."

"I'll leave you now," Gardner said. "The nurse will show you how to feed your baby. He won't get much nutrition yet, but the closeness will be good for him."

But as Joanna went through the motions, letting the nurse undo her gown and position the baby just so in her arms, watching as her son, her living child, searched blindly for her nipple, then found it, and latched onto it firmly with his mouth and sucked, as Joanna heard the nurse exclaim, "Oh, what a smart little fellow you are!" she seemed to hear and see and feel all of this, even the bite of the baby's mouth on her nipple, as if from behind a barricade of sorrow. It was not a whole, entire sensation. It did not have the quality of reality.

The day after the birth, nurses helped Joanna out of her bed and into a chair, where she sat, groggy and stupid with the aftereffect of the anesthesia used during the delivery. In the afternoon they began to take her for hourly walks, drunken, painful little shuffles out into the corridor, then down the corridor, a longer way each time. Gradually her mind cleared while her body remained a clumsy, heavy bulk dragging from her shoulders.

The nurses brought her her son, and she held him as he slept or gazed up at her with his wide unfocused look. Her milk had not come in yet, and her breasts felt hard and uncomfortable against his small supple body. In spite of herself, she kept sagging; without the use of her abdominal muscles it took immense effort to sit holding him, and she often was afraid she would simply slump over and crash onto the floor.

"You'll feel more like yourself tomorrow when more of the drugs have worn off," the nurse promised.

In the very early morning of the next day the nurses came bustling in with their charts and thermometers and sharp anesthetic aroma. Madaket woke from her sleep on the cot against the wall, and stretched and yawned and came to Joanna's bedside.

"How do you feel?"

Joanna considered. "More alert. Less completely stupid." The nurses were fussing with her gown, checking the dressing over her abdomen.

Madaket smiled. "Great. I'm going to get some coffee."

"Coffee," Joanna said, and suddenly she was salivating. "I'd love some coffee."

"You'll have some right away," a nurse said. "Juice, too. Let's sit you up."

A cacophony of pains blared through Joanna's body as she made her way into the chair. The worst of it was the gas left in her abdomen from the C-section; it wasn't dangerous, and eventually it would disappear, the nurses promised, but for the moment she had no choice but to tolerate it. Madaket returned to the room and indulged Joanna in as thorough a washing up as she could manage, then she creamed Joanna's face and hands and feet and brushed Joanna's hair.

Gardner came into the hospital room and perched on the bed, looking over at Joanna.

"Doing better today?"

"Much better."

He cleared his throat. "The nurses will bring your son to you in a minute, but first I need to get some information from you." He paused. "I'm sorry, Joanna, but I have to ask all this. Would you like to arrange to have your baby buried or cremated, or would you prefer that the hospital take care of it?"

"Take care of it?"

"We would cremate her."

Joanna moaned and Madaket gripped her shoulders and stood behind her, holding her that way, supporting her. "I'll do it," Joanna said softly. "I want to do it. I want her buried, not cremated. I don't know why, but it seems important that she have a proper burial."

"If she's buried here, she'll always be here," Madaket said softly. "Your daughter will always be here on the island. She'll have a place on the earth."

"Yes. You're right. That's it," Joanna agreed, looking gratefully at Madaket. Turning back to Gardner, she asked, "Can she be buried here on the island?"

"Yes. In Prospect Hill Cemetery." Gardner looked at Madaket. "Perhaps you can help Joanna? Call the funeral home and make the arrangements?"

"Of course," Madaket said.

Gardner nodded. "It should be done fairly soon. And if you want a service, you'll need to talk to a minister—"

"All right," Joanna said. "We'll do it. Madaket can do it."

Gardner and Madaket left then and the nurses arrived with her baby boy. Joanna held him with a numbed, muted pleasure. The significance of his existence, the pleasure of his living, came to her cramped and twisted, as if it had forced its way through a stony wall of grief. As soon he was taken away to his incubator, she was washed through with despair. She sat sagging in her chair, head nodding forward like a drunk's, eyes closed as she replayed her dreams of the Chorus Girl, laughing and running. When people entered her room and disturbed her from her fantasies, she wanted to snap at them, to tell them to leave her alone, to let her remain with her dreams.

Three days after her babies were born, Joanna stood in the privacy of the hospital bathroom, hiked up her gown, and studied her body. Her waist hung in wrinkles and folds over a jiggling belly through which a long puckered scar ran from navel to pubis. She looked like a thing that had exploded, she looked like something destroyed. And she was, she was something destroyed.

Joanna and her son were to remain in the hospital for a week. Mostly they slept. In the evenings, friends came to visit, bearing gifts. The baby, as fragile and mewing as a kitten, was held and admired. Pat and Bob, June and Morris, Tory and John, and Claude all gave their condolences about the daughter she'd lost, but advised her to forget about her, to let her go, and enjoy the child she had. Joanna could only promise she'd try.

Doug showed up one evening. After a few moments of awkward conversation, he presented her with a box; Joanna unwrapped it to find a white, powder-soft blanket.

"It's beautiful, Doug," Joanna said, running her hands over it.

"My wife chose it," he confessed, smiling. "But I chose this. For you." He handed her a small gold box of Godiva chocolates.

She smiled. She was genuinely pleased. "Thanks, Doug. It's nice to get a present for myself for a change. I wonder why people don't think of giving the mother a present. After all, we do so much of the work."

"I'm sorry about your other baby, too," Doug told her. He cleared his throat. "My wife and I lost a baby. She miscarried at five months. Not quite like what you've gone through, but . . ."

"Five months," Joanna said quietly.

"Yes. She had to go to the hospital. It wasn't easy."

"I'm sorry."

"Somehow we all get through it."

Night darkened the world beyond her windows, and Joanna and Doug were enclosed in the gentle dome of light falling from behind her bed. It was an intimate thing, lying in a gown in a hospital bed while Doug stood nearby. But he had come in pure and simple friendship.

"I looked in the nursery window at your little guy. He looks great," Doug said.

"Yes. Yes, I think he'll be fine."

"Madaket said you'd probably want us not to work out at your house for a while."

"I think I'll need just a few weeks to get settled in and get my strength back. Is that all right with you?"

"Sure. I've got a list as long as my arm of minor repair work people have been asking me to do. Just give us the word when you want us to come back."

"Thanks, Doug."

"All right, then. I'll be going."

He came very close to her, as if intending to embrace her. Joanna felt blood rush to her cheeks. He did not smile. His eyes were fixed on hers in an intense gaze that seemed purely sexual. As she watched, enthralled, he bent toward her, and then brought himself up short. He patted her hand.

"Take care of yourself," he said, and nodded, and turning abruptly, left the room.

In the middle of the night the nurses brought Joanna the baby for her feedings, and then she had him all to herself. In the private glow of her hospital light, she unwrapped the blankets and unsnapped the hand-sized cotton T-shirt and ran her fingers over the skin, soft as petals, which thinly covered the birdlike ribcage and beating heart. His head, like a hot little softball, fit exactly into the palm of Joanna's hand. His perfect ears lay against his head like shells, and his skin was of a marvelous pearly iridescence, as if the Milky Way had been spun into fabric. When he slept he smiled, and slowly moved his limbs, as if swimming gently through her dreams or memories.

Did he dream of the sister who had floated in warm security beside him?

Joanna's dreams were full of her. She thought of nothing else all day, all night.

Joanna awakened on the fifth day to discover a masculine presence in the room. Her eyes and senses focused on . . . a suit, which meant someone from off island, since a sports jacket was as formal as Nantucketers usually got . . . a rich tweed, hand-tailored over massive arms and bulky shoulders . . .

"Jake!"

"Hi, sweetheart. How ya doin'?"

Pushing herself up on her elbows, she shook her head. "Not very well at all!"

"Come here," Jake said. He sat on the side of the bed and took both her hands in his and looked directly at Joanna. "Tell me about it."

Because of Jake's tremendous power in the network, he'd always served as a good judge of the seriousness of any situation. His presence in this small hospital room seemed confirmation of the significance of what had transpired. Joanna looked into Jake's eyes and saw such generous sympathy that she simply leaned forward, trusting that he would catch her, and he did, and he held her close to him, her face against his chest. He stroked her hair, smoothing it over the back of her head and down the base of her skull as if soothing a child. He smelled of wool and tobacco and the peppermints he ate constantly in an attempt to stop smoking. His arms were muscular and burly and strong, and his embrace was so thorough it was like a kind of homecoming.

"Oh, Jake, I lost a little baby."

"I know. I'm sorry about that."

"Jake," she confessed in a whisper against his chest, "I don't know if I can bear it." Pain pressed relentlessly against her heart.

"I know," Jake said. He stroked her hair.

"It was a little girl. My daughter."

"That's terrible, Joanna. It's just completely unfair." She felt his voice rumble in his chest with repressed anger.

"Everyone tells me to be glad I have another child, as if one could replace the other. People tell me to 'focus on the positive.' It makes me so damned mad!"

"I know. But people don't know what to say. When Emily died, everyone said, 'Be glad she didn't suffer long.' Or 'Be glad you had such a happy marriage.' While all I wanted to do was take apart the universe to get her back."

"Oh, Jake, I don't think I was sympathetic enough when you lost Emily. Forgive me."

"You were fine, honey." He patted her shoulder.

"I thought—a lot of us thought—that you were in a bad mood for a long time, longer than you should have been."

"Yeah, well, I was." He coughed. "You'll be in a bad mood, too. I don't think there's an option. If you're cut, you bleed. Same thing, but on the emotional level."

"So you're still sad about Emily?"

"I expect I'll be sad about Emily every day for the rest of my life."

"Really?" A great sense of relief and rapport swept over Joanna. "Then I can be sad about my daughter. Every day. For the rest of my life."

"I imagine so."

His words seemed a kind of permission. She felt the pressure against her heart increase unbearably.

"Jake, I don't know if I can't stand it."

"I know."

"It hurts so much."

"I know." His arms were sheltering.

It was as if a boulder lodged against her heart moved slightly; something dragged beneath her breast. Hiding her face against Jake's shoulder, she let her face fall open in the tortured grimace caused by grief, and she cried, the high, hideous, keening cry that had been waiting in her heart. Jake did not back away in consternation. He held her tightly. A sea of grief flooded through her. The tears came so fast and hard she was blinded. She could only cling to Jake, her body shuddering and knocking against his as the sorrow poured out of her, drenching her, shaking her, scalding her muscles and nerves and bones.

Finally she was emptied out, shivering with exhaustion. Jake's arms were still tightly around her, holding her to him. The wool of his vest was wet and scratchy to the side of her face. She could feel his heart thudding solidly against her ear. She just lay against him, catching her breath.

"Here," Jake said. "You'd better drink some of this." He poured her a glass of water from the carafe on the bedside table and handed it to her. He looked weary, almost desolate, all the lines of his face drawn downward with sympathy and with his own unforgotten sorrow.

"Thanks." Joanna drank the water, which tasted cool and clear all the way down her throat. She sniffed. For a few moments they only sat together in silence. "Have you seen the Swimmer?"

"The Swimmer?"

"My son. I call him that because I can't think of a real name."

"I haven't checked him out yet, but I will." Reaching into his briefcase, Jake said, "Hey, that reminds me. I brought you something."

He placed two packages, wrapped in white, with stiff gold ribbons and bows, on the bed.

"Jake. How nice." Joanna opened them: a Hermes scarf for herself, and for the baby, a baseball signed by Don Mattingly.

"My sons always preferred baseball to football," Jake said. "It's the more intelligent sport."

"This ball isn't much smaller than my baby's head," Joanna observed.

"He'll grow. He'll be outside throwing it through your windows before you know it."

A glimpse of the future—spring, a little boy in a baseball cap, perhaps a golden retriever?—flashed through Joanna's mind.

"Thanks, Jake. I'm so glad you came. I'm so glad you haven't forgotten me." Tears welled up in her eyes.

"I'll never forget you, kid. You know that. But I'd better go now. I don't want to wear you out."

"Are you going right back to New York?"

"I'm staying here overnight. I'll come back in and see you again in the morning before I go." Jake approached the bed and once again wrapped Joanna in his arms. For a long moment she rested against him, feeling as if she were safe inside some large and benevolent force of nature.

"Jake. It means so much to me to have you here," Joanna told him.

Jake kissed her forehead. "You mean a lot to me, too, honey. I'll be back tomorrow."

She lay back against her pillows, nearly ill with exhaustion. Almost of their own accord, her hands slid beneath the covers and found the long ridge of scar down her torso. Its rough presence somehow was a comfort. Her loss would be like this scar, Joanna thought, the loss of the Chorus Girl would be like the long scar on her skin, always a part of her, embedded in her very life. It would belong to her. And she was glad for that. Sinking into her pillows, Joanna closed her eyes and fell into a healing sleep.

Twenty-One

~

*T*en days after her son was born, Joanna and her baby were released from the hospital. There was much fussing from the nurses over the sweet blue sleeper and sweater and bonnet and blanket and how adorable the little boy looked in them. Joanna had regained much of her physical strength and had begun doing basic beginning exercises to bring her stomach back to some kind of shape, and so as she stood dressed in sweatpants and a long loose sweater and shoes instead of paper slippers, she felt for the first time in months as if she were returning to her original, capable self.

Or, rather, a facade of her original self. Beneath the surface of her skin, a cold and obdurate scar ran across her heart. She could feel it, a ridge of sorrow beneath her breast.

They had given her a little booklet, and inside the booklet were two photos, two copies of birth footprints, and two photos taken just after the birth of her babies. Even in the photograph the tiny girl baby looked dead, or rather not alive, very pale and perfect and infinitely still. Also in the booklet were two birth certificates, and a certificate of death.

They had insisted that she name the babies. When she was pregnant, she'd tested many different names, cute names that made the babies sound bonded, twinned, such as Charles and Charlotte or James and Jane, and names that made them sound separate and individual such as Miranda and Bret or Jonathan and Lilly. She'd settled on Angelica and Christopher just before she went into the hospital, and now superstitiously she wondered if she'd doomed her daughter by naming her Angelica, with its taint of heaven and death and angels.

They made a rather stately and ceremonious departure. Madaket gathered up in her arms the vases of flowers Joanna had received. Gardner came up from his office on the first floor of the hospital building to carry the suitcase and diaper bag and the canvas bag full of free baby gifts from the hospital. Both walked beside Joanna as the nurse pushed her out in a wheelchair, the tiny baby nestled in a light cotton blanket in Joanna's arms.

Gardner opened the hatch door and, taking the vases of flowers, put them in a cardboard box Madaket had brought along for the occasion. Madaket took Christopher from Joanna and gently tucked him into the car seat, then assisted Joanna in stepping up into the Jeep. They had to tighten the seat belt, which had been stretched to its extreme length. Gardner came around and leaned in Joanna's window.

"Well, there you are, happy and healthy and on your way home."

"Yes." It would seem churlish to disagree.

"I'll stop by as often as possible to check on the little guy."

"Thanks, Gardner. Thanks for everything."

"And you'll get as much bed rest as possible, right?"

"Right."

Gardner looked across the seat to Madaket. "You'll be watchdog for me, okay?"

"Okay," Madaket answered, smiling.

"He's a good baby," Gardner told Joanna. "Look how calm he is."

Joanna turned in her seat to look at her son, who seemed impossibly tiny among his straps and paraphernalia. His dark blue eyes were wide and searching, as if trying to see everything at once, and his two small fists were bunched under his chin like a pair of flowers.

"Yes," Joanna said. "He's a good baby." Then she leaned back against her seat and watched the wide outside world pass by as Madaket drove them home.

When she entered her house, she saw that Madaket had made it shining clean and polished. Madaket had put fresh sheets on the bed and opened the windows to let the crisp October air fill the rooms. Joanna walked through her house, just looking at it all, the gleaming windows and glowing brass of the fireplace screens and tools, the rich luster of the furniture and draperies, the intricate lushness of the rugs. She could tell with her intelligence that her house was beautiful, but she felt no sympathetic reaction to it, no visceral response. She was carrying Christopher and he had fallen asleep in her arms and so she took him into the nursery at the front of the house to lay him in his crib, and when she walked into the room, which she had decorated in a mixture of pinks and blues, she realized at once how busy Madaket had been, removing the extra crib and all the dainty pink girlish items which would have belonged to her daughter. She should have been grateful, but she felt cheated, and grief washed up against her. She lay her baby boy in his crib and watched a few moments to be sure he was truly asleep and comfortable, and then she could stand it no longer. She left the room.

In the days that followed, Joanna felt like a long-distance swimmer flailing through a stormy ocean with her heart a heavy dragging anchor and her limbs weighted down. Sometimes she managed to force her head above water, but almost immediately a great dark wave would crash down over her, spinning her helplessly back into the depths.

Joanna was to let Christopher nurse on demand, and because the baby was premature and his stomach tiny, the demand was often. During their first days home, night and day blurred into each other, so that she seemed always moving against a tide. Her body was exhausted by her living baby's cries and her soul was spent and sinking in the dark, oppressive ocean of grief which thrust her continually along in a drenched darkness which was the knowledge of her daughter's death.

Sometimes she dreamed also of Carter. Of Carter with Gloria, both of them sleek and shining and speeding, like bullets, like gleaming submarines, silently moving past her and beyond, while she was caught in the lightless depths by the twisting ropes of her sorrow.

Ten days after she was born, Angelica Caroline Jones was buried in a small casket in a small plot of the Prospect Hill

Cemetery. The minister from the Unitarian Church offici-
ated, saying only a few brief words to the small group gathered there: Joanna, with Christopher in her arms, and
Madaket, and Gardner, and Tory and the Hoovers and the
Latherns and Claude. The day was brilliant with sunshine,
the air full of copper light, and the brisk smell of salt air and
chrysanthemums and leaves just beginning to flame and curl.
It was a day radiant and dancing with light, a day to begin
life. Madaket cried, but Joanna did not. Before they left,
they covered the tiny coffin with a blanket of tiny pink baby
roses.

Very quickly Joanna realized that as much as she loved her
house, it was set up inefficiently for life with a baby. She could
not leave her tiny son alone in the pretty nursery at the front
of the house—it was so far away from her bedroom that
Joanna couldn't hear him if he cried, and it took nightmar-
ish ages to hurry down the long hall while her baby wailed.
Madaket couldn't sleep in her room in the attic for the same
reasons. So for the first two months of Christopher's life, all
three slept in Joanna's room: Joanna in her bed, sometimes
with her baby, Christopher in his crib, Madaket on the chaise
longue. Wolf lay on guard at the threshold of the bedroom.
Bitch scorned them all and slept in another part of the house.
It was infinitely soothing to Joanna to have Madaket with
her in the dark hours.

Even though premature, Christopher was a normal baby,
and as the days passed, he quickly changed from the tiny pale
infant into a solid little creature with his own personality. He
grew eyebrows and eyelashes and fingernails and soft pale
peach fuzz all over his scalp. After the first month, during
which he did very little but eat and sleep, he began to stay
awake longer, to engage in communications with his mother
and Madaket, waving his tiny fat dimpled hands and purs-
ing his lips as he tried to speak.

One day Madaket laid him on a blanket on a soft and
sunny spot of the living room floor, and Wolf approached the
squealing, squirming bundle, in a sideways, cautious walk,
smiling his ingratiating, hopeful, dopey doggy smile. Immediately all of Joanna's senses sprang to attention, and an

electric sensation of vigilance, like a golden living wall, rose quivering within her.

"Madaket."

"It's all right." Madaket knelt next to Christopher, poised to come between the baby and the dog if necessary.

Joanna watched in an agony of apprehension. Extending his neck, ready to recoil, Wolf sniffed the air above the squirming baby. Christopher's eyes grew wide as he became aware of the enormous, gentle, bestial presence above him. Christopher stopped wriggling and went very quiet.

"Lie down, Wolf," Madaket said softly, and Wolf obeyed, placing his huge doggy feet just inches from the baby's body and dropping his great head down to rest. As he did, his breath ruffled Christopher's white T-shirt and his whiskers ever so slightly brushed the baby's hands and Christopher looked startled, then grinned a wide and genuine grin and chuckled with glee. Wolf wagged his tail.

From that day on Wolf and Christopher were great friends, and as the baby began to differentiate the personalities of the creatures who lived around him and played with him, he continually doted on the dog and laughed with delight when Wolf came near—and timid Wolf came near only when invited by Madaket or Joanna.

During the days the baby was winsome and fascinating, and Joanna began to feel that perhaps she had done one thing in the world right. Then toward his sixth week, Christopher became fussy at night, every night, whimpering and crying and finally wailing inconsolably for hours. Joanna nursed him, and tried to give him a bottle of lightly sweetened water when he furiously turned his little face away from her breast. Madaket walked and rocked him. Gardner checked him, and said he was all right, and that probably he had a touch of colic, that inexplicable ailment, as prevalent and infuriating as the common cold, which came and went among babies without any seeming reason. He would get over it, Gardner said. Perhaps they should try music or taking him for a ride in the car.

Joanna thanked Gardner for his help and didn't tell him what she thought the problem might be. But that night, as she sat in the rocking chair in the nursery, with the north wind rising and beating steadily against the house, she admitted the truth, her truth. Madaket had already spent an hour trying to soothe Christopher with sugared water and lullabies and a drive in the car, and now she had gone up to the attic to try to grab some sleep before relieving Joanna. Wolf remained as Joanna's companion. He worried terribly when the baby cried continuously like this, and paced the floor with Madaket or Joanna, and wagged his tail and whimpered in distress. Now, exhausted, he lay in the threshold to the nursery, eyes wide and fixed on Joanna, ready to spring to her bidding.

"Wolf gives you pure, wholehearted, uncomplicated love," Joanna spoke aloud. Looking down into the pinched and wrinkled face of her crying son, she whispered softly, "Wolf can, and I can't." She brought her baby up against her chest and nestled her chin against his tiny hot head, and lightly kissed the infinitely soft peach fuzz on his tender scalp. "But I want to love you that way," she whispered.

Joanna had told the Snowmen to postpone their work on the house until she and the baby were on some kind of schedule that revolved around sleeping at night; she didn't want the sound of hammers and chain saws to interrupt what precious moments of sleep she could grab during the day. Even though Madaket never complained, Joanna suspected that it was hard on her to go for so many days without seeing Todd, but she didn't care. She had no energy for that kind of caring. Sometimes she thought all her kindness had dried up inside her.

"Please, Joanna, come along. It will do you good to get out and see the island. It's so beautiful now. The moors are all orange and red."

Joanna sat by an open window in a rocking chair, her son cradled in her arms. It was morning, a particularly lovely late October morning, with the warm golden air disturbed by only a hint of coolness from the autumn breeze which brushed over her skin like invisible scarves. Yet she disdained it. She was too tired for beauty.

"Christopher's too fussy. I want to rock him and put him down for a nap and get some sleep myself." Joanna felt especially grubby and vile as she sat in her favorite, most com-

fortable, long cotton nightgown, which was stained, in spite
of all of Madaket's best attempts to wash it. Her heavy
breasts, thick with milk, hung down in their nursing bra like
sullen objects. She didn't have the energy to change clothes
simply to ride in the car while Madaket went in to get groceries.

Madaket persisted. "We could put Christopher in the baby
car seat. The movement might help him fall asleep."

Christopher stirred against her breasts and made a small
mewing noise.

"He's almost asleep. I'm sorry, Madaket, I only want to
go back to bed."

Madaket opened her mouth to object, then decided against
it. "All right. I'll be back as soon as I can."

Off she went, her long brown and gold dress swaying
around her rounded hips. Joanna leaned her head wearily
back against the rocking chair and raised her baby so that he
rested against her shoulder. Her arms were tired, her shoulders ached, and she was heart-sore. Outside, the door of the
Jeep slammed with its solid resounding thud and then the engine purred into life and gravel clicked and spattered as
Madaket drove away. Joanna knew she and her son would
not have done so well without the continuous care Madaket
gave them. Madaket was always there, ready to take the baby
and change his diaper or help weak Joanna rise from her
bath. Madaket cooked the meals, did the endless laundry, answered the phone, rocked the baby, rubbed Joanna's back,
hurried into town for groceries, cleaned the house, and took
turns walking the floor late at night when Christopher in his
sixth week went into a colicky period.

Yet all of Madaket's actions were tainted for Joanna,
edged by the conversation Joanna had overheard on the stairs
between Madaket and Todd. She did not know that Madaket
had succumbed to Todd's charms, of course, and it was just
possible that Madaket would remain loyal to Joanna. But
they were both island people, and young and poor, and
Joanna remembered Tory's admonitions. Also, she knew full
well how sexual attraction could cause a person to change her
life.

And why should Madaket not betray Joanna? Betrayal
seemed only another component of nature. Wouldn't it be

simply the easier course to give up hoping and believe the worst? Why not?

Her eyes were closed, and the bitter tears were rising, stinging against her eyelids.

Gravel crackled again, and again a car door thudded. Madaket had forgotten something, the grocery list, a check, the mail. Joanna bit her lip to check her tears. The front door opened, closed, and then she heard footsteps come up the steps. Heavy steps, not Madaket's. A man's.

"Hello?"

Before she could answer his call, Doug Snow came down the hallway and stood in the doorway, his slim, intense masculinity contrasting with all the pastel innocence of the nursery walls. His hair and beard glittered a thousand shades of gold and his skin was bronzed by the sun, so that his blue eyes seemed particularly vivid. Joanna could smell him: the tang of fresh air, dried sweat, movement, leather and denim and hard tools and strength. Facing him as she sat in her chair, she felt lazy and heavy and slow, and she knew that her swollen breasts showed against the fabric of her nightgown. Sensation flowed into her breasts, stung and shoved against her nipples. She wanted him to cross the room and kneel by her chair and put his mouth on her breasts.

"Sorry to bother you," Doug said. "How's the boy?"

"Almost asleep."

He lowered his voice. "I was hoping I could talk to you a minute."

"Of course." She brought the baby down from her shoulder and held him against her breasts, to cover herself.

"It's about the tunnel."

Joanna waited.

"Todd and I were hoping that you'd let him come back at nights to explore it. He'd be very quiet about it. He wouldn't bother you or your baby. He wouldn't need Madaket to help."

Joanna stopped listening. You haven't come for me, she realized with a sudden despairing clarity; your desire for me has not driven you here, nor have you come in ordinary friendship. Why, you haven't been lusting after me, it's only me who's lusted after you. You haven't chosen me. You want to find the treasure and claim it for yourself, and if flirting with me is part of the price you have to pay, then you'll pay it. If charming me makes it possible to manipulate me, then you'll do that. And I interpreted your kindnesses as I wished.

Doug was staring at her, vehemence darkening his eyes, every line of the long thick muscles of his body straining against his clothes. "The kids did find that chest with two rubies in it. It seems a shame to cover it all over when we could be so close to finding the treasure—"

"No," Joanna interrupted him, her voice cold. "I was going to call you. I'd like you to resume work out here in the day again. I'm tired of having the house torn up. I want you to go ahead and cover that floor and finish that room as soon as possible. I'll need it for the baby."

Doug flinched slightly and his eyes blazed. "Look," he began, his voice louder, antagonistic.

"I don't think we need to discuss it any more. Please leave. I'm tired."

He took two great strides into the room and stood before her, a powerful, handsome man, nearly vibrating with suppressed anger. "Joanna, you're not being fair. You have no right to keep us from finding more of the treasure.".

"I have every right. I own this house," Joanna told him coldly. "Now please leave."

Doug stared at her, insolence heating his eyes. He was fiercely handsome, with the braced, keen, virile handsomeness of a lion poised to attack. Fear streaked along her nerves.

"Joanna," he said again, and she thought she heard a threat in his voice.

She raised her chin. "Shall I call the police?"

He looked startled, then contemptuous. "Oh, Christ!" He turned and left.

Later that day Madaket returned from town, and after she'd unloaded the groceries and dry cleaning and shopping from the Jeep, she came quickly up the stairs to see if Christopher and Joanna were all right. Joanna had taken the baby to bed with her and fed him, and they had both napped and now lay together in the tousled sheets. Joanna was on her side, head propped on one hand, looking down at Christopher, who lay on his back, smiling and kicking his legs and waving his arms and cooing to her. This was a tantalizing, seductive thing that he could do, Joanna thought, watching him, for his eyes shone with light and happiness as he looked up at her and he blew bubbles of pleasure each time she spoke.

"Hi, guys," Madaket called, entering the room. She tossed a pile of new and glossy magazines on the bedside table and knelt down on the floor next to the bed. "Here, Joanna, I brought you lots of stuff to look at. Now I get Topher for a while." Leaning over, she fondled the baby, and her speech dissolved into baby talk. "How's my best little apple dumpling sweetie pie?" she asked, touching him gently on the tummy. Christopher shrieked with joy.

Joanna studied Madaket as she played with the baby. The young woman's face was full of happiness and affection, all genuine, Joanna thought.

"Madaket, I'll let you take Christopher off for a while so I can bathe, but first I need to tell you something. Doug Snow came out here and asked if Todd could begin digging in the tunnel again. I told him I want the floor covered over." Was she right, did the brightness shining from Madaket's face dim slightly? "I really do believe that if there was anything else to be found, you and Todd would have found it by now. It's just so unlikely that any other jewels would have gotten separated from that box. I don't want to live with the house in a state of disorder." Why was she making so many excuses? Angry with herself, she said, "Do you understand, Madaket?"

Perhaps her voice had been sharper than she'd intended, for Madaket looked at her in surprise and Christopher went quiet.

"Yes, Joanna, I understand. I'm disappointed, but I understand."

"You can't really think there's more treasure under there."

"I think it's possible."

As if hurt by their voices, Christopher screwed up his face and began to cry. Madaket rose to her feet and lifted the baby up and jiggled him, charming him with baby talk. Joanna threw back the bedcovers and slid her legs over the side of the bed. "Well, I've decided, and that's that. I told him I want them to come out and cover the floor and finish the room."

"If that's what you want," Madaket replied, speaking in a

light singsong voice as she bounced the baby. Then, as if Joanna's decision were of little importance, she said, "I'm going to go change His Majesty's diaper. Then I'll take him downstairs while you shower. Okay?"

"Great. Thanks."

Joanna stalked into her bathroom and threw off her gown and turned on the taps full blast, then stood under the pounding water for a long time, wishing her soul could be washed clean.

Now the days of October and November turned golden and whirled off into the past like autumn leaves and Joanna felt buffeted by the rising wind, the humming, swelling, insistent Goyaesque wind which sped over the ocean toward her house like a dark galleon of ghosts under full sail. Her life was turbulent, her spirits restless, and her body seemed to flap like a scarecrow around the aching core of her soul.

The Snows did not come to finish the floor and the sunporch. They did not come at all. After a week Joanna asked Madaket to call them, and Madaket did, reporting to Joanna that she got only their answering machine. She left messages. Joanna tried several times, also got the answering machine, and also left messages. They were miffed, she thought, and were punishing her. Or perhaps they were deeply angry and insulted and intended never to come back again. In that case, she needed to get names and references for new carpenters so that the work could be finished. But she was too tired, and too busy with the baby, to deal with all that just yet.

Twenty-Two

~

*G*radually, as the days and nights passed, Joanna's strength returned. Her first social outing with her new son was on Thanksgiving Day, when she and Christopher and Madaket were invited to Tory's. The Randalls' drafty house wasn't insulated, and its location high on the 'Sconset bluff exposed it to the wind which gusted off the choppy ocean, so that the shutters closed over the upstairs guest bedroom windows tapped, and the windowpanes on the ocean side rattled, and throughout the house the fireplaces occasionally whistled with wind. Schools of clouds sailed and swerved over the lemony sun, sending flickering shafts of pale cool light through the windows. But a fire of applewood burned in the living room, and in the dining room the food was delicious and abundant, and everyone laughed and gossiped and feasted. They lingered around the table over pie and whipped cream and warmed their hands around their coffee cups.

The Latherns came, and the Hoovers and Gardner, contentedly alone, and Tory's husband, John, was there, and Jeremy, home from boarding school, and Vicki. Joanna leaned back in her chair, holding a drowsy Christopher against her shoulder, secretly comparing Tory's children with Madaket; all three were of an age, and yet Madaket seemed infinitely older but at the same time much more innocent. Madaket wore a long, loose, supple, finely woven wool sweater in a bronze that accentuated her skin over a Gypsyish skirt of blacks and browns and greens and golds. She'd pulled her black hair back with a paisley scarf. She looked autumnal and comfortable and appropriate, as if she were paying homage to the season. Jeremy, on the other hand, wore his sweatpants and a ripped sweatshirt all day. When Joanna first arrived, she'd overheard Tory say in surprise, "Jeremy, you're not wearing your sweats to the table?" Her son had replied, "Get a grip, Mom. It's freezing in here. Besides, we're on vacation." Vicki didn't seem to mind the cold. She wore brief black shorts over fishnet stockings and black knee-high boots along with a black bustier and a black choker. Her fingernails and lipstick were a brilliant crimson and her bare arms and meager chest an anemic ivory. Neither one of the Randall children helped bring the feast to the table or clear afterward; Madaket with easy smiles and graceful quick gestures carried and passed platters while at the same time taking part in the conversation.

The difference is, Joanna reminded herself, that Jeremy and Vicki are Tory's children. Madaket is my paid help, and she has to be pleasant while she helps out, or I might fire her. Obviously Jeremy and Vicki placed importance on Madaket's housekeeper status, for neither one spoke to her, although Jeremy's eyes lingered on the large round bosom which Madaket's loose clothing only slightly camouflaged. Gardner, on the other hand, was kind to Madaket. He sat next to her and throughout the dinner engaged her in conversation about her grandmother's recipes for curative herbal drinks and poultices. Perhaps he wasn't only being kind, Joanna thought, watching, for he seemed genuinely interested, and as the rest of the table joined in, discussing homeopathic medicine and holistic health, Joanna noticed that Madaket could hold her own in such conversation. She really has a field of expertise, Joanna thought. Madaket cited research done by clinics in Maine on the use of castor-oil packs to stop uterine bleeding in pregnant women, and Gardner chimed in, yes, he had heard about those studies. She spoke of the newest books out on herbal drugs. The Latherns and Hoovers looked impressed by Madaket's knowledge, and as Joanna watched, she felt the oddest small shiver of pleasure, pleasure for Madaket, and for herself, a little frisson of pride.

But why do I feel this? Joanna asked herself. Madaket is not mine. She is not my family, not my daughter. My daughter is lying in a coffin lined in white silk under the sere ground.

Suddenly she was exhausted by all the food and laughter and by the pelleting of these emotions against her wounded heart. Christopher cried, and she excused herself to slip into the living room, where she curled up on the sofa in front of the fire to nurse him. No one chided Joanna when later she awoke to find that she and Christopher had fallen asleep together on the sofa.

By December Joanna had enough energy to enjoy the season. She ordered Christmas presents from catalogs and sent out Christmas cards, freely giving out her address now that she had nothing to fear. She rode into town, her baby tucked away in his car seat, Madaket driving, to see Main Street decked out in holiday finery. Together Madaket and Joanna bought a tree and wrestled it into the back of the Jeep and then into the house and its three-footed stand. It was the first time that Joanna had decorated a tree for Christmas, and she and Madaket went wild, buying everything, then hanging lights and old-fashioned shining balls and twisted glass ornaments and candy canes and icicles. They put green and scarlet candles throughout the house. In the evenings Joanna lay in her living room, Christopher in her arms, dozing, soothed by the fragrance of fresh pine, listening to Christmas music on CD. Christopher turned his wide calm gaze toward the tiny multicolored tree lights and smiled.

Her pleasure was only slightly spoiled by a disagreement with Tory, who called early in the month to invite Joanna and Christopher to spend Christmas with the Randalls in their home in New York. When Joanna asked if she could bring Madaket along, Tory became annoyed.

"Can't you go anywhere without her? I'll help you take care of Christopher. I'll ask my maid to give me some extra hours if you think you can't handle the baby by yourself."

"It's not a matter of my needing help," Joanna insisted. "I just wouldn't feel right leaving Madaket all alone at Christmas. She's been so—"

"All right, all right, stop!" Tory interrupted. "I don't need to hear you sing her praises one more time. If you won't come, you won't. And I refuse to invite her to my house. She's only a maid, after all, and you know how I feel about all that.

Besides, I don't like the way Jeremy was looking at her. She's got that vulgar body—"

"—she can hardly help that!" Joanna snapped.

"—and I can just see her getting knocked up by Jeremy and forcing him to marry her," Tory finished.

"Tory, you're ridiculous and insulting," Joanna said.

"And you're a fool!" Tory shot back, and hung up the phone.

Later, Tory called back to apologize and Joanna grudgingly apologized, too, and in the spirit of Christmas they agreed not to fight anymore, but as Joanna put down the phone, she thought that probably the only way she and Tory would avoid fighting would be simply not to speak to each other for a while.

As it turned out, she didn't have time to think about Tory again, for she and Madaket and Christopher were asked to a number of Christmas parties and to the Latherns' for Christmas Eve and to the Hoovers' for Christmas Day and to Claude's for a New Year's Day buffet. She began to feel part of the smug, cozy community who lived on the island year-round.

The month whirled by. Joanna and Madaket had bought presents for each other, and there were presents under the tree from friends as well. When Joanna came down the stairs in her quilted robe, with Christopher bundled in his warm red holiday outfit, she found that Madaket had already made a fire in the fireplace and turned on the Christmas tree lights. Outside, the day was cool and damp and foggy, and the crackling sounds of the fire and its warmth were especially welcome. Wolf ambled in with a huge red bow tied around his neck, and even Bitch condescended to join them, curling up proprietarily on the hearth, her back to the roaring fire, her eyes in slits of pleasure.

Christopher received the most presents—everyone had given something to him, and Joanna and Madaket took turns opening all his boxes of clothes and toys and stuffed animals. Madaket had presented the Latherns and several of Joanna's other Nantucket friends with jars of her homemade jams and jellies and in return they had given her books and a scarf and some earrings and much the same sort of things to Joanna. As she sat surrounded by all her loot, she felt very warmed and pleased and even slightly teary to think that she'd made so many good friends on this island, so many friends who knew about her life, and cared.

When it came time to trade gifts with Madaket, Joanna was excited. First she gave Wolf a great box of assorted dog treats, and to Bitch she gave a catnip mouse which sent the cat into purrs and fits of ecstasy. Christopher's gift to Madaket was a red plaid robe and fleece-lined leather slippers. Joanna's gift to Madaket was under the tree, a large box covered in silver and pink foil; inside were seven sweaters in a rainbow of colors, all long and large and loose, just the way Madaket liked them, and seven matching scarves and twists for her hair.

"This is too much!" Madaket protested, kneeling by the tree, holding the creamy sweaters so that they seemed to pour from her hands.

"No, no, not at all, Madaket. Please. They're so beautiful and perfect colors for you, and I couldn't bear not to get them all." She did not say: and besides, you need them, I know you do, I've seen you biking back from town with your Second Shop bargains in a brown paper bag. "Christmas is about luxury," Joanna said. "You have to accept them."

"Then, thank you," Madaket said. Rising, she approached Joanna and, leaning forward, briefly hugged her and kissed her cheek. Then, embarrassed, nearly tripping over her feet, she said, "I'll go get Christopher's gift now. I had to hide it out in the shed."

She flew out into the hall and through the front door and back in again in only moments, carrying with her something very large and heavy and covered with a blanket. The wind and fog had lifted Madaket's hair into a black halo around her head. Her eyes shone with excitement. Joanna was holding Christopher in her lap as he sat looking out at the cheerful disarray of the room with its mess of wrapping paper and presents and the rainbow of sweaters spilling out of the box beneath the Christmas tree. Madaket put her present on the floor and lifted the blanket off.

A large and marvelously beautiful wooden rocking horse stood before them. He was carved of pale pine, and his coat was polished to a sheen, and his sculpted mane was accented with gold, as were his black saddle and his elegantly braided tail. Real leather reins hung from glistening gold rings in his mouth and he smiled a handsome horsey smile with his long rectangular white teeth.

"Oh, Madaket," Joanna breathed, amazed.

"Todd built him. I designed him, and helped sand him, and painted him. And put the rings in—they're attached to a dowel and I'm sure Christopher won't be able to pull them out." Lovingly she pushed the horse's back and he rocked gently back and forth on his curved rockers.

"He's beautiful. I've never seen such a beautiful thing."

"Now for your present!" Madaket took the last present from under the tree and put it on the sofa within Joanna's reach, then lifted bottom-heavy Christopher into her own arms and perched on the edge of the sofa to watch Joanna open her gift.

Carefully Joanna peeled back the red and green wrapping paper to find a framed, ten-by-twelve-inch, pen-and-ink drawing of her house. It was perfect. The lines were drawn with sure authority, and every detail captured. Underneath, in flowing calligraphy, was the title: "Joanna's House." In the corner the name Claude Clifford was signed, and Joanna caught her breath. She knew the kind of prices Claude could command for such a drawing.

As if reading her mind, Madaket said, "Claude gave me a deal. Because he likes you so much, you know."

"I don't know what to say, Madaket. This is an amazing gift." She looked up and saw Madaket's eyes shining with delight. "Thank you," she said, and turned her head away, to hide her tears.

Just then the telephone rang; the Latherns calling to wish her Merry Christmas. Soon after that a knock sounded on the door and Gardner came in, wearing jeans and a camel-hair blazer that made his sandy hair blaze like sunlight. Joanna and Madaket had invited him for Christmas breakfast since he was alone now, and he had walked down from his house at the other end of Squam Road. They traded gifts. Gardner gave Joanna several books about Nantucket's history, and to Madaket he gave a large and very beautiful book of Dutch prints of flowers and herbs. Joanna gave Gardner a silk tie, and Madaket shyly presented him with several jars of her jams. Then they adjourned to the dining room for a holiday feast. Gardner held Christopher while Joanna and Madaket cooked and served eggs scrambled with peppers and feta cheese, and her country fried potatoes, and bacon, and Madaket's special almond Christmas bread, and fresh coffee, and champagne mixed with fresh orange juice. After that, Gardner went home and they napped until it was time for Christmas dinner at the Hoovers'.

On Christmas night Joanna fell into bed in a state of happy exhaustion, certain that nothing except Christopher's most serious entreaties would waken her. But almost as soon as she sank into sleep, she was jolted awake by an awareness of something—a sound, a slight change in the air?

She sat up in bed. Dark lay all around her except for the night-light glowing from the bathroom, which slightly illuminated the cradle where Christopher lay. The windows were black with night. She looked at the clock on her bedside table: it was not quite midnight. She'd been asleep only about thirty minutes. Throwing back her covers, she tiptoed over to look down at her baby, who lay on his back in angelic repose, arms flung upward, small chest rising and falling evenly. The bedroom was very warm, the floors warm to her bare feet.

She heard a noise, so slight it was almost imaginary. Perhaps Madaket was down in the living room watching television. Quietly Joanna went out into the hall, which was still dark. She peered down the stairs: darkness. She started to call out Madaket's name, and then some instinct stopped her and sent her down the full length of the hall. Staying in the protection of the heavy draperies, she leaned against the window and looked down at the driveway, which was brightened by lamps on either side of the front door.

The Snows' red pickup truck sat in the white gravel. The engine was running and the truck vibrated gently. As her eyes adjusted to the semidarkness, Joanna saw that Madaket was sitting inside the cab of the truck, talking to Todd. It was too dark to see them clearly, she could make out only movements and the flashing of white teeth, and shadows. It didn't seem that the two young people were in a lovers' embrace. It looked as if Madaket was on the passenger side. It did not seem that they were touching. Still, why was Todd here? At midnight on Christmas night? Were they exchanging presents? What had they discussed while they worked together as conspirators, building Christopher's rocking horse? How close had they become?

A feathery touch brushed against Joanna's hand, making her jump and nearly cry aloud. It was only Wolf. Then from her bedroom came Christopher's high wail. Joanna held her breath. Perhaps he'd fall back asleep. She looked out the window. Madaket and Todd were still apart, still talking. Christopher cried once more, then steadily. Reluctantly Joanna left her watch post to return to her bedroom. Gathering her baby up in her arms, she checked his diaper—dry—and shushed him and soothed him and then sank into her rocking chair and nursed him and burped him, then rocked him, singing lullabies. And after all that time, and after she lay him back to sleep in his cradle, Madaket still did not return to the house. Joanna crawled back in her bed and lay on her side, keeping watch through her eyelids for a change in the light, listening for the soft opening and closing of the front door. But the next thing she knew, it was morning and the December sun was shining thinly through a layer of white clouds.

And all that day, and all the days that followed, Madaket did not mention her midnight meeting with Todd to Joanna, and Joanna did not ask.

How many other times had Madaket secretly met Todd? She wouldn't ask.

In January, Joanna received an invitation to join a mothers' group that met weekly at different homes. She had little energy for meeting new people, but her mind nudged her for information about such humble topics as teething and feeding and crying patterns, so she forced herself to go. It could only be good for her, she suspected.

And it was. Once there, she immediately was overcome with a deep sense of humility. Listening to the other mothers, she realized she had no right to complain. Most of the women were juggling care for their baby with caring for at least one other child, and some of them also worked outside the home, leaving the baby with a relative or a neighbor or a less than satisfactory baby-sitter. They all loved their infants ferociously, and they all felt that they loved their babies insufficiently, that somehow they were failing their children. Joanna sat listening, holding small Christopher in his pure cotton Baby Dior romper, and realized how spoiled she was, and how blind she had been to what good luck she truly had.

She did not speak to the other mothers of the baby girl who had not lived, but when Joanna was in this group, the thought of Angelica lingered with her, a ghost child nestling near. Among these women her sorrow would be understood and accepted and even shared. Joanna could almost feel the extra weight in her arms.

One frigid February afternoon Joanna returned home from a mothers' afternoon get-together to find her answering machine blinking. Madaket took Christopher off to the nursery, and Joanna sank down into her chair, and put her feet up on the footstool made for her by Doug Snow, and leaned back. She hadn't spent much time in her study recently, and she looked around with pleasure at her computer and her printer and her waiting Rolodex. She pressed the play button.

"Joanna, hello, dear, it's Justin. Just wanted to tell you we'll be sending the galleys of your books off at the end of this week. Hope you can plan to clear your calendar and get them back right away. One's scheduled to come out in June, the other in September. We're thinking about some publicity; perhaps even an author's tour. It would help sales immensely. What do you think? Call me."

"Joanna. Jake here. How's Christopher? Hey, I saw Justin today for lunch and we have some ideas cooking. Some TV tie-ins, which would keep your name and face in front of the audience over the spring and summer and be a great buildup for the fall and your return. I'll call again."

A delicious warmth flowed through Joanna. She hugged herself and smiled. Her books! And an author's tour! *Fabulous Homes*! The world opened up before her. Oh, what fun! She'd take Christopher and Madaket, and Madaket, who had traveled no farther than Hyannis or Boston on a school trip, would get a chance to see the country. She'd take Madaket to a Broadway show, to a nightclub in New Orleans—

But wait.

First, Joanna insisted to herself, *first* she had to settle something between herself and Madaket. What connection did Madaket feel to Todd? What plans did they have, exactly, concerning the discovery of any more treasure? Were they conspiring against Joanna? Or was Madaket trustworthy? Joanna needed to know, because she felt beholden to the young woman and increasingly fond. Even though no amount of money could have bought the kind of care Madaket had given, still it was money, Joanna reasoned, that could best express her gratitude. Now was the time.

There were no directs flights to New York from Nantucket, so Joanna made an appointment with a jeweler on Newbury Street in Boston. She told Madaket only that she had some business to attend to there, and using the breast pump, she expressed milk into bottles for the young woman to give Christopher. With the baby carefully tucked into his car seat, Madaket drove Joanna to the airport. Joanna felt oddly unreal in her sleek hose and slender clothes, the first work clothes she'd donned since her pregnancy.

"You look glamorous," Madaket told her as she entered the airport.

"I just hope no one spits on me," Joanna replied, for she was wearing her black mink coat and hat against the winter cold.

The flight went well and took only forty-five minutes. Joanna took a taxi directly to the jewelry shop. An elegantly uniformed security guard stood frowning in front of the shining brass doors. He eyed Joanna coldly before nodding curtly at someone inside, who pressed a button which released the electronic locks. Entering this rarefied atmosphere where the jewels and the jewelers exuded the same iciness, Joanna was glad for her furs. Mr. Vandermeer greeted her with a European bow and led her to a luxuriously appointed private salon, where she sank onto a George Cinq settee and sipped Hu Kwa tea before getting down to business.

Joanna opened her purse and took out a black velvet jewelry box. Inside were the two rough-cut rubies. Mr. Vandermeer actually smiled as he studied them under his magnifying glass. When at last he lifted his gleaming bald head, he said,

"These are top-quality rough-cut rubies. I could pay you thirty-five thousand dollars."

Joanna shook her head and sighed.

Mr. Vandermeer sighed, too, then said sadly, "Each."

"Very well. That seems a fair price." Joanna sipped her tea while the jeweler called in various employees to deal with the paperwork. In a remarkably short period of time, she had a certified check for seventy thousand dollars and a stamped bill of sale. She shook hands with Mr. Vandermeer and went back out into the bright winter day. Two blocks of walking brought her to a branch of one of the banks with which she had accounts. She went in and deposited the check in her checking account. No use to open a special money market account for it, she decided, she'd be writing a check to Madaket almost immediately.

She had some free time before her flight back, so she walked along Newbury Street, looking in the windows at the fashionable shops. People passed her on the sidewalk without a second glance. Had her face been forgotten so soon? She grew tired more quickly than she thought she would and went into the Ritz for tea. The gracious room was filled today; it seemed she was the only one alone. Pairs and groups of friends bent toward each other over the tea tables, and the air was sprinkled with soft laughter and the hum and buzz of intimate talk, and Joanna looked and listened with envy, suddenly pierced through with longing for the bustle and perfume of city life. She couldn't wait to get all this treasure business settled, and proof the galleys of her books, and gear up for a book tour. Her figure, while not yet in its original shape, was slimming down very nicely, thanks to the nursing. But she could be more diligent about shaping up. She'd heard there was a health club in Nantucket. Perhaps she should start working out, to build up her strength and flatten her tummy. And then she would have to buy some fabulous new clothes!

Madaket and Christopher were waiting in the airport. Madaket was holding Christopher up and exclaiming, "There's Mommy! There's your mommy!" To her delighted surprise, Joanna's heart jumped at the sight of them, her almost-family, waiting eagerly only for her.

"He really missed you," Madaket said. "He didn't like his bottle at all."

Joanna leaned over and rubbed her nose against her little boy's. "Hi, Christopher. Did you miss me?"

"Bbuuhh," Christopher said, blowing bubbles of joy at the sight of his mother. He waved his fat arms bulkily in the padding of his snowsuit. Christopher had Carter's piercingly clear blue eyes, rather startling in a baby, but the expression in those eyes was winsome and sweet and terribly yearning, as if Christopher were trying to talk.

Joanna grabbed her baby and kissed him all over his face, smooching him ecstatically, and Christopher laughed a deep hearty baby chuckle and cooed and wriggled for joy.

"God, I'm just spurting milk!" Joanna whispered to Madaket.

They raced to the car.

"You drive. I'll nurse him right now." She buckled herself in and hastened to unfasten all the buttons and snaps on her clothing. The baby's toothless bite on her nipple brought a surge of relief. "Did he cry?"

"No, but he fussed a lot. I was busy entertaining him!" Madaket steered the Jeep out of the airport parking lot and toward home. "How was your trip?"

"Successful. I'll tell you about it later." Joanna stroked the side of Christopher's head as he nursed. His skin was as soft as silk.

"Joanna, I have some good news for you."

"Oh?" Christopher clamped his fist around her finger.

"The Snowmen returned today. Just showed up about ten o'clock and started pounding away on the sunporch floor. The trapdoor is all covered over with subflooring now, and they said they'll put in the tile tomorrow."

"Oh. What a surprise." Joanna looked over at Madaket to watch her profile as she spoke. "How very odd that they showed up the day I was off the island."

"It is a strange coincidence, isn't it?" Madaket agreed. She didn't seem ill at ease, and yet Joanna wondered: had Madaket called the men and told them it was safe to return to the house because Joanna was gone for the day? Joanna studied Madaket. She'd come to rely on the young woman so completely she'd stopped really seeing her. She was beautiful, exotically, erotically beautiful.

As they pulled into the driveway, the Snowmen were leaving in their red truck. They'd been alone in her house, Joanna realized. Suddenly she was overwhelmed with fatigue.

"I'm tired," Joanna said as they entered the house. "I think Christopher and I will spend the evening in bed reading magazines."

"All right. Shall I bring your dinner to your bedroom?"

"That would be nice."

Madaket went off to the kitchen. Later, after she'd brought Joanna's dinner up on a tray, she went up the stairs to her attic room.

Joanna played with Christopher, and looked at magazines, and nursed Christopher again, then slid into her wide bed with Christopher next to her and fell asleep. When the baby woke her for his night feeding, it was two in the morning but bright with a high cold winter moon. Joanna nursed and changed the baby, then tucked him into his crib. The lazy evening had left her restless and she'd been having unpleasant dreams. Pulling her heavy down robe on, she went down the stairs, planning to fix herself a cup of chamomile tea.

The overhead kitchen light was too glaring when she flicked it on, so immediately she flicked it off and crossed the room to turn on the small light above the stove. As she moved around the kitchen in the soft cottony light, she realized that Wolf wasn't around, following her every step with hopeful eyes. That was odd. No matter that he slept in the attic with Madaket; if Joanna got up in the night, he always heard her and came down to accompany her, especially when she was eating.

She checked the back hall door. It was unlocked, and Madaket's parka was gone. So even in this weather she was out walking at night, Wolf undoubtedly by her side. The kettle whistled. Joanna poured her tea, then walked through the dark house, looking out the windows. Under the silver moonlight the property around her house rambled off in a tangle and blur of bushes and moors. It was still another two months before the bulbs would be piercing up through the cold ground. Madaket had described it all: crocuses and snowdrops would come first, then the tulips grouped under the windows in the shelter of the front of the house, and finally the daffodils scattered wildly across the back lawn and iris and lilies in the garden. It would be beautiful.

She spotted Madaket at the front of the property, walking slowly around the long rectangle of earth she'd dug and fertilized and worked for a garden last fall. Wolf was by her side. Probably she was planning her spring planting. On the dining room windowsills and in rows in the pantry, small boxes of seedlings and ceramic pots of herbs sprouted. Madaket intended to set them out when it was warm enough. Marjoram, tarragon, parsley, mint—Joanna couldn't name them all. In the sunroom, too big for a sill, sat fat tubs of Madaket's grandmother's ancient and rather gnarled geraniums with stems as thick as fingers and leaves as large as saucers. It made Joanna oddly melancholy to see the plants waiting so patiently, so mutely, through the night, their scalloped leaves angled for the morning sun.

She was cold. Carrying her tea with her, Joanna hurried back up the stairs to the warm oblivion of sleep.

Twenty-Three

⁓

The next morning Joanna sat at the kitchen table, nursing Christopher, while Madaket puttered around, squeezing fresh orange juice and stirring a pot of hot cereal and honey for Joanna's breakfast. It was a mild and oddly oppressive February day; the white sky seemed unusually low and the ocean looked heavy and dark and sullen, and the wind, when it came, was sudden and forceful.

"It's so strange out there today," Joanna remarked.

"They're forecasting a storm," Madaket replied cheerfully. She was wearing one of the sweaters Joanna had given her, a brilliant turquoise, over a long brown skirt, and thick brown stockings and her work boots. "Here's your breakfast. Want me to take the baby?"

"No, thanks. He's not quite finished. I can eat and feed him at the same time."

Madaket took a mug of coffee and sat down at the other end of the kitchen table with a pad and pen. "I'm going into town this morning to stock up on supplies. Food. And a lot of videos. If it really blows, we might be stuck out here for a few days. And of course if it gets bad, all the planes and ferries will be canceled and the grocery stores will be empty."

"You sound happy about it."

"I love a good storm. Do you want some books from the library?"

Joanna shifted Christopher to her shoulder and burped him. "I want to buy some books at Mitchell's. If we're really going to get a big storm, perhaps I'd better go in with you while I can. Christopher can nap in his car seat."

"Great. I'll be ready anytime. Candles," Madaket said, writing her list. "Flashlight batteries. Do we have enough diapers?"

"I think so. This makes me nervous. I'm going to see what the weatherman says."

Joanna went off, Christopher snug in the crook of one arm and a hot cup of decaf in the other hand. Sinking onto the sofa, she set her mug on the end table and switched on the television and watched for the weather forecast. Christopher flexed his muscles eagerly. He was gaining weight, becoming a nice little bundle, plump and sweet-smelling in his blue terry-cloth romper. He had stopped crying every evening, had taken to sleeping several hours at a time during the night, waking Joanna for a feeding only once, and in the mornings he was active and happy and eager to play. She held him facing her on her lap, and put her hands under his arms, supporting his torso so that he seemed to be standing on her legs. He loved this. His eyes brightened while, with enormous effort, his fists clenched, his entire body tensed, he attempted to pull himself up, as if he thought he could stand on his own.

"Big boy," Joanna cooed. "What a big boy." Christopher shrieked with pleasure.

According to the Weather Channel, a major storm was headed their way this evening, or it might veer off into the Atlantic. National weather forecasters weren't always accurate about Nantucket because it was so far away from the mainland. Joanna finished her coffee and headed upstairs with Christopher. She changed his diaper and carried him into the study with her.

Her desk was piled with notes she'd been scribbling to herself about ideas for *Fabulous Homes*. Vaguely she heard noises downstairs: the front door opened and slammed shut, Wolf barked joyfully, voices rumbled. The Snowmen had arrived. They'd probably finish the floor in the sunporch completely today. Good. Joanna had bought a little red automatic swing for Christopher. She could have Madaket assemble it and put it out there, and she would call the cable people to ask them to send someone out this week to move the television cable from the living room to the sunporch.

She turned to her work. Families. She'd made a memo to

herself about the definition of the word "family," which came from the Latin *familia,* meaning servants in a household, or just household. The first definition in Webster's dictionary was "all the people living in the same house." She wanted to do some research and have CVN's Research and Graphics Department create some models, drawings, perhaps three-dimensional reproductions, of ancient houses, Roman houses, when the servants lived in the same house as the family they served. Also, she thought, scribbling rapidly, medieval homes. Castles and forts were lived in by the servants as well as those they served. Now, to the twenty-first and even twenty-second centuries: as more women joined the workforce, it became more important to have good, trustworthy, live-in help, which often meant, in the cities, at least, having a self-contained apartment for the nanny or cook or housekeeper.

She wrote as fast as she could with her right hand while with the left arm she jiggled Christopher against her body. When she glanced at him, she saw that he'd fallen asleep. He was so perfect, so lovely . . . and he was getting heavy. Quietly she padded down the hall and into the nursery, where she lay him on his tummy in his crib. He sighed a sweet high baby sigh and scooted up so that his little diaper-padded bottom stuck up in the air; his current favorite way to sleep. Joanna covered him with a light thermal blanket and stood watching him. Why was it that a baby's sleep was so particularly hypnotic and pleasing?

"Joanna," Madaket whispered from the door. "Are you ready to go into town with me?"

Joanna left the side of the crib and went out into the hall, pulling the door shut behind her. Now the nursery would stay cozily warm, without the long hallway leeching out the heat.

"I've changed my mind. I think I'd better stay here, Madaket. There's some work I want to do, and now that Christopher's settled in for a nap, I think I'll have some time to concentrate. Let me give you a list of books I want you to buy. Just charge them to my account."

Together the two women went into Joanna's study, and Joanna wrote a few titles on a sheet of paper, and Madaket took the list and some signed checks from Joanna for the groceries and gas for the Jeep and some fresh flowers for the house.

"I'll be back by lunch. Doug and Todd are working in the sunporch. They think they'll be through today."

"Good." Joanna was not completely comfortable with this arrangement of relaying messages and knew she needed to talk to the men directly. But *Fabulous Homes* was on her mind, and she didn't want to break the flow of ideas. She sat down at her desk. "I'll see you later."

She was aware of Madaket's steps as the young woman went down the stairs, and she heard the front door slam and then the rumble of the Jeep's engine and the crackle of gravel. Because the house was so large, she'd installed a monitor in the nursery, so that she could hear instantly when Christopher awoke or cried, and now she heard only the faint regular sounds of his breathing.

She focused on her work, but felt blocked and stalled. It seemed that motherhood had plugged the channels of her brain with molasses; she knew the good ideas were there, waiting in the crevices of her mind, but it took her true labor to force her way through the sweet muddle and laze of her head to find anything. She needed more coffee. Even if it did mean encountering the Snows.

Hurrying downstairs, she entered the kitchen and was surprised to find it empty. She looked into the sunroom. It was crowded with equipment: sawhorses, a tool chest, sheets of plywood, a new roll of carpet. But Doug and Todd weren't there. She'd heard them come in only a few minutes ago. Where were they?

She went back into the kitchen, picked up her mug, took a carton of skim milk from the refrigerator, poured, and stirred. She put the milk back in the refrigerator and lifted her mug to her lips. Outside, the white sky had become tinged with an ominous gray and the ocean was leaping and frothing.

A thunderous boom split the air, shaking the entire house.

Beneath Joanna's feet the floor moved, throwing her to her knees. Her mug flew out of her hand and across the room. She threw her hands out to catch herself as she fell. The noise was so tremendous she thought a jet had fallen from the sky, through the roof, and into the house. Through the kitchen door she saw the hall floor burst open, its golden boards cracking apart and flying upward. One wall of the kitchen groaned and shuddered and broke open, flames flashing up from beneath the floor.

For a split second she knelt, stunned. More explosions roared through the air. Her mug lay shattered on the floor, the coffee spilled in a wide black shivering puddle.

Her mind jumped forward and signaled: Fire. Danger. Christopher.

Stumbling, she pushed herself up and raced out into the hall. A jagged hole yawned in the middle of the wide boards, and from it tongues of fire leapt upward. On the other side of the hallway, the living room was crashing inward, part of the second floor above it was groaning downward, and she could see part of the attic as the fire twisted up to the sky. Bits of flaming rubble, timber, burning wood, shot up as blast followed blast through the roof. Black clouds of smoke billowed through the house. She ran along the margin of the hallway, past the fiery hole, up the stairs, into the nursery.

Christopher was in his crib, screaming with fear. Joanna grabbed him up. She took a precious few moments to cradle him against her shoulder, murmuring, "There, there, darling baby, it's all right, Mother's here, it's all right."

She stepped back out into the hall, then stopped, trying to think. The center of the house was consumed with flames. More of the house was giving way as she watched, walls and floors cracking, screaming, as if the fire were eating off chunks of it, chewing it down into its burning belly. The back of the house was now a fiery pit, and the front stairway was rippling with flames. Oily smoke obscured her vision, rolled over her face, smothering her, making her cough. The noise was terrifying, as if a train were passing over them. Christopher screamed and thrashed in her arms. Heat blasted toward them.

She ran back into the nursery and with shaking hands swaddled her baby in blankets, taking care to cover Christopher's face, but not too tightly. She pulled another blanket over her head and shoulders. She was moving as fast as she could, but already the air in the nursery was hot and thick with smoke and she was coughing spontaneously, continuously. She took time to look out the window: no. She and the baby would not survive a jump from this height. She had to face the fire.

Now flames were billowing up through the hall as if blown by the winds of hell. Wood crashed around her, bits of ceiling and draperies fell or floated upward on the inferno's breath. But the front stairway still held, although the inner wall was a sheet of fire. Just a few feet farther down the hallway, the antique mahogany trestle table, with its silver bowl filled with white letters to be mailed, and its orange and blue porcelain vase of dried hydrangeas, tipped and slid and disappeared in the flames. Then the lopsided coatrack, one of Joanna's treasures from the dump, fell. Soon the stairs would go.

She had no choice. Coughing, her eyes weeping from the sting of the smoke, she tightened the blanket around her face, leaving only enough room to see out of, and clutching her baby tightly to her breast, she plunged down the steps. Flames grabbed for her. She felt a searing pain as the hand holding the blanket over her head was scorched by the heat. Each breath was agony, as if she were swallowing glass, and she was dizzy, and the walls around her were sagging and bending so that she couldn't see clearly.

She reached the bottom of the staircase. Between her and the front door a wall of fire raged. The house roared as it was ripped apart, crashing into the central core of the fire. Frantic, she looked behind her, but saw only fire. The heat was intense. Desperate for air, she took a few steps back up the front staircase toward the remaining front hall and bedroom where the fire hadn't completely taken over. She looked helplessly down at the inferno. She couldn't go through the flames. But she had to; it was the only way out. Without realizing it, she'd sunk to her knees, and kneeling, she coughed racking coughs, trying to clear the smoke from her lungs. She couldn't think clearly. She was too dizzy to stand. She couldn't get back to her feet. A smothering sensation came over her, she felt her eyes bulge, and she tried to crawl forward on one elbow, holding her baby with the other arm.

A figure loomed toward her through the oily thick smoke. Madaket was crashing toward them through the flames. Joanna felt Madaket's arms embrace Joanna and Christopher, she felt herself and her baby being dragged through the flames. They were in the fire. Then they were going out the burning front door to safety. She fought not to lose consciousness, but her nose and mouth burned and it hurt to breathe.

It felt like the end of the world. She was aware of lying on the ground, on the gravel. Her arms were still around Christopher, her body curled over his. She could feel the heat and hear the crackle of burning wood, the scream and crash of falling lumber. Beneath her cheek the driveway was gritty and cold. It scratched her skin. Christopher was crying. Her breath burned in her throat. Someone near her was keening shrilly in pain. Then the noise stopped.

"Joanna, oh my God, Joanna." June Lathern was there, weeping and babbling, her voice shrill with hysteria.

"The fire department's on its way. An ambulance is coming." Morris Lathern's voice was calmer. He rolled Joanna onto her back, and loosening her hold from the baby, took Christopher from her arms. Christopher screamed.

"He's all right, Joanna," Morris said. "June has him now. He's perfectly all right. Can you breathe?"

Joanna tried to say yes, but made only a hideous sound that felt as if it ripped apart the tissues of her throat.

"I'm going to carry you now," Morris said. "Just a little ways, to get you away from the heat."

Joanna felt herself being half lifted, half dragged, and she heard Morris grunt with exertion, and felt the effort and strain in his chest and arms.

"Go back to the house and get blankets to cover them," he said to his wife.

Joanna heard Christopher's crying subside and then dim as June went away.

A hideous stench, a smell like that of cooked meat, assaulted Joanna's senses, filling her with terror. "Madaket," she cried.

The word was unintelligible, but Morris understood. "I'm going to her now."

Joanna lay on the ground on her side. Above her something large and black flew across the sky, dipping and flapping. The air roiled and trembled with fiery cannonades of thunderous sound, as if all the devils in hell were doing battle. Wrenching her body around, she faced her house. It was writhing with fire. Flames flared from the roof and poured out the windows. Great black clouds of smoke billowed up into the sky. Black flags of burned material floated upward on waves of hot air.

An enormous crash shook the air, followed by a pandemonium of sounds as beams, furniture, ceilings, walls, and floors collapsed in the fury of the fire. Sparks flew upward like brilliant orange birds, and instantaneous explosions ripped the air.

She was aware of the scream of sirens slicing through the air as a red fire truck, enormous and gleaming, raced into the drive. Behind it came another, and then an ambulance. The earth shook beneath her.

The fire chief, bulky in his black and yellow slicker and helmet, jumped out. She could not move anymore; she felt her consciousness fading, melting in the waves of heat.

The fire chief yelled, "What happened?"

From somewhere nearby Morris shouted back, "I don't know!"

"Anyone else in there?"

She didn't hear the answer.

She was aware of being strapped on a stretcher and slid into the ambulance. Gardner was there. June was there, with Christopher. The last sight she saw before they closed the ambulance doors was her house, now completely transformed into a towering frenzy of orange and black and purple flames. Huge sails of black smoke lifted off and swept toward the ocean.

Later, she understood she was in the hospital. Her throat was on fire. People moved around her and pricked her arms.

She awoke in the late afternoon. Pat was sitting on a chair with a book. Immediately she came to the bedside.

"What happened?" Joanna asked, but to her horror, only a croak emerged from her painful throat and mouth. A scream swelled in her chest.

Pat leaned forward. "You're okay. Christopher's okay. The smoke burned your throat and respiratory passages, but you'll be okay."

Where's Madaket? Joanna asked, mouthing the words, beseeching with her eyes and her hands.

"Madaket's alive," Pat replied. "Now close your eyes. You have to rest."

They brought her the baby to nurse at some point in the evening. She was thirsty, but could have nothing to drink. Tubes in her arms gave her necessary liquids.

She fell asleep, and woke in terror, screaming, thinking that it was happening again. The nurses came and gave her more shots.

She woke again in the late morning. She was in a hospital room. Milky sunlight poured through the window. In a chair near the bed, Pat sat reading a magazine.

"Hey, there. You're awake," Pat cried, looking up.

"The baby—" Joanna croaked. Her throat was sore and parched.

"Right here." Pat gestured to a portable crib. Christopher was there, wearing an unfamiliar white garment, covered with a light blanket. He was on his tummy, bottom in the air, sleeping peacefully. "He's okay. Not the tiniest part was burned. I'll tell the nurse you're awake."

"No, wait. Pat—"

But Pat hurried away, shutting the door behind her.

Joanna looked around, looked down to see her right hand wrapped and taped with white gauze. The hand that had held the blanket closed around her and Christopher. She felt her face with her good hand. It was smooth and unbandaged. No pain. Because of the blanket around her, she'd come through the flames intact.

Pat returned, followed by Gardner. He looked terrible, pale, with dark circles beneath his eyes, and tired, and somber. But he smiled as he approached the bed.

"Good morning."

"Gardner. It hurts to talk. It hurts to swallow."

"You inhaled smoke, hot air, soot, and it burned your throat. You have minor tracheal swelling. But we didn't have to intubate you. We'll keep you on liquids; you'll heal fast." He came close to the bed, took her wrist in his hand, and took her pulse. "You'll be fine."

"And Madaket?"

His forehead creased. "She's in Boston. Intensive care. Mass General Burn Center."

"Oh, Gardner!"

"She'll live. She'll be all right."

"But was she—"

"She sustained severe burns."

"How severe?"

"What you would know as second-degree."

"When will she be back on the island?"

"Not for a month or two. We'll see. She has to be isolated for a while—burns can easily get infected."

"Is she in pain?"

He paused. "She's on pain medication."

"Gardner. I have to know. How bad—"

Gardner hesitated. "Her face sustained full burns. Her hair—is gone. Her scalp was burned. Her hands were burned. About eighteen percent of the rest of her body sustained partial burns."

Joanna moaned with pity. "Dear God."

"But she was lucky," Gardner continued. "Her jacket and all her heavy wool clothing protected most of her body."

"Think how much she loves you," Pat said, her voice husky with wonder. "Joanna, she saved your life. And Christopher's."

"Yes."

"She went right into the fire to get you out."

"What about Wolf? And Bitch?"

Gardner shook his head. "I suppose there's a chance, if they were outside . . . If they were inside, their bones will be buried in the rubble."

"What happened?" Joanna asked. "Does anyone know?"

Pat looked at Gardner, who nodded. She took Joanna's unbandaged hand in hers. "Doug and Todd Snow used dynamite."

"Dynamite!"

"The fire chief talked to Mrs. Snow. Doug's brother is in construction work. Doug got some dynamite from him. Doug and Todd told Helen that they'd found part of Farthingale's treasure in a room underneath the screened porch. They thought there was more." Pat looked questioningly at Joanna.

So that was it. Closing her eyes, Joanna admitted, "It's true. When they began work on the sunporch, Doug and Todd found a trapdoor leading to a cool cellar beneath the porch. Todd and Madaket went down. They found a room with brick walls, and a small old metal chest with a lock on it. We opened it together, the four of us, Todd and Doug, Madaket and me, and we found a pouch with two rubies in it."

"Are you sure they were rubies?" Pat asked.

Joanna nodded. "I've taken them to Boston. To a jeweler's. I sold them."

"So you really did find the Farthingale treasure." Pat shook her head in wonder.

"Yes. I'm sorry I didn't tell you, Pat. I didn't tell anyone— I was so tired, and worried about continuing the pregnancy to term, and I wanted to avoid publicity and all that fuss. The others agreed to wait until I was ready before telling anyone else. And in all honesty, I had so much else going on I just didn't think about it. But I did let Todd and Madaket explore the tunnel."

"There was a tunnel?"

"Yes. I never saw it. Leading toward the ocean. Madaket said it was mostly caved in. Todd and Madaket spent quite a few nights digging around in the sand, sifting, opening up the tunnel. They hoped there would be more chests there. Something." Bleakly she continued. "I didn't realize how important the idea of more treasure was to the Snows. How tempting. It didn't mean much to me. I told them to cover the trapdoor. I wanted the room finished. Dear God. If only I'd . . ." She looked up at Gardner. "How are they?"

He shook his head. "Last night after the fire was completely extinguished, they used backhoes to pull away the heaviest debris, then a crew of men shoveled, and—they found the bodies."

"Both dead?"

Gardner nodded.

"My God. This is all so terrible. I can't take it in. Doug and Todd . . . dead." She put her hands to her face. "I feel guilty," she whispered.

"You're not to blame for this, Joanna," Gardner insisted.

"Should I have given them the rubies?" she wondered

aloud. Raising sorrowful eyes to her friends, she confided, "I called Morris and asked him a theoretical question about finding treasure; he said anything found in my house belonged to me. But if I had given them the rubies . . ."

"If you had given them the rubies, they would still have looked for more treasure," Pat replied. "It would only have whetted their appetites."

Gardner said, "The fire chief told us what Helen knew: Doug and Todd planned to blast open the brick wall between the main basement and the little dirt cellar so they could go on looking for more treasure even when the sun-room floor was covered over. They didn't mean to injure you; they said you never go down in the basement. They planned to create only a small opening, and to use the dynamite when you and Christopher and Madaket had left the house in the Jeep."

"They just misjudged the amount of dynamite to use," Pat concluded.

"And now they're both dead," Joanna said. "Todd and Doug—" She began to weep. "I can't bear it."

"You need to rest now," Gardner said.

"We'll be back later," Pat assured Joanna, and approaching the bed, she wrapped her in a long and disconsolate embrace.

From the portable crib a soft wail rose.

"I think you've got a hungry baby here," Gardner observed. "Want him?"

Pat released Joanna, who wiped her eyes and replied, "Yes, please."

Pat lifted the tiny bundle from the crib and put Christopher into his mother's arms. "I've got to make some phone calls. I'll leave you alone with your little boy. Okay?"

Joanna looked at Christopher, awestruck. The baby gave her a huge toothless smile and began to make bubbles of joy.

"Oh, yes. Sweet darling," Joanna cooed. Her baby cooed back.

Gardner watched them fondly for a moment. "I'll be back, Joanna. And I'll keep you informed about Madaket's condition."

"Wait, Gardner," Joanna entreated. "Tell me: how long do I have to stay in here?"

"I'd like to keep you at least another night."

"But—"

"You've had a bad shock, Joanna. You'll be able to rest better here."

"Can I get up and move around?"

"Of course. Just be careful with that hand."

"Can I talk to Madaket on the phone?"

"Not yet. The pain medication is keeping her pretty foggy."

"Listen, hon." Pat patted Joanna's arm. "Everyone's going to be all right. You and Christopher and Madaket are alive, and now you have to regain your strength. As soon as you can get out of here, I'm taking you and your baby back to my house. Everyone wants to see you, everyone's offering to loan you baby cribs and everything you'll need. It's going to be all right. It's going to be just fine."

Pat kissed Joanna's cheek, then she and Gardner left the room.

Joanna put Christopher on the bed and, unfolding his blankets around him as if peeling back the petals of a flower, she stripped him and studied the perfect pink rose of a body. Christopher waved his arms and legs slowly, and blew bubbles, and his eyes were shining and his tiny dear face glowing with love for his mother.

"Oh, my baby," Joanna exclaimed, and buried her head in her son's fine powdery scent and kissed his little wriggling body all over. Christopher latched onto Joanna's hair with his fists. That this perfect plump soft baby flesh could have been . . . scorched . . . *burned* . . . or worse . . . The moment of explosion flashed over Joanna again and she closed her eyes and rocked in the memory. Horrible, horrible. But Christopher squealed and began to make little fussing noises, pointing out that he was hungry, and Joanna opened her eyes and brought herself back to the moment, this moment, safe and intact with her lovely baby alive and needing breakfast. And here she was, safe and intact, able to feed her child. It seemed miraculous. Her milk pressed at her nipples.

Quickly dressing Christopher, she sat back up against the pillows and brought the baby to her breast. Christopher gave a happy groan of pleasure when Joanna's milk rushed out, and as he nursed, he stroked Joanna's breast in little circling motions. It gave Joanna immense comfort to comfort her child. Afterward Joanna moved down into the bed. She was very tired. She lay her baby near her, snuggled in a cove between her outstretched arm and her breast. Christopher lay placidly looking around him. Joanna dozed.

But only for a few moments. Then, behind her closed eyes, it happened again: the house shuddered and exploded and she and her baby were trapped inside the house. She came awake, gasping.

In the afternoon she was allowed to sit in a chair and to receive visitors.

Pat returned. Bob was with her, and they brought a vase of spring flowers and a suitcase of new clothes for herself and Christopher. Pat hugged Joanna. "Bob's been busy. Everything's going along fine."

"I've already talked to Walt Rinehart. Your insurance covers it completely. When you get some energy back, you can start thinking about building yourself the perfect house," Bob assured her.

June and Morris arrived with an enormous bouquet of flowers. "You can come live with us awhile," they said. "We're interviewing girls to help you take care of Christopher when you feel up to buying clothes or—or anything."

The fire chief arrived. "I'm sorry," he said. "There really wasn't a thing we could do but stop the fire from spreading, and we were lucky to do that with everything so dry. We had three tankers out there, and fourteen men, and we floated a pump in the ocean and pumped about nine thousand gallons of water. But your house was old, and the wood was seasoned. The fire started in the basement, and fire burns in an upward V. Fire loves old wood. It just gobbled your house up. Even if we could have gotten out to Squam sooner, it wouldn't have mattered. Your house was pretty much gone in ten, twelve minutes."

Joanna thanked him through numbed lips.

The fire chief was her last visitor. When he left, a nurse appeared. "You're looking a little fatigued. I tell you what. I'd just love to play with this darling baby. Let me take him awhile and show him off to the other nurses, and you take a little nap," she cajoled.

Wearily Joanna smiled and let her child be lifted from her arms. She closed her eyes and let her head sink back into the pillows. At once her vision was flooded with a pageant of all the possessions she had lost: her airy, bright study with its shining wood file cabinets, her computer with so much of her mind stored in it, her boxes of letters and cards from readers, her pretty pastel wire baskets holding correspondence and memos, the framed photos of Christopher at birth, of her mother and father on their wedding day. All gone. Her wide bed, smooth sheets, deep rugs, candles and chairs and crystal and costly vases and mirrors and armoires and new clothes, gone, all gone. Her treasures from the dump, so lovingly restored. Madaket's beautiful lamp and oil painting. Madaket's potted herbs. Christopher's rocking horse.

And all she had not possessed: Wolf. Bitch. Todd. Doug. All consumed by the fire.

Twenty-Four

The next day Joanna and Christopher were checked out of the hospital, driven to the Hoovers', and settled in the bedroom which had belonged to a daughter, now grown and gone, with the understanding that in a few days, whenever Joanna felt like it, she and her baby would move to the guest suite above the Hoovers' garage. For now, she wanted the comfort of people nearby. She was on a mild sedative, which didn't prevent the nightmares at night, but did postpone a squall of emotions which flickered at the edge of her thoughts. Christopher flourished, not minding where he slept or when he was fed or who held him, and Joanna held him almost all the time, except when sleeping, because it calmed her to have the baby safe in her arms.

Joanna called Gardner her first day out of the hospital to find out how Madaket was. "I want to see her," Joanna told him.

"I think you should wait a few days," Gardner advised her.

"Why? Is she lucid?"

"Sometimes. She's on morphine for pain. And . . . she looks . . . different now. You have to understand."

Joanna's voice trembled. "You're afraid, when I see her, I'll be frightened or upset and scare her."

After a pause, Gardner replied, "Yes. But I'm thinking of you as well, Joanna. You need to regain your strength."

"Gardner, if she cared enough for me to save my life, I think I can care enough to go see her. She needs to know"— why hadn't she said this before?—"I love her."

Again, a pause. Then, "Yes, of course. You're right. I'll go with you. We'll fly up on Friday."

* * *

For a few days Joanna did nothing more than take care of Christopher and sleep. She was aware of commotion in the house as, all through the following days and evenings, people arrived with gifts, secondhand donations, the necessities of daily life. The women from her mothers' club brought baby clothes and baby equipment; someone loaned a crib. They left cards of sympathy and support, messages offering to take care of Christopher whenever Joanna needed, and she was stunned by their generosity, and deeply grateful in a way she could not find the words or energy to express. June, who was tall like Joanna, donated two suitcases of clothing for Joanna to wear until she could buy a new wardrobe, and Claude Clifford presented her with a totally impractical, sinfully gorgeous silk and cashmere nightgown and robe in gleaming emerald green. The accompanying note read, "Darling Joanna, please wear this. It's so important to look good when you're depressed!" This brought a brief smile to her face.

Marge and Harry Coffin, who owned the bakery where once Madaket had worked, phoned one morning and asked if they could impose on Joanna for just a few moments. She agreed, and they arrived at the Hoovers' house that afternoon. Both verging on retirement, the couple were a lookalike salt-and-pepper set, both round, rosy-cheeked, white-haired. They wore similar beige down coats which they did not remove as they seated themselves in Pat's living room.

"We've come about Madaket," Marge Coffin said. "You know she used to be our employee at the bakery."

"Yes. She told me how much she enjoyed working for you."

"How is she?"

"I haven't spoken with her yet. Gardner Adams told me she is stable, recovering—" Joanna's throat closed. "She's alive. She will live."

Marge Coffin's eyes were as blue as robin's eggs. "We're tiring you. We won't keep you. We wanted to give you this. For Madaket."

Harry reached into his jacket pocket and brought out a piece of paper. He handed it to Joanna. It was a check for a thousand dollars, made out to Madaket. Joanna looked up, confused.

"We took up a collection," he said, his voice gruff with emotion. "It's from the community. Everyone. Teachers and kids at the high school, and people she worked for, and merchants. Everyone gave a little bit."

"I know it's not much," Marge told Joanna. "But we thought every little bit would help. We thought you might have insurance for the hospital bills—"

Joanna nodded confirmation.

"Thank God for that. Still, she'll need so many things." Marge cleared her throat. "Tell her that they've started a collection box at the high school for clothes. Everyone knows the kind of thing Madaket wears, and people are bringing in what they think might work. There'll be an announcement about it in the paper."

Harry Coffin continued. "They're starting a fund at Young's bike shop. So when she's out of the hospital, there'll be money for a new bike for her."

"This is all so generous," Joanna said, brought to the point of tears. "But I thought . . . that Madaket was . . . considered . . ." She stumbled over her words, unable to find the right phrase.

Harry Coffin finished for her. "She's odd, but she's one of us."

Marge smiled gently. "Comes a time when you believe we're all a bit odd, those of us who make our homes here."

"We sent her flowers, too, and one of the high school girls is going around with a great big get-well card for everyone to sign."

"It will mean so much to her," Joanna told them. Her voice was choked with emotion.

"We don't mean to be intrusive," Marge began, "but we wondered—"

"Yes?"

"Will you be staying here?"

"I'll be at the Hoovers', yes."

Harry cleared his throat. "Are you planning to remain on Nantucket is what we meant. We would understand, if after losing your house, you went back to New York."

"What we mean," Marge rushed on, "is that if you do, well,

please tell Madaket she can live with us."

"I'll tell her," Joanna said quietly. "But I plan to remain here. When I find the strength, I'll rent a house until I can rebuild. Please don't worry. I'll take care of Madaket."

"That's good to know," Harry said.

"And let us help you," Marge urged. "We care for Madaket, too."

"Yes. Of course. I'll tell her. I know she'll be grateful. It will mean so much to her, I know. I think she'll be suprised."

Four days after the fire Joanna and Gardner climbed into a small commercial airplane and flew to Boston. The predicted storm front had come through the night of the fire, and now had passed on, leaving the ocean dark and choppy and the sky full of turbulence and peevish leftover winds that swatted and slammed the spunky plane as it bounced over a roller coaster of gray air all the way up the Massachusetts coast. It was rocky enough to make some of the passengers use the paper bags supplied for the purpose. One woman wept quietly with terror. Joanna only closed her eyes and sagged into her seat. She wasn't afraid they would crash.

They landed safely enough. Gardner gently ushered her through the bustling airport and out the glass doors to the line of waiting taxis. Joanna sat silent with apprehension as they passed through the Callahan Tunnel and wended along Boston's crowded streets and avenues, finally entering a congested, narrow street shadowed by looming buildings. Suddenly a paved courtyard opened up on the left and Massachusetts General Hospital rose up into the sky with a vigilant and stony dignity. On either side of its tall central tower long brick arms projected, so that the hospital seemed literally to reach out with open arms, welcoming, offering sturdy hospice.

Inside the hospital, Gardner quietly shepherded her through the wide central corridor thronging with nurses and doctors and lab technicians and visitors carrying flowers and bandaged patients out for a spin in their wheelchairs. The core of the building housed the elevators which Joanna and Gardner rode to Bigelow 13 and the Sumner Redstone Burn Center. The doors slid open. Joanna took a deep breath and stepped out.

The hall was wide and smooth and glossily clean. Gardner took Joanna by the arm and led her to the nurse's station.

"Hey there, Dr. Adams, how're you doin'?" The receptionist, a sensationally gorgeous black woman, greeted them with a smile.

"Hello, Rosalyn. I'd like you to meet Joanna Jones. She's come to see Madaket."

"That's great. I'll get Lisa to take you in." Picking up the phone, she pressed a button, spoke briefly, then told them, "She'll be right down."

"How'd you do on your phlebotomy exam?" Gardner asked, and as he stood chatting with the receptionist, Joanna found some of the chill thawing from around her heart, and her breath melting more deeply into her lungs. She realized that she'd been unconsciously envisioning a grim, unnatural, exigent place, where caregivers with deeply furrowed brows rushed through air shivering with the moans of people.

"Hi, Gardner." A nurse in green scrubs approached them. She was young and pretty, with tangles of curly brown hair; perhaps in order to offset any nuances of flirtatiousness given off by her unavoidable good looks, her expression was solemn, almost formal, and her movements efficient and deliberate. She held out her hand to Joanna. "I'm Lisa Hale, the charge nurse."

"Hello. I'm Joanna Jones."

The nurse shook Joanna's hand briefly but firmly. "I'd like to tell you something about Madaket's condition before you go in." Her eyes flicked to Gardner quickly, then back. "I'm sure Dr. Adams has already described some of this to you, but I'll go over it, just so you're not alarmed. Madaket's in our Bacterial Control Nursing Unit. It's necessary to protect a burned patient from infectious germs, to which the patient is susceptible because the skin, which usually protects the body from infection, has been broken. Also, these units house special laminar flow vents which keep the air sterile and the temperature and humidity comfortable for the patient. Burn patients tend to feel cold; they have difficulty maintaining body temperature because their skin is injured."

Lisa paused and waited, gauging Joanna's reaction. "I understand," Joanna told her, nodding.

The nurse nodded in return. "Madaket is also on a respirator. She has tubes in her throat, because of the swelling in her tissues, and she's not going to be able to talk. She won't be able to write messages to you either, because her hands are bandaged. She's going to be groggy. She's on morphine for the pain. And she's going to look dirty to you. That's because we put silver nitrate on her burns, and contact with air turns it black. But she's not dirty; her wounds are cleaned every two hours. All right?"

"All right."

"This way."

Lisa turned and Joanna and Gardner followed. At the door to the large room housing four BCNU units, they stopped.

"Just look a moment, Joanna," Gardner said.

Joanna complied. All four beds were surrounded by transparent walls of clear plastic suspended from metal rods and extending to the floor. In the bed nearest her a man lay unconscious, swathed in white gauze from head to toe. Across the aisle from him were two empty beds. On the fourth bed lay a still white figure covered with white blankets, head and chest and hands bandaged in gauze. Her arms were strapped into long foam-cushioned metal troughs hanging from a metal bar ringing the bed.

The nurse must have followed Joanna's eyes. "Her arms are kept raised to prevent swelling," she informed her.

Madaket was lying very still. She didn't even seem to breathe. Outside the plastic room a computerlike monitor flickered. Tubes snaked from the wall at the head of her bed and into her nose and arm. Gardner put his arm around Joanna to steady her.

"Take your time. Look at her now. Prepare yourself before you talk to her."

"Yes. All right."

"Remember, you don't want to frighten her."

"No."

They approached the bed.

"Hello, Madaket." Joanna leaned against the plastic sheet, looking in.

Madaket opened her eyes. They were dazed with pain, dark holes of suffering sunk inside the white, mummylike wrappings.

"Oh, Madaket. My dear." Joanna turned to the nurse. "Could I touch her?"

"Yes. First you'll need to wash your hands and put on gauntlets."

"I'll be right back," Joanna assured Madaket, and hurrying after the nurse, washed her hands with pHisoHex and slid on the enormous thin plastic gloves the nurse handed her; they enveloped her from fingertip to shoulder. Returning to the bed, Joanna waited while the nurse parted the plastic walls at waist level, making a slit through which Joanna pushed her arms. For a moment she stopped, unsure just where to touch the young woman, and then her emotions took over. She needed desperately to touch Madaket. She wanted to pick the young woman up and hold her in her arms. She wanted to comfort and console her, to take the pain away.

"Her upper arm?" Joanna asked the nurse. "Here? Will it hurt her here?"

"Around her elbow's best. You can see—she wasn't burned there."

Joanna lay her hands on Madaket's arm just above the elbow, and felt through the plastic the yielding cushion of Madaket's live flesh, and choking back tears which had suddenly clotted her throat, she caressed the unburned skin.

"Madaket. Sweetie. How can I ever thank you? You saved my life. You saved Christopher's life."

Madaket's eyes were black but shining, intense, it seemed to Joanna, with a desperate need to hear and speak and connect. Joanna's words came out in a rush, she couldn't say it all fast enough. "Madaket, listen, you're my daughter now, you're my family and Christopher's, I think you've always been. I love you like my own and I loved you that way before the fire but didn't realize. I'll take care of you always. When you come out of the hospital, you'll live with me as long as you want to. I'll take you to Europe, I'll buy you your own car—oh, Jesus, Madaket, how could you have done that, run into the fire?"

Gardner put his arm around Joanna and pulled her back

upright and Joanna realized she had been bent almost double in her anguish. "Easy there. Don't frighten her. Tell her about Christopher," he suggested quietly. "Tell her about where you're living now."

Joanna nodded. She took a deep breath. Her throat convulsed with her efforts not to sob. She leaned back in toward Madaket. "Christopher is fine, perfect, not a mark on him. All because of you." Madaket's eyes were avid. She tried to think of something, anything. "And we're staying at the Hoovers', in their guest room, and people are so kind, so many people have brought clothing and baby equipment. Madaket, Marge and Harry Coffin came by. They brought a check for you from the community, from everyone on Nantucket. A thousand dollars! The high school's collecting clothes for you. They are all so concerned about you. Everyone sends their best wishes."

Madaket's lips moved, but the tubes prevented any communicable sound from forming.

"What?" Joanna leaned over.

"I think she's asking about Bitch and Wolf," Gardner said.

"Oh, Madaket, I don't know. I don't think—"

"We think they were in the house, Madaket," Gardner said, leaning against the plastic toward the young woman's face. "But I'll go back out and look in the area. Just in case." He put his hand on Joanna's shoulder. "All right. We should go. You rest, Madaket. You're in good hands."

"I'll come back soon and as often as I can," Joanna promised, and leaning forward, she pressed a kiss onto the plastic sheet. When Madaket closed her eyes deep within the bandages, it looked as if a light had been extinguished.

Out in the hall, Joanna conferred with Gardner and the charge nurse.

"How long will she need to be here?"

Gardner cleared his throat. "The doctor on charge told me it should be about a month. We have to see how she heals and whether or not she gets infected."

"Can I come visit her?"

"Of course," Lisa replied. "Probably it will do more good for her if you come when she's out of the BCNU and can communicate."

"When will that be?"

"I'd say she'll be out of BCNU in about three more days. Her burns are actually minor, at least compared to what we get here. I tell you what. I'll give you our phone number and you can call us here every day to check on her condition."

"Thank you. Thank you for everything. I appreciate all you're doing." Joanna turned to Gardner. "Tell me, please. How will Madaket look once she's healed?"

He reflected a moment, then answered, "I think her hair should grow back all right. Her face will be quite scarred."

"You've seen the burns?"

"Yes."

"Will she need skin grafting?"

"There's always that possibility. It takes a long time for skin to grow back, so it will be a while before we can determine what is necessary or desired."

"Gardner, tell me the truth. Will she ever be as beautiful as she was before?"

A pensive smile fell across Gardner's face. "I think so."

"If you'll excuse me," Lisa said, handing Joanna a slip of paper. "Here's our phone number. I must go. I've got a meeting . . ."

"Of course. Thank you. I'll be calling you."

Lisa nodded and hurried off. Joanna took one long look at the doorway to the room where Madaket lay, then said to Gardner, "There's nothing we can do for her now, is there?"

"No."

"Then I guess I'm ready to return to Nantucket."

Then together in a companionable and meditative silence Joanna and Gardner retraced their steps through the hospital and out to a waiting taxi which took them to the airport. In the echoing lobby they sank into molded plastic seats and waited for their flight to be called.

"Are you okay?" Gardner asked.

"Yes. Just very tired." Joanna studied the physician's face. "You look tired, too." A thought occurred to her. "Have you been seeing your regular patients as well as flying to Boston?"

"Yes," he admitted.

"Oh, Gardner, no wonder you're exhausted."

"It's only the traveling that fatigues me. Practicing medicine is what keeps me sane."

An almost maternal affection rushed through Joanna as

she realized how powerful the compassions of the heart were behind Gardner's handsome face. The fire, the deaths of Todd and Doug, the injuries to Madaket, all this had touched many people, she realized, and she patted Gardner's arm in a gesture of comfort, and found that the gesture also brought some little comfort to her.

Once again the plane ride was tempestuous, and Joanna closed her eyes in reaction, and to her surprise awoke from a deep sleep as the plane was touching down in Nantucket. Gardner had driven to the airport, and they found his Bronco in the parking lot and rode together in peaceful exhaustion to the Hoovers' house.

The front door opened before they could knock. Pat stood holding Christopher upright against her nubby black sweater with one arm, and with the other she manipulated the baby's hand so that he waved at Joanna.

"Mommy, Mommy, you're home!" she squealed, then laughed. "What is it about babies that makes a person talk like a cartoon character? Joanna, you look exhausted, come in out of the cold. You, too, Gardner. You both could use a drink, and I've got a bouillabaisse and some homemade bread waiting for dinner."

Gardner helped Joanna take off her coat, and Pat placed Christopher in her arms and Joanna went off into the guest bedroom to nurse her baby. Pat brought her a glass of warm apple cider. Joanna watched her son as he nursed, blissfully happy to hold his familiar weight in her arms again. She ran her fingers over the delicate fuzz of his scalp and down the perfect, glistening, silken pink of his cheek.

"Joanna?" Pat approached her softly. "There's a phone call for you. It's Tory. Can you talk? We've got a portable phone, I can bring it to you."

"Yes, please," Joanna answered, and when Pat had brought her the phone, said, "Hi, Tory."

"Oh, Joanna!" Tory was crying. "We just returned from Mexico and heard the news. I can't believe it. How are you?"

"I'm very tired." She discovered she had no energy for conversation.

"Oh, Joanna, I'm so sorry, I'm so sorry! I can't believe this!

After all your hard work, to lose everything like this!"

"Tory," Joanna said quietly, "all I lost was a house."

Late the next afternoon Jake arrived. He'd just heard the news from a friend of Tory's and had chartered a flight from New York and rented a car and appeared at the Hoovers' front door, as laden with bundles as Santa Claus. Pat and Bob invited him in and they all settled in the living room with drinks. Christopher had been fed and was awake and bubbling and wriggling happily in Joanna's arms, and Joanna sat on the sofa holding her son so he could watch while Jake unpacked before Joanna's surprised eyes: an enormous box of Godiva chocolates, five just-published hardback novels, a four-ounce bottle of Joy, four complete baby outfits, a snowsuit, and all sorts of clever toys for Christopher. A brightly colored daisy full of clicking beads especially pleased the baby boy, who grinned beatifically at it and tried to maneuver it into his mouth for further inspection.

Laughing at the sheer excess, Joanna leaned across and kissed Jake lightly on the cheek. "Jake, thank you. What a lot of loot!"

"I had my sons help me pick the toys and clothes out," he confessed.

"Everything's perfect. Oh, it's so kind of you. And to fly here again like this . . ."

"Actually, I've got an ulterior motive."

"Oh?" Laying Christopher on his back between them, she rattled the daisy above his tummy, and the little boy squealed and reached out his chubby hands, trying to grab it.

"Not to sound frivolous, Joanna, but it seems to me the universe is sending you some pretty clear signals that you shouldn't be here. This place is hazardous to your health. You should come back to New York."

"You know that was always my plan, Jake. But I can't come yet."

"Are you sure?"

Joanna looked up, surprised.

"I think Bob and I have suddenly discovered things we have to do in the other room," Pat said, smiling. "Call us if you need anything." The Hoovers left the room.

"Perhaps you'd like another year off," Jake suggested. His

tone was mild but Joanna felt his eyes on her face, reading her reactions.

"I don't know. I don't think I want an entire year off. The show . . . I don't know what to say. Everything is so topsy-turvy right now—"

Jake reached across the sofa and gently touched Joanna's cheek, stilling her words. "Hey. I'm sorry. I didn't mean to pressure you. I just want you to remember you've got a world waiting for you."

Jake's hand on her skin was so large, so male, so much more sturdy than anything she'd felt in a long time. For a moment she was caught in a spell. The starched edge of his shirt cuff lightly brushed her chin. Joanna met Jake's eyes, seeing how the dark brown was flecked with gold and bronze and deep pure light, and in that moment she was entirely suffused with the memory of Jake's tantalizing and mysterious Fourth of July kiss. She had often wondered what Jake had meant by that kiss. Was it only the lighthearted whim of a summer's eve? Jake was not a capricious man.

Her thoughts made her shy, and she was glad when Christopher twisted, so that both Jake and Joanna bent to move the baby away from the edge of the sofa.

"He can turn over," Joanna told Jake. "He can move at the speed of light when he wants."

Jake leaned back and took a sip of his drink. "Have you thought about *Fabulous Homes* at all? How you'd envision it next season? If you'd change it?"

All thoughts of romance vanished; suddenly her mind clicked on. She picked Christopher up and held him in her arms. "Oh, Jake, have I ever! I want a whole new format. I've been thinking about the restoration of old homes. In some cases an old house is like a mountain, with a record of its years built in like eras of the earth. For example, I remember a house in which hideous 1960s silver foil wallpaper covered five other layers of wallpaper, then plaster, and underneath all that, horsehair used as insulation. I've been considering adding a segment called 'Fabulous Homes Past and Future.'" She leaned forward as she talked, feeling an old elastic energy revive within her. "I know someone on the island who has a microwave oven built into a wall which still has the original eighteenth-century beehive baking oven in it.

Another friend has an Indian room, a tiny cubbyhole built to hide valuables. And of course, so many houses have, as mine did, cool cellars. Root cellars." At the thought of her own house, her energy dried up. She sagged back against the sofa. "I don't know if I can do it, Jake."

Jake ignored this lapse into despondency. "You say a segment about past and future. How would you work that into the present format?"

"Oh, I want to change the format," Joanna told him. "I think the show would be better broken up into segments, past, present, and future. The function of rooms in houses has changed considerably: colonial homes used to have birthing rooms, and Victorian homes had good parlors and daily parlors. Now houses are being built with specific rooms for computers or media or exercise equipment. I'd like to write and produce the shows, and perhaps do the intro and a short segment, but have other hosts for each different segment. Some Alistair Cook type to talk about historical houses and a slick young thing to talk about contemporary homes and future designs. You know, Gloria actually would be great for that. She's as shiny as stainless steel and she is knowledgeable. The show needs a new look, not the same leisurely stroll through just one house. I don't like it, but TV today moves fast."

"Right," Jake agreed. "Clips and segments and bites. Here. Let me take him awhile."

He reached out for Christopher, who had been squirming restlessly in Joanna's arms and Joanna handed him to Jake, who laid him along the length of his thighs. Christopher was at once entranced by Jake's thick fingers, and clutching one finger tightly with his entire hand, he tried to pull it toward his mouth for a good experimental chew.

"Sweet," Joanna said, watching her son, then continued, "I'd like to play around with that format, inserting bits, flashing close-ups on details. Show an antique kitchen and a state-of-the-art kitchen side by side, perhaps have a psychologist discuss how cooking and family life have changed. Or remained the same. Also, there should be a home-decorating segment, with one room showcased each week, say a living room, with eight different styles of chairs shown in the same spot, so the viewers can see which they'd like best in their home. I think we'd get great sponsors for that bit."

"Sounds good." Jake's voice boomed in his enthusiasm, and Christopher's eyes widened with surprise.

"Also, Jake, I want to include in each show a brief bit about about alternative homes. Hospices, soup kitchens, AIDS houses, halfway houses for the mentally ill making the transition back to the world, foster homes, communes, shelters, safe places for battered women . . ."

"Not quite what your audience is used to," Jake reminded her.

"I know. But I'm determined. I'll stick it in the middle, I won't go overboard, I won't scare off the advertisers. But I believe it might be a way for the show to help somehow. To raise public consciousness."

Jake considered. "It's worth trying. We could run an address at the end of each show for charitable donations."

"Oh, Jake, that's good."

"When were you planning to start production?"

"I've already decided on several locations, and I've laid the groundwork, talked to the people, gotten some verbal commitments. I'll need some secretarial help for the letters and contracts and logistical arrangements. If we can get the preliminaries done in April, we could start shooting in May. Oh, Jake." Once again her own thoughts braked her to a full stop, and she looked across at Jake with troubled eyes. "All my notes are gone. All my names and addresses and phone numbers and locations. It's all gone." She felt as if she'd just been shoved out of an airplane. All around her, space whirled in a great confusion, and in response her stomach churned and her vision blurred. Sinking back into the cushions of the sofa, she closed her eyes.

Jake's voice was reasonable, encouraging. "I'm sure Gloria has duplicates of most of the names and addresses in her files. And once you sit down with the list, you're bound to remember other contacts, and when you come up with the name, Gloria can dig up the rest."

Joanna shook her head. Her eyes were still closed against the dizziness. "I don't think I can do it."

"Well, give it a try," Jake advised her equably. "I'd hate to see Carter and Gloria get it."

Her head cleared. She opened her eyes. "What do you mean?"

Jake was dandling Christopher on his knee and the baby was bubbling with pleasure. "I mean that Carter and Gloria want to do FH themselves."

"Excuse me? It's *my* show! I conceived it! I initiated it, I breathed life into it! God, Jake, it's called *Joanna Jones' Fabulous Homes*!"

Christopher turned his head and gazed at his mother with amazement.

"I know you did. I'm just telling you what's going on right now. Carter and Gloria are talking to people at the network. They want to take over the show."

"Well, they can't have it." Greatly agitated, Joanna rose and paced the room, rubbing the palms of her hands together as if kindling her thoughts. "Look. This is complicated. I can't come into New York yet, not with everything in such utter chaos here. And I've got to spend as much time with Madaket while she's recovering as I can. You must understand that."

"Of course."

"Give me two months to get organized. And get me a new secretary. I can't work with Gloria if she's going to sabotage me. And get any FH files that are at the network away from Gloria and with my secretary. As soon as you've found someone, I'll tell him what to look for."

"I don't mean to interrupt," Pat said, sticking her head in from the hallway, "but Bob and I are going to have some dinner now. It's a casserole, and there's plenty. Want to join us?"

Joanna threw a questioning glance at Jake, who rose, Christopher in the crook of his arm. "I'd love to. I'm starving." He smiled at Joanna. "And I think we've accomplished what we needed to, at least for tonight."

Over dinner, which tonight Pat and Bob served up in their cozy kitchen, Joanna and Jake conversed amiably with their hosts about babies and children, about television and the future of the entertainment media, the real estate market on Nantucket and the nation's economy, good new books and movies. In the calm of their company, Joanna relaxed. She'd been roused to a state of indignation that was almost alarm over losing her show. She would not lose her show. She had work to do. But as the evening passed, she felt dropped from the heights of excitement to the depths of exhaustion. She excused herself from the table for a while to rock Christopher and tuck him in for the night. When she returned to the kitchen, she felt as if her limbs and nerves and mind were encroached upon by a melting fatigue until it was all she could do to hold her head up and keep her eyes open.

"Are you okay, Joanna?"

Jake's voice seemed to come from far away, as if funneled toward her by a tube of air.

"I'm just so tired." It was all she could say.

"Of course you are," Pat exclaimed. Pushing back her chair, she rose. "You need to go to bed, Joanna."

"You're right. I'm sorry. I don't know what's come over me."

"You've nothing to apologize for," Pat replied.

Jake rose when Joanna did, and met her halfway with an avuncular hug and kiss.

"It was wonderful of you to come, Jake," Joanna said, hugging him to her. "Thank you for all the presents."

"You bet."

"I wish you didn't have to return to New York tomorrow."

"So do I. But I'll be back."

"Jake—" She was frustrated. Overwhelmed with fatigue, aware of the Hoovers' presence, she had no way to ask about his kiss; and how would she phrase her question? It had been only that, one kiss, between colleagues and friends.

Jake's dark eyes seemed deep with emotion. "You get some rest, Joanna. I'll be back soon."

Like a cold person suddenly soothed and comforted by warmth, Joanna nodded, went to her room, and fell asleep the moment her head touched the pillow.

She woke once in the night to feed Christopher, and then they both slept until late in the morning. Jake had gone back to New York. Joanna summoned up her courage and asked Bob to drive her out to Squam. She had to see the remains of her house. She had to face it. Pat offered to stay home with Christopher, and in the early afternoon Bob and Joanna set off in Bob's Mercedes station wagon.

It was a briskly bright February day with the sort of early spring sunlight that made everything seem excessively vivid.

Joanna pulled out her sunglasses to shield her eyes from the glare.

"It was a little more than a year ago when I first brought you out to look at the place," Bob mused as they bounced over the dirt road to her property.

Joanna smiled, remembering. "The moment I stepped inside I knew I wanted it."

They turned in her driveway, down the winding lane, and there before them, with the blue sky and the wide ocean as a backdrop, were the remains of the house, a great hideous mound of blackened timber. Two brick chimneys rose alone intact from the debris.

Joanna's heart contracted.

"Sure you want to do this?"

"I'm sure."

Bob turned off the engine and they got out. Joanna walked around the great pile of rubble which once had been her home. Bob followed behind her, quietly, at a respectful distance. On one side of the house blackened bits of wood protruded from the heaps of ashes and burned timber. On the other side, piles of sand bordered an area which had been dug out, then hurriedly filled back in, after the bodies of Todd and Doug Snow had been found and removed.

It was a scene of terrible desolation.

Joanna turned her back on it and looked out at the ocean, where the water bobbed gaily, tossing up little waves that glinted with light. She walked around the edge of the moorland bordering the cultivated lawn, looking down at the brown and gray, brittle, winter-withered shrubs. Overhead, a gull called and swooped.

Quietly Joanna declared, "I loved that house, Bob."

"Yes. I know you did. Well, you can build a replica, if that's what you want."

"What I want is for the fire never to have happened."

"That," Bob told her, "is one thing you can't have."

Twenty-Five

⌐

*J*oanna could not seem to get enough sleep. Every morning she would awaken to Christopher's cries, rise and feed him, drink a cup of freshly ground strong coffee in Pat and Bob's kitchen, enjoy a bite or two of toast and marmalade, dress for the day, call to check on Madaket's condition, then lie down on the bed with Christopher, instantly falling back asleep. Many days she didn't leave the Hoovers' house. Sometimes she didn't even change out of her green cashmere robe, but shuffled around the guest bedroom, which had become her own snug, safe world. Whenever Pat offered to take Christopher out for a stroll, Joanna accepted, intending to use the free time for the myriad things she needed to accomplish, but, returning to her bedroom for a pen or list or phone number, she'd feel overcome by exhaustion and would collapse on the bed and fall into a heavy sleep until Pat and Christopher returned.

Partly this was because she didn't rest well at night, haunted as she was by nightmares of the fire. Every night, before her eyes, her letters or a favorite sweater or one of Christopher's innocent toys would spontaneously ignite, shooting flames and curling into ashes while she stood helplessly watching. The fire would flare up, a writhing wall surrounding her and her child. Heat would sear her skin. The monstrous roar and crackle filled her ears. She would awaken panting, heart thudding, overwhelmed with terror and grief.

More than that was the simple sense of hopelessness that weighed on her these days. Sometimes she lay staring at the wall, thinking of the Chorus Girl, and her grand old house, and her dreams of family life, and her belief in Carter's love, and even her belief in Doug Snow's interest in her as a woman. All had somehow been torn away from her and consigned to a hazy never-never land.

She disliked herself for being so maudlin. She chided herself for giving in to self-pity. She'd always been strong, a survivor, she'd always picked up her burdens and tossed back her head and carried on. She urged herself to get on with it; but all she wanted to do was to sleep.

Jake called to tell her that *Fabulous Homes* had been bought for syndication with another cable TV network; now five years of old shows ran on a local station every Saturday afternoon at three o'clock. That Saturday Joanna determined to watch it, hoping some architectural style she'd loved a few years ago would catch her eye now and fire her inspiration. Instead, she felt her breath knocked from her lungs. How slender she'd been only a few years ago, how young and sleek and glowing! She didn't have to look in the mirror to realize how much she'd aged in only a year. Sometimes she found herself exhausted by the sight of how she used to be.

It was hard to know what to do with her anger. For anger was there, a dark vein twisting around all her other emotions, webbing up her heart in a net of fine and cutting threads. If only the Snows were alive, so she could sue them and berate them and hate them for all the losses they had caused her, for the damage they'd done to Madaket. But the worst damage they had inflicted on themselves, and Joanna could not separate her anger from her deeper pity.

The officiating minister called Pat Hoover to ask her to let Joanna know, if the question arose, that Helen Snow, Doug's widow, Todd's mother, would prefer it if Joanna did not attend the funeral and burial service, and Joanna respected the woman's wishes.

The day of the funeral Joanna got out of bed only to care for her baby. Other than that, she lay curled on her side, playing desultorily with Christopher when necessary, and when he slept, closing her own eyes. But she was not sleeping. Nor was she thinking, really. She let her thoughts drift, and it was a kind of dreaming that she did, in which Doug and Todd stood before her, whole and healthy and vigorous with life's normal greed. They had wanted Farthingale's treasure. She had wanted Blair's husband, and then she had wanted Helen's. She thought of the sandy ground beneath her house. She thought of the sandy ground in which the bodies of Doug and Todd would be put to rest.

Joanna awoke from violent dreams the day after the funeral and found that while she'd slept, her subconscious had been working furiously, and during the night had woven a new obsession into her thoughts. Joanna left Christopher with Pat and drove by herself to the cemetery and walked across the dry, winter-crisped grass to the plots where the new mounds of earth lay side by side, for father and son.

The day was bitterly cold and a great flat barricade of clouds walled up the sky, dulling all available light. Joanna knelt to place her offering of spring flowers at the foot of the graves, then stood for a long time, trying to empty herself of all thoughts of anger and retribution and also of lust and insult. So much had gone wrong between her and the Snows. She could not believe it was entirely their fault, and as she stood in the bitter cold, she made a resolution, and before she left the graves, she spoke aloud to Todd and Doug. She made them a promise.

As soon as she walked into the house from her visit to the cemetery, Joanna called Helen Snow and asked if she could pay a brief visit to her the next afternoon. After a moment's hesitation, with a voice weary of emotion, Helen agreed.

The next afternoon Joanna once again left her baby with Pat, and drove out to the western area of the island known as Madaket, to the Snows' home. To what had been Doug's home, and Todd's, and now was only Helen's.

The small gray-shingled ranch house sat on a slight slope of land with a sweeping view of the water, and Joanna saw that at this end of the island, all around the sheltered harbor, ice laced the shoreline with a frosty embroidery. The Snows' driveway and yard were crowded with cars and trucks, including the red pickup, and with boats covered with tarps, waiting for the winter's end. Shrubs rattled under the windows.

She knocked on the door. Helen Snow answered it almost at once, and nodding brusquely in greeting, stood back for Joanna to enter. The front door gave immediately onto the living room and Joanna saw that the ranch house was compact but cozy and bright. A multicolored rag rug lay before a fireplace. Pictures of Todd and Doug and others paraded across the mantel. Facing an enormous color TV were a much-used sofa and a scuffed vinyl reclining chair, which probably had been Doug's. Helen indicated with her hand a rocking chair with a braided rag cushion, and Joanna sat down there, her coat still on, her muffler still wrapped around her neck.

"Thank you for letting me come," she said.

"I don't know if you've met my daughter, Chrissy." Helen spoke tonelessly as she sank onto the sofa next to a sullen-faced teenager.

"I haven't. Hello, Chrissy."

Chrissy's nod was curt. For a moment the three women only looked at each other. Both Helen and Chrissy had Todd's blond hair and blue eyes and both were quite lovely even now with their eyelids swollen from tears and their faces drawn with grief. Helen had a French delicacy and paleness to her skin and bones, and she was very slender; she had the looks of one who might easily have been called "Princess" by her parents and by her husband.

Joanna took a deep breath and began. "I want to tell you how terribly sorry I am about Doug and Todd."

Helen only stared, and now Joanna understood that Helen's eyes held the absentminded, faraway gaze of someone on sedatives.

"I should have realized that the thought of finding more treasure in the house was tempting. I was so afraid of publicity, of a commotion at a time when I needed peace and quiet. And then with the baby—the babies . . ."

Chrissy spoke up, her voice cold and shaking with emotion. "They found rubies."

"Yes," Joanna agreed. "But they never found anything else. I let them dig. You must know that. Todd and Madaket spent many nights looking, and they found nothing but sand."

Helen spoke. Her voice was high and almost singsong, like

a child's. "In any case, they were wrong to take dynamite to your house. I asked them not to. I told them it was wrong, dangerous. They promised they wouldn't use it when you and your baby were in the house. They meant only to cause a small explosion, enough to crack through the brick wall." She was beginning to tremble bodily. "I told Doug. I begged him. You've never used dynamite before, I told him, but he said his brother had told him just what to do. It would be short and sweet, he said, you'd never know."

"Don't, Mom." Chrissy put her arm around her mother.

Helen's lower lip quivered. From a pocket in her cardigan she drew a handkerchief and twisted it in her hands. "I'm sorry your house burned down. I really am. I don't know what to do about it."

Joanna leaned forward. "Oh, Helen, please. That's not why I'm here. Listen. Please. I took the two rubies to Boston a few weeks ago and sold them. I want to give you some of the money. Thirty-five thousand dollars."

"I don't want your money."

Chrissy jerked her mother. "Mom."

"I don't think of it as my money," Joanna explained. "I was planning all along to give part of it to your son and part of it to Madaket. I just didn't get around to it with the baby and all that happened."

"I can't take your money."

"I want you to know that if you don't want the money, I'm planning to donate it to the Nantucket Conservation Foundation, in Todd and Doug's name."

"We want the money," Chrissy said. "For God's sake, Mom!"

"You don't have to decide now," Joanna told her. "Just think about it."

"I don't understand why you're doing this," Helen said.

"I only wish I'd given them the money before," Joanna told her. "I can't tell you how sorry I am."

"You're lucky you can just give away that much money," Chrissy said accusingly.

Joanna looked at her. "Yes, I am. I'm lucky in many ways that I'm only now discovering."

"We could use the money," Helen admitted softly. "We really could use it, especially with the funeral expenses. And now that Doug won't be working . . ." Her voice broke off in a sob. "Working!" she cried, and shook her head at her words, and dropped her face into her hands.

Joanna opened her bag and took out an envelope. The check was enclosed, made out to Helen Snow, but she handed it to Chrissy, who opened it, and took the check out and stared at it in wonder.

"Mom," Chrissy said. "Look."

Helen looked at the check through her tears.

"This is so generous." Her voice was thick with effort. "I don't know what to say. I never expected . . . Thank you."

For a long moment the three women sat in silence. Then Joanna rose. "I'll see myself out."

She crossed the room in silence and quietly pulled the door shut behind her as she left the house. But when she reached her Jeep, she heard her name called. "Miss Jones!" She turned to look.

Chrissy ran out of the house and down the walk and stopped on the other side of the Jeep. She was wringing her hands near her heart in an anguish of emotions, and her eyes spilled over with tears.

"We really *are* grateful," the young woman said. "This means I can go to college. I want you to know that. We couldn't afford for Todd to go to college, and he knew how much I wanted to, and he loved me, and I'm going to miss him so much, but I know he would be glad about the money."

Tears streamed down Chrissy's face, and she shivered unaware in the cold. Joanna thought her heart would break open.

"Thank you for telling me. It helps to know."

They stared at each other across the hood of the Jeep for a long moment, then Chrissy ducked her head and ran back into the house.

It amazed Joanna that her act of generosity brought her such enduring pleasure. She was financially comfortable, because she had worked very hard for many years and because she'd saved her money. But she was not so wealthy that thirty-five thousand dollars meant nothing to her. If she'd kept it, she could have contemplated not working for a year, while she enjoyed her baby. Or she could have put that money into a trust fund for Christopher when he was grown—for his college education.

She'd considered all this before she gave the money to Helen Snow, and she'd even warned herself that once the money had actually been transferred, she might experience regret and anger.

Instead, she felt as if weights had been taken from her shoulders. Her spirits lifted, her heart grew lighter. She knew she had done the right thing.

Ten days after the fire, Madaket was released from the plastic bubble and into a private room in the Burn Center. Joanna packed a suitcase for herself and one for her baby and one for *Fabulous Homes* and flew with Christopher to Boston. She checked into a Holiday Inn near Mass General, set up a temporary base, and then with her baby in one arm and a bag of presents in the other, she went to visit Madaket. And visited her every day.

There were things about which to be glad and grateful: Madaket hadn't developed pneumonia or infections, both common with burns. Her scalp was covered with a fine bristle of black hair and the doctors promised that Madaket's thick hair would grow back. Even the most damaged skin on the side of her face and hands was recovering.

On the other hand, Madaket would never look like she had before the fire. As the days went by and the dressings were removed, the scarring of Madaket's face was revealed. A giant patch, a continent of injured flesh, spread across her left temple and cheek from her hairline to her nose. Eventually the angry burgundy and crimson would fade but in its place would be new skin of a different shade and texture than the rest of the skin on her face. Madaket was no longer beautiful. Because of the scar, her face was shocking, painful to look at. The first time Christopher saw Madaket after the fire he made abrupt little startled movements and burst into tears. Joanna continually fought to keep herself from wincing when she looked at Madaket's flesh and especially to prevent pity or shock from showing in her eyes. Each day as the new skin grew, the nurses left more of the area open to the air, and in spots where the skin was weak and sensitive, it broke open; the nurses dabbed Mercurochrome on those spots, adding yet another vivid, unnatural hue to Madaket's multicolored face. It would be months, the doctors said, before the wound healed enough for them to evaluate the necessity and possible benefits of skin grafting.

In the early days of Madaket's recovery, Joanna refrained from speaking of Todd, or the fire, or the money from the rubies. Madaket was no longer dulled by painkillers, but she was far from her normal self, and spent most of her time either sleeping or staring blankly at the television.

"Is Madaket depressed?" Joanna asked Lisa Hale, the head nurse, one day as they stood together in the hall, far from Madaket's room and hearing.

"Of course," the nurse replied sensibly. "Wouldn't you be?"

"Because of her appearance?"

"No, I don't think that's the case with Madaket. She spends very little time looking in a mirror. I think it's more a matter of simple exhaustion. You must understand that even though she was helped with morphine, she experienced a debilitating amount of pain. It will take a while for her body to recover from that. I think it's just a matter of time. Be patient with her."

"I will," Joanna promised, but she found it hard. It was such a drastic change to have energetic Madaket reduced to a silent hull. If it had not been for the way Madaket played with Christopher, Joanna would have been seriously worried.

Instead, she really did try to be patient, and because it made her restless to simply sit in the hospital room, she set up a makeshift workstation there, and while Madaket held Christopher, Joanna made notes and memos which she had faxed from her hotel to the network in New York. Jake had hired a new secretary for Joanna, an older, efficient, quiet woman named Louise, and most mornings and afternoons Joanna began and ended her day in long conversations with Louise. Justin mailed her the proofs of her first book. Every day when Joanna walked from the hotel to the hospital, she carried Christopher in her arms, a diaper bag over one shoulder, and a loaded briefcase on the other. And it was odd, but she was very happy as she walked. She felt quite balanced.

Two weeks passed this way. More and more of the bandages were removed, revealing new, thin, fragile skin stretching tautly over the burned area. This skin was tight and dry, Madaket said; the itching drove her wild. At first the nurses and Joanna, and later Madaket herself, helped soften the new skin by smoothing on lanolin cream.

The morning finally came when Joanna arrived to find Madaket sitting up in bed, squeezing a rubber ball.

"I see they've given you some toys to play with," she laughed, depositing Christopher on the bed and bending over to undo his snowsuit.

"Physical therapy," Madaket replied. "I'm supposed to keep squeezing it so the skin growing over my knuckles won't pull and hurt when I move my hands."

"I'm glad to see you're diligent about it."

"The faster I get well, the sooner I can go home."

"Can it be you're bored with this lovely hospital?" Joanna teased. When Madaket only groaned in response, she continued, "The Latherns are off to Europe for a month, and they're giving us their house to stay in while we decide what to do."

Madaket flashed a look of concern that was balm to Joanna's heart: she cared about this, she had healed enough to care about something.

Madaket asked, "Aren't you going to rebuild on your property?"

"Yes, of course. But we have to live somewhere while the new house is being built."

"Oh. Right." Madaket relaxed against her pillows.

"Madaket," Joanna said, curling up at the end of the hospital bed and idly moving Christopher's feet and hands in a kicking and waving game he enjoyed, "do you think we could talk a little now?"

Madaket shrugged. "All right."

"I mean, are you feeling that you're on the way to recovery?"

"I guess. Whatever that means."

Joanna looked at Madaket, who was staring at the blank television screen hanging from the ceiling. "There's so much we have to talk about. The fire. And your animals. And Todd."

"What is there to say?" Madaket asked, her voice monotonal.

Joanna thought a moment. "A lot. There's a lot to say. We haven't talked about how sad it is that Todd is dead. You haven't told me what this means for your life."

"I don't understand." The young woman turned her black-eyed gaze to Joanna.

"Madaket. I thought you loved Todd."

"I did." She drew in a long, shuddering breath. "And it sucks that he's dead." She flashed a passionate look at Joanna. "That's all I can say about his death. I can't . . . I don't want to . . . deal with it now. I can't. I just . . . can't."

"I understand, I think."

Madaket looked down at her hands. She'd stopped squeezing her rubber balls and now began again. "I did love Todd. I adored him. I idolized him. He was like some kind of god to me. But he could be a jerk. He was kind of an idiot, too."

Shocked, Joanna let an uncomfortable laugh escape. "Why do you say that?"

"For one thing, he really thought he was going to find some more jewels. I did, too, at first, but after a few nights digging in the sand I could tell we wouldn't find anything else. But he was so—romantic—about it!"

"I need to tell you, Madaket—" Joanna hesitated, afraid to cause some sort of emotional upheaval that would cause Madaket to deteriorate back into her invalid self; but from sheer need she plunged on. "I overheard you talking with Todd the night of my dinner party for Justin. I overheard him trying to convince you to steal any other stones you found."

She'd expected Madaket to be embarrassed or angrily to protest her innocence, but the young woman only smiled ruefully and said, "Oh, Todd was always talking about that."

"But it seemed—it seemed he was seducing you so that you'd come around to his point of view."

Madaket was still smiling, and nodding her head. "That's another thing he did all the time. It didn't mean anything. I knew it, I always knew it, and on some evolved level of his Neanderthal mind Todd knew it, too. Todd was just a lover. Put him near a female and he'd try to get in her pants. Rather like the stories I've heard about my father."

"But would you have—?" Joanna stopped, afraid to upset the other woman.

"Would I have helped him steal? If he had promised to love

me, would I have helped him steal?" Madaket grew thought ful. "I don't think so. I never took him seriously. I knew what he was like. I never told him I would." Again her dark eyes rested on Joanna. "Did you think I'd steal from you?" Without waiting for Joanna's answer, she continued, talking slowly, musingly, "Perhaps I would. If it would bring back Todd. What can I say? I *didn't* steal from you. I certainly did n't know what Todd and his father were planning. They did n't give me a hint."

Joanna felt tension lift off her shoulders. She inhaled a cleansing breath. "Good. I'm glad to know that. I needed to hear that from you. Todd is—was—so persuasive. And you did seem so—so much in love."

"I think I was only infatuated." Her face grew wistful. "I was fun flirting with him. I'm going to miss that." A shud der ran over her visibly, and she put her hands up, covering her face. When she spoke, her words were muffled. "I'm so sorry that he's dead."

"I want to tell you what I did, Madaket. I sold the two ru bies you and Todd found, and got seventy thousand dollars for them. I've already given half of that to Helen and Chrissy Snow—and I'm giving the other half to you. Thirty-five thou sand dollars. For you to use however you wish."

Madaket regained her composure and with great care wiped the tears from her face. Solemnly she stared at Joanna. "Wow. That was really generous of you. I'm sure Mrs. Snow and Chrissy can use that. But, Joanna, you don't have to give me that money. It's not necessary."

Joanna smiled. "It's necessary for me."

Madaket nodded thoughtfully. "I can understand that, I guess."

"You could make a down payment on a piece of property on Nantucket."

At this, Madaket looked surprised, and then she dropped her eyes to the bed, and Joanna sensed a shrinking in of her spirit, as if Madaket were actually shriveling before her eyes.

"Madaket?" Reaching over, she touched the young woman's arm. "What is it?"

Madaket had been sitting up in bed with her legs stretched out underneath the sheets and now she brought her knees up to her chest and wrapped her arms around them, hugging

them, defending herself. She looked very young. "I thought
. . . it was only that you said . . . you've said several times,
when I was in the bubble, that I'd always live with you. That
I would be, well, like your family."

"Oh, but I meant that! I mean that. I do!" Hastily Joanna
slid off the rumpled sheets, picked a startled Christopher up
in one arm, and moved to the top of the bed, to sit down next
to Madaket, whose spirits suddenly seemed as fragile as her
new skin. "It was only that I overheard you telling Todd that
you'd buy property of your own, if you could. But you don't
have to use your money for that. You can save it and use it
for whatever you want in the future."

"Thank you," Madaket said softly.

"Oh, Madaket, I meant everything I said. I do love you like
a daughter, and I do want you to live with me and stay with
me always."

"Thank you," Madaket said again, and this time she raised
her dark eyes and looked at Joanna. Her breath came out in
a long shiver. "I'm glad."

Joanna felt tears rise to her own eyes. "I'd hug you, but I'd
probably knock your bandages askew," she said frivolously,
and Madaket chuckled and Christopher eased the tension of
the moment by shrieking gleefully and waving his arms at
Madaket, who took him in her hands and bounced him on
the bed.

"So you see, we did have a lot of things to discuss," Joanna
said, modulating her voice to a commonsense tone. "A lot of
things to set straight. I'm sorry if I insulted you by asking if
you were planning to steal anything you found, but it was
something I needed to know. I've never had anyone I could
completely trust before."

Madaket looked levelly at Joanna. "Well, now you do,"

Joanna smiled. "And so do you."

Twenty-Six

$\sim$

$\mathcal{A}$s the month of March progressed, Madaket's face and hands and chest healed completely. The new skin, stretched so thinly over her wounds, broke open in several places, was dressed with bacteriostatic medicines, and grew again. The unmitigated itch of all this made Madaket irritable, and she was also restless, bored with the hospital, eager to get out of there, and she mentioned this, it seemed to Joanna, a hundred times a day.

"Soon," the nurses promised. "Very soon."

"I kind of like it here," Joanna told Madaket one late afternoon as she prepared to return to the hotel. Sunlight as pale as sheets of parchment fell from the windows into the hospital room. Christopher squirmed and wriggled on the bed as Joanna bundled his limbs into his puffy snowsuit.

"You do? You're kidding!" Madaket scoffed.

"I really do. It seems kind of—homey."

"Wait a minute," Madaket said. "Hold on. Homey? Homey?" She held out her hands to hold Christopher one last time before he left for the day, and automatically Joanna handed him to her.

Then, pulling on her coat and floppy hat and gloves, she looked around. "Yes, homey. I guess what I mean is, it makes me think of the network. I'll take you in to see it sometime. Then you'll understand. It's got the same marvelous electric sense of urgency, people hurrying through corridors, phones ringing, people arguing and laughing and shouting for each other, equipment and cables everywhere, huge message boards with thousands of notes thumbtacked to them."

"Have you read some of the boards here?" Madaket asked. "Charts for things like 'fasting bloods.' Like something from a vampire movie."

"You're just stir-crazy, and I don't blame you." Joanna pecked a quick kiss on the top of Madaket's bristly scalp, and took Christopher from Madaket's arms and, calling goodbye to the nurses as she went, set off through the labyrinthian hospital halls, down the elevator, and out to the streets.

After the warmth of the hospital, the frigid air hit her skin like a slap, but as Joanna detoured around taxis and cars in the hospital's courtyard and turned down the narrow canyon of Fruit Street, she felt the sheer motion warming her blood. And then she came to North Grove Street and stood, suddenly overcome with a heady sense of the fullness of life. Holding Christopher against her, her briefcase and diaper bag pulling at her shoulders, she stood on the sidewalk and just looked and listened, breathing in the sensations of the city as if they were expensive perfumes. Beneath her feet the cement walk shuddered from the thunder of traffic along Storrow Drive, while overhead a subway car rumbled its way to the Charles Station T stop. Sirens wailed, horns honked, taxi drivers cursed and spat tobacco out the window, buses migrated past her, hissing and howling like steel-skinned dinosaurs. It was fabulous. She loved it, and felt tears sting her eyes, tears of homesickness for New York.

Christopher wriggled against her impatiently, and so she sniffed and turned down the street, heading for her hotel. She saw a homeless woman hunched over a grate against the cold. She put a twenty-dollar bill in her cup.

During the last two weeks of March, as Madaket's strength returned, so did her impatience, and the day came when Joanna arrived at the hospital to find Madaket pacing the halls in her hospital gown and the new robe Joanna had bought her. Joanna had given much thought to the selection of this robe; wool would chafe Madaket's skin, and Madaket would scorn anything satiny or sexy. Joanna had thought she'd found the perfect garment in the thick velvety terry cloth in a luscious shade of deep turquoise. But the robe's simple span of unbroken color somehow counterpoised in unfortunate contrast Madaket's ravaged hands and face. The burned area was at last entirely covered with new skin, and the doctors predicted that eventually that area would be paler than Madaket's original skin, but now it was still a savage glare of crimson. There was no color on earth that could help that.

Partly to entertain Madaket and keep her thoughts off her raw and itching skin, but also with the hopes of encouraging the young woman to envision her future, Joanna attempted to interest Madaket in various projects. She spent hours at a travel agency, garnering sheaves of glossy travel brochures which she took to the hospital and spread all over Madaket's bed. "Let's plan an itinerary, and when you get out of here we'll spend a few months roaming the world. Where would you like to go? Paris? London?"

"I don't think I can face the thought of traveling anywhere yet, Joanna," Madaket said somberly. "I'll have to get used to people flinching from the sight of my face, or staring horrified at me, before I can travel."

"Sounds like you need to develop thicker skin," Joanna said. "Hey. That was a joke. Come on, smile."

Madaket grinned and rolled her eyes.

Another day, Joanna said, "What would you think about starting college in the fall? I'll pay your tuition. I'll help you study for the high school equivalency exam."

"I've never been interested in college."

"All right, then, what about career-oriented courses? In the culinary arts? Or homeopathic medicine?"

"Joanna, to do any of those things, I'd have to live off island. And I don't want to do that. I never wanted to do that. I just want to be on Nantucket. I just want to go home."

One evening, when Madaket had complained about the hospital food, Joanna brought in tacos and burritos and tostados and tortillas and even, hidden in a Styrofoam coffee cup, a margarita for herself. By this time Madaket spent as little time in bed as necessary, and so they flattened the electric bed and lowered it to an appropriate table height and spread food out over the white cotton sheets.

"I've weaned Christopher," she announced to Madaket, raising her cup in a toast. "He's eating solid foods now. He's wild about applesauce."

"What a good boy." Madaket had Christopher on her

knees. He was the one person who could always get her to smile.

"Listen, Madaket, we've got to make some plans. You'll be sprung from here soon. I've been talking to Justin from my fancy office over at room 1215 in the Holiday Inn. They've arranged an author tour for me in the last two weeks of June. When my question-and-answer book comes out. Seven cities. New York, of course, and Chicago, San Francisco, Seattle, Dallas, Kansas City, and Philadelphia. I think you should come with me. You could help with Christopher, but more than that, you could see the country. And honestly, Madaket, I'd love to have you along."

"That's nice of you, Joanna. And I don't mean to be a drag. But I just want to go home. The idea of traveling anywhere is abhorrent to me right now."

"I understand." Joanna couldn't keep the disappointment from her voice. Now what, she wondered in a silent, private frenzy, was she going to do about a nanny to help with Christopher on the trip?

As if reading her mind, Madaket assured her, "I'll stay on Nantucket and take care of Christopher for you. As you said, he's weaned. And it would be difficult for you to travel with a baby, and frankly, Joanna, it wouldn't be that great for Christopher to be dragged through all those airports and hotels. He doesn't need so much exposure to germs. Not to mention a totally turbulent schedule."

Joanna feigned intense interest in her taco. Madaket was speaking as if she had almost equal rights to Christopher, equal authority in how the baby was nurtured. Joanna was touched by this, and pleased, and amused, and also slightly affronted. Christopher was *her* child! But if she meant what she'd told Madaket, that Madaket was now part of her family, then Madaket had rights to Christopher, too. Had she really meant all this?

Yes, she thought, she did. It would take some time getting used to the thought of truly sharing her little boy, but it seemed a blessing that Christopher might have some other person on this earth to love him as her own.

At the end of March, six weeks after the fire, Joanna flew up to Boston, checked Madaket out of the Burn Center, and brought her back to the island in a humming, vibrating, eight-passenger plane. Madaket's hair, grown back enough by now to look like merely a very bad punk cut, was covered by a floppy blue velvet hat. Joanna glared at the other passengers who blanched or gaped at Madaket's scarred face, but Madaket didn't seem aware of the other people. She pressed her eyes to the window, eagerly watching the island come into view. There it was, the jewel of the sea, green and golden land curving in blue water, the beaches and stretches and arms of sand, the lighthouses, the town with its steeples, the ribbons of roads winding through the moors, the green pine trees, the soaring gulls. As they landed, they saw a young deer grazing near the runway, and two large hawks lifted away from their perch on an evergreen to fly away from the airplane's noise.

Madaket turned to Joanna. "Oh, isn't it beautiful!" Her eyes were brilliant with tears.

It was a cool, windy day with the sun high in a yellow sky and a breeze buffeting them as they walked together across the airport parking lot to Joanna's Jeep. Madaket's clothes, an assortment of new garments donated by the community or bought with care by Joanna, fell in loose layers around her body exactly as her clothes had always done. The rest of her new wardrobe was waiting for her at the Latherns' house, where they would live for a few weeks. Madaket tossed her overnight bag into the passenger side of the Jeep, then said, "Joanna, I'm going to walk."

"Oh! Are you sure? Aren't you tired?"

"Not at all. I'm so glad to be back. I just want to walk and look at everything."

"Would you like me to pick you up somewhere?"

"No, thanks. I'll just come to the Latherns' when I'm ready. I probably won't be back until after dark."

"All right. Well, here—at least take some change, then I'll know you can call me if you get tired. And remember, you very well might get tired after being inactive for so long."

"I know. Thanks." Madaket was chafing with impatience.

"Madaket. You know, the house was burned to the ground. It still looks—wounded—out there."

"Fine, I won't go there. Anyway, I want to walk on the moors."

"Good. We'll go to my place, our place, tomorrow. Okay?"

"Okay. Bye now." Madaket shoved the coins in her coat pocket and almost sprinted away.

Joanna felt a surge of envy. How lucky Madaket was, to love this island so much, so that returning here immediately renewed her spirits. Joanna loved Christopher, and her spirits were lifted by his darling adoring face, and her work was both a solace and a pleasure, but she still felt oddly lethargic about much of the rest of life. She knew she should turn her thoughts to building a new house on her property, but she hadn't yet been able to summon any enthusiasm for the project. Perhaps with Madaket home, she'd feel more excitement.

The next morning, after fortifying themselves with hearty breakfasts, the two women agreed to go together to look at Joanna's property. Madaket slipped into the harness of a Snugli and adjusted it over her back, and Joanna maneuvered Christopher into it.

"Wow! He's getting heavy," she told Joanna.

"My big boy," Joanna cooed, rubbing noses with Christopher.

They set off down the road. Madaket's head was covered and shaded by her floppy hat, and even though the day was mild, she wore gloves and a scarf around her neck and the lower part of her face because the hospital had impressed upon her the necessity of keeping her skin protected from the sun at all times for at least a year.

As they turned down the white gravel drive, Joanna's heart began to jolt with trepidation. This was never an easy moment for her, seeing the ruins of her house. She'd had the worst of the debris cleaned up; she'd hired a crew to bulldoze and shovel and haul off the rubble; she'd had them knock down the two remaining useless chimneys. The bricks that could be saved were stacked, waiting to be incorporated into a new house. Still, the property had a wounded look about it. Where once the house had stood was now an expanse of black and charred ground covered with the sand dug from the cellar where the Snow bodies had been found. Wolf and Bitch had also died in the fire, and Joanna worried that when Madaket was confronted with the actual remains of the fire, she would break down in some way.

But Madaket only walked around the vast expanse of blackened earth, solemnly studying it before turning toward the front of the property and then running and kneeling on the ground. Feverishly she raked with her hands at the straw-colored mulch she'd spread over her garden. Joanna drew near.

"Look!" Madaket cried. She'd uncovered masses of tight swords of green just breaking through the hard ground. "The daffodils! The tulips! They're up! They'll be opening soon! And my little chives have peeked through! And my sweet marjoram!"

Joanna knelt next to her. Christopher was laughing and hopping against Madaket's back, rocking the Snugli, excited about Madaket's excitement.

"Look," Madaket said, pointing. "Here. Touch."

Until that moment, Joanna had considered selling her Squam property and buying a house in a completely different location—it would be easier and quicker than having something new built, and the difficult memories could be better forgotten. But when she saw Madaket kneeling in her garden, talking to her plants as if they were her relatives, she knew she had to stay here. And she found that obligation oddly comforting. It seemed a good thing to have any reason at all to remain anywhere on the earth.

They couldn't stay forever in the Latherns' house. It was essential to have some kind of orderly home base before she left on her author's tour in June, and accordingly Joanna and Christopher and Madaket went looking at rental houses with Bob.

Finding a suitable temporary home turned out to be more difficult than Joanna had realized. Many of the older, larger houses were Greek Revivals, with architectural details and spaces that reminded her of her home, and walking through them felt at once familiar and odd. They made her sad; sometimes they made her shiver. They were also just more house, more space and impedimenta, than she wanted to deal with right now. Of the newer houses, some were designed for summer living but would be hard to keep warm in the winter, and others were too expensively furnished or inconveniently arranged for family life.

One day Bob showed Joanna and Madaket a rustic two-bedroom cottage at Quidnet. Joanna saw the light in Madaket's eyes and rented it. Madaket loved it because of the location: the house looked right out at Sesachacha Pond, and its one picture window was always full of water and sky. Also, the homely little cottage was close to Joanna's property and Madaket's garden. Joanna considered the furniture and equipment functional, comfortable, and clean, and easily replaceable if something should get broken. The walls of the cramped bedroom she shared with Christopher were covered with a wallpaper bizarrely printed to look like pine logs, complete with knotholes. The floors throughout were carpeted in a tough loopy shag of an ambiguous green-brown color; Joanna had it cleaned, then shrugged her shoulders: it would be perfect for Christopher as he crawled and dropped his graham crackers and knocked over his bowl of stewed peas.

So they moved into the cottage, which they not wholly in jest referred to as "the shack," until a new house could be built in Squam. They studied blueprints and books on architectural styles. They toured various model houses. But nothing sparked their desire. Early every morning, and late at night, and every spare moment she had, Madaket spent at Joanna's property, working on her garden.

Joanna worked as efficiently as she could in the cramped, makeshift office she set up at one end of her ugly rented bedroom. While Madaket played with Christopher, she continued the groundwork for the sixth new season of *Fabulous Homes,* talked to her secretary at the network, held telephone and fax conferences with Justin. She'd scheduled the taping of the first two FH shows during the last two weeks of May. Two more would be shot in June; she'd return briefly to Nantucket, then go off on her author's tour. Then more FH shoots. The calendar hanging from a nail above her desk was slashed and scribbled with colored inks demarcating different shoots; this was as gorgeous to her as any Renoir.

A few days later the phone rang. It was a terrible early May day, cold and windy and rainy and gray, the kind that made people curse Nantucket. Christopher was sniffling and fussing, his tiny nose was chafed, and his bottom, too. Madaket had taken the Jeep into town for groceries and liquid baby aspirin. Lackadaisically playing with Christopher, Joanna lounged across her bed, still wearing the sweat suit which she remained in so often it was beginning to feel like her second skin. She hadn't yet gone shopping for clothes to replace all she'd lost in the fire.

She answered the phone. Jake's voice boomed over the line. "Look, Joanna, I've got a proposition to make. I want to fly out to Nantucket and have a good long talk with you about an idea I have. Friday night okay?"

Joanna smiled at his familiar voice. "Friday night's fine."

"Great. Let me take you out to dinner."

"I'd love that."

"Can you make a reservation for us? Someplace nice."

"Sure."

"I'll rent a car and be at your place around six. Okay?"

"Jake, I can't wait."

After they'd said their goodbyes, Joanna called a restaurant, then, cheered by the pleasure of Jake's voice, called Robert Miller's and made an appointment to have her hair done—everything, color, conditioning, a trim and style—perhaps she'd have it cut into one of those short, sleek, chic styles so popular lately. Then it occurred to her that she had nothing to wear out on Friday night. She dressed and when Madaket returned from shopping, left Christopher with her and drove into town.

The sky still hung low and gray, but Main Street was a cheerful sight; all up and down in the shop window boxes, daffodils and hyacinths bobbed, drinking in the rain. She parked and walked up Main Street. The stores and boutiques were opening for spring and summer and full of the newest styles. Her pulse quickened. She hadn't indulged in a good fit of clothes shopping for a long time; she was more than overdue. All afternoon she tried on silk dresses and challis skirts and white shirts and long loose cashmere sweaters and shoes and hose and hats. She bought everything, including lots of clothes and a wonderful wide-brimmed spring hat for Madaket.

Friday evening Jake and Joanna sat at a corner table in the Boarding House. Joanna sipped a strawberry daiquiri the color and texture of her new creamy silk evening suit. Jake had his usual Scotch. The wind and rain had disappeared, leaving the island cleansed. The air was sweet and mild, the trees flowering, the air fragrant. It was almost warm enough to eat outside, but Jake had preferred the privacy of an inside table.

"You look wonderful," he told Joanna.

"You look pretty good yourself," she replied. And he did. He looked somehow younger.

"You can thank my daughter-in-law for that," Jake said. "She made me a grandfather a few weeks ago—a little girl. Named her Emily, after my wife, and it's the strangest thing, Joanna, but this baby looks so much like Emily it's amazing." He cleared his throat. "I think I've finally been able to cope with Emily's death, now that I see some of her is carried on. The baby has a way of smiling—" He shook his head, unable to continue.

Joanna put her hand on Jake's arm, touched by his confidence. "That's lovely, Jake."

"How's Christopher?" Jake asked. "And Madaket?"

"Christopher is pure sunshine," Joanna told him. "That's one of the lovely things about having a baby around, I guess. No matter what's going on in the rest of the world, just seeing the people he loves—and being fed—keep him happy."

"Not a bad philosophy for any of us," Jake said thoughtfully.

"Madaket's doing surprisingly well, too. She's so glad to be home, and so glad to see her garden . . . She's amazingly resilient."

"Madaket isn't as greedy as the rest of us," Jake surmised. "Like Christopher, she's grounded in a few basics."

The waiter appeared beside them to take their order, and when he'd gone off, Joanna leaned toward Jake and said eagerly, "Tell me about the network."

"All right. What do you want to know?"

"Well, let's see . . . how's Dhon? Is he still with Perry? And does everyone still hate the new executive from the West Coast, what was his name—Mack?"

"Mike."

"Mike. And how's the fall lineup looking? And—"

"Hang on," Jake ordered, laughing. "I can't keep up with you."

They leaned toward each other, passionately discussing the network, and the people who worked there, and *Fabulous Homes*, and the waiter set before them lobster ravioli, and medallions of beef in a buttery garlic sauce, and a crisp salad and hot freshly baked bread, and they talked and laughed together as they had so often before. Joanna was aware of the curious and envious looks flashed their way by the others in the restaurant and she remembered how much she liked it, being slightly celebrated and admired.

"You look pleased with yourself," Jake remarked over coffee.

"I am." Joanna tossed her head just to feel how light it was now. That day she'd had her hair trimmed in this prep school boy's cut, which was wonderfully becoming. "I haven't had such a lovely evening in a long while."

"Do you miss New York?" Jake asked.

"You know, Jake, I do. Although I haven't had much time to think about it, with working on the show and taking care of the baby. Not to mention the fire."

"Are you going to rebuild?"

"Yes—if I can ever decide on what I want. I've looked at floor plans and blueprints until my head aches. I can't seem to find anything that thrills me. Not the way the house did when I first saw it standing there, so square and powerful and . . . enduring. *Enduring*. Well. All right," she announced, leaning back in her chair, "you might as well tell me how Carter and Gloria are. Don't worry, Jake, whatever the news is, I can take it."

Jake studied her with his dark, shrewd eyes. "Carter's going through with the divorce from Blair. He and Gloria were living together in an apartment on West Seventieth. They were agitating to coproduce their version of *Fabulous Homes*. As you know, I scotched that." He paused for effect. "Then Gloria ran off with the new vice-president in charge of advertising. He's a lot younger than Carter, closer to Gloria's age."

"You're kidding!" Joanna exclaimed. "Poor Carter." She nodded her head, and then felt a slow, immensely pleasurable grin spread across her face. She was so *satisfied* by this news. "Serves him right."

"Well, he's available again. Now more than he ever was."

"Are you implying that he and I could get back together? Forget it." Joanna shook her head.

"Oh, come on. Don't tell me you don't still love the guy."

Joanna sipped some coffee and considered. "Honestly, Jake, I don't. I don't feel anything for Carter anymore. I don't even hate him."

"If he shows up at your door someday, you might feel differently."

"No, I'm sure I wouldn't." Laughing, she said, "It's as if loving him was an illness, a fever, but now I'm immune. I can search my heart and not feel a thing." She leaned forward. "Please. Let's change the subject."

"All right," Jake agreed.

"You mentioned a proposition when you called," she reminded him.

"A proposition. Yes, I did." He shifted in his chair. "It's not professional, Joanna. It's personal." He spoke slowly. "It's more in the nature of a proposal than a proposition." Now he looked at her steadily. "I wonder what you'd say if I asked you to marry me."

Joanna stared.

"I've missed you." Jake's voice was soft now, so that she had to strain to hear him. "I missed you for a long time before I realized why. I've thought about this a lot. If you'd been excited about seeing Carter again now that you know he and Gloria have broken up, I wouldn't have broached this. I'd have proposed some new format for FH. But Carter never was good for you, and you don't seem to care for him like you once did. I'm not saying you could care for me passionately, the way you cared for Carter. But maybe you could care for me . . . somehow."

Joanna looked at Jake, really looked at him, as if seeing him for the first time, which in a way she was. The muted noises of laughter and conversation and silver clinking against china drifted around them like a gentle snow, and like a figure in a paperweight she was surrounded by the magic of this moment.

"I do care for you, Jake," she said honestly, talking

through her thoughts. "But . . . I've never thought of you *personally.* I mean, I've always thought of you sort of as a Symbolic Persona: The Boss."

"I can understand that. I always thought of you as the Joanna of *Fabulous Homes,* and then as Carter's girl. Sorry. Woman. Not until you left did I realize how much I liked having you around. How happy it made me to see you."

"Jake, I really don't know what to say. It's going to take a while for this to sink in. I'm flattered, obviously. But—I'm so surprised I can't seem to think."

Her cool ringless hand rested on the table and Jake covered it with his large warm one. "Joanna, let me press my case. I'm forty-nine. My health is excellent. I'm well off financially; you know that. I'd like to adopt Christopher, raise him as my own." A smile broke over his face. "I can give you some good references on that score from my two kids. I've been attracted to you for a long time, but just didn't know what to do about it. But now—life's gotten short. For me; for you, too, I think. I want to be happy, and it would make me happy to be married to you, and I think I could make you happy, too."

Joanna studied his familiar face, trying to analyze her feelings. "I need some time to think," she told him.

"Then think. Take all the time you want."

"Joanna! How are you! And Jake!" June and Morris Lathern entered the restaurant and swooped down on their table. The intimate mood was broken. The four chatted about the gorgeous spring weather, then the Latherns went off to their own table. The waiter brought Jake the check. Jake and Joanna left the restaurant and went out into the mild dark night.

"Want to walk a bit?" Jake asked.

"Sure. Let's go down by the water."

Side by side in a companionable silence, they crossed over the cobblestones toward Easy Street and sank down together on a wooden bench looking out at the harbor. Flocks of ducks paddled amiably along, looking for handouts. Occasionally a pair of lovers or a family strolled by and stopped to feed them bits of chips or popcorn. The sky seemed infinitely high and luminous. Jake reached out and took Joanna's hand. A complicated charge of emotions raced through her and she kept very still, letting her body sort it all out. His hand was warm and hard and large and steady. Reliable. Not displeasing. Not at all displeasing.

She turned to look at him. Beneath his beautifully tailored clothes, he was a stocky, solid, earthy man who enjoyed all his appetites. Feeling her gaze, Jake turned, too, and studied her face. Pulling her close to him, he kissed her mouth. His breath smelled of garlic and wine and coffee and his kiss was tender, then increasingly ardent. A warm desire flushed through Joanna, and her body felt suddenly vulnerable and voluptuous. She'd been so obsessed with maternal sensuality that she'd almost forgotten other kinds of desires and indulgences. Now she gave herself over to the sensation of his great strong arm around her, the pressure of it, the weight and bulk. She put her hand on his chest, and let the kiss intensify. Yes, her body signaled her, oh, yes, she could make love with this man.

Jake was the one to pull away. He seemed slightly shaken and a bit shy. A group of schoolgirls passed by them, giggling. Jake kept his arm around Joanna. Tentatively she lay her head on his shoulder. His large, firm, steady shoulder. They sat that way awhile, looking at the lights of the boats on the water.

"Madaket!" Joanna said suddenly, sitting straight.

"What?"

"If you and I were married, we wouldn't live on Nantucket all the time."

"No," Jake agreed. "We wouldn't. I have to be in the city. You will, too, once you get your show going again. But we could build a great summer house on your land and spend weekends in it. Christopher could grow up with the best of both worlds, New York and Nantucket. Madaket could live with us, travel with us . . ."

"I don't think so, Jake." Joanna moved away from the pleasure of his embrace and, leaning her elbows on her knees and her chin in her hands, stared out at the water, thinking furiously. "She won't want to leave the island. It's her life. And I can't just leave her, not now, not after all she's done—"

"Well, give yourself some time to think about it," Jake advised. "You don't have to decide everything right now."

"Yes, I do," Joanna said. "If I have any integrity, any

sense of responsibility in the world, I do. Jake, remember what Madaket did for me. She saved my life. She saved Christopher's life. She risked her own life, and she—destroyed her own beauty—for us. I owe everything to her. I can't possibly let myself think of abandoning her."

"But if you married me, that wouldn't be abandoning her . . ."

"Please, Jake." Joanna rose. "Don't press me on this. Don't try to make me change my mind. I can't. I won't. I can't leave the island. I want to stay here. I have to stay here and make a home for Madaket."

Jake studied Joanna. "For the rest of your life?" he asked.

"Yes." Joanna was determined. "For the rest of my life."

Twenty-Seven

$\mathcal{I}$t was raining again. May had been an inordinately dismal month, windy and cold and bleak. Joanna parked her Jeep in front of the hardware store and turned to Christopher, strapped into his car seat in the back.

With a cheerfulness she didn't feel, she cooed, "Hang on, now, sweetie, Mommy's got to get your chariot rigged up."

Stepping out onto the sidewalk, she rushed to pull out the stroller and set up the canopy which would protect her baby from the rain. Hurrying as strong winds sent curtains of water lashing over her, she fiddled unsuccessfully with the brake lock, which, with almost malicious timing, tended to jam. By the time she'd wrestled the contraption into submission, she was drenched from rain and sticky with perspiration.

"Damnation!" she swore under her breath, giving the stroller a furious jerk. Opening the Jeep door, she found Christopher wailing. She'd just returned from four days in South Carolina, where she and her crew shot the first FH show in the new series. Working again had been pure, unadulterated bliss. She'd trotted around on her high heels like a prima ballerina back *en pointe*. Energy had flowed ceaselessly through her. She'd been clever. She'd been charming. She'd been brilliant. Even the most minor technical problem caused a blissful sense of challenge. She had actually felt the pure clean lines of creative acumen emerging from the hormonal fog she'd been buried under the past year. She'd been purely flawless at work, delighting the cameramen and hosts equally, solving lighting or angle or design problems quickly, working with the streamlined efficiency of a Concorde jet slicing through the atmosphere.

She returned to find that Christopher had developed some kind of separation anxiety—about Madaket. He cried when Madaket left the room, and glared at Joanna when she tried to hold him. It had taken her three days to get him used to her again, or perhaps, she thought, to coax him into forgiving her, for she could tell by the way he looked at her that he recognized her. He was furious with her for abandoning him, she decided. And in two more days she had to go off for another shoot. So she tried to keep him with her every minute she was on the island so that he would understand how much she loved him, and feel secure in the reliability of her love.

This morning Madaket had to see Gardner for a checkup on her healing scars, and Joanna had to check out a possible location for an island office. Her work was simply too complicated and the paperwork too voluminous to be contained in a portion of the shack.

"All right, all right," Joanna murmured, lifting Christopher into her arms and kissing him. As she bent, a thin stream of rain spilled from the hood of her rain slicker right onto the baby's forehead. Christopher gasped, then wailed. "Poor baby, Mama's sorry," she murmured, grabbing a diaper from the bag and drying his head, but he'd been insulted and he would not be consoled. Somehow Joanna maneuvered his chubby, eight-month-old, furiously wailing body into the stroller, pulled the plastic canopy over his head, grabbed her briefcase and diaper bag, and pushed off toward Easy Street, grateful she had only a block to go.

She turned off into the trim, neat yard of a quaint brick and shingled building with a bow window on the first floor. Rain lashed the roses clinging to the white picket fence, and despondent flowers whipped by the wind hung their heads over the slate walk. Bob Hoover was waiting for her just inside the open door.

"Let me help you," he said, and together they got the stroller up the steps and in out of the rain. Once inside, Joanna looked around. The door opened onto an entrance hall barely large enough to hold them, with a side door opening to a real estate office on the ground level and steps leading directly to the second floor. Rescuing Christopher from behind his plastic shelter, she lifted him into her arms and followed Bob up the stairs.

The Realtor unlocked another door and stood back for Joanna to enter. She tossed her wet hood back and looked around. The wide bright room was large and newly refinished, with the clean scents of paint and polyurethane lingering in the air.

"Plenty of electric outlets," Bob pointed out, moving around. "Two walls of built-in shelves and a long worktable. All you'd need would be a chair and your equipment and you're set."

Joanna crossed over the gleaming pine floors to look out the window.

"Great view of the harbor," Bob said.

"Yes," she agreed, although right now the rain obscured everything. She looked up and down the narrow one-way street. "In the summer the parking would be impossible," she observed.

"Not really. You'd just have to park a few blocks away in the residential areas and walk in."

"That would be a drag with piles of papers, especially in the rain." She jiggled Christopher in her arms. "And I'm not sure I'd like those stairs."

Bob leaned against a spotless white worktable that ran along one wall. "Joanna, are you sure your heart's in this?"

"Of course!" she snapped. "What a question."

"It's just that everything I show you is wrong. That office space out of town you didn't like because it had no view. The rooms in that great old house near Children's Beach were too noisy."

"I'm sorry I'm being difficult," Joanna said, feeling around in her pocket for a zwieback. Christopher was no longer crying, but recently he'd started teething and often fussed unless he had something to gnaw on.

"Joanna, it's not that you're being difficult. It's just—at one time you worked quite happily on a screened porch."

Joanna set Christopher on the worktable. It continually surprised her how heavy a baby could be, how her arms could ache. Perching on the edge of the table with one arm firmly around her child, she looked directly at Bob. "Pat's been talking to you, hasn't she?"

"Pat always talks to me," Bob responded, shrugging, and then he dropped all pretenses. "Joanna, we're worried about you."

"You don't need to be. Honestly, Bob. I'm fine."

"We both think you're making the wrong decision to stay here just because of Madaket."

"Look, Bob, Pat and I have been over and over this ground. Everyone in Madaket's life has left her. Her parents, her grandmother, and then in the fire she lost Wolf and Bitch. I asked her to give up her garden at the house she'd lived in with her grandmother. I just can't leave her, especially now after all she's done for me."

"Didn't she just turn twenty?"

"That's not the point."

"What is the point?"

Joanna was silent.

"Let's be blunt. You're afraid Madaket will be alone all her life because she'll never be able to get a husband."

Joanna shook her head. "I don't think Madaket ever thinks in those terms. 'Get a husband.' "

"All right, then, you think no one will ever love her because of her scarred face."

Joanna glared at Bob. "That's right. I do think that. I also think Madaket has never had anyone of her own and now she never will. She's never had anyone she can trust. I want her to be able to trust me. Bob, she saved my life. She saved Christopher's life. The least I can do is stay here with her and help her get her own life on to some kind of track." Christopher dropped his zwieback. Joanna picked it up.

"But why can't you marry Jake *and* take care of Madaket?" Bob asked.

"Because Jake wouldn't live here all the time, and I don't want even to suggest to Madaket that she move to New York."

"There's got to be some way to work it out. If you really want to be with Jake. I think you're being a bit of a martyr, Joanna."

"Perhaps I am. I think I'm just being responsible. *Committed.*"

"You should be committed," Bob punned, trying to lighten the atmosphere, "if you're going to stay on the island with Madaket merely out of a sense of duty."

Joanna was intense. "But that's where you're wrong, Bob, and I feel very strongly about this. No one cares about a sense of duty anymore, but I do. I want to. I'm obligated to Madaket, and I'm obligated to Christopher, and I'm going to stand by them both."

"Even if it makes you unhappy?"

"But it *won't* make me unhappy. In an odd way, it's deeply satisfying, knowing at last I'm truly part of someone's life. I like knowing that I'll have responsibilities, a strong connection. An *enduring* connection."

"What about your connection to Jake?"

Joanna fiddled with one of Christopher's socks which had gotten twisted around his foot. "I just can't let that matter as much."

"Why not? Because he could make you happy?" When Joanna didn't reply, Bob continued: "That's not healthy thinking, Joanna. That's superstitious."

"You can say that, Bob, but I've tried—" Her voice broke. Taking a deep breath, she began again. "I've tried as hard and as long as I know how to live life the way I want it, to make my dreams come true, and all I've done is wreak a terrible havoc and damage to people's lives. No, I can't live for my own happiness anymore. I need to make amends somehow. I need to make someone else happy."

"At the expense of your own happiness."

"Yes! If that's what it takes!"

"And what about Jake's happiness?"

"Maybe he'll be willing to wait. A year or two. A lot can happen in a year or two."

"Yeah, like he'll find another woman."

"I have to take that chance." She sighed. "Besides, we're constantly in touch while we're collaborating on FH. So could I please stop mooning around like an orphaned cow and concentrate on finding a decent office?"

"Back to my original point: you won't be able to find an office you like because you're so unhappy. Look, at least think about talking to Madaket about all this."

"No! Are you kidding? Did Madaket talk it over with me before she ran into the fire? I'm not mentioning Jake to her, and if you're any kind of friend, Bob, you won't, either."

He held up his hands, palms-out in surrender. "All right.

Just as long as you know what you're doing."

Christopher was squirming now, uncomfortable on th
hard surface. Joanna lifted him into her arms.

"Look. This place is fine," she said. "I'll probably take it.

"It's available immediately."

"Great. Give me a day to think it over. I'll call you."

They went back down the stairs and Joanna went throug
the ritual of strapping her baby into the stroller. Just befor
they set back out in the downpour, she turned and gave Bo
a peck on his cheek. "I'm grateful that you care about me,"
she said. "I appreciate it. I'll be fine."

But once she and her son were tucked back into the Jeep
a familiar melancholy settled over Joanna, and she felt he
face pulled into despondent lines. Driving back to the shac
at Quidnet seemed to take longer with each trip. Now wit
rain streaming down and the windshield wipers clicking mo
notonously, the road stretched on forever. Christophe
fussed, frustrated and bored beneath his various safety straps
then subsided into sleep, exactly what Joanna didn't wan
him to do. He was cranky if he didn't get a long afternoo
nap, but Joanna needed to change into dry clothes and ge
some work accomplished, which she couldn't do with th
baby left out in the car, but if she took him out of the car seat
she'd wake him, and then he'd be fussy and demanding and
incapable of falling back to sleep with his schedule so inter
rupted. Even if Madaket played with him in the living roon
or bedroom, he'd be noisily fretful, and Joanna at he
crowded desk in her cramped bedroom would be wrough
with guilt . . . babies made the smallest act complicated.

Madaket had said she'd bike from the doctor's office ou
to Squam to check her garden. Anyone else would be force
inside by this rain, but not Madaket. Joanna decided to driv
out and pick her up.

By the time she came to the Squam Road, the rain had di
minished to a spattering of fat drops and the sun was mak
ing its first appearance in days. The long ruts in the dirt roa
were puddled with water, which splashed up against the side
of the Jeep. She turned onto her private driveway. Bushes an
shrubs, lushly swollen with rain, drooped against the sides o
the Jeep. Her stomach tightened. Never again would sh
enter her property without thinking of Todd and Doug, es

pecially Todd, so young and handsome and vital—so greedy for all life had to offer, and who could be enjoying all life had to offer if she'd only given him one of the rubies. So much had been lost here; she thought this particular segment of earth would always be haunted by the loss of so many possibilities. She remembered the delight she'd felt each time she saw her sturdy storybook house standing forthright against the sky. Now there was only empty space.

As she brought her Jeep to a halt, the sun flashed out from behind clouds. The outlines of the charred black rectangle of earth where the house had once stood were softened and obscured by the lacy tangle of grasses, vines, and wild berry bushes reclaiming the land.

At the far end of the property, Madaket was standing in her garden. It had been untouched by the fire, and healthy green shoots gleamed in even rows. Someone was with her. Gardner. They were absorbed in conversation. Both were wearing yellow rain slickers, which gleamed glossily in the misty light. Joanna turned off the engine and slid out of the Jeep as quietly as possible, trying not to waken Christopher. The air smelled fresh and sweet.

"Looks pretty good," Joanna called, crossing the gravel to the grassy lawn. "Hi, Gardner."

The physician waved. Madaket smiled. Her hair was growing back nicely, lying full and gleaming over the curves of her skull, shining like ebony beneath her rain hood. But something else had happened . . . Joanna couldn't quite figure it out . . . something about Madaket had changed. The wretched scar was still as shiny as always, and yet Madaket looked . . . well, beautiful.

Something had happened.

Joanna stopped. Stood still, waiting.

"Joanna," Madaket said, her eyes brilliant, her face more alive than it had ever been. "We have something wonderful to tell you." She took Gardner's hand and together they walked toward Joanna.

Twenty-Eight

～

$\mathcal{J}$oanna stood waiting in the sodden, quickening earth
Madaket smiled shyly at Joanna, then turned her gaze a
Gardner, who said with a quiet pride, "Madaket and I are in
love."

"Oh, wow," Joanna exclaimed. "Wow. My gosh
Madaket." Searching the young woman's face, she found
sheer happiness shining there. "Oh, this is amazing. It's
lovely. Oh, Madaket, Gardner. I'm stunned. I'm knocked of
my feet."

"So are we," Gardner admitted.

"Well, let's go home and get inside where it's warm. I'm
soaked and frozen, and I want to hear everything, and I can'
think properly out here in all this damp."

"We'll meet you at the shack," Madaket said.

"Great."

Joanna hopped back in the Jeep. "Christopher," she said
to her sleeping son, "you'll never guess what happened. The
most amazing news. Madaket and Gardner are in love. I'm
just dazzled! What do you think?"

Her little boy only snored, and she drew up in front of their
shack, and stepped out, and lifted Christopher out, and his
head fell heavily against her shoulder; not even the wet slick
surface of her raincoat against his bare cheek woke him up
In their bedroom she settled her baby on his tummy and gen
tly stripped off his hooded sweatshirt and sweatpants, and
tucked a blanket over him, and stood for a while, watching
and listening, as she always did, partly to be certain he was
comfortable, but more simply for her own pleasure.

She pulled off her own rain gear then and wrapped herself in a bulky, fleecy sweater. She could hear Madaket in the kitchen, making coffee, but when she went out into the large open living room, she found Madaket and Gardner standing by the stove, entangled, kissing. She cleared her throat.

The lovers drew apart and they all carried in coffee mugs and sugar and a pitcher of milk and napkins, and Madaket poured the coffee and Gardner sank onto the sofa and watched her every move with the happy obsession of a man who cared in all the world only about putting his hands on her again. Finally Madaket sat down beside him, and they smiled at each other and held hands, looking as if they'd just discovered uranium and had been struck idiotic by their find.

"All right," Joanna said, sinking into a rocking chair. "Tell me."

Gardner and Madaket smiled at each other.

"We've hardly told each other yet," Madaket said shyly.

"We're going to get married," Gardner said.

"Married!"

"Well, not immediately," Madaket said soothingly. "Not until the fall at least."

"But I didn't even know you two liked each other!" Joanna protested. "This is all so sudden."

"I fell in love with Madaket the moment I saw her," Gardner admitted softly, flushing bright red to the tips of his ears. "At my office. When I came out to the reception room and met her."

"Remember how he came running out the side door and told us he would stop by to check your blood pressure?" Madaket's face glowed with pleasure as she spoke.

"I would have come by to check your blood pressure if you'd lived at the other side of the island," Gardner confessed. "I was still engaged to Tiffany, but we were both unhappy. We weren't even really in love, Tiffany and I. We were infatuated with a vision of what should be. I thought it would all be worth it, and Tiffany is really a nice person, and good-hearted, and deserving of love . . . but when I saw Madaket it was like . . . like a blind man seeing for the first time. I knew then, really knew, what I was missing with Tiffany. It really was love at first sight," he concluded happily.

"Did you feel this way, too?" Joanna asked Madaket.

"Oh, no. I mean, how could I? He was a doctor. I was a housecleaner. It never occurred to me that he even *saw* me." She turned to gaze adoringly at Gardner. "Whenever he came to the house, I always enjoyed seeing him. I looked forward to his visits. I liked listening to him—he has such a nice voice. And I liked looking at him. His beautiful hair and, well, he has such a nice"—crimson darkened her face; her scar glowed—"body," she whispered in conclusion.

"And we got along," Gardner pointed out, rescuing Madaket from the embarrassment of her admission of desire. "We talked a lot, and had so much to say to each other."

"That's true, yes," Madaket agreed. "And you were genuinely interested in what I knew."

"We're very compatible," Gardner declared.

"But it was when I was in the hospital in Boston that I knew."

"Knew that you loved Gardner?" Joanna asked.

"Knew that Gardner loved me." Now her other hand went to Gardner, and he reached for her and they sat close to each other, both hands clasping. "Even when I was not quite conscious and partly blinded by pain, I knew. I could tell by the way he touched me." Tears welled in Madaket's eyes. "And when I could see, I could see his face, when he looked at me I could see how he cared."

Joy burst like fountains within Joanna's heart. "I wondered," she said to Gardner, "why you were at Mass General so often. I guess I just assumed you gave that kind of attention to all your patients."

"I'm afraid I rather ignored my other patients for a while," Gardner confessed. "But I needed to see her. To see for myself that"—his voice roughened with emotion—"she stayed alive, and returned to health."

"We spent so much time talking. Well, I spent so much time listening, at first. It helped the time pass. It kept me from focusing on my pain. He told me about his family, and their pets, and medical school, and his vacations as a child, and even Tiffany. He even talked about Tiffany."

"How did you know Madaket wanted to hear all that?" Joanna asked. "How did you know how she felt?"

"She reached for me," Gardner said. "The first day her arms came out of the troughs, she reached for me."

"We held hands," Madaket said. "Sort of. I could feel—something—his steadiness, his strength, even through the bandages and the wounds."

"But I didn't want to tell her how I felt, to talk about the future, until she was strong, and well, and back where she felt steady. I wanted her to have real choices. So I waited until now."

"This is all so marvelous," Joanna said. "I'm so happy for both of you."

"It's an amazing thing," Madaket said thoughtfully. "I don't know if I can explain it, how it feels to realize that someone you've known and admired suddenly becomes someone you love and desire."

"I think I can understand," Joanna replied. And she thought of telling Madaket about Jake, about Jake and his declaration of love and his offer of marriage, and her own surprising eager emotional response; but Joanna waited. Now was the time for rejoicing in what Madaket and Gardner had found.

In spite of her best intentions, Joanna discovered she could not wait very long. Something in the way Gardner and Madaket brightened when they saw each other, in the way they couldn't stop touching one another, made Joanna wild to be with Jake, and one day only a week after Madaket and Gardner had told them about their marriage plans, Joanna interrupted them.

"Madaket. Gardner. Could I talk with you a moment?"

They'd just finished lunch and were all roaming between the shack's kitchen and the crowded living room.

"Sure." Madaket sank onto the sofa, holding Christopher on her lap, and Gardner settled so close to her he seemed to be vying with the baby for that spot.

They looked at her expectantly. Joanna took a deep breath. "Last month Jake asked me to marry him. I didn't tell him yes—I told him I had to think about it." She skated over the truth; someday she'd tell Madaket everything, so that Madaket would know that she truly came first in Joanna's life. "I've thought about it, and I've tried to be rational about it, and I've arrived at the knowledge that in fact I do want to marry him. Desperately." She felt her face flush and tears rush to her eyes. "Oh, God!" she laughed. "I really love him!"

"That's wonderful, Joanna," Gardner said.

"Well, for heaven's sake, Joanna," Madaket exploded, "what are you waiting for? Think how Jake must feel! Why not call him and tell him?"

Joanna looked at Madaket and saw only happiness in her eyes, and she heard only impatience in Madaket's voice. Madaket was not threatened by Joanna's love for Jake. She was purely happy, and baffled by Joanna's reluctance, and even bossy in the way that one can be only with one's family. So there was to be no either/or in the love between them, no choosing between people. There was to be no leaving, no loss. She smiled at Madaket, and reached for her hands, and met her eyes. "You're right. Yes, I will. Right now!"

She rose, intending to head for her bedroom and the privacy of the phone there, but suddenly, struck through with an idea, she paused.

"No," she said slowly, speaking to herself as much as to the others as the plan unfolded in her mind. "I don't think I will call him." She turned and looked at Madaket, a smile of conspiracy in her eyes. "I think I'll leave Christopher in your care, and take the first plane to New York, and show up on Jake's door, and surprise him."

"What a good idea, Joanna," Madaket said.

Joanna was gripped by a sense of urgency. "I'd better hurry. What time is it? Madaket, will call you the airlines and make me a reservation on the first plane out of here? I'll pack."

"Sure, Joanna. Here, Gardner, hold Christopher." Madaket grabbed up the phone while Joanna raced into her bedroom. She grabbed a canvas carryall from the top shelf in her closet and filled it with clean underwear, socks, and a silk shirt; she would wear her jeans and loafers and silk sweater and navy blazer on the plane. Then she reached for her robe and was struck with paralysis. She would spend the night with Jake—she hoped. But she had no nightgowns that were even slightly sexy. The silk nightgown Claude had given her after the fire had gotten stained with breast milk, and the cashmere robe was stretched from constant wearing and soiled from baby spit.

Madaket stuck her head into the bedroom. "Bad news, Joanna. The last shuttle to New York has already left. I tried to connect you through Boston, but nothing will get you there tonight."

Joanna stared at Madaket. She could wait, of course. She'd waited a week already. She could take tomorrow to go shopping, to buy some attractive new nightgowns . . .

"Charter a flight," Joanna ordered. The words were out of her mouth almost before she thought them.

"Right!" Madaket replied, her face lighting up with a smile.

Joanna turned back to her closet and tossed the old nightgown and robe into the bag. Jake didn't want to marry her because she had great clothes.

She rushed into the bathroom to gather up her toiletries. Perfume, toothpaste, toothbrush . . .

"I've got someone!" Madaket called. "He wants to know how soon you want to leave."

"Now!" Joanna called back.

"You got it!" Madaket yelled.

Joanna hastened to her bureau, opened the top drawer, and grabbed up the satin jewelry bag she'd bought to hold the few pieces of costume jewelry she'd purchased or been given since the fire. She tossed the bag into her carryall, added her cosmetics bag, and checked her reflection in the mirror. She was clean, alive, glowing; she'd never looked better.

"Let's go!" she announced. Madaket bent over Christopher, zipping him into a lightweight hooded sweatshirt.

"Shall we take my car?" Gardner asked.

"Can't," Madaket replied. "We need the baby seat. But you drive. I've got the car keys." She tossed them to Gardner and they all rushed out into the bright spring evening.

Madaket settled Christopher into his car seat and fastened the seat belts, then crawled into the front seat beside Gardner. Joanna sat in the back, talking to Christopher. "I have to go off again, little guy, but you know I'll come back soon, I always do. And Madaket will take good care of you."

Christopher blew bubbles and shrieked and banged his hands on the plastic beads on his car seat so that they rattled and clattered. He seemed to have picked up Joanna's mood.

The evening air as they sped through it was cool but clear "You'll have an easy flight," Madaket predicted as they hur tled along the road toward the airport.

"I hope so. God, I wish I could just be there. I feel really a little insane. Like I'll explode, truly explode, if I can't ge to Jake right now."

"I know how you feel," Gardner said. "That's how I fel when I made up my mind to tell Madaket. I had to leave my office, I had to ask my nurse to reschedule all my poor pa tients. I've never done anything so irresponsible in my life."

"You're both being so wonderful about this. I'm so grate ful."

"The charter plane is at the east end of the airfield," Madaket informed Joanna. "The pilot's name is Will Turner He said he'd be waiting for you at the Nantucket Airline: gate."

"Great. Thanks." As they pulled into the parking lot Joanna leaned over and kissed her baby boy on his cheeks then turned and planted a fat smooch on Madaket's head "Don't get out. I'll find him myself. God, I'm so excited think I could fly there without the plane!" She jumped out o the car the moment it slowed in front of the terminal. "I love you all!" she shouted, and raced off.

Streaking through the entrance and along through the long, well-lit building, Joanna came at last to the counter where Will Turner waited. She introduced herself, and wrote him a check on the spot, and just as they headed out to the gates, Joanna heard her name called. It was Madaket.

"Here," she cried, rushing up to Joanna and putting a paper bag in her hands. "I got this for you. It's dinnertime and you haven't eaten since lunch, and you won't have a chance to eat, and the flight takes about an hour—"

"Oh, honey, thanks, but I'm too excited to eat."

"I know, but once you're in the plane it will help to have some food. You'll be edgy and nervous and this will help pass the time." Madaket looked at the pilot. "There's stuff in there for you, too. Since you were good enough to come a a moment's notice—"

"Thanks," Will Turner said, and headed off for the gate to the airfield, and Joanna hurried after him, turning to blow Madaket a kiss.

"I've already checked the plane for takeoff," Will said as he handed Joanna into the twin-engine Cessna.

The little plane shot down the runway and lifted up into the air. Below them, the outline of the island came into view, then drifted away as they flew toward New York.

"I gather this is a good emergency, rather than a bad one," Will said.

"It is," Joanna told him. Then a new thought hit her—what if Jake wasn't in New York? Or what if he was in New York but with another woman? Why shouldn't he be? She'd made no promises to him, and she'd asked nothing of him. "Or I think it is," she muttered to the pilot. "I hope it is. I guess you never know with love, do you?"

"Oh, it's love," Will Turner sighed. "Well, you're right, you never do know."

Joanna dug into the paper bag and found two Styrofoam cups of coffee. Madaket was right; it did help to pass the time. She fussed with the little containers of sugar and cream and handed a cup to Will, and drank her coffee and toyed with a sandwich and still they weren't there. The engines of the small plane droned steadily, and she put her head back and closed her eyes and tried to rest. But she couldn't rest. Beneath them the ocean spread in vast darkness.

"Talk to me," she said to the pilot. "Talk to me about anything."

Will cleared his throat. "Well, uh . . ."

"Tell me about your home. Your family."

"This is my home," Will said, patting the instrument panel of his plane. "This is my family."

"Then tell me how you started flying."

That was the right question to ask. Will regaled Joanna with tales of his love for flight, which began in childhood and continued right up to the moment. The buzz of his words calmed her for a while, until the lights of New York came into view, and then she was overcome with an irrational urge to shout, "Shut up, shut up, just get us to New York!"

She was relieved when Will curtailed his monologue in order to turn his attention to the routines of landing. Joanna took her compact from her purse and looked in the mirror; not an efficient way to judge her makeup since the lights inside the plane streaked her face with shadows, and as she at-

tempted to refresh her lipstick, the little craft shuddered and
bumped. She brushed her hair, which didn't need it, then
brushed it again. Finally she subsided against her seat, eyes
closed, as they descended toward the landing lights.

She knew where Jake lived. He had a handsome apartment
in the East Eighties. She'd been there often when Emily was
alive; they gave wonderful parties. She tried to remember if
she'd been there since Emily's death, and decided she hadn't.
Jake's children were grown. He would be lonely in all that
space.

The plane touched down, bumped, skidded, then settled
firmly against the landing strip. She opened her eyes and
watched the blue lights flash by the windows of the plane as
they slowed, the little plane sputtering just outside the windows. They decelerated to a crawl. In the distance, the lights
of jumbo jets in line for takeoff moved in a stately procession.
Blasts from other planes in transit hit their little plane so hard
it rocked. They seemed to be idling at the edge of the airfield.

"What are we waiting for?" Joanna asked.

"There's a lot of traffic here tonight. We've got to wait our
turn to approach the terminal."

Joanna closed her eyes again, and crossed her arms over
her chest and forced herself to take deep breaths to calm
down. She could call Jake. His home number was unlisted,
but she knew it. But the shuttles that made the New
York/Nantucket run, and this small plane as well, were sit-
uated in a small building apart from the regular terminals and
she wasn't certain where the pay phones were. It would be
quicker simply to run out, hail a cab, and jump in. Besides,
she didn't want to call Jake, she wanted to surprise him.

It was a torturous eternity before the plane slowly crept its
way across the dark pavement and into the civilization of
lights and ground crew and buildings. Will let down the door,
stepped out, and handed Joanna down. Reaching for her
bag stowed at the back of the plane, he gave it to her and told
her good luck.

"Thanks," she said. "Thanks for everything."

Then she raced off. Through the small, rather shabby terminal, which was mostly shut down for the night. Out the
front doors, to the street.

Which was dark and empty. No taxis awaited.

She looked left and right. Left led only to a barren dark expanse of airfield and looming plane hangars. To her right, far away, the enormous complex of La Guardia sprang up, with ramps and cement walls and dark holes in the stretch of land she'd have to cross to reach the outer limits of the multilevel terminal.

She raced back into the small building behind her and rushed through it, searching frantically for the pay phones. She found them. She'd call a cab. But the hard plastic covers for the telephone directories hung emptily from their chains. She dropped coins into the machine, punched in the numbers for information, and waited. Finally someone answered, gave her a number for a taxi service, and clicked off. Frantically she dialed, and begged for a taxi to be sent to her, then hurried back outside where, to her amazement and joy, a taxi appeared almost instantly.

She threw herself into the backseat and barked the address at the driver.

As they pulled away from the airport and entered the stream of cars headed for the city, Joanna once again took out her compact and checked her face. Her face, that face, which now, according to the kind of light cast by the lamps they passed, showed her in either an orange or a blue glow, that face was pretty much set. Lipstick would help, and eyeliner, but on either side of her mouth a pair of parentheses was indelibly indented, and the appealing slant of her eyebrows was changing, sinking into a downward slant. She looked tired. Well, she should, she'd had quite a year. And Jake knew what she looked like and had asked her to marry him anyway.

The cab began to lurch; a sure sign they'd entered the checkerboard grid of city stoplights and double-parked cars and one-way streets and general traffic congestion. They were almost there. She glanced at her watch: it was a little after nine o'clock. Wednesday night. Jake would be home. Should be. She was familiar with his routines. He would have left the network and taken a cab to one of his clubs, where he would have eaten a large meal and had a Scotch or two with it, while perusing piles of memos, files, and reports from the briefcase he carried with him everywhere. He'd take another cab to his apartment after dinner and settle in to watch

television. CVN had a block of comedy shows they ran on
Wednesday nights from eight until eleven, the latter show
aimed at more mature and sophisticated audiences. For re
laxation, Jake would be watching those.

But where? She didn't know. Did he stretch out in bed and
watch television? Or sink into one of the leather chairs in hi
den? Would he have showered, would he be in pajamas? O
a robe? Perhaps, saddened by Joanna's rejection of his mar
riage proposal, he would have started dating one of the many
bright young things who worked at the network. Perhaps h
had one of them in his apartment now, and was plying he
with liquor and admiring her flat stomach and pert breasts
Why should Joanna believe that she was the only woman fo
him? Jake was a man of great appetites. Jake wasn't one t
wait around, nursing his wounds. He was a man of action
he got things done. He was a hot-blooded, warmhearted
man, who liked to eat and drink and laugh, and therefor
who undoubtedly liked to make love. The more she though
about it, the more certain Joanna became that Jake would
have moved on after Joanna's rejection.

It was quite probable that he had a woman with him now

What if Joanna knocked on his door, and he opened it and
was wearing mussed clothing with lipstick on the collar and
a young woman half-undressed on his sofa?

"This is it, miss," the cabdriver called, startling her from
her thoughts. Jake's apartment building rose up before her

"All right," Joanna said meekly. She paid the driver
picked up her bag, and stepped out of the cab.

The doorman politely asked Joanna her name and whom
she'd be visiting. For one wild moment Joanna wanted to
clutch the man by his lapels and beg him to tell her whethe
or not Jake Corcoran had a woman with him tonight.

"It's Joanna Jones. For Jake Corcoran."

The doorman spoke into the intercom.

Perhaps Jake wasn't even home.

"Go right on up," the doorman said, and held open the
door.

She crossed the small foyer, stepped into the elevator, and
pressed the button. Her heart knocked against her chest. Th
door slid open. In this building each floor belonged entirel

to one owner, and Joanna stepped off onto the fourth floor
and into Jake's entrance hall.

He was waiting there, a perplexed smile on his face.

"Joanna. What a surprise."

He was wearing suit pants and a rumpled work shirt, with
his tie yanked down and his sleeves rolled up. A familiar
sight. He'd been running his hands through his hair again,
and it stood out in a dark halo around his head.

"Yes, I wanted to surprise you," Joanna told him. She
could tell that he was happy to see her. "Jake. Jake, I want
to change my answer to your proposal. If it's not too late."

Jake shoved his hands into his pants pockets and eyed her
with a lazy smile. "And what did you want to change your
answer to?"

"Yes. I want to say yes."

A smile broke out over his face. "That's the best news I've
had in a long, long time, Joanna."

"Oh, Jake, I'm so—excited and exhausted!" Joanna confessed. And he laughed, and took her by the arm and with
the other hand took her bag, and led her into his living room
and shut the door to the outside world behind them.

They sat on the sofa and talked. Joanna told him about
Madaket and Gardner, and on the strength of that news Jake
rose and went into his kitchen, and she followed him and
watched while he took a bottle of Perrier-Jouet from his refrigerator.

"I always keep one cold, just in case," Jake said as he un-
corked the bottle and took out two crystal flutes, and Joanna
smiled with delight at this new bit of insight into Jake's life—
what a wonderful man he was, what an optimist, always to
have a bottle of champagne ready, always certain, even after
all life had tossed him, that on any normal day life might give
him something to celebrate.

Returning to the living room, they sipped champagne and
talked, or rather Jake listened to Joanna with a new light in
his eyes, and Joanna told him all about Madaket and Gardner and Christopher and *Fabulous Homes* until at last she realized that she was talking faster and faster, almost babbling.
She was nervous, in spite of the effects of the champagne,
about the next step of intimacy with Jake. About going to bed
with him. Odd thoughts flashed through her head: she'd got-

ten so stretch-marked from her pregnancy, what if Jake
found her body unattractive? Or what if her body didn'
work, somehow, for him or for her?

Then suddenly Jake's arms were around her and his mouth
was on hers, and he was leading her to the bedroom, and no
turning on the lights, but letting in a gentle glow from the
hallway, and delicately, slowly, helping her out of her clothes
and onto his bed. It was covered with soft goose-down comforters which surrendered, seeming to melt to the shape o
Joanna's body. Jake took off his clothes and lay next to her
His skin was warm, his thighs shockingly large and muscular, his chest matted with hair, his torso fleshy to the touch
She had only held her little baby over the past many months
and now Jake seemed like a giant to her.

"Are you all right? Is this all right? Am I going too fast?"
he asked.

"Yes, no, oh, Jake," Joanna answered, greedily pulling
him to her.

Jake kissed her and ran his hands over her body, learning
its lines and swells and hollows. He rose up above her. She
parted her legs. He entered her. He was wide, big. He could
wedge himself into her only so far before she shifted her hips
to stop him.

He asked, "Am I hurting you?"

"Yes," she admitted. He withdrew slowly, and as he did,
she felt her muscles and skin contract, as if trying to keep him
"No," she said. He entered again, a little way. The pressure
was intense and painful and delicious. "Just there," she said,
and Jake stayed, just there.

He was supporting himself on his arms above her, and his
face was next to hers, his mouth against her ear. She had
brought her knees up so that she could find some purchase
on the comforters with her feet to help her bear the brunt of
his wide penis. He smelled so good, so Jake-like and familiar and safe, an aroma of coffee and Scotch and ink, and yet
he felt so unfamiliar, so excitingly strange.

"This is going to take us a while," he whispered, moving a
millimeter farther into her.

"Yes," she agreed in a sigh.

"We'll have to work on this a lot," he told her.

"I know."

"I love you, Joanna," Jake said.

"Oh, Jake. Oh, Jake, I love you," she replied.

They lay in silence then, adjusting themselves by degrees to the contours and desires and limitations of their bodies together. Finally Jake said, "Joanna, I can't—" and he pulled back, but as he did she felt him swell even more, so that he was like a boulder wedging against her. She felt the ripples of his pleasure radiate into her body. She shuddered with a delicious pain, and when he lay next to her, exhausted, catching his breath, subsiding, holding her to him, his chest heaving against her, she lay like a woman who has just emerged from a dream and awakened to the fullness of life.

Part Three

Twenty-Nine

~

The courts of the Commonwealth of Massachusetts were
housed in Nantucket's town hall, a modest two-story brick
building on Broad Street. Its main, front door faced oddly
away from town so that most people, approaching it from the
center of the village, used the side doors to enter. Inside, a
gloomy long corridor punctuated by doors to the Assessor's
Office, the Town Clerk's Office, the Registry of Deeds, and
other town boards and commissions stretched straight between side entrances with staircases to the second floor. There
the upper hall repeated exactly the long straight run, institu-
tionally bland, with offices on each side opening to the Registry of Motor Vehicles, the Courtrooms, and the Judge's
Chamber.

On a bright early June afternoon a group filed into the
courthouse and up the stairs to the second floor: Joanna,
Madaket, Jake, who carried Christopher, Gardner, Pat and
Bob, June and Morris, Claude and his new beau, Larry,
Gardner's sister Norie, and Marge and Harry Coffin. The
women wore fluid, pastel dresses and romantic hats trimmed
with flowers or lace or silk bows. The men wore sports coats
and ties and Christopher wore a pale blue sweater over his
white cotton romper.

No benches or chairs lined the long hallway for the waiting crowd, but an officer of the court, smiling above his dark
suit, assured them they wouldn't have to wait long. He lingered to chat about the fine June weather. Everyone talked
at once, and then the door opened and they were summoned
into the courtroom.

Judge Julius Cohen, who came several times a week from Boston, sat in black robes behind his high bench. He peered down at them through thick black-framed bifocals.

"Will the parties concerned please approach the bench?" he directed.

Joanna and Madaket went forward. The witnesses solemnly clustered in a half-circle.

The judge stared down at the two women in stern silence. A hush fell over the room. Even Christopher, who'd been squirming in Jake's arms, trying to get a look at this new room, went quiet, eyes wide as he looked around.

Judge Cohen studied the forms before him.

"Joanna Jones?"

"Yes." Joanna smiled.

"Madaket Brown?"

"Yes, sir." Madaket smiled, too.

The judge looked them over, taking his time, then spoke. "You, Joanna Jones, have petitioned this court to adopt Madaket Brown as your legal daughter."

"That's right, Your Honor."

"And you, Miss Brown, are twenty years old and understand that we are therefore waiving the social services procedures."

"Yes, Your Honor."

"You want to be adopted by this woman."

"I do."

"I see you want to change your last name to Jones, also."

"Yes."

"Very well. By the powers vested in me by the Commonwealth of Massachusetts, I declare that you, Joanna Jones, have now adopted Madaket Brown, to be known henceforth as Madaket Jones, as your legal daughter." He slammed his gavel down, once, hard.

Then he smiled.

Joanna couldn't help herself; she was crying. She pulled Madaket to her in a warm embrace. The two women hugged tightly, then Joanna took Madaket's face in her two hands and looked at her as if she'd just arrived in the world and was brand-new.

"Hi, Mom," Madaket said.

"Hi, kid," Joanna whispered through her tears.

Gardner raised the camera hanging around his neck and clicked pictures. Judge Cohen rose from his seat to lean over and shake hands. "Congratulations," he said to the women.

It was the end of the day, and no other cases were waiting, so the judge and his officer didn't mind letting the others take their time snapping photographs: Joanna and Madaket and the judge, Joanna and Madaket and Christopher, Joanna, Madaket, Christopher, Gardner, and Jake, then all the witnesses, and then the entire group, including the judge and his court official.

Then the crowd clattered out of the courtroom, down the stairs, and out into the sunny afternoon.

Of all the people invited to the adoption ceremony, only Tory declined to attend, not because she didn't approve of it all, which in fact she didn't, but because her life had suddenly fallen apart. That spring Tory discovered that her husband had a mistress, had been involved with her for several years now, a thirty-year-old journalist named Madeline. John was leaving Tory to marry Madeline because she was pregnant. John insisted they sell their New York apartment and the 'Sconset house; they would divide the profits equally. John would use his share to buy a new home for himself, his new bride, and their new child.

At the end of May Tory flew to Nantucket for the gloomy task of readying the house to be shown to prospective buyers. Joanna had just returned from taping an FH show in Cleveland, and Saturday evening she drove out to 'Sconset with a picnic dinner and a bottle of wine. She had Christopher with her, too, even though Madaket had offered to take care of him; she wanted to be with her baby every second she could.

The sun was shining and the grass was green and tulips were blooming, but it was cold inside Tory's house. A brisk breeze sifted through the walls and windows from the ocean and Tory built a fire in the living room fireplace to offset the chill. She poured them each a glass of wine, and then Joanna carried Christopher and they walked through the spacious old house. As they opened doors and stood gazing in at the many rooms, it was as if they were actually revealing true and living scenes enacted there not so very long ago.

"Remember how this house sounded the year Jeremy was fourteen?" Tory asked. "He had several friends come to visit and they were all as clumsy as colts, and so goofy." She ran her fingers over a patched area in the wall of the upstairs hall. "They played touch football up here one rainy day. Someone—I think that big cute Bowles boy—tackled Jeremy and drove his shoulder right through the wall." Suddenly she turned to Joanna, her blue eyes wide with alarm. "How am I going to live without all this? Without them?"

"You'll find a way," Joanna assured her. "I did."

"Oh, you're totally different," Tory snapped, and shaking her head bitterly and wiping at her eyes with a handkerchief, she moved on to another room. She stopped at her daughter's bedroom door. "My children are growing away from me. They never call me from boarding school. I don't know what they're doing. I don't know what time they go to bed at night. They don't want me to know."

"That's only natural," Joanna reminded her.

Tory drifted into Vicki's room. Nostalgically she ran her fingers over the ice cream twists of her daughter's canopy bedposts. "I'm going to sell the furniture. Everything. I'm going to tell Rafael to come take everything and sell it all."

"Tory—"

"Really, I am! Vicki doesn't even like her canopy bed anymore. She thinks it's too 'infantile.' She wants to find some drug addict and travel through Europe with him; her goal in life is to sleep on the floor of a train station with her backpack for a pillow."

Joanna laughed. "It's her age. She'll change." Crossing the hall, she entered the guest bedroom, pulled back the crisp white curtains, and looked out the window at the blue Atlantic. "I stayed here three years ago," she mused aloud. "When I saw my house for the first time."

"I always liked the wallpaper in this room," Tory commented from the doorway.

"And the view. Such an amazing view."

Tory came to stand next to Joanna. She stared out in silence for a few moments, then said, "Yes, I used to love the view. But do you know what? Now it terrifies me. So much emptiness. So much cold water to drown in."

"Oh, poor Tory . . ." Joanna began, but Tory let the curtain fall and walked away.

Returning to the living room, they set up their picnic dinner in front of the fireplace. Joanna made her way across the rug on her hands and knees, checking for sharp objects, and satisfied that the space was safe, she took Christopher from Tory's arms and let him crawl.

"Look at him go!" Joanna laughed, delighted by her baby's healthy antics. "Too bad they don't have a baby Olympics."

"All mothers think their baby's precocious," Tory replied with a sniff.

"I hope I can be as good a mother to my child as you were to Jeremy and Vicki," Joanna said.

"I was a good mother," Tory agreed.

"Remember the great board games you all used to have on the porch?"

"I'll never forget them."

"What will you do with them all?"

"Donate them to the Second Shop."

"Why not keep them? Someday you'll have grandchildren to play with."

Tory shuddered. "Oh, wonderful, just what I want to look forward to, life as a feeble old grandmother."

"Tory, grandmothers don't have to be old and feeble anymore," Joanna began, but Tory was indignant and the two friends finished their dinner in an uneasy truce.

The fire died down as they cleaned up the remains of their picnic, and they went out of the house. Tory locked the door behind them. She couldn't bear to stay there alone, and besides, it was cold, so she had booked a room at a local inn.

The two women stood looking up at the gracious old Victorian. "This is a wonderful house, Tory," Joanna said. "I'm so sorry you're losing it."

"I'll never come back to Nantucket again in my life," Tory swore.

"Yes, you will," Joanna told her. "You'll come stay with us in our new house some summer."

Tory only looked glumly at Joanna in reply.

Joanna kissed her friend and watched her drive off, then tucked a drowsy Christopher into his car seat and set off herself for the little rented shack in Quidnet, thinking as she drove of the sheer serendipity which had changed so many lives.

If Joanna hadn't known Tory, and hadn't stayed at her house three years ago, and hadn't driven along the Squam Road from the east, rather than from the west, from town; if she hadn't turned down the wrong driveway and seen the storybook house; if she hadn't bought the house and needed a housekeeper and hired Madaket—would Madaket still have met Gardner? Possibly. They both would have lived here on Nantucket anyway. But perhaps they would not have had so many occasions on which to become acquainted, and to see each other over and over again, and to fall in love.

It would be a summer full of ceremonies celebrating the entanglements of love. First, Joanna adopted Madaket as her legal daughter, making it clear that no matter what else happened in their lives, their bond to each other would remain. Jake and Joanna would be married in August and Jake would adopt Christopher as his legal son. Then Christopher would be christened. And Madaket and Gardner would be married in September.

Their wedding would be beautiful. Joanna had begged Madaket to let her plan and give the wedding, for after all she was now Madaket's mother, and Madaket had agreed. It would be fabulous, Joanna declared, with acres of white satin, white linen, gardenias, white tulips, baby's breath, and champagne. *She* would give Madaket away. Madaket had decided not to take Gardner's name when she married him. She would keep her last name: Jones.

Somehow, in the midst of all this, Joanna had to travel to twelve different states and tape twelve shows for the fall and winter; finish her book tours; choose a design and a contractor for the Nantucket home; supervise the transformation of Jake's apartment into a home for herself and Jake and Christopher, with a guest suite for Madaket and Gardner—or for Jake's two sons and their families. Her life had never been so complicated. She had never been so happy.

It wasn't all sheer sweetness and light, however. Jake's younger son, Gabe, was twenty-four. He and his girlfriend, Jane, were delighted that Jake was going to be married again, that he'd found someone to love and care for him after the loss of his wife and his years of mourning. Paul, the older son, at twenty-six had just become a father himself; he and his wife, Celia, only professed delight, and only briefly. Their concern was financial. If Jake married Joanna, who would inherit his estate when he died? Furthermore, would Jake's own flesh and blood, his sons and grandchildren, be subjected to financial loss in favor of Jake's adopted new son? *Furthermore,* when Madaket became Joanna's legal daughter, did she thus become eligible to inherit some of the money that should rightfully go to Jake's sons and grandchildren? Tempers flared. Phones rang. Faxes cascaded to the floor. Joanna and Jake met with lawyers and began the tedious work of drawing up prenuptial agreements.

Once Jake had made it clear to his family that their inheritances weren't threatened by Joanna or Christopher or Madaket, everyone became more amiable. Jake invited his sons and their wives to La Cirque, where he officially announced his engagement to Joanna, and in turn the sons and their wives gave dinner parties to honor their father and his fiancée. Because the parties were in the city, where Joanna was fitting them into her crowded work schedule, she left Christopher on Nantucket with Madaket. Another task looming before her was the choice of a New York nanny. And a live-in housekeeper; Joanna liked Jake's current help well enough, but the woman came only once a week and couldn't give them the time that Jake's new and complicated family life would require.

Madaket had asked to have Christopher stay with her during the summer. It would be best for him, she pointed out, while Joanna flew around the country producing her shows. Madaket had moved into the house Gardner was renting on the Squam Road. The large guest bedroom there held only Gardner's beloved Fender Telecaster, a chair, an amplifier, and a music stand. He'd played with a rock group in high school, he confessed to Joanna, and at times he found playing his guitar brought him a solitary and melancholy consolation as nothing else could. But now that Madaket was in his life, he had no need for consolation of any kind. He suggested they turn the extra bedroom into a room for Christopher. He took on the task of moving Christopher's furniture from the rented shack to his house.

What more could any mother ask, Joanna thought, than that her child be cared for by someone who loved him as much as Madaket did and, even better, who was living with a doctor? Occasionally she was pierced through with jealousy of Madaket's constant loving presence in Christopher's life; Christopher might come to love, to trust, to need, Madaket more than his own mother. At other times she only marveled at the sheer good fortune that had brought into her life and her son's this young woman, who loved them as her own. Joanna reminded herself that with summer's end, she and Christopher would be living in New York with Jake and they would all have to cope with a new set of faces and personalities.

With Joanna's adoption of Madaket, and Madaket's engagement to Gardner, another group of relatives entered Joanna's life: Gardner's parents and sisters. When Madaket married, Joanna would become Gardner's mother-in-law. Madaket would have sisters-in-law. And Christopher would have a grown brother-in-law. An entire constellation of relationships blossomed around Joanna. Christopher's sisters, Constance and Eleanor, had come to visit their brother during the spring. They'd come separately, and acted as if they'd been raised in different families. Constance, a few years older than Gardner, was also a physician. She had the same mass of curly, unruly, glowing hair that Gardner had, and the same lanky, ambling build, and the same direct look and easy smile. Eleanor, nicknamed Norie, was the baby of the family; she looked it, too. Plump, roly-poly Norie tied her long brown hair back with pastel ribbons and wore waistless dresses that ended at her thighs and baby-doll shoes with straps. When Joanna first met Norie, she'd thought the young woman's wardrobe was some kind of a joke, but fortunately she didn't mention this to anyone; Joanna came to understand that Norie chose her clothes with deliberation and care. Norie worked in a day-care center, taking care of babies and children, which Joanna privately thought was appropriate, since Norie was so childish herself. It was Norie who resented Madaket, although Norie would have resented any woman who entered Gardner's life; she wanted her brother all to herself. During the weekend she spent with Gardner and Madaket, Norie had been aggressively rueful, and she snubbed Madaket, and misunderstood her every sentence, and made it clear that nothing Madaket did was right. Then, to everyone's surprise and relief, Joanna stopped by to meet Norie, and the young woman had gone into raptures over Christopher. She'd taken him from Joanna and flirted and cooed to the little boy. Christopher had responded with his most beguiling gurgles and grins, and by the end of the evening, Norie said, "Look, Madaket, when you have Christopher over the summer, I'll come over and take care of him for you so you can have some time to yourself. Or to be with Gardner. You guys could go out to dinner."

"Thanks, Norie. I appreciate that. I know I'll be glad for some help."

"Lucky boy. He has a girlfriend so soon," Gardner said to Christopher, and Norie glowed at the compliment in her brother's words.

It's possible that she and Madaket will be friends, Joanna had thought, watching the young woman. Especially when Madaket has children; then Norie will come help.

And so here they all were, a party of fortunate people bound by acquaintance and circumstance and good luck, ready to celebrate the first in an absolute festival of celebratory occasions. Much discussion had gone on about just where to hold the reception after the adoption ceremony. Joanna's shack was far too small, Gardner's house didn't have enough furniture, and Joanna didn't feel she should impose on the Hoovers any more than she already had.

At last, with brilliant inspiration, she decided to hire a cruise ship. Now the group walked over the smooth pavement and bumpy cobblestones through the town, past the A&P parking lot where tulips bloomed and the great birch tree towered, beneath the lush green overhang of trees to Straight Wharf and the waiting boat.

It was a fifty-seven-foot power yacht, trimmed out in brass and teak. They assembled on the upper deck on chairs and benches cushioned in navy-blue and white stripes, around tables where the caterers had set out flowers and champagne and food. The boat shuddered around them as the engines rumbled into life, and slowly they moved out into the harbor.

For the first hour or so everyone mingled, exclaiming ove
the view or the gorgeous clouds streaked by the sinking sun
but before long the group broke into small clusters: they al
had so much to be discussed, thought out, and planned. Bo
told Madaket and Gardner about various houses he though
they'd be interested in buying, and Joanna bounced Christo
pher on her lap as she considered with Jake how they'd sched
ule the shooting of the next few shows of *Fabulous Homes
Jake and Joanna would be married quickly and quietly in
New York in August and take a honeymoon in Paris, leav
ing Christopher with Madaket and Gardner. They'd ap
proved the plans of a new, environmentally conscious
ambitious young architect, and by the end of the fall their new
home would be built on the Squam property, a vacation
home complete with solar panels and a swimming pool and
cabanas, and a separate guest cottage connected to the main
house by a glass-roofed greenhouse for Madaket, so tha
Madaket would always have a reason to come home
Christopher would be christened in October. ·

Now Pat came to Joanna, arms outstretched.

"Let me take him for a while," she said, reaching for the
baby. "I used to see him every day and now I never get to.
don't want him to forget me."

"I think he needs changing, and he's fussing for a bottle,"
Joanna said, relinquishing her baby into Pat's arms.

"I'll take him below into the cabin. We'll fix him all up
won't we, snookums?" Pat's voice slid into the sweet goo o
baby talk as she nuzzled Christopher's downy head.

"Can I help?" Norie appeared in front of them, looking
hopeful.

"That would be great," Pat replied easily. "Here, you play
with him and I'll find his bottle and a fresh diaper." The two
women disappeared into the cabin.

Free of the weight and care of her son, Joanna rose and
found Madaket, who now was standing at the bow of the
boat. Joanna had asked the captain to take them out into the
Sound and east, around Great Point, then down along the
eastern shore of the island, so that they could see Joanna's
land from the water. Joanna slipped her arm around
Madaket's shoulders, and Madaket slid her arm around
Joanna's waist, and in companionable silence they looked ou

at the coastline. A gentle breeze made the long blue ribbon on Madaket's hat flutter and sent the hems of Madaket's and Joanna's light dresses dancing.

They passed around the tip of Great Point, and then as the boat motored steadily south, they saw the scrubby green of tenacious beach plants and the angular gray geometrics of houses rise above the long stretch of gleaming sand.

It was difficult figuring out just what land belonged to Joanna and what to other people, for from this view there were few markers. She recognized the houses on either side of her property, but there were no fences, and the wild moorland spread in an unruly tangle of roses and brambles and low bushes. The beach shone golden as far as she could see.

"Look," Madaket cried, "there's my garden!"

Joanna squinted, peering against the brightness of the setting sun. Up past the shore and the steadfast luxuriance of seaside roses and ivies and heathers, past the large irregular patch of damaged and blackened ground being reclaimed by wild vines and tough grasses, near the winding white ribbon of the gravel drive: there it was, Joanna could see it, Madaket's garden, small rows of tender greens cultivated and flourishing in the midst of the patient and resilient earth.

All around the boat the ocean flowed deep blue, and above them the sky shone in layers of pure blue light. The straight, sleek stream of a jet cut a line of white overhead.

"That plane's way up there," Madaket observed.

"Yes. On its way to England or Europe. Maybe you'll go there someday with Gardner."

"Maybe." Madaket shrugged beneath Joanna's hands. "Maybe not. I'm not wild to go anywhere at all, really. You can travel and send me postcards." She grinned. "And bring me presents."

Joanna smiled in reply. "All right. That sounds good to me."

She would travel. She had come to understand that was one place where she belonged, where she felt at home: in a state of movement, from one location to another, in a train or a plane or a Jeep or a taxi or a ferry, or even physically in her study as her mind voyaged along electronic thoroughfares. And her home base would remain here, with Madaket and Nantucket and Angelica's memory and grave, as well as in New York, with Jake and Christopher, and also at the network, where recently she had reclaimed her office space, dumping a briefcase full of notes and papers and computer disks onto the welcoming wide surface of her lovely desk.

"Goodness!" Her new secretary, Louise, had goggled at the abundance of paperwork cascading before her. Then, to Joanna's immense relief and satisfaction, Louise had actually rubbed her hands together in greedy anticipation. "What a lot of work to do! We'd better get busy."

The phone had rung then, and Joanna had heard a shriek in the hallway. The makeup man, Dhon, raced into the room, waving his hands, babbling euphorically. Since she'd been gone, he'd added a ring to his nose and dyed his hair green.

"Can you have lunch with me today? I have gossip that will make your ears hot."

"You bet," Joanna had laughed, delighted; at lunch they'd gossiped and giggled like school kids.

Why was she thinking of the network now? Joanna wondered as she stood in the fresh air on the deck of the cruise ship, with her arm around her daughter. The sun fell on their shoulders and into the sea so that the water seemed strewn with jewels. Beside her, Madaket's face was lambent with light and emotion, and Joanna smiled to surmise Madaket's thoughts: of Gardner, and their future, their wedding, their children, their home. I'm not like Madaket, Joanna realized. I don't crave one single place on this earth to be mine. I don't need one home—or rather, I need many. I need Christopher, and Jake, and Madaket, and the network and this island, and the vast, light-flung sky, and a vehicle to carry me through.

From the distance came the deep resonant rumble of the jet's engines as it disappeared from their sight. In her euphoria, Joanna silently saluted the jet and thought that the very sound of movement was just one of the many things to which she belonged.

Against the backdrop of an elegant Cornwall mansion before World War II and a vast continent-spanning canvas during the turbulent war years, Rosamunde Pilcher's most eagerly-awaited novel is the story of an extraordinary young woman's coming of age, coming to grips with love and sadness, and in every sense of the term, coming home...

Rosamunde Pilcher

The #1 *New York Times* Bestselling Author of *The Shell Seekers* and *September*

COMING HOME

"Rosamunde Pilcher's most satisfying story since *The Shell Seekers*."

—*Chicago Tribune*

"Captivating...The best sort of book to come home to...Readers will undoubtedly hope Pilcher comes home to the typewriter again soon."

—*New York Daily News*

COMING HOME
Rosamunde Pilcher
_____ 95812-9 $7.99 U.S./$9.99 CAN.

MARGARET... DAISY... DALE...

From the surf of Maine to lakeshore Milwaukee to Canada's Pacific mists, each of the Wallace women—a mother and her two daughters—is looking across her treasured home waters to the horizons of change...

These three women—warm, funny and courageous—are about to ride a bittersweet merry-go-round of joy and pain, love and illusion, reconciliation and rediscovery, in this classic bestseller that has won the hearts of women everywhere.

Three Women at the Water's Edge

A NOVEL BY NANCY THAYER

"COMPELLING, ABSORBING AND RICH."
—Publishers Weekly